DEATH ROE

DEATH ROE

JOSEPH HEYWOOD

THE LYONS PRESS

GUILFORD, CONNECTICUT

AN IMPRINT OF THE GLOBE PEQUOT PRESS

Copyright © 2009 by Joseph Heywood

The Lyons Press is an imprint of The Globe Pequot Press.

Designed by Sheryl Kober

Library of Congress Cataloging-in-Publication Data

Heywood, Joseph.
  Death roe : a woods cop mystery / Joseph Heywood.
    p. cm.
  ISBN 978-1-59921-428-3
  1. Service, Grady (Fictitious character)—Fiction. 2. Game wardens—Fiction. 3. Upper Peninsula
(Mich.)—Fiction. I. Title.
  PS3558.E92D43 2008
  813'.54—dc22

                                                              2008024499

Printed in the United States of America

10 9 8 7 6 5 4 3 2 1

To past and present detectives of the
Michigan Department of Natural Resources
Wildlife Resource Protection Unit and its predecessors,
who operate without fanfare or recognition,
and seek to bring light to darkness.

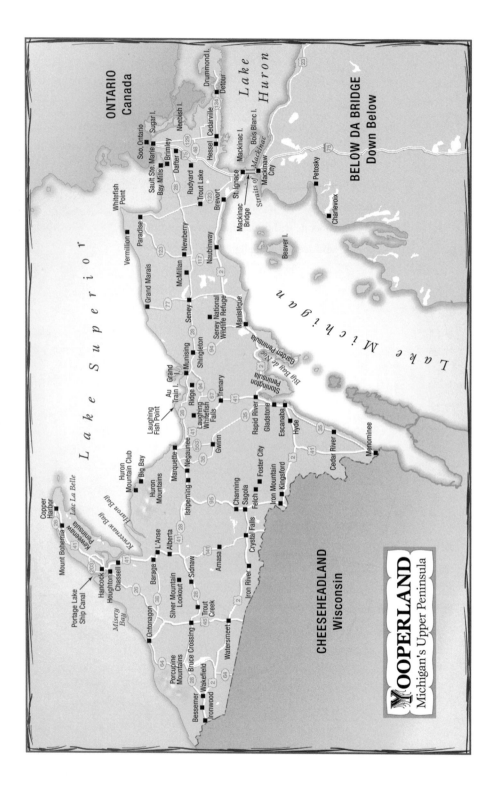

PART I
THE UPPER PECULIAR

Singularity is almost invariably a clue. The more featureless and commonplace a crime is, the more difficult it is to bring it home.
—Sherlock Holmes, "The Boscombe Valley Mystery"

MONDAY, OCTOBER 4, 2004

Carp River, Mackinac County, Michigan

Grady Service had found a vantage point under the canopy of a cluster of white cedars, and sat on a low bluff watching the dark riffle through his thermal imager. Four individuals on the far bank were using long spinning rods, methodically arcing long casts across the gravel: They would cast, reef and reel, reef and reel, the classic Yooper salmon-snagger's twitch. Testosteronal splashes told him they were using not lures but spiders, large treble hooks with one-ounce chunks of lead soldered to them, a jury-rigged grapple used to foul-hook the Chinook salmon trying to spawn on the gravel beds below.

It was cool, first light, clouds rolling over, a hint of rain in the air, and he had watched at least six fish snagged, hauled to shore, and stashed. As it began to grow lighter, the snaggers gave indications of calling it quits before anyone could see them at work. They had come in at 4 A.M., two hours ago, and had worked quietly and efficiently the whole while.

While they collected their gear, Service moved west, hopped and slid down a century-old log slide, and made his way across flat boulders to the far side of the river. He cut east, climbed up into the woods, and searched until he found the carcasses of kings, gutted, eggs stripped out, meat tossed aside. *Odd*, he thought. *They took only the eggs. Most snaggers took the whole fish.*

The snaggers were walking ahead of him, hiking east in silence toward the campground. The group's aural discipline and demeanor suggested they were professional violets, not amateurs. *Violet* was Service's term for violators of fish and game laws.

The campground was nearly empty. In years past during this season it was usually overflowing, but two-dollar-a-gallon gas and a stone-dead economy were keeping downstate fishermen closer to home this fall, and mostly he was encountering homegrown outlaws. The four people went to a pale blue recreational vehicle and carried their gear inside. They had worked and departed in silence, good discipline, all signs of a veteran crew.

He gave them a few minutes to settle in, approached the living-quarters door, and knocked. It opened immediately and a light came on. The man before him had matted gray hair, more salt than pepper. He had bright blue eyes, an almost cherubic face, wisps of whiskers on a receding chin.

"What?" the man asked, squinting like he had just been awakened.

"Sir, would you please bring out the fishing gear and the salmon roe you just took inside?"

The man studied him, started blinking wildly, and broke into a huge grin. "*Hooy na ny!*" he said. "No fucking way! I can't believe this!" he said. "It's *you!*"

"Sir, please step outside."

"Okay, okay," the man said, stepping down to the ground. He looked to be early forties, gaunt, leather-skinned, spry. "You don't remember *Benny*?"

The man was stalling. "Get the others out here with their gear—all of it. Right now! I'm not going to repeat myself."

The man yelled something in Russian and there was muffled scrambling inside. Three teenage girls emerged, carrying rods. Service looked at the man. Russian? He probed his memory. He had once threatened to ticket a sixteen-year-old Ukrainian immigrant. Had to be more than twenty years ago. The boy had been serving as the lookout for a shining crew, his job to blink a red light if he saw a game warden coming. He had failed. Service had wrenched the light away from the startled boy and put him on the ground in almost the same motion. The crew had hired the kid in Macomb County, offered him fifty dollars in cash, some cheap booze, and cigarettes for the weekend. The kid had been petrified and Service had let him off with a warning if he would agree to testify against the others, which he had. But the others had pleaded guilty and paid their tickets without protest. The kid had been spared court and a ticket.

"Baranov," Service said.

"You got good memory," the man said happily.

"They called you Blinky."

"*Da*, I work light for *slovachy—bastards!*"

Service studied the girls, who sat down at a picnic table. All under eighteen, he guessed, but these days it wasn't easy to judge.

Some professional crew, he thought. "Where are the eggs?"

"What eggs?" one of the girls challenged with a shrill bark and started talking to the others.

"*Konchaj bazar*," Service said menacingly in Russian. "Stop talking." He had studied the language in college, retained smatterings, enough to operate rudimentarily.

The man turned to the girls and nodded at the RV. One of them went inside and came out with a sagging clear plastic bag, which she handed to Baranov, who held it out to the conservation officer.

Service set the bag by his boot. "A lot of charges here, Blinky. You've got possession of illegal equipment, taking fish by illegal means, improper disposal of litter. The fine on the fish alone is ten bucks an inch or ten bucks a pound, whichever I decide. I cut you a break that first time, and hoped you saw the light, but apparently you didn't figure it out."

"Many people do this thing," the Ukrainian whined. "*Many*," he added.

"And many get caught. It's against the law," Service answered. There was a silver spider attached to each line. "You got more spiders?"

"Inside," the man said.

"Get all of them—and your mold, too."

He had not seen silver spiders in almost ten years. The new generation of snaggers poured tubular molds that vaguely resembled lures and hung oversized hooks a couple of inches behind them. Some tried to skirt the law by using legal one-ounce rigs, but it was the way they used them that gave them away. They could always claim they were fishing legitimately, but a game warden only had to watch the retrieve to know what they were up to. Legal-weight torpedoes were a halfhearted subterfuge; spiders were blatant, in your face.

The same two girls went back inside and came out with a plastic tackle box and a cardboard box. "Open them," Service said.

The tackle box held a dozen shiny spiders; the cardboard box contained a mold and coils of pencil lead to be melted down.

"What's the deal with the eggs, Blinky?"

"We Ukrainians believe the eggs cleanse our blood. Was, for long time, you know, food of serfs and peasants *before* food of czars and fucking Kremlin bosses."

Service had the group follow him back to the fish carcasses. The girls scooped the gutted fish into the clear plastic bags and they all trooped back to the campground, where Service measured each of the six fish and took down names. The girls were Alexandra, Alla, and Anina. They gave their ages: twelve, fourteen, and sixteen. The eldest had challenged him. The others were quiet, calm, showed no nervousness. They were either used to this, or not aware of the trouble they were facing.

Service looked at them. "No school today, girls? It's Monday."

"Leaks in school roof," Baranov said disgustedly. "Will open again Wednesday. The schools have no money. The people have no money. How much this will cost?" he asked.

"Six fish at thirty-four inches each, give or take, round it off to two hundred inches, times ten bucks, let's say two grand in restitution—just for the fish. Additional fines and costs I can't cite because each county has its own scale, but we're talking illegal gear, illegal taking, and illegal disposal. I could write you for over-limit, but that's moot because everything you're doing is illegal. It won't be cheap, Benny. I'm also taking the spiders, the mold, and your rods."

"You leave us nothing to fish with," the man protested.

"You weren't fishing, you were *snagging*," Service barked back.

"Okay, is mistake. Give us break, yes? Life is not so easy."

Something in the man's voice intrigued Grady Service. He was right about life being tough. Michigan's economy was in the crapper, its unemployment among the highest in the country. "Why would I give you a break?" he asked.

The man shrugged.

"You had one chance from me already," Service said.

"Yes, of course," the man said disconsolately. "Benny does not forget."

"Your English has improved," Service said.

"My girls," the man said. "I am citizen now. My girls, they insist I must speak good American."

Grady Service had lost his son and girlfriend last spring and the wounds were still raw. Baranov's girls were underfed, dressed shabbily, dull-eyed, and looked hungry. The thought of his soon-to-be-born grandchild living this way made his stomach turn.

"Things tough, Blinky?"

"Michigan," was all the man mumbled, and Service understood. He had recently seen college students in Houghton wearing T-shirts that said MICHIGAN IS DYING.

"You got a job?"

"No more. Fifteen years I was in GM plant, Novi, UAW, union card, everything. Then job was gone, *pfft*. Union, *bah*! Three years now, I have no work."

"You're a citizen?"

"Yes, of course. But with ticket, maybe now they change minds, deport me to Ukraine, give my darling girls to foster homes. They are all born here, all real Americans—same as you."

"Any arrests or tickets since I gave you your warning?"

"No, honest to God. Benny Baranov is honorable man."

"Honorable, but snagging. There's a major disconnect."

"For food, sir," the man said in a pleading tone. "For my family. You must understand."

Sir? "Bullshit. You threw the meat away." Violets who knew they were in trouble always adopted an obsequious, oddly formal tone.

"*You* would eat such rotting shit?" the man countered.

"No way," Service said. "The fish are full of contaminants, the eggs too."

The man shrugged and looked downcast, but mumbled, "But legal to eat, yes?"

Service asked for the man's driver's license, and sat down at the picnic table.

"You moved out of Detroit?" Service said, holding up the license.

"Capitalism: No work, no money; no money, no rent, no food. In Soviet Union they pretended to pay workers and workers pretended to work. In United States there is no faking. No job, you starve democratically."

The license listed an address in Onaway, which had a long reputation for hard-core DNR violators. "More work up this way?" The northern part of Michigan was even more depressed than southern regions of the state.

"More natural food north," the man mumbled. "In the *taiga*."

"You poaching your food?" Service asked.

"Sometimes," the man admitted. "Girls must eat."

There was resignation in the man's eyes as Service wrote the ticket, tore off Baranov's copy, and held it out. "You can call the court to find out the amount of the fine, and what to do. You have to pay it within ten days, but you can do it by mail. If you don't pay, a warrant will be issued for your arrest, and when we find you, we will take you to jail."

The man took the ticket, folded it without looking at it, rammed it into his trouser pocket.

Service's gut was churning. Was the guy hurting or was this a line of bullshit? He made his decision quickly. "Okay," Service said. "Keep the rods, but fish legally with them. I catch you again, there will be no mercy."

"*Spasibo*," the man said, raised his arms, herded the girls inside, and closed the door. Service heard sobbing through the thin walls, cut spiders off the lines of the rods, took out one of his business cards, left it under a reel, collected the spare spiders, mold, fish, and eggs, and headed for his truck, which was more than a mile away, on the other side of the river. *Poor bastard,* he told himself as he hiked. But he had not made the choice for the man and there had to be consequences, or what was the point of the job?

The salmon would die after spawning, but someone had to ensure they would have the chance to reproduce. *Your job, your responsibility,* he lectured himself. Nature had a way of balancing things; only man could permanently skew the balance, which made him wonder what man's purpose was in the big picture. Having had the thought, he said "Bah!" out loud and kept hiking.

How did an out-of-work autoworker afford an RV that had to have set him back at least a hundred grand off a lot?

This past summer he had learned that his late son's girlfriend Karylanne Pengelly was pregnant and due in late December. She was a junior at Michigan Tech in Houghton. He thought about the baby, and the prospects of being a grandfather, and told himself, no way was his grandchild going to end up like Baranov's daughters.

Almost four years earlier he had met DNR fire officer Maridly Nantz and they had fallen in love. She was a wild spirit, who also had wanted to become a conservation officer. Less than two years ago they learned that he had a son by his previous marriage. Now Nantz and his son Walter were dead, murdered. And she had left him an unimaginable fortune he didn't want, without consulting him. Whatever else lay ahead, he was resolved to take care of his grandchild with what she had left behind. He had a lot of regrets in his life, but this grandchild was *not* going to be one of them.

2

MONDAY, OCTOBER 4, 2004

St. Ignace, Mackinac County

Sergeant Milo Miars was in civvies. He was short and fit and had intense eyes, like steely-gray BBs, and sported a clean shave and a fresh whitewall haircut. They met outside Lehto's pasty shop on US 2. The sergeant had called while Service was driving away from the Carp River, asking for an immediate meeting with a demanding tone of voice. Until this fall, Grady Service had reported directly to Captain Ware Grant, the senior officer in the Upper and Northern Lower Peninsulas. Though he had been a detective in Wildlife Resource Protection—the DNR's special investigations unit—for a couple of years, he had not had to deal with the organization other than to forward case reports. This was about to change.

"You did a helluva job last summer," Miars said.

Service had helped solve a case in which a pair of killers had been ambushing and murdering game wardens all around the country. Ironically it had been Limpy Allerdyce who had stepped in and eliminated one of the killers. Though it could never be proven in a court, Service knew the truth, and it perplexed him. Did he owe the old poacher now? Allerdyce, a felon, was one of the most notorious and successful poachers in the U.P., and possibly the state. Service had already sent him to Jackson Prison once. He decided the best thing to do was ignore that it had happened. "It was an experience I could have done without," Service told his new supervisor.

"You working any cases now?"

"The usual stuff. I'm pretty clear."

"Good. We're going to send you down to Vanderbilt, undercover. We've got a dirty elk guide down there, but we can't seem to get anything on him."

Service shrugged. He had never handled an elk case before and found the proposition mildly interesting. He wasn't sure how he felt about performing undercover, but having worked with federal undercover agents, he had some definite feelings about protocol and procedure. "If I work UC, I'll be the one to serve the warrant when the time comes."

"We don't work that way," the sergeant said.

"I won't do it any other way. If I'm going to go inside, I want to be able to look a man in the eye and tell him why when the cuffs go on."

"I'll have to take that up the line," Miars said.

"You do that. When do you want me in Vanderbilt?"

"For the December hunt. We'll brief you about six weeks ahead and make sure you have a tag. You'll stay in a camp near there, hunt deer, and hang out in the bars so you can get to know the local personalities."

"I don't do the barfly thing," Service said.

"The pasties here any good?" Miars asked, eyeing the shop and ignoring Service's comment.

"Best in the eastern U.P.," Service said.

"Shall we order?"

"Not hungry," Service said. He rarely ate pasties. His first impressions of Miars were ambivalent. Did he want to work for the man, or was it time to hang it up? He had more than enough time in and money to retire.

"Call me once a week and check in to let me know what you have going. I'll make arrangements for the place in Vanderbilt, and we'll put you in there a few days before the gun-opener."

"What're the dates?" Service asked.

"Late elk is December seventh through the fourteenth. More than forty thousand applications, and only a hundred and twenty-four got drawn in the lottery. This year there'll be a lot of angst out there. There's a lot of meat on an elk and a lot of trophy-only hunters."

The timing should be okay, Service decided. The baby was due December 28. Service nodded, and started to walk away, but the sergeant caught his arm and turned him around. "You've got the reputation of a cowboy. You've had some unreal successes, but in this unit we play it by the book, and we talk straight, no bullshit. That work for you?"

"Yippie-kay-ay," Service said, earning a sarcastic chuckle from his new sergeant.

He got into his truck and drove back toward the Carp River. There would be other violators out on a day like this, and he wasn't going to miss them. As he drove he called Information and got the number for Onaway Public Schools. A woman answered. "This is the DNR," he said. "Are you open today?"

"Closed until Wednesday morning," she said. "The roof is leaking all over our classrooms."

Service thanked her. Baranov hadn't lied about that. He then ran computer checks to see if Baranov had been in trouble with the law, including DNR tickets. The man's record was clean. He had told the truth about the kids not being in school. And he'd said he'd had no tickets, another truth. He was glad he had given the fishing gear back to the man. Anyone could make a mistake.

3

TUESDAY, OCTOBER 12, 2004

Moran, Mackinac County

It had been eight days since he had worked the Carp River and today was to be a pass day, what civilians called a day off. He had been sitting on his porch in the morning sun when his cell phone began to vibrate.

"Service here."

"Benny Baranov. I call court just as you tell me. They say it is fortune to pay tickets, but I am thinking maybe you and I can make trade, yes?"

"You've got something to trade with?"

"You know bank boys?"

"A family named Bank?"

"*Nyet, nyet*, bank boys, bank boys—okay?" Desperation palpable in the man's voice.

"You'd *better* have something. Where and when?"

"You know scenic overlooking place west of St. Ignace?"

Service knew it. "Yep, on US Two."

"*Da*, good. Three o'clock?"

"I'll be there."

"Look for RV."

Was this Baranov's sole vehicle, and if so, how did he afford the gas? Something in this didn't add up. A deal in the offing? He reminded himself that the Ukrainian had not lied during the initial contact. *Keep an open mind,* he told himself as he got dressed and headed east.

Service found Baranov sitting on a ten-gallon plastic bucket in front of his RV, staring out over the spartan-green spans of Big Mac Bridge and the gunmetal-gray slick of the Straits of Mackinac.

"Beautiful view," Service said when he got out of his unmarked Tahoe.

"I think it is easier for a rich man to appreciate beauty than a poor man."

Service said, "You want to philosophize? I didn't drive all the way over here to gawk at scenery."

Baranov invited him inside. The interior of the RV was clean and neat.

"Where are the girls?" Service asked.

"In school," the man said.

"I guess they got the leaks fixed. I called the school and they verified your story."

Baranov looked hurt. "I would not lie. My children are important. They will finish school."

"You mentioned a trade."

The man took a deep breath. "Vodka?"

"No, thanks," Service said. Drinking on duty had contributed to his father's death. It would not happen to him.

The man reached into a huge cooler and pulled out a bottle. "Okay?"

"Knock yourself out."

The man got a loaf of dark rye bread and a jar of pickles out of the small refrigerator and set them out with a brick of jalapeno cheese and a plate of sliced sweet onions. He poured himself a full glass and drained it. It was a cool fall day, but the man was sweating.

"You nervous?"

"I have no money," the man said, his voice cracking.

"If you don't pay the ticket, they'll issue a warrant and it will just get worse."

"What is Benny to pay with?" the man shot back. He thumped his chest. "I have *nothing*."

"It must cost a fortune to operate this rig."

"From time to time I have a little money. Until two weeks ago, we live out of this. Now I have a *dacha* until end December. Then is back to RV, home on wheels."

"Life can be tough."

"You have good heart," Baranov said through a squint. "You give me break long time ago. This time, you give rods back. You are not prick."

"Yeah, I'm a regular bleeding heart."

"I have no money to pay tickets now!" Baranov keened.

Service heard panic in the man's voice. "You can work something out with the court."

"I don't know when I will have money again."

"I'm not a bank."

"I ask from heart—you drop ticket, please."

"Why would I do that?"

"Bank boys."

"Never heard of them."

"Not family. Is term. Means boys on bank of river—collectors."

"Collectors of what?"

"Salmon eggs."

"For what?"

"Caviar. The company gives bank boys money for eggs."

"What company?"

"Piscova."

Service felt himself flinch. "The outfit that contracts with the DNR to operate weirs and harvest eggs, for the Fisheries division?"

"Yes, Piscova."

"Why would they be buying eggs on the side?" It was illegal to sell or buy eggs, or any wild game or game parts.

"I hear things."

"This sounds like bullshit. . . . What do you think you've heard?"

Baranov poured another glass of vodka, took a bite of bread, a bite of cheese, and drained the glass. "It is said they bring eggs from New York factory to Elk Rapids."

"So?"

"New York eggs come in containers that say 'Not for Humans to Eat—Bait Only.' "

"You've heard this?"

"Yes, of course."

"From whom?"

"Bank boys. Some do other jobs for company."

"The bank boys collect eggs for Piscova?"

"They take to company. They are like prick foremen in auto plant, yes?"

"How do you know this?"

"I am egg boy. Egg boys give eggs to bank boys. Bank boys take eggs to company."

"They've paid you for eggs?"

"Every fall since I am losing job."

"How much do they pay?"

"Two dollars, one pound, this year three dollar, thirty cent. Not many fish, eggs worth more, *da*? Supply, demand—law of capitalists."

Service took out a cigarette and lit it. "That seems like a pretty decent price."

"Is hard work to harvest eggs."

"And risky with game wardens out and about."

"Yes, of course, this is true."

"Who does Piscova deal with in New York?"

"Company has a plant there."

"You're telling me that Piscova ships bait eggs from its plant in New York to its plant in Michigan?"

"That is what is said."

"Why?"

The man pursed his lips and hunched his shoulders. "I don't know."

Grady Service felt something stir deep inside his gut. He had always had hunches and often played to them. "This is what you want to trade in exchange for making your ticket go away?"

"*Da.*"

"Not enough, Blinky."

The Ukrainian looked past him, sucked in a deep breath, and sat up straight. "I take you to see this thing happen, okay?"

"Explain."

"You see them buy eggs from Benny."

"One of them is here?"

"They are all over state—is *big* network."

A statewide network? Was Baranov bullshitting him? "When?" Service tried to keep excitement from overwhelming his skepticism.

"Bank boy is tonight in bar in Moran. I bring eggs to him, he weighs eggs, pays cash, deal is done"

"The eggs I took from you. You were going to sell them?"

"Yes, of course."

"But now you have no eggs to sell."

Baranov paused a long time before speaking. "I have eggs."

"From when?"

Baranov looked past Service at a wall, took a deep breath, and said, "Today, yesterday, day before. I meet bank boy tonight. I need money to pay fines."

Which meant Baranov had gone back to snagging despite his promise to stop. "How much do you have?"

"Eighteen kilos, maybe more. Maybe one hundred twenty dollars."

He tried to do a quick mental calculation. Eighteen kilograms was about forty pounds. "That's a lot of dead hen salmon."

"Yes, of course."

"I should cuff your sorry ass and take you to jail right now. You *promised* me, no more snagging."

"You have no evidence. There are no eggs here."

"You promised to go straight."

"I have three darling girls depend on papa," the man said. "What would you do?"

They were not exactly little, but Service understood the point.

"You are not interested?" the man asked.

"I'm thinking on it." Officers faced difficult decisions: Make an immediate arrest, or trade for something larger down the line. This felt like one of those times to look to the future.

"Okay, *if* this is real. Otherwise, no deal."

"No bullshit. I take you to get eggs and you watch me sell. I keep money and you see how bank boys work."

"I said okay." Was he making a mistake? "Where are the eggs?"

"Not far. We take RV."

Baranov drove the RV west to Epoufette and parked behind a store fronting US 2, which was boarded up and padlocked in front. A prominent hand-lettered sign said OUT OF BUSINESS. The Ukrainian opened a padlock on the back door, went to a freezer, took out clear plastic bags filled with red eggs and two bags of ice, carried them out to the RV, and put them in the cooler. Service made a mental note to find out who owned the out-of-business building and follow up. He was tempted to probe Baranov for why and how he was using the place, but his gut said to stay focused on the eggs in the cooler for now.

They arrived on the outskirts of the village of Moran around 5 P.M. and parked down the road from a bar called So Soo Me, the name in blinking neon. *Stupid name*, Service thought. It seemed that some bars in the U.P. tried to outdo each other with their insipid names.

"You take the eggs inside?"

"No; first I go in, have drink, make small talk. After some time, we come outside, I give eggs, he weighs, he pays, and then we leave."

"You expect me to walk in with you?"

"No, I go first, you follow later. I must be alone to do this thing. It is rule."

"If you're lying to me . . ." Service said, not finishing the sentence.

"Baranov is man of honor."

"Yeah, right."

Service got out of the RV and watched Baranov drive away. He half expected the man to rabbit, but he watched him pull into the parking lot in front of the bar and get out. Service popped out his false teeth, put them in a plastic container in his pocket, and followed the Ukrainian inside.

The bar was quiet and dark, with the usual garish beer brand and Green Bay Packer signs, a few for the Red Wings, no colleges. An orange-and-black sign behind the bar said WELCOME TO BULLDOG COUNTRY. There was the face of a cartoon bulldog staring out, its teeth bared. Who the hell were the Bulldogs? Baranov was at the bar with a clean-shaven man with short white hair, and a black chook on the bar in front of him. He watched the two men down shots, get up, and stroll out.

After a decent interval, Service put on his coat and followed, cracking the door before stepping out and going to the corner of the building. Service watched the man wearing the chook come out of the RV with the egg bags, take them to a red truck, open the cap, take out a scale, weigh the bags, put the scale and eggs inside, close the cap, and lock it. Baranov stood beside the man, watching. The man tookout his wallet, handed cash to the Ukrainian, and went back into the bar. Service wrote down the plate number and vehicle description.

Baranov went back to his RV.

Service walked down the road and waited for Baranov, who soon pulled up and showed him the cash from the sale.

"Who was that?"

"Big cheese."

"Your usual contact?"

"No, this one is called Vandeal."

"Where's your usual contact?"

"No longer employed," Baranov said.

"They fire people?"

"Capitalism," Baranov replied, as if the one word explained all the peculiarities of America.

"How do you know this Vandeal is a big cheese?"

"I have heard his name more than once."

"Who is he?"

"Big cheese," the Ukrainian repeated.

When they got back to Service's Tahoe at the scenic pullout on US 2, Baranov poured another shot of vodka for himself.

Service got into his Tahoe and ran the plate through the state computer. The 2004 red Ford pickup was registered to one Willem Vandeal, with an address in Elk Rapids. Service stared at the computer for a long time. He ran Vandeal for warrants and wants. Nothing. He called Station 20 in Lansing and asked them to run Vandeal through RSS, the Retail Sales System, to check for any licenses, hunting or fishing, and to run another check for any DNR violations in the past. Again nothing. On paper Vandeal was squeaky clean, but he had seen the man buy the eggs and he knew such practices didn't start overnight. His gut was telling him to go with this.

Decision made, he went back to Baranov's RV. "Okay, we almost have a deal," Service said.

"What is *almost*?" the man asked. He looked pale. "You tell Benny we *have* deal."

"I'm not reneging. Just tell me what rumors you've heard about why the eggs are shipped from New York to Michigan."

The man looked into Service's eyes. "The best vodka is pure. The cheapest is mixed, you understand? But even the cheapest in cost can make very high price when demand is high."

The company was mixing eggs fit only for bait with those cleared for human consumption? New York's eggs were contaminated. Service was pretty sure Michigan's salmon were also filled with crud, but they had not yet been banned by the FDA or EPA for food. Was this possible? Was it possible that such a case could fall into his lap so easily?

"You have my number. You hear anything more, you call."

"There is reward for this?"

"Your reward will be in heaven."

"I am atheist. God is dead."

"Your ticket will be erased—that's reward enough. Tell me honestly, how much can you make selling eggs?"

"Last fall, seven thousand dollars."

Service did a quick mental calculation. He had no doubt the money was undeclared and therefore tax-free. "That's about three and a half tons of roe."

"Of course, I move from river to river and it costs much to keep this American pig on road."

"Typical business type," Service said. "Always complaining about operating costs and the bite into profit." Service had more questions. "Piscova's the only one who buys eggs?"

"Now," the Ukrainian said. "Years ago, I hear many paid for eggs and meat, mom-and-pop, you understand? But these Piscova guys, they convince them to find other business."

"Convinced them how?"

"You be careful," Baranov said as Service opened the door.

"How's that?"

"Benny hears Piscova has powerful friends in Lansing."

"You've heard that?"

"Many times."

"Names?

"No names, just fact."

4

TUESDAY, OCTOBER 12, 2004

Newberry, Luce County

Lieutenant Lisette McKower's Tahoe was in the parking lot of the Newberry district DNR building. Grady Service found her in her cubicle, hunched over a computer, scowling.

"Ain't being an el-tee just grand?" he quipped as he plopped down in a chair.

She lobbed a pencil end over end at him. McKower had been his sergeant before her promotion to lieutenant. At one time they had both been COs and had worked closely together. Too closely: There had been a brief affair, the only time he had ever gotten involved with a married woman. After a period of sore feelings, they remained close friends, and he suspected she had played a role in his promotion to detective, something she adamantly denied.

"How are you doing?" she asked. Out of respect for his privacy most officers no longer asked about the loss of his girlfriend and son, which had happened April 28—one hundred and sixty-eight days ago today. That he knew the precise number of days disturbed him, but he was not sure why.

"Good days and bad," he said. "I keep turning around to tell her something, only she's not there to hear me."

"I think she hears you, Grady."

He had never married Maridly Nantz and had loved her in a way he never thought himself capable of. Now she was gone, murdered in her pickup truck, and his son with her. The memory choked him.

"It will get better over time," McKower said.

"Sounds like herpes," he said.

She rolled her eyes. "You are hopeless."

"Put it on my headstone."

"What did you put on Maridly's?"

This was a sore point that continued to irritate some of his friends and colleagues. He had delayed a memorial for Nantz and Walter. After the memorial he and Luticious Treebone, his best friend of more than twenty years, had taken the ashes to a camp in west Chippewa County and dumped some of them in a creek filled with spawning brook trout. He and Maridly had talked only once about death and she had made him promise to dump her ashes in the most beautiful place he saw. He decided to put some of their ashes in each beautiful or meaningful place he encountered and now carried them in the truck at all times. Only Treebone knew what he had done. "I didn't come here for a goddamn lecture," he said sharply.

"Point taken. Why *are* you here?"

"I need a landline."

"Help yourself," she said. "I'm the only one home today."

"What do you know about Miars?" he asked.

She raised an eyebrow, sat back in her chair. "Milo? Solid, quiet, thorough—a good guy, but a little cautious. Be glad Zins hung it up."

Until retiring at the first of the month, Zins had been the lieutenant in charge of Wildlife Resource Protection.

"What about Zins?"

"He's a self-serving prick with the common sense of a slab of slate. He only spent two years in the field as a CO and two as a sergeant before his first lieutenant's job. Very smart, very glib, very political. Wouldn't take a shit if he thought it was a bad political move. You and Miars get off on the wrong foot?"

"Just curious," he said. He was weighing whether to tell Miars about Piscova, and what he had learned. Was Baranov bullshitting about the company having powerful friends in Lansing? He knew Piscova had a longtime contract with the DNR to harvest eggs for brood stock in hatcheries and for research purposes, and this required friendly intermediaries. The almost throwaway comment from the Ukrainian had set him on edge.

"Put your teeth in before you get on the phone," McKower said.

"Thanks, Mom."

"You never had a mom. You hatched from a dinosaur egg."

He smiled at the word *egg* and left her to her computer.

His first call was to Miars. "This is Service. Can we meet?"

"Why?"

"I have something I'd rather not talk about over the telephone."

"I'm heading to the RAM Center to meet the chief and your captain."

The Ralph A. McMullen Conference Center, or RAM, was used by the DNR for meetings. The site had once housed a Civilian Conservation Corps unit but had been taken over by the DNR around the time of Pearl Harbor. It was located on Higgins Lake, about ninety minutes south of the Mackinac Bridge.

"When's the meeting?"

"Tomorrow, zero eight hundred."

"I'll drive down."

"*You're* not invited."

"I'm inviting myself."

"Cowboy," Miars muttered. "The subject of the meeting *is* you."

"Good," Service shot back. "All the more reason for me to be there." *A meeting about him?* He felt a knot in his stomach. He hated political shit. And despite having some successes as a detective, he still preferred being a conservation officer with his own territory. He was born to be outside, not sitting in damn offices developing cases and plans and filing goddamn reports.

"I don't like this," his sergeant said.

"Piscova," Service said.

"What was that?"

"You heard me."

"What *about* them?"

"Something I heard," Service said. "I don't want to talk about it on the phone."

"Whatever it is, stay away from them. Piscova is out of bounds for you."

"We'll see about that," Service said, and hung up.

What had Baranov said about the company having powerful friends in Lansing? Did that include the DNR, and, if so, was Miars included? Zins? The chief? The director? This case had started on a hunch and had seemed full of promise. Was it about to turn to shit already? Or was there no case at all? *Be cool and keep it together,* he cautioned himself.

Service walked down the hall to the office of the irascible fish biologist, Harvey Ghent, who had been with the department forever and was nearing retirement. "Hey, Harv, you ever work with Piscova?"

"Back when I was handling salmon. Now I'm a warm-water maven. Why?"

"You know the name Vandeal?"

Ghent smiled. "Sure. Willem Vandeal's the plant manager for the company down in Elk Rapids. Why?"

"Just one of those somebody-knows-somebody-who-knows-somebody deals."

"Gotcha," the biologist said and went back to scribbling on a yellow legal pad.

Service asked, "Is the company private?"

Ghent looked up at him. "Yeah. Guy named Quintan Fagan owns it."

"Okay, thanks. I won't bother you anymore."

Vandeal was indeed a big cheese. Had Baranov known how big and played it cagey with him? Impossible to tell.

He called CO Candace McCants. "It's me," he began, "checking in." Recently she had been taking care of his dog and cat when he was away.

"They're fine, Grady. They like attention."

"I don't know how long I'll be gone this time."

"Not to worry. They're fine. Really."

It bothered him that his animals would be happy with someone else, but he had enough to worry about and tried to put it out of his mind. "Okay. I'll call when I get back."

"Be careful. You're not Superman."

"Right," he said. Why the hell had she said *that*?

RAM Center tomorrow; tonight he needed to think and prepare. Why was Piscova off limits to him? He would grab something to eat at Brown's Hotel, and hole up for the night in the district office conference room. Newberry was an hour from the bridge and the RAM Center ninety minutes below the bridge. Michigan conservation officers rarely thought in terms of miles, and always measured distances by time.

5

WEDNESDAY, OCTOBER 13, 2004

Ralph A. McMullen Conference Center,
North Higgins Lake, Roscommon County

The RAM Center was one of those places you could drive by and not think much about. The buildings were set back under a canopy of leaning cedars and fragrant pines, and the whole complex didn't look like much to casual passersby, but more DNR business got done at the so-called Campus-in-the-Woods than in Lansing, and senior DNR officials yo-yoed back and forth from Lansing so often that some of them swore they'd worn permanent tire tracks into the interstate.

It had been here years ago that former longtime Republican governor Sam Bozian, aka Clearcut, had angrily confronted him. Service had been working as the governor's son's field training officer and had seen the boy fall apart in a semi-tense situation with a biker group. It had not been the boy's fault; he had simply been unsuited for law enforcement work and cripping him along only would have increased risk for the boy and the officers he would have to work with. Recognizing his own shortcomings, the boy had made the decision to withdraw from training. Bozian had taken it as a personal affront and become Grady Service's enemy. Bozian was now gone from the state, out of politics, and working in the private sector at some fat-cat Washington job. The state was still paying for the damage Bozian had done as governor.

Service parked his truck, locked it, and strolled through the packed parking lot toward the administration building, which had a stone facade against dark wood; a faded official seal of the state hung over the entrance. No money in the state budget to even spruce up their signs and symbols.

A woman was standing outside and smiled when she saw him. "Grady Service, ghost of the north woods," she greeted him. "Make your skin crawl to be in this place?"

"I just think of it as a cedar swamp," he said.

Angie Lemieux was in her mid-seventies, and had worked in the center's kitchen for at least thirty years. "It can be a swamp all right," she said.

"Have you seen the chief, Angie?"

"He was at breakfast with Captain Grant. They've got the Whitetail Room for the morning."

The Whitetail Room was small, with a fireplace and a conference table. Usually the chief worked in a larger space with larger groups.

Service got to the building and looked through the frosted window. Chief Lorne O'Driscoll and Captain Grant were sitting on one side of the conference table, and Sergeant Milo Miars and Lieutenant Zins were sitting opposite them. Zins was in civvies, the others in uniform. What the fuck was Zins doing here? He'd retired two weeks ago. Service immediately regretted not having a change of clothes or a uniform with him. At least he had his teeth in. He had gotten injured last Easter, had all his teeth pulled, and was still not used to his dentures.

He tapped his knuckles on the window and the chief waved him in. "Sorry to intrude," he greeted the chief.

"Is it important?"

"Possibly."

"Take a seat. There's coffee."

Service poured a cup and sat down, wishing he could smoke. The other four men stared at him and said nothing.

Service looked at Miars. "You tell them this was about Piscova?"

The sergeant nodded. Zins immediately glared.

Service asked, "Does the company pay the DNR to run the weirs and collect eggs?"

Chief O'Driscoll said, "They provide all the services our hatchery people and biologists need, and they pay for the eggs they collect to use for themselves. Why?"

Service walked them through what had happened, including witnessing Vandeal collecting and paying the Ukrainian immigrant for his eggs.

"Why didn't you confront Vandeal right there?" Zins asked imperiously.

"I think there's something bigger going on," Grady Service said. "How many eggs does the Fisheries division need? It seems to me that the company's collecting a helluva lot more than we need, so what're they doing with the surplus? The eggs belong to the people of the state, right?"

"How big a harvest?" the chief asked.

"I don't know yet, but if my informant is correct, they're collecting all over the state every year. My guy's been doing it for at least three years. Sergeant Miars said Piscova was off limits to me," he added.

Zins glared at Service. "Loose cannon. Piscova pays the state for the eggs and meat it sells."

Service glanced at the retired lieutenant. He was tall and distinguished-looking, too damn slick for a game warden. He thought about pushing some buttons to see how Zins would react, but the chief said, "Could you use a smoke?"

Service nodded.

"Let's step outside."

The two men walked onto the wet grass. Dead leaves were already stacked up and crisping, turning the lawn to gold and red. The chief said, "The Wildlife Resource Protection Unit has been quietly investigating Piscova. There are rumors that perhaps some Fisheries employees are a little too *cozy* with them. It's strictly an internal matter. We're not aware of any law or contract violations, only potential ethical concerns."

"Meaning I should leave this alone?"

"No," the chief said. "Every investigator can choose to take a case in any number of different directions. Miars and Zins chose to look internally. What do you propose to do with what you've got?"

"I thought I'd call New York, see what they know, if anything, and decide the next step from there."

"All right—but no action beyond inquiries with New York unless I give you the green light."

"What about Miars?"

"He has his own work. With Zins gone, he's running the unit now."

"Did he and Zins get anywhere with their investigtion?"

"Not really."

"How long were they at it?"

"Eighteen months."

"What if my work leads me back inside?"

"We'll cross that bridge if you get to it."

"I report to Miars. Do I tell him what's going on in my case?"

"Not for the moment. Let's keep it between us."

"Miars isn't going to like it."

"Nobody likes being kept in the dark," the chief said, "but sometimes it's necessary. You want to sit in on the rest of meeting?"

"Miars said it's about me."

The chief smirked. "It's not. Zins is just handing over the reins. It's a good opportunity for Ware and me to get up to speed on details of the special investigations unit." Ware was Captain Ware Grant, his previous boss.

Which meant he had the investigation all to himself, and he had a pretty good idea what that meant. "I'm expendable," he told the chief, who answered with raised eyebrows.

Why had Miars told him the meeting was about him? To threaten him and keep him away? "I think I'll get back to work."

"Suit yourself," the chief said, and went back inside. Before parting the chief stopped and looked at him. "We're *all* expendable in this profession, Grady. The key is to know what's important and what's not."

Service wandered over to the garage area to find Billy "Fuzz" Fazzari, who had worked at the center for at least forty years as a maintenance mechanic. From time to time Fazzari had driven up to the Mosquito Wilderness to fish with him. Service considered him a friend.

Fazzari was puttering with a leaf blower and smoking a cigar that reeked enough to gag a vulture.

"How they hanging, Fuzz?"

Fazzari was short, a little overweight, and balding. "Geez, the Great Grady Service. You lost?"

"Had a meeting."

"I remember the time you and Clearcut went nose to nose out in the parking lot. Boy, you pissed him off. What can I do you for?"

"You ever hear of a company called Piscova?"

"Sure. Their head guy Fagan is here all the time with Fisheries people."

"What's he like?"

"Glad-hander to all who can help him, a dickhead to those who can't. He can't do enough for them Fisheries folks."

"Enough what?"

Fazzari shrugged. "I don't know. I just hear talk. You know, maybe trips to Florida and to his hunting camps, lots of free booze, maybe some broads from time to time. I figure it's just talk, eh."

"Anyone from Law Enforcement ever ask you about him?"

"Nobody asks a grease monkey shit."

"Thanks, Fuzz."

"Sorry to hear about your lady and your son, Grady. I met Nantz when she was up here for some kind of training. She was a pistol. We all liked her."

Maridly Nantz, a former fire officer, had started at the DNR law enforcement academy in Lansing a couple of years ago, but had been attacked by a dirtbag, seriously injured, and forced to drop out before graduation. Nantz had spent some of her recuperation time living with Chief O'Driscoll and his wife in East Lansing. She was scheduled to begin the academy again this fall, but that wasn't going to happen now. The thought made his stomach flip.

"Thanks, Billy." He did not want to think about Nantz and Walter right now, but the more he pushed thoughts of them away, the more they seemed to intrude.

Cripes, even the RAM Center's mechanic had an opinion about Fagan and Piscova. Why had Zins and Miars gotten no place in eighteen months? *Rhetorical question,* he told himself. The answer was politics, which meant a minefield for which few people had an accurate map.

6

WEDNESDAY, OCTOBER 13, 2004

Cedarville, Mackinac County

Instead of heading for home, Grady Service drove north up I-75 past St. Ignace and turned east on M-34, toward Cedarville. He needed some computer advice, and Joe Colyard was the man to help him. Colyard, nearing fifty and still charging, was a CO who had just transferred into the area from downstate last year. Service had known Colyard for years and had always considered him a solid officer. He was also one of the most knowledgeable when it came to computers. Colyard was six-foot-six with a teenager's waistline and a voice that bowled people over, even when he was happy, which was most of the time. Throughout the force he was known as Growler.

Cedarville was located at the head of the Les Cheneaux Islands archipelago, a string of islands that had been home to some of America's neufiest families for more than a century. Marquette Island, the largest in the chain, had its own private airport. Lots of locals worked as caretakers for absentee estate owners, and were often rich and reliable sources of information to game wardens.

Service called Colyard at home and got his wife, Pam, whose volume equaled her husband's. "How's it feel to be mingling with the rich?" he asked.

"Give it a break, Service!" she shot back.

"Growler around?"

"He said he was going to patrol the Pine River today. Has reports of snaggers over there."

Service thanked her, looked up Colyard's cell-phone number, and buzzed him.

The voice that answered made Service move the phone away from his ear.

"What?!"

"Service."

"Call me back in five, okay?"

"Where are you?"

"Join the twenty-first century and look at your frigging AVL!" Colyard shouted before hanging up.

Service flipped up the computer screen and touched it several times to take him into Mackinac County via the automatic vehicle locator. He saw Colyard's icon about five miles up a two-track that dead-ended at the river.

Service arrived at the site to find Colyard with six men around him, all of them yelling and trying to talk and Colyard drowning them out. "I don't give a shit *how* the last frigging officer interpreted the frigging rules. You gotta frigging one-ounce torpedo and you're jerking it like a frigging bird dog won't get in the water, and that's the action of snagging. I don't give a shit whether you've got a frigging fish on the end or not. You're attempting to take by unlawful means. *That's* the frigging law, asswipe!"

"Discussion group?" Service said to announce his presence.

"Ain't no *discussion* here," Colyard said. "These wads claim the last CO said they have to have a fish in possession for it to be a violation."

"Only if you're fishing legit methods," Service said. Heads immediately dropped.

"Don't run!" Colyard bellowed as Service saw one of the group bolt. He reacted immediately, took one step, felt a sharp pain in his upper calf, and went down on all fours with searing pain. Colyard glanced at Service, flew after the fleeing man, took out his baton, and struck the runner on the outside of the knee, sending him sprawling. He immediately rolled him on his face, pulled his hands behind him and cuffed him, while the man started screaming, "They're too tight, they're too tight!"

Colyard dragged the man over to Service and looked at his colleague. "Does the detective got him a boo-boo?"

"Something popped in my calf."

"Ice, elevate, heat," the other officer said.

"I'll try to remember that," Service said. He struggled to his feet, but when he tried to take a step, pain shot through his leg again. He wavered and Colyard caught him by the arm. At that moment the other five snaggers all fled like cockroaches under a sudden light.

The one on the ground moaned, "My leg is killing me."

Colyard laughed out loud. "Your stupidity is killing you. Where the hell do your buddies think they're going? I've got all their frigging drivers' licenses."

Service said, "I guess this isn't working out the way they'd planned."

Colyard said, "I love it when they run!"

Service limped to his truck and got in.

Colyard said, "I've got ice in the cooler in my truck," and went to retrieve it. Service took a blue latex glove from the box of them he carried, filled a glove with ice, and used duct tape to secure the makeshift ice bag to the back of his leg.

"Stylin'!" Colyard said with a deep laugh. "We'll wait for the jerkwads to come back, stroke them, and send 'em on their way." He looked down at the man on the ground. "Any of your crew got outstanding warrants?"

"My *leg!*" the man keened.

"Don't be a baby. They don't write warrants on frigging body parts, bug-brain."

"Let me have some more ice," Service said. "I'm gonna take off. I'll stop along the way and get more."

"Bullshit. After I get done with this mob, we'll head over to my place and let Pam play doctor with us."

"Us?"

"I'll think of something for me," Growler said. "I love sympathy sex! What the hell are you doing over this way?"

"I need computer advice."

"For what?"

"Questions for New York wardens."

"What kind of questions?"

"Salmon egg processing."

"Hmm. Talk to their environmental branch law enforcement people."

"I'm cold," the man on the ground said.

"Yeah," Colyard said. "Guess you didn't run long enough to frigging heat up."

"You hit my leg," the man protested.

"Don't remind me, jerkwad. I was aiming at your frigging skull," Growler said. "My aim ain't what it used to be."

"I'll get a lawyer," the man said.

"Good—you'll need one: resisting arrest, attempting to flee, fishing with illegal methods . . . he'll have plenty of work to do. Just lay there and shut your piehole."

"Interesting bedside manner," Service said from the truck.

"Took years to develop," Growler said. "Can you believe they actually *pay* us to have all this fun?"

Joe Colyard was a happy man, up to his neck in the job in the woods and relishing every minute of it. Service envied him.

7

WEDNESDAY, OCTOBER 13, 2004

St. Ignace, Mackinac County

Miars called as Service started to cut west just north of St. Ignace. "Where are you?"

"On Two, headed toward Iggy."

"Meet me at the Castle Rock Parking lot."

What was Miars doing back in the U.P.? He lived near Roscommon, two hours below the bridge. Castle Rock? Tourists were told it was an old Indian lookout, which was pure bullshit. The land had been bought by a local just before the Great Depression, who turned it into an enduring tourist attraction of absolutely no historical significance. The rock was a 200-foot high column of limestone. The first time Nantz saw it she called it every white man's dream—a big white woody. *Nantz*, he thought, shaking his head.

Service didn't get out of his truck. Miars did and signaled for him to roll down his window. "The chief told me you're working on something for him."

Service said nothing.

"Captain Grant also told me you're anything but a cowboy. He says you're more like a shit-magnet," Miars said with a grin, and stuck out his hand. "I guess we got off on the wrong foot. Sorry about that. I never had a legend reporting to me before."

"No problem," Service said, not sure he meant it. "And can that legend crap."

"Piscova," Miars said. "Zins and I have been on the case for a year and a half, but Zins was a political animal and scared shitless of stepping on toes in the Fisheries division or anywhere else in Lansing. We got allegations of too-cozy connections between the company and some inside people, and as soon as we started looking into them, Director Teeny started sending some not-so-subtle messages to back off. Zins wouldn't let me do shit after that."

"You think the director's involved?"

"I'm not ruling out anything or anyone, but you need to understand that if your case swings inside, it could get down and dirty in a hurry."

Grady Service could not understand why Governor Lorelei Timms had not yet replaced DNR director Eino Teeny, a Bozian appointee, and the former governor's political stooge.

"Grapevine says Teeny's desperately looking for a position outside the state, but nobody wants him," Miars confided. "The governor gets the balls to dump him, I'll drive down to Lansing and personally escort the man out of the Mason Building." The Mason Building was home base for the Department of Natural Resources, in the state capital.

"You'll be part of a large contingent," Service said. This Miars seemed different, more relaxed and open. "How'd the case start?"

"Whistle-blower said the contractor gave one of the Fisheries guys a new boat. Then an auditor reported Piscova was in arrears for payments to the state for three years of its contract. Six months later the same auditor declared there was no problem. Now you see it, now you don't."

"I heard something similar about connections," Service said, deciding to cooperate. "But nothing about contract audits being whitewashed."

"Been rumors for years," Miars said.

"I never heard them."

"Now that you're in the unit full-time, you'll hear and smell every fart from Lansing. What exactly do you have?"

"I laid it out at the RAM."

"Do it again. I'm in a different frame of mind."

"I pinched a guy taking salmon eggs. He told me about selling them to a guy who works for Piscova, claimed there's a statewide network. I watched him make a sale. Turns out the buyer was Piscova's plant manager from Elk Rapids."

"Willem Vandeal?"

"That's him."

Miars sighed. "Bozian stripped the state and invited all the bloodsuckers in on the feed. Where are you going with it?"

"Thought I'd call New York."

"I've got a contact over there," Miars said. "Name's Heygood."

"Environmental side?"

"Nope, Fish and Wildlife—but he can point you."

"You want in?"

Miars said, "The chief told me to stay out of your way. And he's right. I've got the unit to worry about now. You need help, you call."

Was Miars backpedaling? "The more we know about what each of us is doing, the better off we both are."

"I buy that, but for now I'll let you proceed on your own."

"Let's drive down to the Troop post by the bridge and borrow a landline. You can at least call your buddy, and let's see how far we can get."

Sergeant Miars stared at the latex glove taped to Service's calf, but said nothing as they walked into the Michigan State Police post on the north side of the Mackinac Bridge. They borrowed a phone and Miars called Heygood and jotted down some notes while they talked. The most scribbling took place after he said the name *Piscova*.

"Environmental conservation officer Roy Rogers," Miars said. "He's got something going with Piscova. My friend doesn't know what, but he says Rogers is a tiger." He held up a telephone number.

Service made the call and reached Rogers on the first try. "Roy Rogers, for real?" Service greeted the man. "Detective Grady Service, Michigan Department of Natural Resources."

"Lame stuff. It's Roy Rogers the third," the man said. "My old man's idea of a joke. People call me 'Trip,' for Triple."

Service put him on speakerphone and introduced Miars.

"I stumbled on a thing with a company called Piscova," Service began, outlining what he knew for the New York officer, including the mention of egg packaging from New York containing product-not-fit-for-human-consumption labels.

"Hmm," Rogers said. "How long you had this?"

"Couple weeks," Service said, "but Sergeant Miars has been on an internal investigation a bit longer, looking for possible improprieties between the contractor and the department." He didn't want to give the New York man a specific time frame because it seemed embarrassing.

"You on the case full-time?"

"As of this morning," Service said, not sure yet that there was a case.

"Good. I think you and me are playing in the same sandbox. We know shit is going down, but so far, no luck in nailing anything specific. We're trying to get federal and state warrants to look at Piscova's processing operations here and over there in Michigan. There are rumors of paper bags full of cash floating around. Might be good to hit both plants at the same time."

"I'll have to talk to my chief," Service said.

"Okay, do that. We also found some Michigan Fisheries seals at one of our hatcheries. Nobody can explain how they got there, or why. We heard someone was opening the hatchery gates at night but we could never prove it, and the plant manager denied it and quit."

"Michigan seals in Piscova's New York plant?" How the hell had they gotten there? Only state biologists possessed such seals.

"I hear you," Rogers said. "How do you want to play this?"

"You think you can get the warrants?" Service asked.

Rogers chuckled sarcastically. "Let me 'splain something, Detective. This is New York State. We don't take kindly to environmental shitwads," Rogers said. "We'd publicly burn them at the stake if it wouldn't degrade air quality. I'm asking to get into both plants," Rogers added, "but I think I'd like to see the Michigan operation firsthand. You got a problem with that?"

"Works for me. Call when you have paper."

"I was going to hit the New York plant, but I think I'd rather look at yours. I'll send one of my people to serve the warrants on this end. Next Tuesday work for you guys?" Rogers asked.

Service looked at Miars, who nodded.

Rogers said, "We'll coordinate with the state, and fax directly to the county seat. You guys can pick up the warrants, if you don't mind."

"We're happy to take care of that," Service said.

"Give me a contact number and I'll call you back. What's the closest airport to Elk Rapids?"

"Traverse City."

"Good, we'll meet there. I'll call later with flight times."

"We'll pick you up," Miars said.

Service punched the button to break the connection and looked over at Miars. "*We'll* pick him up?"

"You might as well be there to see what New York's warrants get us," said Miars. "It could help your side of the case." Miars studied him. "You're not at all the way some people say."

"I know," Service said. There were times when he didn't know himself.

8

TUESDAY, OCTOBER 19, 2004

Traverse City, Grand Traverse County

It was very early morning; Service got to the Cherry Capital Airport an hour and a half before the New York environmental CO's flight was due and stationed himself just outside the baggage-claim area where he could smoke unmolested by Traverse City's infamous antismoking zealots.

Miars was in Bellaire picking up search warrants filed jointly by the states of Michigan and New York. New York had probable cause from interviews with several of Piscova's employees at their New York plant, and Service had a statement from Baranov and had witnessed Vandeal buying eggs from Benny. Federal warrants were also being issued in Grand Rapids, but they would not get to them in time and were largely redundant to his way of thinking. It was complicated enough to work with another state's agency. Bringing in the feds usually turned the simplest cases into quagmires. Not having to mess with the feds could make this case easier to flesh out.

The flight's arrival was announced and passengers soon began flowing into the baggage-claim area, milling around and waiting for the carousels to spit out their bags.

A man and a woman came toward him with carry-on bags over their shoulders. The man was six foot, stocky, head shaven clean as a genie, a goatee that was more shadow than hair. The woman was thin, dressed in government black—a jacket over a knee-length black skirt, scuffed low black heels.

"*The* Roy Rogers?" Service greeted the pair.

The man grimaced. "Call me Trip. Detective Service, meet Special Agent Zhenya Leukonovich of the Internal Revenue Service."

The woman nodded blankly, didn't offer a hand. She had a long face with prominent cheekbones, brown eyes, acne scars barely covered with makeup, gold post earrings, and a haircut Nantz used to refer to as a feminist buzzsaw, or a Lezbe-on-our-way 'do. The memory made him smile. The Nantz view of life and the world was no-holds-barred. She could crack him up with no more than a slightly elevated eyebrow.

"You alone?" Rogers asked.

"Miars is picking up the warrants. He'll meet us at the plant."

"You are alone?" the IRS agent asked.

Was she not listening?

"Aren't we all?" Service said, watching her for a reaction. Nothing. No visible personality.

Rogers asked, "You think your informant is legit?"

"It got you here quick enough," Service said. "How'd you get onto this?"

"Pure serendipity. A pickup truck schmucked a PT Cruiser with a woman and three young kids almost at the Pennsylvania border. Nobody hurt, but the pickup driver bailed, and bugged out. There were four seventy-five-pound containers of salmon eggs in the back of the truck, which we traced through the license plate and VIN to Piscova. When we called them, they claimed the vehicle had been stolen, and they had a police report to back it up. The hatchery deal I told you about? That happened a year before the truck incident."

"Was the vehicle reported stolen before or after the crash?"

"After, but not long enough after to make it obvious they were covering their asses."

"But suggesting it," Service said.

"That's affirm."

"And?" Service added, suspecting the New Yorker had more to tell.

"The state troopers who responded to the wreck found twenty grand in cash in the truck."

"Ergo the IRS," Service said. "That's it?"

"So far."

"Is the New York plant shipping eggs to Michigan?"

"We've interviewed a couple of Piscova employees since we last talked, but we haven't been into the plant yet. It's possible it could be legit—that they're sending contaminated Lake Ontario eggs to bait shops or bait processors here—but when we see the two plants, maybe the evidence and records will tell us something else.

It *could* be legit; we need to keep that in mind before we go stepping on somebody's foreskin."

"Michigan eggs are also contaminated," Service said.

"In fact that's true, but it's a question of degree and official scientific evaluation. Your eggs are still legal for human consumption," Rogers said. "Our eggs will turn you into a glow stick."

Service's gut told him there was something the other two were holding back, but decided this wasn't the time to press.

9

TUESDAY, OCTOBER 19, 2004

Elk Rapids, Antrim County

They were just leaving the airport when Miars called on the 800-megahertz radio. "Twenty Five Fourteen, Twenty Five One Oh One."

"Go, One Oh One."

"I just did a drive-by, counted six vehicles in the lot. The plant's on Meguzee Point at the end of the peninsula south of town. Only one road in and out, a long private driveway, and an open gate. We'll wait out on US Thirty-One. I've got help with me."

"We'll follow you in," Service said. "Twenty Five Fourteen clear."

"Miars," Service explained. "He's got two of our officers with him. We can use the extra eyes, arms, and legs. That makes six of us." He and Miars had discussed whom to bring along and the sergeant had called COs Venus Wire from Grand Traverse County and Bruce "Earthquake" Polonich from Antrim County. Wire and Polonich often worked together and were known as thorough, aggressive officers who could keep their mouths shut. According to Miars, both had cooperated with the Wildlife Resource Protection Unit on numerous occasions, and both wanted to be detectives.

"Does the company know we're coming?" Leukonovich asked from the backseat.

"Nope. We're gonna swoop in and go through the door."

"They may refuse to open," Rogers said.

"The door *will* open," Service said. "One way or another."

Service slowed as he passed Miars, who was parked in front of a boarded-up café on US 31. Miars pulled out, passed, and turned east down a narrow road that veered south.

The plant looked new, the grounds well maintained. "Look anything like their New York plant?" Service asked Rogers as they roared into the parking lot.

"This one's bigger," the officer said.

Polonich, Miars, and Wire were already at the door by the time Service and his passengers caught up.

The door was locked and Polonich pounded on it with the side of his fist. A woman came to the window beside the door, cracked open Venetian blinds, and mouthed, "We're closed."

Miars took out his cell phone and called the office on the other side of the door.

A woman answered, "Piscova."

"This is Sergeant Miars, Department of Natural Resources. We have warrants to search the premises. We're not standing out here to suck up UV rays. Open the door."

They could hear things bumping against the metal door. Miars shouted into the cell phone, "If you barricade the entrance, everyone in there is going to jail. Now open the damn door!"

It took a few moments, but the door swung open and a twenty-something young woman stared at them. She was wearing blue jeans and a baggy gray sweatshirt with electric-colored sequins that said HOTTY! There were three office chairs beside the door. Miars handed her the warrants. "We're here to search."

"I have to call the boss," the woman said.

"Do what you have to do," Service said calmly. "How many people are here today?"

"Eight," she said, "counting me. I'm trying to catch up on my filing." The others took off through the plant to round up workers and make sure no one ran off.

Service looked around the office and saw a six-foot-tall green safe pushed against a pale yellow cinder-block wall. "We'll need that safe opened," Service said.

"It doesn't open. It's old, and I guess they haven't gotten around to getting rid of it."

"Where's the combination?" Interesting use of pronouns, he noted. *They* haven't gotten around to getting rid of the safe, not *we*. He guessed she was new.

"What's your name?" Service asked.

"Alma . . . Alma DeKoening."

"How long have you worked here, Alma?"

"Three months."

"And the safe never opens?"

"Not that I seen. The combination got lost years ago. The safe belongs to Mr. Fagan."

"The owner?"

"Yes, the chief executive officer. My boss is Mr. Vandeal. He's the plant manager."

"Tell your boss when you get hold of him that the safe has to be opened."

"He's gonna be kinda sore," she said. "Mr. Vandeal's grandson is playing peewee football in Petoskey today."

Service said, "We don't get that safe open, he's gonna be in jail for resisting, and you'll be there with him." He could see that she was shaking, and added, "Relax, Alma. We're just trying to do our job, just like you. There's nothing personal in this. Call your boss and help us out, and we'll make this as easy as we can, okay?"

"Yessir."

"Good," he said.

Rogers came into the office from the warehouse area. "Nothing back there. They're cleaning equipment and waiting for a weir shipment. What do we have up here?"

"This is Alma," Service said. "She's been here three months and she's trying to be helpful. She's gonna call the boss and get the combination to the safe over there."

Rogers glanced at the safe and said, "We could blow it up."

The woman's eyes widened as she snatched up the phone.

"Any New York containers out back?" Service whispered.

"Not so far."

"How many people?"

Miars said, "Seven. They said they're waiting for weir shipments today—part of the contract with the state. They'll ship the eggs on to your hatcheries."

Alma put down the phone. "Mr. Vandeal and the company lawyer will be here in an hour. He said I should give you whatever you need."

Service and Rogers exchanged glances.

Rogers joined Leukonovich, who was already beginning to open file drawers.

Service plopped down at the desk closest to the safe and began going through it. In a large side drawer he found an old, dusty Rolodex. There was another on Alma's desk. Why two of them? One that didn't get chucked? The office was immaculate and organized, not the sort of place where things wouldn't get pitched when they'd outlived their usefulness. Something overlooked, maybe? Time would tell. Service went out to the Tahoe, brought back a dozen cardboard boxes, and assembled some of them. The first thing he packed was the old Rolodex.

Just before Willem Vandeal arrived, Service found a small, yellowed piece of paper with some numbers scrawled on it, stuck inside the main drawer of the desk. He peeled it off and looked at it. A lock combination?

Vandeal was wearing a bright orange jacket with the words HEAD COACH, ELK RAPIDS JUNIOR FIGHTING ELK in black-and-white script over the breast. The man was short and trim, fiftyish, with short white hair, the same man he had seen with Benny Baranov in Moran. Trailing behind Vandeal was a woman in an orange-and-black tracksuit and Nike running shoes. Her hair was matted and she looked like a good sweat had been interrupted.

"What's going on here?" Vandeal asked. Calm demeanor, voice even, no sign of stress—like they got search warrants every day.

Alma handed him the papers and he passed them to the young woman without looking at them. "Who are you people?" he asked.

Grady Service made introductions.

"We have DNR people in and out of here all the time," Vandeal said. "Why're New York and the IRS here?"

Roy Rogers said, "By law, all we have to do is give you the warrants."

"I understand that," Vandeal said, "but what about common courtesy?"

"We *are* being courteous," Rogers said.

Vandeal was beginning to redden. "Look, we're trying to rebuild a football program in this town and today's game is a big one. I'm the head coach and I had to leave my kids on the sidelines."

The woman with Vandeal looked at him, nodded, and handed the paperwork back to Service.

"How old are the kids?" Service asked.

"Fifth and sixth graders," Vandeal said.

"They have a lifetime to get over one game."

"Well, it's beyond me what the heck this is all about. I don't like being called away like this."

"So sue us," Service said, making a play on the name of the bar where he'd seen Vandeal buy the salmon eggs from Baranov. Vandeal didn't react. "We need for you to open your safe," Service added.

"Sorry, but the combination to that thing got lost years ago, and only Quint can open it. It's his, from the old days."

"Can you call him?" Rogers asked.

"I can try. He's not easy to reach."

"Do what you can. Meanwhile, do you mind if I take a crack at it?"

Vandeal gave him an amused look. "Suit yourself."

He opened the safe on the third try and Vandeal's mouth hung open and Alma said, "Wow, I've never seen the inside before."

The girl's astonishment aside, the safe looked relatively empty. There were two pale blue metal boxes on the bottom, both about eighteen inches long and six inches wide. Service bent down to pick one up and found it to be inordinately heavy.

Vandeal was on the phone. Service heard him say, "They're here right now and they just opened your safe."

It took some effort, but he got one of the metal boxes onto a desk. There was no dust on it. It had a key lock. Service looked at Vandeal. "Key?"

"No idea what that is," he said. "Must be Quint's."

"You talked to him. Where is he?"

"Lansing, on business."

"He's always in Lansing," Alma added, earning a disapproving look from her boss.

Service got a paper clip from Alma, straightened it, and began trying to solve the lock. Miars came in, saw what was going on, and asked if he could try. Service offered him the clip, but Miars brushed it aside, borrowed a pencil from Alma's desk, and began gently poking at the lock. After several minutes, he turned to Service and held out his hand. "Scalpel, please."

Service gave him the paper clip.

The lock opened immediately.

Vandeal said, "I don't know anything."

"You haven't seen anything yet," Service said.

"I don't know anything," Vandeal repeated.

Miars looked at the box, picked up something, and held it up. "Silver dollar," he said. He counted, his lips moving. "I count forty of them, and these." He held up a shiny gold coin.

Zhenya Leukonovich stepped over to Miars. "May I?" She took the coins, studied them, looked back at the men, and held up the silver dollar. "This is an 1895 P in what one might call fine condition. It's worth approximately ten thousand dollars." She put down the dollar and held up a gold coin. "And this is a 1967 Krugerrand, an original. Each contains one full troy ounce of gold, which yesterday was selling at four hundred and thirty dollars an ounce on the international market. A lot of people hoard these things as a hedge against bad times."

Service hoisted the second box out of the safe and Miars opened it. It was filled with Krugerrands. Leukonovich counted all the coins and looked at the men. "The approximate value is five hundred thousand dollars, and there are two hundred and fifty Krugers, for another hundred K."

Service turned to Vandeal. "Six hundred grand in rare coins, and you *don't know anything about it*?"

"I told you, the safe and everything in it belongs to the boss, Quintan Fagan."

"I'm, like . . . totally blown away," Alma muttered.

Vandeal's lawyer had been reading the search warrants and had said nothing until now. "You can take anything that has to do with plant operations," she said, "but the coins are not covered by the writ. They stay."

Service looked at Leukonovich, who nodded.

"And they'll be right here if we look again?" Service said.

"They're the personal property of Mr. Fagan," Vandeal said.

Venus Wire came into the office from the warehouse. "The weir shipment is here. What should we do?"

"If you don't let my people process them, the eggs will go bad," Vandeal said. "They're for the state."

Miars said to CO Wire, "Watch what they do, talk to the people about the process, take notes."

Wire disappeared as Service's cell phone buzzed. He popped it open. "Service here."

"Service, this is Jeff Choate from Fisheries. I coordinate the Piscova contract. What's this bullshit I'm hearing about search warrants?"

Interesting, Service thought. Wagons being circled so fast? And why such a blatant attempt at interference now? Was Choate part of it? "This isn't part of the hatchery business," he told the Fisheries man.

"If you disrupt our egg shipment, I'm going to make life miserable for you," the man said.

"You got a problem, call Chief O'Driscoll," Service said.

He was trying to sort out the connection and overreaction when his cell phone rang again. "Detective Service, this is Director Teeny, and I want to know what you think you're doing, harassing a valued state contractor?"

"We're not harassing anyone, Mr. Director. We're gathering evidence as part of an authorized investigation."

"I authorized no such investigation," Teeny said.

"Talk to Chief O'Driscoll," Service said.

"Lorne hasn't said anything to me about this," the director said. Service thought he heard him sputter at the end of the sentence.

"Just doing our job," Service said, closing his phone. He stepped outside and called the chief, who answered on the second ring. "We're at Piscova in Elk Rapids. I just got calls from Jeff Choate and the director, demanding to know what we're doing."

"What did you tell them?'

"That we're here as part of an authorized investigation. I told them both to call you."

"Find anything yet?"

"That depends on your definition. We found an estimated six hundred thousand dollars' worth of rare gold coins in a safe in the office. The plant manager don't know nuttin', claims they belong to the owner."

O'Driscoll paused before speaking. "What do the coins have to do with our investigation?"

"Not sure yet."

"Will your warrants stretch to cover the coins?"

"The company's lawyer says no."

"Anything else?"

"We're just getting into the paperwork, but I found an old Rolodex. No idea what's in it yet, but we'll take it along. You think we should grab the the coins?"

O'Driscoll took a long time to speak again. "Better leave them. Take photographs, do a formal count, and get an affadavit from the Piscova people, verifying the count."

"Okay, chief."

"Where are you taking the records?"

"Lieutenant Bosk told Miars we can have some space at the District Five HQ in Gaylord." Brett Bosk had joined the DNR about the same time as Service, had been a solid CO, and was respected as a lieutenant as well.

"Good. Everything by the book, right?"

"Absolutely, sir."

Late in the afternoon they began to carry boxes out to the trucks. Roy Rogers nudged Service and asked the girl Alma to step outside with them, turning on his tape recorder.

"What's your job here?" Rogers asked.

"Quality assurance manager for Piscova," she said.

"Caviar Queen and bookkeeping too?" Rogers said.

"It's a lot of work, but the pay's not bad."

"What happened to Roxy?"

The woman looked at Rogers for a moment. "Ms. Lafleur? She retired in August."

"Retired. Did she move?"

"I don't know. I never met her," Alma said.

"Have you got an address for her?"

"I can look it up, if you guys haven't taken my Rolodex yet."

Service nodded. Rogers said, "We can look it up ourselves. Thanks."

The woman went inside. "Who's Roxy?" Service asked.

"Don't really know. We heard the name from one of our inspectors. There was a woman named Roxy—the New York plant people called her the Caviar Queen. She went to the New York plant several times a year to inspect eggs."

"Caviar queen?"

"The egg lady," Rogers said.

Vandeal came outside. "I just talked to my grandson. They won a close one. Are you people about done here?"

"Let me get the receipts for you," Service said. Why wasn't Vandeal more concerned about the subpoenas?

Vandeal took his time reading the lists before signing and dating each page.

The young woman with him handed Miars a business card, and Miars handed it to Service. It read CONSTANCE ALGYRE, ATTORNEY AT LAW, and listed a Traverse City address, several phone numbers, and an e-mail address.

"Thanks, Connie," Service said.

"*Ms.* Algyre," the woman said icily.

He turned to Vandeal. "What's Shamrock Productions?"

"One of the boss's side businesses."

"Fish business?"

Vandeal shrugged. "Video production. Mr. Fagan has a lot of outside business interests."

Loading complete, Service dug out the old Rolodex that he'd found and located an address for Roxanne Lafleur. She lived on Smokey Hollow Road in Traverse City.

Service walked over to Venus Wire. "You know where this is?"

"About halfway up the Old Mission Peninsula. Take M-Thirty-Seven north past Mapleton to where the road splits and bear right. That's Smokey Hollow Road. You want me to show you the way?"

"Thanks, no. You guys get the stuff back to Gaylord. Thanks for everything."

"Not a problem," Wire said. She was about thirty, muscular, smiled easily.

Rogers asked, "Is it out of our way?"

"No, it's fairly close."

"We've got rooms in Gaylord," Rogers said.

"We can swing by the address before we head to Gaylord."

Service walked over to Miars. "Rogers wants to visit the old quality assurance manager."

Miars said, "I'll order pizzas for about eight people at the district office. We can get together there and start going through all this stuff. Call me when you're an hour out and I'll place the order."

TUESDAY, OCTOBER 19, 2004

Old Mission Peninsula, Grand Traverse County

It was closing dark by the time Service found the address, a driveway through a stand of towering maples, oaks, and white pines, a sagging, heavy link chain across the driveway.

"Nobody home," Rogers said.

"Maybe, but let's take a little walk."

He parked the Tahoe on the road and the three of them walked almost a third of a mile back to an expansive house overlooking the East Arm of Grand Traverse Bay.

"Five thousand square feet easily," Leukonovich said.

"Gotta be millions for a place like this," Service added. It immediately struck him that with his inheritance from Nantz, he could afford such a place, and the thought made his stomach roll.

They walked around the house. No lights inside, no sign of life.

"Let's talk to the neighbors," Service suggested.

It took four houses to find someone who knew Lafleur. The woman's name was Harris and she was one of those rare people who showed no fear of cops. "Roxy? She's gone."

"Gone—like on a trip?"

"Just gone."

"Missing?"

"All I know is that she retired, closed up the place, and left."

"With her husband?" Rogers asked.

"She never married. Worked all those years at some fish business up in Elk Rapids. House like that, I figure she must've owned the company."

"What's she like?"

"Private. She never socialized, but I'd see her out walking her kids now and then, and she was always friendly."

"Kids?" Service asked.

"Three chocolate Labs. They're pretty much her whole life."

"No idea where she might be?"

"I saw her car loaded up, and there's been no mail in her mailbox. I assume she arranged to have it forwarded."

They thanked the woman for her help, and returned to the Tahoe.

"We'll talk to the post office Monday," Service said as they headed east toward Gaylord.

"Those people are kinda hinky about addresses," Rogers said.

"They can be managed," Leukonovich said from the backseat.

TUESDAY, OCTOBER 19, 2004

Gaylord, Otsego County

The group met at 8 P.M. but there was minimal discussion. Instead, they divvied up paperwork from the plant: Rogers took the contracts; Miars got records pertaining to state weir operations; and Leukonovich, the financial reports. Service carefully dismantled the old Rolodex, took the cards to a copier, and began copying each one. The Rolodex contained more than a thousand entries: DNR contacts from both New York and Michigan; Piscova's suppliers and service providers; lawyers, insurance agents, and bankers; others in various aspects of the fish business in Michigan and other states; and, most important, the names of employees, most of them no longer with the firm.

Copies made, Service began looking through the pages one at a time, making piles by category. Around 11 P.M. he walked into the conference room and announced, "I need a smoke." Rogers walked outside with him, Service lit up, and handed Rogers a stack of copies. "New York DNR employees." Rogers looked through the stack, pulled one out, and shook his head.

"Something I should know?" Service said.

"Garrick Bindi," Rogers said. "He worked at one of our hatcheries and got canned for stealing equipment. That was two, maybe three years back. Same plant where the manager resigned. Since then we had an informant call and claim it was Bindi, not the manager, who used to unlock the gates and let people in to steal eggs. He got paid in cash, they didn't take many each time, and nobody picked up on it until we got the tip, began looking at our data, and there it was. Pretty damn clever. You can steal a shitload if you're not too greedy. I think I mentioned this earlier."

"You forgot details. Did you bring charges?"

"Had an informant's claim and no evidence. We brought him in and talked to him several times, but he played dumb. About a year ago he boogied."

"Foul play?"

"More likely he split because he didn't appreciate the heat." Rogers tapped the sheet again. "If this means anything, I've got a pretty good idea who he was letting in."

"Based on the card? There are a lot of your state employees in that pile."

"Bindi's the only worker bee. The rest are people with pull who could do things for Piscova—contracts and such. He stands out as the oddball."

"If he's gone, there's not much you can do unless he screws up, and somebody grabs him for something else."

"Yeah . . . unless somebody from Piscova knows where he is, or admits to the egg thefts."

Service looked at his New York counterpart. "The Caviar Queen?"

"Could be," Rogers said.

"Where'd you get her name?"

"Lemme have one of your smokes. I quit the damn things two years ago, but right now I need something to settle my nerves." Rogers lit up and inhaled deeply. "Finding twenty grand in that wreck wasn't enough to bring in the IRS," he explained. "I mean, they might have sent over a junior agent, but instead, they sent Leukonovich, who is like their big-case hound dog."

"Why?"

"It's taken me a while to get it out of her, but she says the IRS got a tip from a former subcontractor who claimed he got stiffed by Piscova. He also told the IRS that he knew a woman who had personally transported bags of cash back and forth between New York and Michigan. Said he had dates, times, and details."

"Roxy, the Caviar Queen. Why didn't you tell me this earlier?"

"I'm making my way in this case like a blind man with earplugs. Until you called, we were nowhere. We needed time to get comfortable with each other, yes?"

Service took a sheet out of his pocket and handed it to the New Yorker. "Addresses for the Caviar Queen. It lists the house we saw on the Old Mission Peninsula, another place in Florida, and a camp in the U.P., in Northern Marquette County. No phone numbers, just addresses."

"She's sure not here," Rogers said, scanning the page. "Her place in Florida was listed as Sugar Sand Estates, and someone had written Pensacola Beach in parentheses. What kind of budget do you have for this case?" Rogers asked.

"Unspecified, but I've got enough to call one of our people and have them visit the Marquette address."

"I'll talk to Zhenya, see if she can get one of her people to check out Florida."

"Who called the IRS about Piscova?"

"Zhenya's a team player—the IRS team, period. She plays things close to the vest and she isn't saying, but I overheard her say something about a Greek during one of her phone calls."

A Greek? Service went back to his papers, pulled the stack of former employees, and handed half to Rogers, who raised an eyebrow. "Better than nothing," Service said.

There were more than a hundred names, and it took a while to sort through them.

"You don't have to have a Greek name to be Greek," Rogers pointed out.

"Read," Service said.

He found two names right away: Vasilios Kefalis and Theo Trisagios. A notation said Kefalis died in 2000. He set aside the sheet for Trisagios.

"Prokos?" Rogers said.

"That's Greek."

"Tassos Andriaitis?"

"You bet."

They found five names in all and looked at their titles: Trisagios had been a truck driver; Prokos, the plant engineer; a woman named Litsa Agonas worked in contract liaison; a man named Belafis had been a janitor; Andriaitis had held the title of processing supervisor.

"Let's talk to our IRS colleague," Service said. "But let me do the talking."

Leukonovich came outside with cup of coffee. "It's a lot warmer inside," she said. "Cold disagrees with Zhenya."

Like all reptiles, Service thought. "We're outdoor guys," he countered. "We've been looking at employee names from an old Rolodex and I found a note linking Roxy the Caviar Queen to a certain man with a Greek name."

Leukonovich took a measured sip of coffee. "You called me outside to tell me that? Why is this significant?"

"There's a list of dates and dollar amounts on the entry for one of the Greeks and a mirror entry on Roxanne Lafleur's record."

"I see," Leukonovich said. "Which person?"

Service handed her the sheets and watched her go through them, reading deliberately, but lingering over one more than the others, before looking up. "There are no dates or amounts on any of these."

Service took the pages from her, pulled out the one for Prokos. "The specifics are on another sheet."

"Are we sharing?" she asked, looking him in the eye. "Or are we not?"

"Very good question," Service said. "*Are* we?"

She shook her head, and a smirk formed. "You don't have dates or amounts," she said. "You were fishing for a name."

"*Nolo contendere*," Service admitted.

"According to policy, practice, legal casework, and ethics, Zhenya is forbidden to share the names of informants. There is nothing personal in this, gentlemen."

"Understood," Service said. *What kind of woman referred to herself in the third person?*

"Are we done?"

"For the moment," he said.

"What the hell just went on?" Rogers asked after she went back inside.

"I juked her. The sheet she paid the most attention to was Andriaitis. He lives in Baldwin, according to the information here. That's about an hour north of Grand Rapids."

"You think the address is current?"

"We'll find out."

Service called a retired CO named Carl Burke, known to Lake County locals as King Kong. A sleepy female voice answered, "Wha—?"

"Have you got a gorilla in bed there with you?" Service asked.

"Grady Service, what the heck are you doing calling here at this time of night? We go to bed at nine."

"Hand the phone to Carl, Jen."

"Jesus Christ!" a voice boomed into the phone. "Don't you know retired wardens actually sleep at night?"

"I need help, Carl."

"Do I need a fucking pen or something to scribble with?"

"Maybe not. You know everyone around Baldwin and in Lake County, right?"

"If this is a quiz, what can I win?"

"The name Tassos Andriaitis ring a bell?"

"What if it does?

"Bottle of single malt is what it means."

"Fuck that single-malt pussy piss. I'll take a half-gallon of Jack. Tassos Andriaitis has a place on the flies-only water of the Pere Marquette. He's up here early summer, before he heads back to work in Alaska."

"What sort of work?"

"Has his own fish business up there. Does business all over the world."

"Stand-up guy?"

"Nobody in the fish business can meet that standard, but he's a pretty solid guy. Very, very tough and a total asshole about fair play, yada yada, which don't mean he wouldn't put you in the poorhouse with a deal that benefits him."

"Where in Alaska?"

"HQ's in Anchorage, but he has all sorts of stuff all over the state. He works June through December up there, and heads down to his place in Florida. He comes up here to fish and rest for April and May."

"Where in Florida?"

"Pensacola Beach."

"*Really*?"

"I just said so, for Chrissakes. Your hearing going bad?"

"He have girlfriends?"

"What am I, his biographer? I had to two-finger my case reports. His old lady's name is Mel and she'd take off his balls with pinking shears if he strayed. No girlfriends, not Tassos. He's about money and fair play."

"I'll have your Jack delivered," Service said.

"This what you needed?"

"More than you can know. Give my apologies to Jen."

"Hey, Grady, don't never retire, man. It's fucking boring!"

Service closed the cell phone and sat back. "We need to go to Alaska," Service announced.

Rogers said, "I think I donated my snowshoes to the Sisters of the Poor."

"We'll get you some loaners."

"I'll have to clear this with my supervision."

"Me too. Let's do it first thing in the morning and take it from there."

"You gonna share what you learned?"

"In the morning. I need sleep," Grady Service said. What he needed more was guidance for handling a case that was beginning to look like it could be far more complicated than anything he'd ever dealt with before.

What he wanted to do more than anything was start thinking about the upcoming firearm deer season, but it was beginning to feel like this case might override the things he'd rather do, not to mention the things he knew best. It was a disconcerting thought.

Leukonovich and Rogers headed to their rooms at a local sleep-cheap, and Service called Luticious Treebone, a habitual night owl, even though he was now retired.

He and Treebone had finished college the same year—Service at Northern Michigan University, where he'd been a fair student and solid hockey player, and Treebone at Wayne State, where he'd graduated cum laude and lettered in baseball and football. They had both volunteered for the marines and met at Parris Island before serving together in the same long-range recon unit in Vietnam. They had been in hell together, and rarely spoke of it.

After Vietnam they had entered the Michigan State Police Academy in Lansing and spent two years as Troops before transferring to DNR law enforcement. After a year as a CO, Tree had moved to the Detroit Metropolitan Police Department, where he had risen to the rank of lieutenant in charge of one of the city's numerous vice units. Had it not been for his wife Kalina's dislike for the U.P., Treebone would not have transferred to Detroit, but now that he was retired he planned to spend a lot of time at North of Nowhere, the name of the camp Service had bought for his friend.

"You know what time it is?" his friend challenged him.

"Does it matter? I've got what feels like a complicated case developing—involving at least two states, the IRS, environmental violations, fraud, and God knows what else. It feels way out of my league."

"Bullshit. Just grow you a tree."

"Say again?"

"What we did in Vice. You write down people, places, events, and times. Then you connect them all with different-colored lines to see if there's a pattern, see how everything fits. It'll look like a genetically fucked tree when you've got it."

"You want to meet and show me?"

"I said, *we* done it, not me. I had people to do that crap."

"I need help, Tree."

"Man, I hate that tone. North of Nowhere work for you?"

"That works, but I don't know when yet. I've got to go to Alaska. I'll call you and we'll set up a time."

"I don't mind some extra days up there. I'll bring my bow, see what wanders by."

"Black man with a bow and arrow?"

"Man, we invented that shit in Africa. You white boys stole it from us."

Service slept for a few hours in the conference room and was awakened by a presence. He looked up to see Zins staring at him and looking around the room.

"What?" Service asked.

"Stopped by to see Brett. I'm a little early."

Bosk and Zins? Odd couple.

"You look busy, so I'll leave you alone," Zins said, taking a final survey of the room.

Service went into the office area but Zins wasn't there. He found a receptionist in the canteen, making coffee. "You see El-Tee Zins?"

"No," she said.

"He and Bosk pals?"

"Not that I know of. He shows up about as often as the other lieutenants. Zins just retired, right?"

Service nodded, went into the men's room, and splashed his face with cold water to wake up. Afterwards he called Roy Rogers at his motel. "You coming back here this morning?"

"Our flight isn't till late afternoon."

"I'm going to lock the room. I gave you a key, right?"

"Yep. You going to be there?"

"Yep, but I'm going to try to get permission to go to Alaska."

"Okay. See you after I fetch Leukonovich and we grab some breakfast."

Service called the chief at home and brought him up to speed. "I need to go to Alaska to see a man."

"Your investigation, your decision."

"What kind of budget do I have?"

"I'm working on that." The chief gave him an account number to charge his travel and expenses, adding, "That's probably temporary. I'll talk to you soon about a budget."

Service was in the conference room going through names when Rogers and Leukonovich appeared. Rogers went right to work, but Leukonovich got a cup of coffee, came over to him, and touched his shoulder. "Can we talk outside?"

"It's colder this morning than last night."

They stepped outside and she said, "I would beg a cigarette."

Service handed her the pack. She fumbled trying to light it, took a long pull, and exhaled. "Zhenya wonders why you stay in a low-level government position."

"Beg your pardon?"

"You are a wealthy man. You could use your time more productively."

It took a moment for what she was saying to register. "You ran a background check on me?"

"Zhenya makes it a point to know the people she is to work with."

"Is that legal?" He felt angry, but her straightforward approach had put him on his heels.

She shrugged. "Zhenya thinks is odd that a man of such means would be doing this work."

"I haven't always had 'such means,' " he said.

"Yes, but the question remains."

"I like the work?" he offered.

She dropped the cigarette and stepped on it. "You are an interesting man, Detective. Zhenya finds few men interesting. I sense in you a combination of zealotry and passion that intrigues me."

Was she hitting on him, and if so, how was he supposed to respond?

He managed a grin. "Kind of cold out here."

"Zhenya feels no cold in your presence," she said, waiting for him to open the door. When she moved to step by him, she stumbled against him and held the contact before recovering and walking ahead as if they had not even talked. When he found himself staring at her behind, he rolled his eyes and cursed himself quietly.

Halfway to the conference room she turned around and came back toward him. "To be entirely forthcoming, Zhenya would entertain invitations to fornicate, Detective, but you should be forewarned that as a wealthy man, you are going to have females and all kinds of people trying to take your money. You must learn to be very, very cautious."

Her off-the-wall declaration finished, Leukonovich pivoted and went to the conference room, leaving him in the hallway with his mouth hanging open.

12

SATURDAY, OCTOBER 23, 2004

Anchorage, Alaska

The city reminded him of a Copper Country town—weary, worn, beat-up, and filled with feral people genetically wired to survive. He checked into a small hotel called Slimers. His room reeked of water mixed with vinegar and had the mottled color scheme of a rotten stump. He had gotten the phone number of Andriaitis from a group called United Fishermen of Alaska. Andriaitis hadn't seemed overly interested in talking, but had agreed to it so long as Service would "bring your sorry ass up from the Outside." The chief approved the trip without questions, but Rogers got held back in New York for unspecified reasons—budget, maybe.

Service called Andriaitis from Michigan and again from the airport in Anchorage, and arranged to meet him at a joint called Polarpalooza, a converted warehouse with a hundred-foot-long bar and wooden floors worn to the grain by too many calked boots and too much wet slop.

Andriaitis had shaggy white hair and eyebrows, a permanently windburned face, hands the size of baseball gloves, and a voice that crackled like taut canvas in a high wind. He was short and wide with a jaw that stuck out like an invitation to trouble.

"I called King Kong," Andriaitis greeted him. "He says you're an asshole with serious *bullchitna*, but he vouched for you."

Service had no idea what the man was talking about. "He said the same about you."

Andriaitis snarled, tilted back his head, and laughed. "I don't have all night to shoot the shit. I've got five crab rigs to get ready, and if you aren't on top of the help up here, they'll peel the Charmin right out of the crack in your ass."

"Piscova," Service said.

"About fucking time you people wised up. Piscova's been ripping off the state for years and nobody seems to give a shit."

The man seemed too righteous out of the gate, and Service wondered if it was nerves, or something else. "You've known this for years and never said anything to anyone. If Piscova hadn't screwed you over, you'd still be working for them, and we wouldn't be sitting here."

"You talk tough," Andriaitis said, clenching the table. "Want to step outside and see who can back it up?"

Service said, "I'll break both your legs before you stand up."

Andriaitis guffawed, released the table, and waved a hand at a bartender who looked like he wasn't yet sixteen. "Two beers here, and keep them rolling." He turned to Service. "The IRS keeps bugging me to talk, but fuck them. You're right. Piscova and Fagan are shitpiles, but I couldn't say much. I had bills and responsibilities, all that shit, but it wasn't the money that finally got me pissed. It was Roxy."

"The Caviar Queen, Roxanne Lafleur."

"After I seen what that creep Fagan did to her . . . that was all she wrote."

Service knew from experience that maintaining silence sometimes encouraged sources and witnesses to keep talking. He took out his small recorder and set it on the table. "You mind?" Andriaitis shook his head, and Service pressed the ON button.

"Fagan was banging her like an apprentice carpenter with his first claw hammer. She's the loyal type, did everything he asked. And now this."

"This?"

"Cancer. She sampled so many goddamn poison salmon eggs, the cancer got her."

"That's why she left the company?"

"Fagan gave her some cash and told her to clear out."

"The girl who took her place says the company pays pretty well."

"It ain't the actual pay, which is okay, but when the new girl starts fucking Fagan, she'll find herself swimming in cash, and if she skims a bit for herself, who cares? It's all off the books."

"Is that how Roxy got the big house?"

Andriaitis made a face. "Fagan's. He put it under Roxy's name to hide it from the IRS. He has all sorts of arrangements like that. But she managed to build herself a place up north of Marquette with what she got, and that's all hers. Out in the sticks, but that's what she likes."

"Is she there now?"

Andriaitis nodded. "Getting treatment at the regional medical center."

"You called the IRS to get justice for her."

"Right. I knew I'd never get my money from that bastard, so the least I could do was find a way to kick Fagan's Irish balls."

"Talk to me about Piscova."

"How long you got?"

"As long as you can spare."

"Not tonight. I've got work. Meet me at the Climate House at seven bells tomorrow morning. We'll have coffee and talk then, but think about this: The state Budget Audit Office audited Piscova years ago and found that the company owed money—a helluva lot of it—going back several years under the contract. As a result, the state let the contract go to another company, but it turned out that Fagan was a major shareholder in that operation too, and even though his other company got the contract, he began to threaten a lawsuit for breach of contract with Piscova, and the spineless state backed off. The sonuvabitch is like bad breath at an all-night poker game. Next thing, the BAO people decide there were no violations and they sent a bunch of seized records back to Piscova. Of course, there's no way your lot will be able to get them back for another look because they won't exist anymore."

"You're telling me someone in BAO was on the take?"

"Yeah, if free and copious hair-pie and goodies count. So here we have this company screwing the state based on BAO's audit, and next thing you know, they weren't in violation, the records were sent back to the company, the BAO made no copies, and the auditor in BAO wrote an article for a state employees magazine telling everyone what a great fucking company Piscova was—the state's model vendor. Can you believe that shit?"

"What role does Vandeal play in all this?"

"Loyal soldier. You'll never get him to tip, but if Fagan can sell out Vandeal, he will. Fagan's the guy you have to put your laser sight on. And while you're poking around, look real hard at that asshole, Teeny."

Teeny was the former governor's poodle, and still director of the DNR, despite the governor's departure.

Service watched Andriaitis drain his beer and get up. "Here's a good one to sleep on: Fagan got a contract with the state in which he more or less dictated the formula for measuring the fish runs and his harvest. One year Piscova paid less than a thousand bucks for millions of salmon eggs."

Andriaitis took a step and turned back. "The BAO auditor met with Fagan to hammer out the contract before bids were submitted and a state legislator ramrodded a law through to outlaw snagging, which pretty much gave Piscova the whole market."

"The auditor's name?"

"See you in the morning, tough guy."

SUNDAY, OCTOBER 24, 2004

Anchorage, Alaska

Grady Service had expected Sergeant Miars to at least express some enthusiasm over the information he'd shared with him after meeting Andriaitis last night, but Miars only said wearily, "We've been looking at that for eighteen months and were told this is normal contract jockeying between the state and its vendors."

"And Teeny's involvement?"

"*What* involvement? He and Fagan are sometime pals. That's not a crime."

"Was Fagan a pal of Bozian's too?"

"Don't even," Miars said.

"How the hell can there be so much rumor and so many weird events, and nobody seems to give a shit?"

Miars said, "The one-eyed man is king in the land of the blind."

"Is that supposed to mean something?"

"Go to bed. You're starting to foam at the mouth."

His sergeant's dismissive attitude had made for an unexpectedly unsatisfactory conversation, but if Miars felt nothing was out of whack internally, maybe he was right—that a lot of this had been investigated and amounted to nothing. The deal with Piscova and New York eggs, however, was a different animal, and he wasn't backing off anything until he was convinced there was no case. He'd witnessed the egg sale. There was reason to believe the New York eggs were contaminated and being mixed with Michigan eggs. And Roxy Lafleur had cancer. He didn't need anything more to keep going until he got some answers. Miars could think what he wanted, but he was not backing off. No fucking way.

The desk clerk at Slimers was wearing a faded red USMC baseball cap with a golden globe and anchor.

"I need to find the Climate House," Service told the man.

"Look at a map, *cheechako*."

So much for customer relations. "Semper Fi, squidbait." The clerk saluted him with a single finger.

He spotted a hooker outside the hotel and went over to her. "I'm about to be lost," he said.

"Lost is my specialty," she said. She was in her twenties, thin, wearing a peach-colored coat and a floppy-brimmed hat with a pheasant feather in the hatband.

"Not *that* kind of lost," he said quickly.

"I'm not good enough for you, *cheechako*?" she challenged.

The day was not starting out like he had hoped. He pulled out his badge and flashed it. "Okay, enough nice-nice. Where's the goddamned Climate House?"

"Chill, big dude." She pointed in a direction. "You can walk it, twenty minutes tops."

"What the hell is *cheechako*?"

"Newcomer," she said, "meaning green as snot. Have a nice day."

The place looked out on something called Ship Creek, and Andriaitis was already seated in a booth and dumping sugar into a cup of coffee. He had bags under his eyes.

"Long night?" Service said, sitting down.

"One of my captains had his appendix blow up. We packed his butt off to the emergency room and I spent the night on the phone trying to find someone to take his place. Finding a body isn't hard. Finding a *good* one is. There's all kinds of politics around king-crabbing now. Lots of volunteers to get involved, most of them not worth a shit."

"You want to put this off until you're rested?"

Andriaitis grinned. "I rest in Florida with the wifey. I'm in Alaska to make money, and that means work. You think about what I said last night?"

"Which part?"

"I'm in no mood to dance the smartass this morning, and I don't feel like spoon-feeding your dumb ass, so fire away, and if you're too fucking ignorant to know what questions to ask, tough shit. You want breakfast?"

"What's good here?"

"This joint ain't about good. It's about fuel."

Service ordered scrambled eggs and elk chops, and after receiving permission from Andriaitis, turned on his recorder.

"Lafleur's cancer," Service began. "How bad?"

"Stage three, which ain't good, but she's just finished a round of chemo and she's optimistic."

"You're saying she got it from the eggs?"

"Seems like, but you know how that science shit works: There aren't many cases where the experts can or will say, Yep, A caused B. Fuckers can't agree on anything."

"How could she not know the eggs were contaminated?"

Andriaitis shook his head. "In her mind, she was just sampling, know what I'm saying? When good money's involved, most people can convince themselves of anything."

"What exactly does a caviar queen do?"

"Besides ridin' the boss's pony? She spent a lot of time at the New York plant and selected eggs to be sent to Michigan, where she supervised the caviar production."

"Bait eggs?"

"They mix Lake Ontario eggs with Lake Huron and Lake Michigan eggs in Elk Rapids, and ship that shit to the East Coast and to Japan. Roxy tasted eggs in New York and tasted the mixed batches in Michigan—a real double dose. Fagan didn't trust anybody else and sent Roxy, whose main job was to haul cash. She'd taste eggs in upstate New York for shipment to Michigan, and go on to New York City to collect cash for shipments from Michigan to the customer."

"What sort of quantities are we talking about?"

"Up to fifty tons a season."

Service had once read that two hundred and forty hen salmon had to be processed in order to harvest a million eggs at a weir. He had no idea how much a million eggs weighed.

"Who bought the eggs in New York?"

"I don't know. She always met her contact in a hotel in Manhattan, took in a Broadway show, and flew home the next day. But if I was a betting man, I'd put my money on the Crimea Group. That outfit controls a helluva lot of fish-related business on the East Coast, and they have the Caribbean cruise-line caviar business sewn up tighter than an Arab virgin's snatch."

Andriaitis inhaled a half piece of dry toast. "Fagan is a piece of work. Here he is shipping eggs filled with fucking mirex from New York to mix with our eggs, which the FDA says are still good for people, but he's no dummy, so he gets it written into the contract that in the event levels of contamination go up in Michigan eggs, he doesn't have to pay as much for them, which is peanuts to begin with, *and* he doesn't even have to dump those that are bad because it would be too damn dangerous for his employees. What a total crock of shit! He knew the EPA and FDA didn't do that much testing, and didn't test eggs at all—just fillets—so he hired some geek-ass science company in Detroit or Fort Wayne, or somewhere, to test Michigan eggs, and they spit out data showing higher-than-previously-reported PCBs. He presented the report to the state, and announced his payments to the state were going down. Meanwhile, he continued to sell the same salmon meat and eggs, but his cost had dropped and his profit had gone up. It's unreal; he'd worked both ends with the state whipsawed in the middle. I don't like the man, but you have to hand it to him: The sonuvabitch is damn good at what he does."

Service was trying to take in all the information and having trouble sorting it out. "The state wrote this into the contract?"

"I told you last night—the auditor from BAO spent a lot of time with him, and they worked it all out according to Fagan's specs. Aren't you listening? Man, you wouldn't last five minutes on a boat in the Bering Sea."

"I'm not on a boat." Andriaitis was a pain in the ass, but he also seemed pretty sure of what he was alleging. Was it verifiable, or was this just someone with an old grudge, spouting off?

"I called the IRS because I heard they nailed Fagan's ass in Florida for some sort of cash problem," said Andriaitis. "I did a little snooping and found that he'd pled guilty on two counts, and this made me think the feds would love another shot at him. The IRS is the elephant in the room, but an asshole like you from the state, you've got shit clout. Your whole department is tainted, and if this ever gets out, that'll be the end of whatever reputation you people have—which ain't all that good, in my opinion."

"What's the auditor's name?"

Andriaitis took a drink of coffee. "Langford Horn. He was a Bozian appointee and moved up to assistant director of BAO. Now he's the BAO director, its number-one honcho. His negotiation of the Piscova ten-year contract looked like a great deal for the state in terms of incoming revenue. It hasn't worked out that way, but he knows everybody in town and everybody knows him. Bozian's shadow still hangs over Lansing."

"What about Teeny's relationship with Fagan?"

"That's a little murky, but I hear Teeny's trying to get a job teaching at some small college near Seattle, and Fagan's made a fat donation to endow some sort of chair to sew up Teeny getting the job."

"We hear nobody wants Teeny."

"Neither does the college, but they want Fagan's money, which means it's a done deal, mark my words."

"How do you know so much?"

"Working in the fish business is like working in a whorehouse. You get to see everyone at their worst, and most whores would rather gossip than turn tricks."

"Do you think Roxy will talk to me?"

"She's been waiting for someone to open their eyes. She'll talk if I tell her it's okay, but nobody better try to beat up on her. She's good people . . . just got caught in something she couldn't handle. She'll tell you everything, but she won't testify in court. Hell, she may not live long enough for that to happen. You fuckers are so far behind Fagan, it may take you ten years just to get your boots on the right fucking feet."

Service was tired of the man's bullying. "Well, thanks a lot for talking to me. I'll talk to Roxy and make sure she gets a fair shake." He turned off the tape recorder.

The man looked surprised. "No more questions?"

"The state gave Fagan a monopoly?"

"Sealed it up for him. Before that Fagan had a crew that visited mom-and-pop fish houses and bait shops all over the state and convinced them to get out of the business. Hell, everybody was dealing eggs and illegal salmon in those days."

Service had heard rumors, but few cases had ever been proven, and after a while, the rumors had simply stopped. Was this why? "Fagan bought them out?"

"Sometimes some money got exchanged, but more often, he took one of his muscle boys with him to clarify the leave-behind message: Quit the business, or else."

"Nobody ever complained?"

"The cocksuckers were all dealing illegally. Who were they gonna cry to? Technically, Fagan was illegal, too, because of a loophole in state law, but the state senator passed a law outlawing snagging, and then the state attorney general issued a ruling that the state could legally sell salmon eggs and meat, which made the state's deal with Fagan legit. Those two things and his strong-arm tactics sewed it up for Fagan. What else?"

"I'm *cheechako* when it comes to this stuff."

Andriaitis tipped his hat back and grinned. "It takes a smart man to admit he don't know shit. King Kong said you were the real deal, and I guess I'm starting to buy that. When you get back to Michigan, call me anytime. I'm thinking that you're about to drown in red tape and the paper jungle, and it ain't gonna be fucking pretty, but call me, and if I can, I'll help you hack your way through. Roxy's a fine woman. Kick Fagan's ass for her, and for me."

What was the relationship between Roxy and Andriaitis? He was going to extraordinary lengths if it was mere friendship. He and Candi had the same kind of thing. Would he go this far for her? He couldn't answer his own question, but it reminded him he owed some people in his life phone calls.

He used his cell phone to book an afternoon flight home and walked back to the hotel under steady wet snow.

14

MONDAY, OCTOBER 25, 2004

Slippery Creek

It was 10 P.M. and Miars was waiting for him when he landed at Sawyer International Airport, twenty miles south of Marquette. It was late October, most of the leaves on the ground turning an ugly brown. Miars had driven Service's truck from Traverse City, and a state parks manager from Lansing had ferried the sergeant's truck to the Marquette regional DNR office for a conference; the parks man would catch a ride back to Lansing with a colleague.

Service drove toward his camp, too tired to talk. Miars was not the sort to flap his gums when he had nothing to say.

Newf nearly knocked him over when he walked into the cabin, and Cat started screeching. Miars stepped back from the bedlam. The dog was a Canary Island mastiff, what the Spanish called a Presa Canario, 165 pounds of muscle, an unappealing mix of brown, gray, and ocher, all slopped together like cheap cake mix in a bowl. He had found the cat years ago in a cloth bag with seven kittens someone had dumped in the creek. Why the one survived was beyond him, but she had turned into a feline misanthrope that he'd never gotten around to naming. Her screeches were like sharp fingernails down a slate board.

"Now that's what I call a welcoming committee," Miars said.

"They're both pissed. The way they see it, I was put on earth to take care of them and nothing else."

Miars laughed.

Since moving back to his cabin after Nantz's death, he'd brought in some army surplus cots for visitors. He slept on a narrow mattress on top of end-to-end footlockers.

"It ain't fancy," he told Miars.

Service made a pot of coffee and sat at the table, scribbling notes. When the coffee was done he poured a mug for the sergeant, and related some of what he had learned from Andriaitis in Alaska, focusing primarily on the Piscova contract and the BAO's involvement.

Miars listened attentively.

"Langford Horn," was the sergeant's only response.

"Spit it out."

"Horn and Teeny have a hunting camp between Pickford and Cedarville. The place used to belong to a millionaire from Chicago who shot himself one hunting season. His widow never wanted to come back, and sold it to Teeny and Horn for peanuts."

"They're pals?"

"Tight as ticks, and Bozian is one of their golfing cronies."

Service looked at his sergeant, flipped open his cell phone, and hit a speed-dial setting.

"Whit, this is Grady Service. Is Lori available?"

Governor Lorelei Timms came to the phone. "I don't know whether to be astonished or petrified," she said in lieu of a greeting.

The way he'd met the governor had been a fluke, but Nantz and Lori had become friends, and the governor had become his biggest fan. He hated asking her for anything, but the truth was, he liked her.

"Langford Horn?" he said.

"My kids are great, Whit's great, our sex life could use a jump start, the job is a pain in the butt, and I have a new allergy. Other than that, things are fine," she said. "We don't talk for months and of course you're Mr. Let's-Get-Down-to-Business. There's more to life than work, Grady."

"Yes, your gubernatorial excellency. What about Langford Horn?"

"What about him?"

"You tell me."

"Am I going to be sorry you asked?"

"It's highly probable."

She sighed. "Horn is the definition of charming and smarmy. He was one of Bozian's favorites. He's looking to move elsewhere, and make no mistake, he'll land on his feet. He knows everyone and he's good at working deals and angles."

"Have you heard Teeny wants to teach at a college out west?"

"He'd like to teach in-state, but nobody wants him. How'd *you* hear about the out-West thing?"

"Sources."

He heard her sigh and chuckle. "It's true. I talked to someone from the college the day before yesterday. They told me that they've gotten a sizable donation to underwrite a chair for Eino to teach natural resource issues."

"The donation is from a guy named Fagan," Service said. *The day before yesterday?* Andriaitis was *really* connected and wired into everything.

"Quint Fagan?"

"You know him?"

"*Of* him. His company has a long-term contract with your agency, something to do with salmon eggs."

Service was impressed both by her memory and the breadth of her knowledge. "Is he one of your contributors?"

"I can't say for sure. Most of these business politicos play both sides to hedge their bets."

"He's dirty, Lori. *Really* dirty."

"I see," she said. "I assume this is not something to talk about in detail over the phone."

"Nope."

"Okay. I'm sure you'll pay me a visit when there's a reason to talk in detail."

"Yes, ma'am."

"And I should verify if Fagan contributed to my campaign."

"I would."

Service hung up and looked over at his sergeant who was looking back, wide-eyed. "You called the *governor*? Are you out of your flipping mind! What we think and what we can prove in a court of law are two different things."

"The governor is my friend, and I don't want her caught by surprise."

"You're supposed to be apolitical."

"I am, but I also believe in fairness." Miars shook his head and Service added, "We are going to put Fagan's ass in jail."

"We're both more likely to get fired and lose our pensions."

"We'll see," Service said. "Maybe there's nothing here, but if there is, it's our duty to do the hard things. That's what they pay us for."

"They don't pay us to commit professional suicide."

"I'm not thinking about politics, or suicide," Service said. He laid out the situation with Roxanne Lafleur for his sergeant.

The sergeant's attitude changed immediately. "Caviar is food. The Food and Drug Administration regulates that. We need to talk to someone at the FDA."

"You want to go with me to talk to Lafleur?"

"If it won't spook her."

"She doesn't have a phone, so we'll just have to see."

"I can't believe you just picked up the phone and called the *governor*," Miars said, shaking his head with obvious disbelief.

15

TUESDAY, OCTOBER 26, 2004

Huron Mountains, Marquette County

Service and Miars swung by the regional office first thing in the morning to pick up the sergeant's truck and a county plat book. Service found that Lafleur had 120 acres off County Road 510, near the Little Pup River.

The property fronted a hilly section of County Road 510 and with most leaves down, Service could see the building a couple of hundred feet above the county road. There was a chain across the grassy two-track driveway, so he continued down 510 to find a place on state land to stash the truck. They walked back to Lafleur's driveway and found a mud-covered sign on the ground that read CAVIAR QUEEN. A new plywood sign had been crudely painted, but was on the ground beside the pole-barn garage. The new sign said DEATH ROE. It had crudely painted skulls and crossbones above and below the letters. Service looked through a door into the garage, and saw a dark green Chrysler minivan inside.

The narrow two-track went past the pole barn, morphed into a sculpted path, and meandered its way up to the house, which was small and built on the crest of a hard-rock ridge. Service saw steel beams beneath the platform and figured the place wouldn't get blown off the mountain by high winds. Dogs began raising a ruckus when they were fifty feet from the house, and Service grabbed his sergeant's arm and thrust him ahead.

Miars gave him a quizzical look, but went ahead. Three chocolate Labs came bounding out the door and circled the sergeant, tails wagging, tongues hanging out, butts gyrating happily. A woman stood in the doorway and Service walked through the dog pack toward her. He had suffered a lifelong fear of all dogs until Newf came along, and though she was helping him conquer the irrationality, it still overcame him at times.

"Ms. Lafleur?"

She didn't look sick. She had short blond hair, a great figure (if on the thin side), and looked like she could run a marathon at a moment's notice.

"Grady? Tas called and said you'd be coming."

How had Andriaitis called her? She had no phone. Service introduced Miars, and she invited them inside, telling the dogs, "Stay outside and go potty for Mommy."

The interior was warm and homey, with a long window looking westward toward lines of tree-covered ridges and bare rocky outcrops. The house sat on the ridge like the crow's nest on a ship. "Impressive view," Service said.

"Coffee?"

She went to make a pot and Miars said, "This is something. You've got to be a genius or a fool to build up here."

Service said, "Sometimes they're the same thing." Miars grinned.

The woman let the dogs in and they immediately lined up and sat in front of Service, staring up at him with expectant yellow eyes.

"Now, girls," Lafleur said from the kitchen. "We talked about this." The dogs wagged their tails in unison. She came back with coffee and said, "Meet Stella, Ella, and Bella—my kids. They're just five, and very sweet."

"You see any wolves up here?" Miars asked.

"Just tracks," she said, "but the kids know to stay near the house."

Service wanted to get the conversation on track, but decided to let her take the lead for now.

"Steel beams?" Miars said.

Lafleur nodded. "We won't blow away to Oz, Sergeant."

"No, ma'am. I just wondered. It's a terrific place."

"I designed it myself," she said proudly. "My dream house."

Service saw an opportunity. "The sign by the garage suggests otherwise."

She pursed her lips. "I was devastated when I did that, but I never put it up."

"You just finished chemotherapy? You look pretty strong."

"It could have been a lot worse," the woman said. "I've had a pretty good life. You have to expect some rough times."

"Could you tell us about your job?" Service asked.

She squinted at Service. "The details are boring. I assume you want to know the real stuff."

"If you feel like talking." Service set the recorder on the table and turned it on. He had decided to record and transcribe every interview in the case in order to have a record, and to help his own porous memory. He had not yet determined how he was going to get the transcription done.

"You went all the way to Anchorage to see Tas; that tells me it's important and that you're serious."

"It is, and we are," Service said.

Lafleur poured coffee for them, picked up her cup, and sat back. "I started working with Quint when I was in my early twenties, and it was a lot of fun. He was just beginning, and we had lots of people with enthusiasm."

"Your relationship grew to be more than work," Service said.

She rolled her eyes. "We were wild. We were together all the time and it just happened. We were both kinda randy, if you know what I mean."

Service nodded. He knew. He and Nantz had been the same.

"I guess I was pretty good at whatever he gave me to do, and eventually he promoted me to quality assurance manager for caviar. Everybody called me the Caviar Queen. I oversaw processing and production of the eggs, from selection, to flavor control, to packaging. Of course, we made caviar only during the fall, but when the season was on, it was nonstop."

"You went back and forth to New York."

"The plant is in Harrytown. I was there several times each egg season."

"To do what?"

"Quint wanted me to decide which eggs were closest in size, flavor, and color to Michigan eggs. Sometimes they were indistinguishable on all parameters, and sometimes they looked like they came from a different species. Once in a while I couldn't find enough, and we had to ship all Michigan eggs; that made Quint really sore because it cost him."

Lafleur shut her eyes. "When we first started mixing the eggs he told me it was simply a matter of 'attenuating taste'—his term. What he wanted me to believe was that the New York eggs would add some sort of counter-flavor to the Michigan eggs, making them more desirable to consumers—kind of like sweet and sour, or something like that."

"You agreed?"

"Of course not. From the beginning I thought it was all about money, and eventually he admitted it, and I didn't protest. We were making a lot of money and I was having a really good time. What was there to protest?"

"You also went to New York City sometimes."

"Quint had a deal with the Crimea Group. They're owned by Semyon Krapahkin, and he's quite a story. Came to the U.S. from the Ukraine when he was a boy and built a fish business that's one of the largest in the country. He has ships, processors, farms, retail shops, seafood restaurants—you name it. That's where I learned about the Brotherhood."

"The brotherhood?" Service asked.

"Brotherhood of the Reeds. That's what the sturgeon poachers along the Volga River call themselves, but it applies to the whole network that smuggles beluga eggs out of Russia."

"Krapahkin is a member of this brotherhood?"

"Technically, no," said Lafleur. "Before the Soviet Union split up he was getting caviar directly from the Soviet government. After the breakup the government had other priorities, and exports weren't high on the list, so Semyon had to deal with the Brotherhood. Over time the new Russian and Ukrainian governments began to get their acts together and clamped down on the Brotherhood in order to reduce the loss of national resources. With sturgeon eggs getting harder to obtain, Semyon had to find egg sources elsewhere. That's when we got involved. Quint heard Krapahkin was looking for other caviar sources to augment his product line, and he went to him with the idea of salmon caviar, but the Ukrainian didn't like the price. That's when Quint came up with the idea of blending eggs from two sources to lower his cost, and therefore, the price. Once he did that, Krapahkin began to take all we could send."

"About a hundred thousand pounds a year?"

She nodded. "Like I said, fall was *real* busy, and it was all cash. I'd go to New York and Crimea would give me a bag with nine thousand dollars in cash, and I'd take it back as luggage. Sometimes I went back and forth every other third or fourth day to collect money. Crimea always paid promptly, and the count was always right."

"How much money?"

She closed her eyes. "I don't really know. A lot. We always had three to four hundred thousand in the office safes. I gave the money to Quint, and I assume that's the cash we had in the safes, but I don't know that for sure. Quint had a lot of things going that he didn't talk to me about."

"The cash was at the Elk Rapids plant?"

"There, at the Old Mission Peninsula house, and at the house on the Grand River in Grand Ledge. Quint never puts everything in one place."

"He lives in Grand Ledge?"

"That place is strictly for politics and entertainment. His family is in Whitehall."

"You were the only one to pick up the cash?"

Lafleur paused and pursed her lips. "Mostly me, but sometimes Quint went, and also Gary Hosk brought us the money a few times."

"Hosk?"

"He's an assistant prosecutor in Barry County now, but years back he was one of Crimea's lawyers." Service felt his temperature rise. Every time he learned something new, the case grew more convoluted.

"Did you meet Langford Horn?"

Lafleur rolled her eyes and her face reddened. "Horny Horn? Quint set me up with him, gave me fifty grand and told me to get the man whatever he wanted, which turned out to be mostly the same thing Quint wanted. Between the two of them . . ." Her voice trailed off.

"Do you know anything about Piscova buying a boat for Horn?"

"No. I bought the boat with cash, but Piscova paid the fees at the marina, and sometimes paid for repairs. They stored it at the plant during the off-season. The cash, of course, was from a business that doesn't officially exist, so there's no record, and no trail of any kind."

"Horn helped Fagan with his contracts."

"Langford wrote the contracts based on what Quint wanted. Horn knew contracts really well, and between them, they structured them to provide max bennies for Piscova."

"You saw them do this?"

"They met at the house on the Old Mission. I cooked and, you know . . ." she said with a shrug. "I didn't mind," she added. "I was young and full of myself."

Service looked over at Miars, whose eyes were bulging.

"The house on the Old Mission?"

"It's Quint's, but it's in my name. He'll sell it and take the cash and put it into stop-and-robs in the Ann Arbor–Ypsilanti area. He already owns about twenty of the things. He also probably owns fifty houses around the country. He buys everything with cash and usually puts assets in other people's names so the IRS won't know. Quint gave me cash for the Old Mission place, but I went out and got a mortgage, and acted like I was anyone else going through the process. All I did was take the cash I needed out of the stash every month and make the payment."

"When did the cancer show up?"

"I was having some strange feelings all last year, so I finally got my act together and went for a checkup, and that's when they found it."

"Last summer?"

"June."

"And you retired the following month."

"I had already paid for this place and I had some cash squirreled away. I was so angry with Quint I couldn't talk to him, and I told him I'd go to the authorities. He magnanimously decided to grant me a monthly stipend—cash, of course—and to pay for my medical bills."

"Do the doctors think the cancer was caused by the mirex eggs?"

"Doctors can rarely tell anyone the specific cause of their cancer. Back in the early eighties the FDA set a safety level of one hundred picograms per kilogram as the safety level for mirex. A picogram is one trillionth of a gram. When Quint had Jensen Labs test Michigan salmon contamination, he also had them test the eggs, and the eggs showed much higher than the meat—like a million times higher. Quint never showed that egg data to the state, but I stopped sampling after that. I guess it didn't make any difference. The damage was done."

She laughed out loud. "The irony is that at one time, mirex was being used as a pesticide to kill fire ants. Well, it sure put out my fire! Our sex life ended after I learned about the mirex levels, and Quint was not very happy with me."

Lafleur suddenly looked tired. "Excuse me," she said, "but I have to take a couple of naps a day as part of my recovery. We can talk more later on, if you'd like."

"We'd like that," Service said. "If you could write down names and dates and places, as many as you can remember, we'd appreciate it—and the name of the convenience store chain."

"I can try," she said. "Is Quint going to jail?"

"Yes, ma'am."

Miars inserted uneasily, "We're going to do our best."

"How do we contact you?" Service asked.

Lafleur smiled. "I have a track phone with prepaid minutes. This way nobody can bother me." She gave him the number.

As they walked back to the truck, Miars said, "You can't make promises like that."

"The hell I can't," Service said. "Did you hear that *shit*?"

They rode back to Marquette in silence and Service dropped Miars at his truck. "We need to sit down and review where your internal investigation has taken you."

Miars looked perturbed. "How about you take care of the egg mixing and I'll take care of the other stuff?"

"I think we'll both be stronger if we combine forces."

"I'm not so sure. You haven't seen what I've seen or been through what I've been through. Your case could be open and shut—if you can pull together the evidence."

It was an unsatisfactory conclusion, but on his way to Slippery Creek Service decided that Miars was probably right, and that his sergeant was nervous about pressing the internal investigation. Still, if there was a way to take the case back inside, he was determined to do it.

When he got to the cabin, Candace McCants was sitting outside in the cool air with a cup of coffee, smoking a small cigar. "I'm here to inform you that your animals and I are having an affair," she said with a big grin.

Candi had been a CO for more than seven years. She was five-six, 160 pounds of muscle, afraid of nothing, and gifted with an inordinate amount of common sense. Born in Korea, she had been adopted by a family in Detroit when she was twelve and joined the DNR after finishing a police academy at Kalamazoo Valley Community College.

"My dog and cat are females."

"Don't quibble," she said. "Take love where you find it. How's Karylanne doing?"

Take love where you find it? What the hell was wrong with Candi?

Karylanne Pengelly had been his late son's girlfriend. He died before learning she was pregnant.

"Good, I guess. She's tired all the time."

"Full class load at Michigan Tech, preggers, and tired. Duh, Service. You need to talk to that girl regularly."

"I do," he said.

"When was the last time?" McCants shot back.

He held out his hands in submission.

16

Marquette, Marquette County

Service called Rogers in New York and told him what he had learned in Anchorage from Andriaitis, and from his visit and talk with Roxanne Lafleur. He left out everything bearing on the internal situation in Michigan, even though he wasn't sure why he withheld that part. Maybe because Michigan was family and New York wasn't.

Rogers said he was still plowing through paper taken from the plant and added, "We're familiar with the Crimea Group. We had a conference with U.S. Fish and Wildlife last spring. They're investigating Crimea for unrecorded shipments of Russian sturgeon roe. Apparently poachers in Russia have killed several wildlife agents and their families, and Crimea's implicated."

"Fish and Wildlife close to warrants?"

"That wasn't the impression they left me with, and I haven't talked to them since then. They briefed us only to alert us that the Russian and Uke authorities have been squeezing poachers pretty hard, and they expected Crimea would start looking for product alternatives."

"Salmon eggs, for example."

"They never said, but if your information is accurate, Crimea has been in the red roe business for a long time, well below the feds' radar."

"This thing's layered like an onion," Service said.

"All we can do is peel it back one layer at time," Rogers said.

"Too many players," Service said. "IRS, Fish and Wildlife, you guys, us."

"Don't forget FDA, EPA, state police agencies, and the FBI. At some point it could take input and assistance from all of them."

Grady Service kept thinking about dead Russian wildlife agents and their families. "Crimea sounds like the old mafia."

Rogers laughed. "They're totally *new* mafia. The Eye-ties and Sicilians are pretty much *finito.* I think the feds are moving cautiously on Crimea because these new outfits are not like the old boys. The Sicilians had a lot of rules and didn't involve civilians unless they were forced to. The Russians and Ukrainians have no rules or compunctions, and they think Western cops are a bunch of pussies."

Service said, "We've got evidence pointing to Crimea."

Rogers said, "But what if Crimea thinks the caviar they bought is legit?"

"They're paying cash," Service reminded the New Yorker. "*Under* the goddamn table."

"So they can only be tagged for financial irregularities—but that doesn't mean they know they're buying and selling *contaminated* eggs, which I remind us both, we have not yet actually verified. Until we have some of Piscova's product in our hands, this is all hypothetical. When we get the caviar, the FDA's got a DNA template that will detect mirex. If there's even a trace, we're good to go, because fish out your way don't have mirex in them."

Service said, "We need to intercept a shipment." He was suddenly sorry he had gone along with New York's push for fast action. If Fagan was as good as Roxy and Andriaitis said, he'd lay off the illegal business until the subpoenas and what they led to were over.

"Or grab some from Crimea—at the other end."

"Which means we have to pull in more agencies."

"The inescapable reality of law enforcement in the twenty-first century."

Service hung up and realized even more than before that he was in over his head. He knew how to deal with assholes breaking the laws during deer season. But this was new territory, and he didn't like any of it.

He called Tree's cell and found him at his camp in Chippewa County. They made plans to meet that night. He also called Karylanne, but her answering machine said she was in class until after four.

McCants answered her cell phone, and Service said, "I'm taking Newf and Cat with me to see Tree."

"They'll be just fine with me."

"I think they need some male attention."

"Don't we all," she said icily.

What's her problem? he wondered. If something was bugging her, why didn't she just spit it out? Nantz would have.

17

WEDNESDAY, OCTOBER 27, 2004

North of Nowhere Camp, Chippewa County

Newf loped down the two-track toward the cabin a quarter-mile down the road while Service undid the lock to the chain gate. He parked beside a giant red cedar at the end of the narrow road, and saw lights in the tiny cabin. He let Cat out, smelled burning charcoal, went looking for his friend, and found him in the shed south of the cabin. A small doe was hanging from a ceiling beam, its hind hoofs barely off the unpainted plywood floor. The back straps had been cut out and were in a pan on a two-by-eight shelf. Tree's arms were covered with blood and he grinned when he saw Service.

"We'll grill the straps. Mr. Weber's already going."

Newf came into the shed and sniffed the blood pooling beneath the deer.

Tree growled, "Don't be snackin' on my deer, dog."

Newf barked at the massive Treebone, but backed away.

"I passed on three dandy bucks," Treebone said, picking up the pan and plastic bag with the heart and liver and heading toward the cabin with Service in tow, Newf bounding around them like a shepherd with ADD.

Service had bought the camp and given it to his friend as a gift earlier in the year. At the time the camp hadn't had power or a drinking-water source. What power it had now came from a small generator Treebone had installed. He had also sunk a well on the property.

Service watched as his friend dropped the heart and liver in the sink, ran cold water on them, trimmed off some fatty deposits, slapped them on a carving board, sliced them paper-thin, threw them in a bag with flour, pepper, and cornmeal, and vigorously shook the bag. Service grabbed an onion and a bowl of mushrooms, chopped them, and diced half a dozen garlic cloves. He put the vegetables in aluminum foil, made a tent, dashed some olive oil on them, added salt, pepper, and some butter, and pinched the tent closed.

The two men stepped onto the porch. Service put the back straps on the grill, sprinkled them with salt, pepper, and Montreal Steak Seasoning, set the foil tent beside the meat, and closed the cover. Treebone uncorked a bottle of cheap Crane Lake cabernet sauvignon and poured some into enameled tin cups.

"Define dandy," Service said.

"Big six, small ten, and a *monster* ten."

"Very sporting to take a doe."

"Gotta let them genes fill the pool," his friend said.

"Maybe you ought to let Chewy know."

Buster Beal was a biologist in the Escanaba office, a man who loved white-tailed deer, took care of the herd as a sacred responsibility, and killed them with equal fervor during rifle and archery seasons. Beal was well over six foot, burly, hairy, and known throughout the DNR as Chewy, after the hirsute *Star Wars* character.

Treebone exhaled loudly. "So that motherfucking killing machine can whack my pets!"

"Pets?"

"My property, my animals. You got a case yet?"

"We've got an asshole mixing contaminated Lake Ontario salmon eggs with clean Michigan eggs and selling them as caviar to a New York City outfit that may or may not be Ukrainian mafia. And they're not your *pets*."

"That ain't so much."

"With at least one state BAO man and some DNR personnel, including the director, possibly on the take—or at least in the know—and all the egg deals are in cash and off the books."

"Now it's getting complicated."

"You said something about making a tree."

"Eat first, work later."

Service went to get Chinet plates, looked in a cooler, and found four eight-inch brook trout. He looked over at his friend. "Are you poaching during closed season?"

"Just a couple for breakfast, man. Most of 'em are gonna die over the winter anyway."

"You *know* better."

"Just this once," Treebone said. "Man, you gonna stroke me?"

"The law's the law."

"And you game wardens wonder why everyone thinks you're a bunch of chickenshit pricks."

"We embrace the love," Service said.

"Learn how to make your own damn tree," his friend grumbled.

"Now *that's* chickenshit," Grady Service said.

The meat was tender, the veggies a bit underdone. Tree mumbled with a full mouth, "I love this shit. You're not *really* stroking me."

"Technically you're within the possession limit. The rules don't say you can't legally possess in the off-season. Of course, you took these earlier this year, right?"

"No man, first thing this morning."

Service rolled his eyes and Tree said, "Why'd you have to go and open the damn cooler? Write the ticket, man. I deserve it." Treebone took a sip of wine. "You got yourself hard-wired to cop-analog mode: On-off, good-bad, right-wrong. Real talk, yo, you get head-to-head with those other agencies and politicians thinking like that and you're going nowhere, man. Analog is Martian to them boys. See, you can point the weapon, but only they can pull the trigger, hear what I'm saying? These aren't your backwoods perps, bro. You start fucking with organized crime, politicians, and bureaucraps, and there will be a shitstorm with you in the middle."

"The tree?" Service said, trying to focus his friend.

"Tree? Point is, all branches come off one trunk and a cop, he's way out on the end, trying to find light, and the rest of them behind him all suckin' the light out of him."

"What the hell are you driving at?"

"Just this, man: When you out on the end of the branch, you can't do nothing if those further back decide to cut it off. You know a man can't attack in two directions."

"Are you telling me to back off the internal stuff?"

Treebone sighed. "Can't *tell* you anything, but you choose to go that way, they gonna try to cut off your balls, man."

"What happened to the notion that the only thing necessary for the triumph of evil is for good men to do nothing?"

Luticious Treebone put his hand on Grady Service's shoulder. "Man, don't play quote games with me. Edmund Burke was a wiggy motherfucker spoke from both sides of his mouth. He also said, 'People act from motives relative to their interest, not on metaphysical speculations.' You got to come to grips with facts, man. You remember what The Mayor used to have on his desk?"

Service knew his friend was referring to the legendary Detroit mayor, Coleman Young. "Yeah—MFIC."

"Well, you ain't the Motherfucker in Charge, Grady. You best keep that in mind."

Service remembered that Young also had said, "You don't grow balls. Either you got 'em or you don't." He decided to keep this to himself. He picked up the wine bottle and poured a little more for both of them. "Can we seriously talk about how to organize my work? I am at least the MFIC of my own time."

The next morning Treebone walked him through the mechanics of what his friend called a "tree."

If Fagan was as clever as everyone believed he was, he would shut down operations while the heat was on. Unfortunately the salmon runs were petering out, close to done for this year. As Service twisted, trying to get comfortable in his sleeping bag, it occurred to him that Piscova's deal with Crimea might be enough to keep Fagan running the operation. If Crimea was truly a mob-op, they might not appreciate a broken contract. Not a sure thing, but it seemed to offer some hope, and before falling asleep he decided to test his thinking.

Ocqueoc Falls, Presque Isle County

It was just before noon and Benny Baranov was standing in the parking lot by Ocqueoc Falls, which was fancifully misnamed, it being more a gradual series of low steps than a dramatic cascade. "We got a deal?" Baranov asked as Service walked over to him.

"We're getting close and it's looking good."

"I get reward?"

"Your reward is I tear up your citation."

The Ukrainian looked dejected. "My girls could use money."

"The bank boys still working?"

"Yes, late run on this side of state. Fish on west side are stinking, you know?" The man made a face.

"You still taking eggs?"

"Nossir, you tell me no more. I am a man of honor"

"Does the man of honor *know* anyone who might be taking eggs?"

Baranov grinned. "Perhaps I hear a name or two."

"Find out when Piscova makes the next pickup from one of those names and call me. You have my number, right?"

Baranov patted his pocket. "I keep you next to my heart."

"Your heart's on the other side, shithead."

Baranov looked down and grinned. "You make joke."

"No joke. Find out when the next buy takes place, or better yet, when it will take place and where, and call me. Where are the best runs now?"

Baranov scratched his chin. "Best maybe is Devils River at Ossineke. You ask much of Benny. I already have given you bank boys."

"You can do this."

"Then ticket is gone?"

"It's already gone. That's our deal. I just need help, Benny."

Rogers said they needed eggs to test. If Baranov came through, Rogers would get the necessary samples for FDA testing.

19

SUNDAY, OCTOBER 31, 2004

Devils River, Alpena County

Word was out that most salmon runs were in the final stages, but Baranov came through in less than forty-eight hours. A man named Jess Smool would meet a bank boy at an old gravel pit south of the village of Ossineke. Baranov said Smool was assured that there would be a bank boy to collect and pay, but the Ukrainian was unable to get an identity or description.

Service wanted Miars to go with him, but Miars was busy with another case, and Service ended up calling CO Dani Denninger, who had been at the academy with Nantz. He had worked with Denninger last summer and liked her aggressiveness. Salmon-snagging crews were among the nastiest and most upredictable violets conservation officers confronted, and he felt Denninger could handle whatever came up.

They met in the afternoon, sixteen miles from the gravel pit. He briefed her only on the night's task, not the case; like any good officer, she didn't ask questions except about the task. "They're going to meet at dark?"

"Right. This guy Smool drives a 2002 Ford F-150 SVT Lightning. We don't know who he's meeting. Your job is to watch the transaction, give me a description of the other vehicle and driver, and let me know when he pulls out."

"Not a problem," Denninger said.

"Got your night eyes?" Service asked.

"And thermal imager. Once Smool parks I'll creep close so I can see what's going on. What do you want me to do after it goes down?"

"Go back on patrol, or home, whatever you're supposed to do."

"I'm on pass starting tomorrow. I wouldn't mind working."

"We'll see," he said, having no intention of taking her along. But he also began to think it might be better to have two sets of eyes and ears when he got to wherever the bank boy was headed.

At 5 P.M. Denninger bumped him on the 800. Smool had arrived. She gave Service the plate number, and it checked against what he had run through the computer when Baranov first gave him the name.

At 6:15, Denninger called again. "Twenty Five Fourteen, I have a dark-colored Lexus with a female driver. Solo, no pax. I'm less than thirty feet from her and I can see everything," she whispered.

"Twenty Five Fourteen clear," he said, hoping she would stop talking.

Ten minutes later, she called again, out of breath. "I'm boogying to my vehicle, Twenty Five Fourteen. If she goes north she'll have to pass me and I'll pick her up. If she goes south, you'll have her."

Service could picture the young officer hurtling through the woods and grinned, remembering all the times he'd had to scramble.

"Twenty Five Fourteen, I can see her turning south."

"Your ride stashed?"

" 'Firm-ah-tiff," she said, breathing hard.

"I'll be at your position in two minutes. Be on the road. Twenty Five Fourteen clear."

He skidded to a stop, Denninger threw her gear behind the passenger seat, jumped in, and he cranked it up to eighty-five, heading south.

"Run the plate," he said as he sought to catch up and establish the pursuit.

He caught up to the Lexus in Harrisville, where it turned east on M-72. He turned with it, and dropped back to keep it in sight.

Denninger said, "Vehicle is registered to an Alma DeKoening of Traverse City. White female, five-four, one-oh-five, blond hair. DOB, ten thirty-one seventy-nine."

Service laughed. "She's going all the way to TC on Seventy-Two. We can relax."

"Prescience comes with your job?" Denninger asked.

"Something like that."

"If you know what route she's taking, you must know her destination too."

"Not really."

"Geez, and I was actually impressed for a minute."

Service was surprised when the Lexus turned south out of Kalkaska, drove to South Boardman, and pulled into a small mobile home park. They sat on the road with their binoculars and watched. The Lexus sat there. DeKoening got out, was inside for a half-hour, came out carrying her jacket over her shoulder. She opened her trunk and a shirtless man moseyed out of a trailer carrying two white Styrofoam coolers, put them in the trunk, and closed the lid. The man smacked her bottom, the woman got into her car, pulled away, and headed north, back toward Kalkaska.

Service didn't move.

"We're not following her?" Denninger asked.

"Nope. Creep the trailer and see if you can get a plate number."

Denninger got out and ducked into the trees. She called five minutes later: "I can't tell which vehicle goes with which trailer," she said.

"Give them all to me."

She read the plate numbers and gave him makes and model numbers, three vehicles in all, and he told her to come back to the Tahoe. Meanwhile, he started running the plates through the system, and by the time she got back, he had two of the three.

"Is something more going to happen tonight?" she asked.

"We'll see," he said.

"You want coffee?" she asked.

"You have coffee?"

"Always," she said, "two thermoses."

"Hit me."

They sat for just more than an hour, engine off, windows cracked, the night chill slowly crawling in, but a man eventually came out of the trailer and tossed a bag into the back of a pickup.

Service looked at his computer screen: Louis K. Veatch, age thirty-three. Out loud he said, "Okay, Louie, show us the money!"

Denninger laughed. "This has been the weirdest Halloween I've ever had."

Halloween? Service thought. Only two weeks until the firearm deer opener. *Stop thinking about it,* he lectured himself. *You'll be doing something different, something important. And a hell of a lot less fun.* It was not the sort of trade-off he'd make willingly.

20

MONDAY, NOVEMBER 1, 2004

Elk Rapids, Antrim County

It was 3 A.M., and no great surprise to Service that the pickup truck from South Boardman pulled into the Piscova parking lot. The lights were off in the front part of the building, on in the back. He saw a stand of sumac, hid the truck behind it, locked the doors, and headed toward the building on foot.

He tried the door. It was unlocked. He went to a dark side of the building by a cinder-block wall and called the Antrim County dispatcher. "How many Troops on the road tonight?"

"One," she said.

Service told her he needed backup and asked her to have the Troop call on his cell phone. He got back in the Tahoe with Denninger and waited.

The phone blurped a minute later and he explained to the state policeman what was happening. The Troop gave an ETA of seven minutes.

Denninger asked, "Are we going inside?"

"You saw money exchanged for eggs, right?"

"The woman set her purse on the hood of the Lexus, took out her wallet, and gave some paper to Veatch. It looked like money to me."

"Good. Probable cause is solid." The fact that the eggs ended up at Piscova closed the loop. It all seemed to be fitting nicely. He saw Alma DeKoening's Lexus parked in the lot.

"What's the plan?"

"We ID Veatch and I'll take him outside. I'll tell you what to do once we see what we have inside."

The Troop came into the lot with his lights out, got out, and Service quickly briefed him. He was tall, muscled, and eager, and looked like a high school kid—and not a senior.

Service led them through the door into a cloud of fish smell. Several men were dumping bags of eggs onto a conveyor belt that led to a large stainless-steel tub.

Alma DeKoening was leaning over the conveyor belt, picking out eggs and tossing them into a plastic-lined trash barrel behind her. Others were scooping eggs from the steel tub, putting them on things that looked like cookie sheets, and placing them on racks under lights. Service thought: drying racks. Two men were sticking labels on tins. Service saw a half-dozen blue buckets labeled NOT FOR HUMAN CONSUMPTION. SELL ONLY AS BAIT. One of the men was dumping eggs from a bucket into the same container where eggs from plastic bags were being dumped. There were several buckets and bags on the floor. Another man was taking trays of eggs from the rack to a table and putting the eggs into small, unlabeled tins.

Willem Vandeal approached them, huffing, his eyes bugging out. "You aren't authorized to be in here."

"Louis K. Veatch," Service said. He saw Alma DeKoening look over at him and look back to the conveyor belt.

"What's he done?" Vandeal wanted to know.

"Where is he?"

"Veatch," Vandeal called out. A man finished emptying a plastic bag and walked toward them. He was skinny with the shaved-head look that had replaced backwoods Kentucky waterfalls in recent years. He wore blue jeans, a plaid shirt, an earring, a black rubber apron, scuffed black Doc Martens.

"Louis K. Veatch?'

"S'up, dude?"

"Come with me."

"I'm working, dude."

Service saw Vandeal nod at the door and Veatch started outside, fumbling for a cigarette as he went through the door.

Service leaned over to Denninger. He had given her vials for samples in the truck. "Fill ten vials from what's on the conveyor belt, ten from the tank, ten more from the racks, and ten from that guy over there who's putting them in tins. Also, grab an empty New York bucket and a full bag. Give them a receipt when you've got everything we want."

Veatch inhaled deeply and stood still.

"All right, Louie," Service began.

"It's Louis, dude."

"You're in a lot of trouble, Louis. I'm going to take you back inside and you are going to show me the plastic bag you brought tonight."

"No way, dude."

"It doesn't matter, Louis. We'll get fingerprints, and we have photos of you taking the bag out of Alma DeKoening's Lexus at your trailer. We followed you here from your place in South Boardman. So lose the attitude or you are going to be royally fucked."

Veatch seemed to mull over the situation. "S'up, dude?"

The vocabulary of young people had never been particularly extensive in Service's experience, but in recent years it had seemed to shrink even smaller. "Don't play me," Service said. "You're mixing eggs in there."

"Duh," the young man said. "That's the *job*, dude."

"You always do this at night?"

"Yeah, it's the special product line."

"Worked here long?"

"Do I like, ya know, need a lawyer, dude?"

Service recited Miranda rights to the man and added, "We can get a lawyer if you want one, but we'll have to put on the cuffs, take you to jail, charge and book you. Or you can just talk to me here."

"Dude, me and jail don't mix for shit, hear what I'm sayin'?"

"You've been arrested before?" Service asked.

"For what?" the man replied.

"You tell me."

"Nothing big," Veatch said.

Service had his doubts but pressed on. "Then talk to me."

"You sure I'm not going to jail?"

"If you don't talk, you are; if you do talk, you might—but what I want here is information. What happens to you will ride on how much you give me, and how useful it is. What's the deal with Alma DeKoening?"

She had been inside his trailer for thirty minutes, and had been messing with her hair when she came out. "You fucking her, Louis?"

Veatch made a sour face. "Dude, she ain't *my* old lady. She belongs to the *man*."

The young Troop stuck his head out the door. "You'd better get in here!"

Service grabbed Veatch, shoved him ahead, handed him off to the Troop as he went inside, and saw Denninger being circled by two men who outweighed her by a hundred pounds each.

"Back off!" he shouted and charged.

Before he could get there, Denninger had a man on his back and her knee on his throat. Service grabbed the second man, spun him, slammed him against a wall, pulled his hands behind him, and cuffed him.

"You can't," the man mumbled.

Vandeal came over, looking shook. "This is totally wrong," he said.

"No shit," Service said.

"You can't take product."

Service said, "Get out of my face, Vandeal, and tell the rest of your people that if there's any more trouble, they're all going to jail for assault and resisting."

Vandeal held his arms out like a priest trying to settle the multitude.

Veatch tried to twist away from the Troop, who was holding him, but the Troop tripped him and pinned him after one step.

Service hauled Veatch to his feet and frog-marched him outside. "What is your *major malfunction*? That was fucking dumb, Louis!"

"Dude, I'm, like, on probation."

"Running is going to make it better?" Veatch hung his head. "Just talk to me, all right? You've got a thing going with DeKoening."

"Dude, if the big boss finds out, I'm toast."

By the time they got back inside, the Piscova people were all sitting with their backs against the wall like schoolboys on a timeout, and Vandeal said, "Our lawyer is en route."

It was the same lawyer Service had met before, and once again she seemed sweaty and wore the same tracksuit, but her attitude was calm and businesslike. "What's the problem here?" she asked Service.

Vandeal said with a grunt, "*I'm* the client."

Service shrugged and watched the two huddle. The Troop was standing by the boys on the wall and looked like he was hitting on Denninger.

The lawyer came back to him. "Constance Algyre."

"I remember," Service said.

"My client has nothing to say. If you have charges, file them."

"Hardball," Service said.

She shrugged. "It's the client's call."

"We're not charging anyone with anything at this time. We just came here to talk to Louis Veatch and we've done that. There will be warrants later."

The lawyer looked skeptical. Willem Vandeal didn't object.

Service looked at Veatch, who went and fetched a plastic bag filled with eggs. The lawyer blocked Veatch's way and said. "You need a warrant to seize product."

"Probable cause. We watched the company's employee acquire illegally taken eggs from an illegal source and bring them here."

"*Those* eggs are not in the company's product."

Service looked at Veatch holding his bag of eggs and wondered if he had screwed up. Technically the lawyer might be right. Would it be better if they had waited until Veatch's batch was already mixed? "Probable cause," Service said weakly.

"This won't stick," Algyre said.

"Go," Service told Denninger.

"Carry on," Service said from the doorway. A couple of employees showed him the bird.

They drove to the state police post, got evidence coolers and ice, repacked the eggs, had coffee with the Troop, thanked him, and headed for Gaylord.

Denninger nodded off, awoke with a start, and said, "Do you ever sleep?"

"When I have to," he said. "You give that Troop your number?"

She laughed. "You mean pink-cheek boy? No way."

Pink-cheek boy. How had he gotten so old?

When they got to the Gaylord office, Service called Roy Rogers in New York to tell him he had eggs, but offered no details of the seizure. He handed the phone to Denninger to get instructions on how to pack and ship the samples and left the room.

Since something had popped in his leg on the Pine River, his calf had been aching like hell. He had iced it for two days and since then, had tried to ignore the pain and tightness. But tonight it was hurting in such a way that he knew he couldn't ignore it anymore. He took off his boot and sock and saw that the ankle was swollen twice its normal size, the foot a rainbow of ugly colors that suggested internal bleeding. Fuck!

He called Vince Vilardo at home in Escanaba. Vilardo was a longtime friend, internist, retired medical examiner for Delta County, and the only doctor he would go to.

"Geez, Grady, why can't you operate during normal hours?" Vilardo complained sleepily. Service explained what had happened and asked his friend if he could meet him at the hospital in Escanaba the next day.

"Are you out of your mind?" Vilardo yipped. "Get your butt to the nearest emergency room and tell them you need a CT scan. Is there any redness in your leg?"

"I haven't looked."

"Look now."

Service slid down his trousers and looked. The swelling reached above the ankle, but there was no redness. "Looks okay to me," he reported.

"You had any shortness of breath?'

"No."

"That's good—but go and get the scan."

"Or what?"

"If there's a clot in there it could blow up your heart or your brain."

Service grimaced and hung up.

Denninger came back into the room, looked at Service's naked legs, and grinned. "All packed and ready. We can ship first thing in the morning. You want me to leave you alone?"

"I need to go to the emergency room," Service said.

Denninger raised an eyebrow. "What's wrong?"

"Did something to my leg," he said, showing her the discolored foot.

"Totally yuck," she said. "Does it hurt?"

"Not much. Mostly it's swollen. I called my doc in Escanaba and he wants me to get a CT scan."

It took five hours in the ER to get a technician in to do the scan and for a doctor to show up. The doctor declared no clot and told him he could keep exercising. They visited a stop-and-rob to replenish Service's ibuprofen, got back to the district office at 6 A.M., pulled up chairs in the conference room, and tried to go to sleep, but Service kept replaying the night's sequence of events and wondered if he had overlooked something.

21

TUESDAY, NOVEMBER 2, 2004

Lansing, Ingham County

They shipped the evidence by 8 A.M., grabbed a greasy breakfast sandwich at the drive-through BK Lounge, and delivered Denninger to her vehicle in Alpena County.

"You did good," he said.

"Anytime you need a partner, yell," she said, heading for her truck. Last summer he had worked briefly with her and had had the impression she was too cynical for someone so early in her career, but this time she had shown none of that. He was impressed.

He was just west of Alpena when his cell phone buzzed.

"I see you on the AVL," Chief O'Driscoll said. "I need to see you in Lansing ASAP."

"For what?"

"I'll explain when you get here."

It wasn't like the chief to be so mysterious. Service immediately called Miars on his cell. "The chief wants me in Lansing."

"Me too," Miars said.

"Any idea what's going down?"

"I smell a shitstorm," his sergeant said.

"See you there."

The two officers went into the chief's office together and were told to sit.

"You raided the Piscova plant last night?" Lorne O'Driscoll asked.

"I wouldn't call it a raid," Service said as he outlined the chain of events.

"Did you have a warrant?" the chief asked.

"We saw an illegal egg buy and saw the eggs handed off to an individual who took them into Piscova, and he was working on the caviar line. There were New York eggs being mixed with ours."

Service suddenly wondered why DeKoening had given the eggs to Veatch and not taken them directly to the plant herself. O'Driscoll offered Service and Miars coffee from his thermos.

"Our department's assistant general counsel for law enforcement just told us you may be a little into the gray area on this one," said O'Driscoll.

"Will it stand up?" Service asked.

"According to our lawyer, it might and it might not."

"What's going on, Chief?" Service asked.

"Piscova filed suit this morning, claiming illegal seizure, violation of civil rights, the usual litany of wah-wah. The judge has already granted an interim restraining order, which means the seized evidence is to be placed in the court's custody until this gets settled. There will be a full hearing in about ten days."

"The evidence is en route to New York," Service said. "It'll be there tomorrow. Who's the judge?"

The chief remained composed. "Valakos, one of Bozian's golfing pals. Call New York and have them hold the eggs until the court decides what it wants to do."

"This is bullshit, Chief," Service said.

"I know, but Teeny has blown his stack," the chief said. "He's ordering reprimands and all sorts of crap for the both of you. I told him there's nothing I can do."

Service looked at the chief. "I don't understand."

"I knew this was going to blow up," the chief said. "It's just happening sooner than I'd anticipated. Two days ago I talked to the U.S. Attorney in Grand Rapids. Effective October thirtieth, you are reporting to one of his assistants here in Lansing. This way nobody inside the department can touch you. When your investigation is complete, you'll be transferred back. With the IRS involved and apparent Lacey violations, this is appropriately a federal case."

The Lacey Act laid out a wide-reaching law governing the trade and treatment of animal and plant life in the U.S. It had been signed into law in 1900 and amended numerous times over the intervening century. It was the legal linchpin in both federal and state efforts to manage certain natural resources.

"What about Denninger?" Service asked. "Sergeant Miars wasn't with me."

The chief chewed his lip for a moment. "Miars stays where he is. If Teeny can't get at you, he'll come down on Denninger. I'll call her this morning and assign her for the duration of the case."

"You can do this?" Miars asked.

"Our lawyer says it's unusual but entirely legal—there's precedent in other states—and in this case, it's probably appropriate. She doesn't like Teeny or her boss, and she's always been good to law enforcement, even when she has had reasons not to be. The U.S. Attorney is Anniejo Couch. She's been with the Justice Department a long time and is in a preretirement slide. Give her a bump, go see her, and get your marching orders and rules of engagement. She's good people, and won't get in your way."

"What about her boss?" Service asked.

The chief frowned. "Riley Endicott is a card-carrying neocon, and definitely not a wave-maker. But Couch will provide a wall to let you proceed with your investigation. All we can do is gather the facts and present the case."

"Grady's not part of the DNR?" Miars asked.

"Spiritually, yes; technically and administratively, no. When the job is done, we'll bring him home."

The two officers took the elevator downstairs and bumped into Eino Teeny in the lobby. "I've been looking for you," the director said.

Service raised his eyebrows. "Me?" The last time he'd seen Teeny he had been with Governor Sam Bozian.

"You will report to my office immediately."

Service looked at the man. "You're the director of the DNR, right?"

"You bloody well know I am," Teeny snapped.

"Yeah, well, here's the thing, sir: I don't work for the DNR," Service said, and though he knew he was on safe ground, the words felt awful and sent a chill down his spine.

The two officers left the director standing there with his mouth open.

When they got outside Service stopped and lit a cigarette. "This feels pretty weird," he said, holding the pack out to his sergeant.

"*I* still work for the DNR," Miars said. "And I've got twenty years in."

"You could've gone with Teeny if you feel so strongly about it. Do you trust the chief to run interference for us?"

Miars nodded.

"Me too," Service said. "Let's not worry about political stuff and get after these assholes."

Miars said, "I guess you're gonna call on the U.S. Attorney."

Service looked at his sergeant and admitted, "I'm nervous, too."

"Did you ship the evidence right away because you smelled this coming down?"

"I shipped it because it's perishable, and the FDA in New York has a DNA test that will help us determine what we have."

The sergeant nodded as Service headed for his vehicle.

Okay then, Service thought. *Your ass is way out there this time.*

22

TUESDAY, NOVEMBER 2, 2004

Grand Rapids, Kent County

Assistant U.S. Attorney Anniejo Couch looked to be in her early fifties, had hair the color and consistency of dry straw, stood no more than five feet tall, and was squarely built and muscled like a pint-sized linebacker. She wore a baggy pantsuit and square-toed shoes with no heels.

"So, you're my new operative," she greeted Service, leading him into a small conference room off her office and nodding for him to sit.

"Lorne and I go back a long way," she began. "He said you poked your dick into a hornet's nest, which tells me you like pain. Hell," she added, "I like pain too. If I had a dick, I'd probably stick mine in the hornet's nest and stir it like pancake batter."

Grady Service stared at the woman and had no idea what to say.

"The way this will work is you will build your case and charge all expenses to my budget." She handed him a stack of folders. "Forms, procedures, account numbers, and details are in there. When the case is over we'll either tack the expenses onto costs at trial, or the feds will eat them. The state's broke, so they can't handle it. Lorne called a few minutes ago and said there'll be a second officer with you."

"Denninger," Service said.

"Right, the female. You two gonna operate out of your own places, or do you need a place to stay?"

"We haven't gotten that far," Service said. "We just learned about this a couple of hours ago."

Couch said, "If you need somewhere to crash down this way, my brother has a place over by Saranac. It's empty, it's free, and you can use it whenever and for as long as you need it." She went out to her office and came back with a key on a ring. "Make extras if you want, or hide this where you can find it. It's a pretty basic place. My brother bought it to develop as a cross-country skiing lodge, but that lasted one winter. My brother's not good at sticking to anything except my sister-in-law because she has the money. The good news is that there's a sauna and it's got hot and cold running water, a stove, cable, computer line, fridge, and all that good stuff. You'll be about halfway between Lansing and Grand Rapids, with easy access onto I-96. That will help make your life a little easier." She put her elbows on the desk and stared at him. "Lorne briefed me on the case, but I'd like to hear it from you."

Service laid out the case for her.

"Piscova and Quint Fagan," she said, shaking her head and grinning. "You met Fagan yet?"

Service shook his head.

"Total asshole," Couch said. "You got a forensic accountant on your team yet?"

"No," Service said.

"That IRS agent you mentioned, Leukonovich? I've heard of her. Supposed to be good, but you'll also need somebody from state." She scribbled a name on a piece of paper and slid it across the table. "Emma Jornstadt's a little arrogant and weird for my tastes, but she's good at her job. You want me to call her, or do you want to do it?"

"You can," Service said.

"A lot of people think I'm a bitch and just waiting to retire," she said, grinning. "They're half right. I love this work, and I've got no time for anything but ballbusters and hard chargers. You need anything, call. Use initiative and creativity and don't back off Fagan. I'd like a briefing every week or so to keep me in the loop."

23

TUESDAY, NOVEMBER 2, 2004

Saranac, Ionia County

Service found the property on Jackson Road, off Riverside Drive. A line of cotton-woods formed a ragged natural fence along a creek bank behind the house.

He had stopped at a grocery store in Saranac and done some basic shopping for supplies. After a quick tour around the place he decided he liked what he saw. Not fancy at all, but pretty well equipped, and private. The main building was a sort of Dutch colonial A-frame with a sleeping loft that contained two double beds. There was a woodstove downstairs and a stack of wood on the back deck. There were woods twenty yards away and he could see a lot of deadfalls cluttering the creek bottom. A pole barn next to the house would hide their trucks.

Denninger pulled in around the time he was getting ready to grill pork chops on a Weber grill on the deck that extended toward the creek. The young officer walked in and threw a couple of bags on the floor. "Beer in the fridge," Service said. "Pork chops work for you?"

"What the *hell* is going on?" she asked, opening the refrigerator. "Am I in trouble?"

"You didn't ask any questions about our visit to Elk Rapids, but now that you're part of it, you need to know what we're up against."

Denninger popped the tab on her beer, took a swig, and listened intently. When Service finished she asked, "Does this mean I'm gonna have a short career?"

"Hell, no," he said. "You're gonna have an interesting career, but all interesting careers have some major bumps along the way."

"What about my area? Deer season is coming up," she said.

"The chief will take care of it," Service said. He wondered how she was going to handle missing deer season, the highlight of most officers' work year. *Better than me,* he hoped.

"He told me to just get my butt over here, and not to talk to my sergeant or my lieutenant."

"The fewer people who know what we're doing, the better," Service said, accepting a can of beer from her. "There's potato salad and pea-and-peanut salad in the fridge. You want to set the table?"

"I don't like domestic work," she said.

"Me neither," he said.

She smiled. "Great. We'll be Oscar and Oscar."

They talked about the case while they ate, and Service began to lay out the next steps from his perspective.

"Our people on the take?" she asked in an incredulous voice.

"Assumed until we rule it out."

"We're in thin air, aren't we?"

She shook her head.

"Very."

"The first thing we need to do is call Rogers in New York and tell him to impound the eggs," she said.

"Maybe we should wait until tomorrow to make sure he has them."

"First thing?"

"I was thinking more like midday."

She recoiled. "The evidence could be in testing by then."

"Yeah, that *could* happen," Service said, deadpan. "I think we should attend the hearing," he added. "If anything goes south, it's on my shoulders."

"When is it?"

He answered with a shrug. "Ten days or so. I also have the name of a forensic accountant who will join us."

"You talked to Roxy Lafleur a second time?" she asked.

"Not since Miars and I were up there," Service said. "At some point I want to talk to Alma DeKoening and try to get a bead on where she is with her job and Fagan. We saw her drop the eggs with Veatch and go on to the plant. I don't get why she didn't just take them there herself."

Denninger rolled her eyes. "She wanted to get laid."

Probably true, but this didn't explain why she'd left the eggs with Veatch. "I also think we should dig around and look at all allegations of all people on the take. We know from Roxy Lafleur that Langford Horn got a boat. We ought to see it, take photos. We also ought to look at the allegation of women and vacations and all that, one at a time, try to pinpoint who got what, when and where, if anything. We also need to talk to as many former employees as we can find to explore what they might know about the caviar operation."

"And coordinate everything with New York?" Denninger added.

"I'll be the primary with Rogers and New York for now. We need to go to New York at some point and see if we can interview Piscova's customers."

"Can't New York handle that on their own?"

"Good question." He had a feeling he needed to meet with Rogers to work out the coordination and a sense of how he saw the case. "The bottom line is that New York has the case, but they also had no clue about what they had until we stepped in and gave them direction. As far as I'm concerned, that makes it *our* case."

"How long has this been going on?" Denninger asked.

"Miars and Zins had it for eighteen months. Me, less than three weeks."

"Teeny actually stopped you in the Mason lobby?"

"Very unhappy man. I ignored him. I'm guessing he'll soon be out of it."

"You ever get this kind of blowback before?"

"Nothing so blatant. When you piss off people you're more likely to get passive-aggressive crap and a lot of cold stares. I've gotten a whole lot of cold stares about my cases over the years," he added. "Unless they turn out all right. Then everybody's your pal."

"I heard," she said, looking at the paper bags on the counter. "There's not enough real food here. We need to seriously shop. You cook, I'll do dishes. I get the shower first in the morning. I don't wake up fast and I sleep like I'm dead. Where's my bedroom?"

"*Our* bedroom is upstairs. We each get a double bed. There's a sauna out back on the riverbank."

She rubbed her face. "I've been told I snore."

"You cool with this?" he asked.

"I'm pachydermatous," she said.

"What?"

"Oblivious to reactions I create in others."

He laughed. "That's makes two of us."

First thing the next morning Service limped through an hour-long run along the river, came back, and made a pot of coffee and breakfast as Denninger struggled downstairs in flannel PJs and wool socks, trying to will the sleep out of her eyes. Her breakfast was the same as his: one egg, one piece of dry rye toast, one small yogurt, and eight ounces of orange juice.

"Combat rations?" she asked. "I eat *real* food."

"Pretty much."

After eating he called Anniejo Couch. "We'll need some equipment here. Pencils, pens, a computer, a laser printer, a few reams of paper, couple of file cabinets, file folders, three or four white boards, markers, CDs, erasers, paper clips, cassette tapes, several cots and folding chairs . . . the drill. Is there a form to fill out?"

"Next time. I wrote it all down and will make sure you get what you need. I think I can get the stuff there tomorrow afternoon. That work?"

"Thanks."

"Your colleague there yet?" the assistant U.S. attorney asked.

"Yesterday afternoon."

"Good. Anything else?"

"Not for now."

His next call went to Roxanne Lafleur, who sounded tired.

"Grady Service here. You up to talking?"

"I'm sorry, but it will have to be tomorrow morning, early. I have to see the doctor tomorrow afternoon."

Service looked at his watch. It was 10 A.M. If he left now he could be at Slippery Creek tonight and spend the night before driving up to the Hurons tomorrow morning. "What time is good for you?" he asked.

"I'm an early riser. How about eight?"

"See you then."

He called Candi McCants on her cell phone. "You on patrol?"

"Blasting off in a few."

"I'm going to head for Slippery Creek, be there tonight. You want to drop the animals?"

"How long will you be here?"

"Just tonight."

"Why don't you just stay at my place," she said. "It'll be open. Let yourself in."

His next call was to Karylanne Pengelly.

"Hello?" she answered.

"It's Grady. How're you feeling?"

"Beat. This is a lot harder than I anticipated. Are you coming over?"

"I'm downstate."

"Oh," she said.

He heard the disappointment in her silence. "What's tomorrow afternoon look like?"

"Class till four."

"I'll meet you at your place at four-thirty."

"Are you sure?"

"You bet. You want me to cook?"

"Thanks, but I'll take care of that. It gets my nose out of the books."

When he hung up the phone he found Denninger eyeballing him. "*What?*" he asked.

"Do I wear a uniform while we're doing this work?"

"It's your choice."

She came downstairs a while later in corduroys and a sweater. He made more coffee and they sat down at the table together.

"I ordered supplies. They'll be delivered tomorrow. I'm heading up to the U.P. to interview Roxy Lafleur again. Be back the day after tomorrow. I've got some cassette tapes. I want to record every interview and create transcripts. We'll share the typing. I'll type yours, you type mine. Fair enough?"

She nodded. He handed her the cassettes from his first Lafleur interview and his meeting with Andriaitis, and a list of Piscova's former employees. "We're getting a computer and a printer, but you can use your laptop; we'll transfer it to disk and later move it all onto the new computer. Call the former employees, see if their phones are valid. Tell them you're with the phone company and doing a routine line check. Questions?"

"Did you get up and run this morning?"

"Every morning I can," he said.

"Get me up, too."

"Okay."

"Do we find out who the area officer is and let them know we're in the area?"

He thought about this for a second. "No. We don't tell anyone where we are for now."

"Because?"

"You really want an answer?"

She shook her head.

"Is what it is," he said. "We've got Miars, the chief, and each other. Everybody else is suspect until we determine they're not."

"This is sort of creeping me out."

"Me too. You okay holding down the fort?"

"I don't care for that term. How about we call it the resort?"

"Your choice."

"Have you got a plan in mind?"

"Very rough at this point."

She took a pen out of her pocket and grabbed a tablet of paper. "Start talking and I'll start writing. I'll transfer what we have to notepads. If some of my friends call on my cell, what do I tell them?"

"Be creative," he said. "Just don't tell them the truth."

"Sick irony," she said.

"Okay," he said, taking a gulp of coffee. "Ready?"

Dani Denninger nodded and he began to talk through what he knew and didn't know and what he thought they ought to do and in what sequence.

When he was done he went out to his Tahoe and headed north, making a mental checklist of clothes to pack at his place. He would stop briefly at Slippery Creek, spend the night with McCants and the animals, see Lafleur in the morning, and drive to Houghton in the afternoon to see Karylanne. Pulling onto I-96 he sucked in a deep breath and tried to conjure a good travel mind-set.

PART II

ANDANTE

These are much deeper waters than I thought.
—Sherlock Holmes, "The Reigate Puzzle"

24

WEDNESDAY, NOVEMBER 3, 2004

Huron Mountains, Marquette County

Staying with McCants turned out to be a mistake. She had come in just after he arrived and immediately began grilling him about what he was doing.

"So, you're like in the federal witness protection program or what?"

"Assignment," he said.

"The man of few words—as in *way* too few," McCants shot back. "We have taken each other's backs too many times to count."

"I'm covering your six right now," he said.

"Why am I not feeling comforted?"

"You're just tired," he said.

"Don't tell me how I feel," she snapped.

"I can't talk about it, Candi."

"Right," she said, stalking off.

She had gone to bed without another word, gotten up this morning without speaking to him, and departed. He knew she was pissed, but he wasn't at all certain about what.

He arrived at Roxy Lafleur's cottage on time and made his way through the three dogs with a lump in his throat and his heart racing.

The woman's eyes were sunken, her skin drawn tight, her movement slow and labored. Last time she had looked healthy. Not anymore.

"I know," she said. "I don't look so good."

"Have you called your doctor?"

"I'm seeing him later today. You want coffee? It's fresh."

They sat in her living room. She pulled an afghan over her legs and he poured the coffee for both of them. She handed him a slip of paper. "Angle Iron Properties is the name of the umbrella corporation for Quint's chain of convenience stores in Ypsi, Plymouth, and Ann Arbor. Quint thinks he has a way with words. Angle iron is used for support and that pretty much describes his business interests. The whole shebang is in his wife's name so the government can't get at her if they happen to get to him." She sighed and closed her eyes.

"Sounds like he cares about her."

"Please," Lafleur said.

The second item on the list was *Netsuko Hurami.*

"Who's this?" he asked, tapping the name with his finger.

"She's an investigator with the RCMP out of Windsor. She came to the plant several times and wrote all kinds of letters, trying to get information about Quint's investments in Canada."

Royal Canadian Mounted Police. *Great—another complication,* he thought.

"What sort of investments?"

"I've no idea," she said, "but the way she stayed on it, they must be significant."

"Did you talk to her?"

"Only to relay messages to and from Quint."

"You have a number for her?"

"It's in the Rolodex, or was. Look under RCMP."

"You mentioned a man named Gary Hosk."

"Right. He worked for Crimea at one time."

"As a bag man?"

She managed a smile. "That's never in formal job descriptions, is it?"

"How do you know he carried money?"

"He delivered it to me in Elk Rapids, or sometimes at the plant in New York."

"Once, twice?"

"More, maybe half a dozen times, but it was years ago."

"But after the company started supplying Crimea."

She nodded. "He was on retainer to Crimea."

"You mentioned women for Fagan's clients."

"Not formally clients."

"You made arrangements?"

"In Lansing I used a woman named Patricia Allard. She runs a very hush-hush and expensive escort service in the capital."

"Got a number for her?"

"No. When Quint wanted me to get escorts, I used a cell phone that he gave me and, when the transaction was done, I threw the phone away. There was a new phone each time. Quint's very, very careful."

Service lifted his chin and stretched his neck. "That's pretty extreme security."

Lafleur held out the palms of her hands. "How it was. Down in Lansing, Allard's known as Mama Cold."

"Can you describe her?"

"I never met her. All our business was done by cell phone."

"She have cop problems?"

"I'd expect anybody in that business would have potential cop problems."

"Did you ever meet a New York employee named Garrick Bindi?"

"Never met him, but Quint mighta mentioned him. For some reason I think he worked at a state fish hatchery."

"What did Fagan say when he mentioned him?"

"It's kinda vague, but I think Quint called him the gate guard, or something like that."

Another potential fit, Service thought, but finding Bindi would be difficult.

Last time, the woman's dogs had gathered around him. This time they were next to her, staring at her, and he imagined he could sense their concern. "Maybe we ought to call your doctor. I'll drive you to town."

"I can drive myelf just fine," she said resolutely.

"You don't look well," he said.

"I've got cancer," she whispered, and tried to force a grin. "Or it's got me. I'm not sure which anymore." She looked over at him. "Don't worry. This is just part of the process. I'll be okay."

He wasn't convinced, but excused himself, made his way down to his truck, and headed for Houghton to see Karylanne.

Passing through Chassell he got a cell-phone call from Chief O'Driscoll. "I've been trying to reach you."

"No cell coverage where I was."

"We challenged the injunction this morning, but the judge stood firm," said the chief. "There will be a full hearing in two weeks. The judge said that because the allegedly illegally taken eggs were not actually in the mix, we were short on probable cause in seizing finished product. Our lawyers think we may be screwed for this round. You need to contact New York and tell them to hold the samples until we exhaust all the legal steps."

"Roger that," Service said. It sounded like the department's lawyers were in the fight and this was good. Sometimes they opposed the law enforcement division.

"Where are you?" the chief asked.

"Just finished interviewing Fagan's Caviar Queen and now I'm headed to Houghton."

"Make sure you call New York," the chief said, hanging up.

Service called Trip Rogers, who was not in his office. He asked a secretary to go and find him.

"What's the status of the eggs?" Service asked when Rogers came to the phone.

"FDA has them and testing is under way. Why?"

"How long for a result?"

"A week or more. Why?"

Service told the New York environmental conservation officer about the injunction.

"That screws the pooch," Rogers said.

"Partially. We'll at least have results that will tell us something, even if we can't use them."

"You think Piscova will keep the line operating?"

"Not for long. The salmon runs are almost done, and they're contracted only to take eggs from brights."

"Brights" were brilliant silver fish, freshly into the river system. As time passed the salmon began to blacken and fall apart during the process of slow death that came with spawning. "I'm guessing the natural cycle and our little raid will shut them down for now," he said.

Rogers said, "We could try to intercept a shipment at Crimea."

"What would that entail?"

"A call to Fish and Wildlife. They have surveillance on the company."

"If that's the best we can do," Service said.

"I'll make some calls," Rogers offered. "You think your legal people can beat the injunction?"

"Probably not."

"Damn," Rogers said. "Why the hell do our laws make it so damned hard to enforce the laws?"

It was the unanswerable question for law enforcement.

"I'll be in touch," Rogers said.

"Let me give you another number," Service said, telling his counterpart about Denninger and reading off her cell-phone number. He also explained how his chief had pulled them out of the DNR and transferred them to the U.S. Attorney's office.

"No shit? Your chief sounds like he has major backbone."

"So far."

"Make you feel like some high-wire freak working without a net?"

"Something like that."

He called Denninger. "I'm checking in. Everything okay down there?"

"Tip-top. I got the transcripts done this morning and our supplies are being unloaded as we speak. Did you talk to Lafleur?"

"Yes. I've got the name of the convenience store chain, the name of an RCMP investigator who's interested in Fagan's investments in Canada, and the name of the woman who provided female talent for Fagan's pals and associates."

"You want me to follow up on anything?"

He spelled out the name. "Netsuko Hurami out of the Windsor RCMP office. She's in the Rolodex cards I copied in Gaylord under 'RCMP.' Give her a bump and tell her what we're doing and see how she reacts."

"Offer her a trade?"

"Offer her a head-to-head. Tell her the big picture only—illegal eggs mixed with legal ones."

"Why should she care?"

"She may not, but if she's looking for Piscova dirt in Canada, she may be interested in any dirt we have here. Dirt follows dirt. Feel her out."

"Anything else?"

"Not for now. I'll be back tomorrow afternoon."

"There's snow coming into the U.P.," she said. "I saw it on the Weather Channel."

Service glanced up. "I can see it in the sky," he said. "See you tomorrow, I guess."

He didn't like the tone of her voice. She sounded unsure of herself.

25

WEDNESDAY, NOVEMBER 3, 2004

Houghton, Houghton County

Karylanne had a ground-floor apartment in a large house on Garner Street. She was close to campus and could walk while the weather was still good. It had been at least a month since he had seen her, and when he knocked on the door she took a long time to open up.

The apartment was large, sparsely furnished, and immaculately clean. For the second time that day he found himself looking at a woman who looked a bit worse for the wear.

"You look like crap," he said.

She managed a smile. "I'm just tired. Twenty-two credits is a struggle, but I'm fine. Don't worry. I'm getting ready to broil some whitefish. I swear, I'm *always* hungry," she added. Her belly was swollen to the point where it looked like the slightest jostle would make it pop.

He followed her into the kitchen, got a can of Diet Pepsi out of the fridge, popped the tab, and sat down. "Classes okay?"

"The usual grind," she said. "Walter could read something once and get it. I have to pound everything into my brain and hope it doesn't drain away."

The mention of his son made him gulp. "The baby?"

"No problems, though I'm getting kicked on a regular basis. We're still on for December twenty-eighth, and the doctor says everything looks normal and fine. I talked to my mum last night and she's coming down for a couple of weeks after I deliver."

This news bothered him and he wasn't sure why. "I'll be here."

"You have a job to do," she said. "Mum can stay for a month if she needs to, and if we don't kill each other."

"Is that likely?"

"Not really. She'll be so into grandmothering she'll leave me alone." She looked over at him. "You don't look like you're on top of your game either."

"A lot of driving."

"I talk to McCants pretty regularly. She says you've been downstate."

"I have," was all he said.

"I told Candi she could bring Newf and Cat over here. I think it would be good to have company around."

"What did she say?"

"No answer. I think she took it as criticism."

The feelings of others, Service thought, were an endless minefield. He had enough of a challenge sorting out his own. "You seen Gus?"

"Stops by every couple of days. Shark and Limey, too. They all hover." She lifted her hands and wiggled them. "Really, are *you* okay?"

"Just tired."

"We promised to always level with each other," she said, playing back a speech he had given her when he'd discovered she was pregnant and decided to take care of her.

"I've got a case that's sort of complicated," he said.

"As a term paper that report would not make it," she said with a chuckle.

They ate fish and lima beans and a simple mixed green salad and made small talk.

"Still the twenty-eighth, huh?" he said.

"That's *our* date, not the baby's. They have their own clocks. Don't worry. If you aren't here, Gus or Shark or Limey will jump right in."

"It's my job," he said. What he didn't say was that it was more a sense of need than anything else. "I'll be here."

She patted him on the arm. "Relax, Grandpa . . . we'll all get through this."

After dinner Karylanne studied and Service drove over to Gus Turnage's house, had a beer, and watched a Red Wings game with him. "Thanks for looking in on Karylanne."

"She's a good kid; works her butt off."

They sat in silence a long while before Gus said, "Messy case?"

"Very."

"You'll wear them down," his friend and colleague said.

Service wished he was as confident. He should have been less impulsive and postponed the raid on the plant, but when you were a game warden, you had to act fast or risk the evidence disappearing.

Stop making excuses, he told himself. *You fucked up. Not your first time—won't be your last. Accept it and move on.*

Hastings, Barry County

He called Barry County assistant prosecuting attorney Gary Hosk an hour after leaving Houghton and made an appointment to see him. Hosk asked him to come to his house on Algonquin Lake near Hastings and gave him directions.

Service pulled up to the house at 6 P.M. and went to the door. A man with a florid face greeted him at the door with a martini glass in hand. He wore an expensive blue cardigan, a button-down shirt, and a loose tie. "Service? What can I do for the DNR?"

The man led him into his den, which was filled with shelves of books and a giant television. "Want a drink?"

"Diet Pepsi."

The two men sat down. Service said, "You used to work for Crimea."

"Who told you that?" the man asked with a start.

"It's part of an investigation."

Hosk began to shake. "God," he whispered. "Oh . . . my . . . God." The man obviously had been imbibing for a while.

"I'm just looking for some information," said Service.

The man's head dropped. "I swear I didn't do anything illegal."

Serious overreaction. "Nobody said you did."

The man tried to pull himself together and looked up.

"You used to deliver bags of cash for your employer to Piscova plants in New York and Michigan."

"I delivered bags. I never knew what was in them."

Service was skeptical. "What if it was coke?"

"It wasn't," Hosk insisted, shaking his head repeatedly.

"Approximately nine grand in cash, per bag. No law against that," Service said. "Is there?"

"No."

"You ever meet Semyon Krapahkin?"

"He was the boss."

"You met him?"

"Once in a while."

"Who gave you the packages?"

"Krapahkin's assistant, Oleg Bauman."

"Not the boss?"

"No, never."

"And you had no idea what was in the packages?"

"I never looked. A lawyer is well schooled in learned ignorance."

"Did you handle the contract with Piscova for salmon caviar?"

"No, my job was to provide legal services, especially where immigration and visas were concerned. Not contracts."

"But you knew there *was* a contract."

"Absolutely not. All I knew was that Crimea did business of some kind with Piscova. I never knew the details."

"All you knew was your own narrow little world."

"Good lawyers learn to focus," Hosk said, trying to make a joke.

"You're probably going to get a subpoena," Service said. He wasn't sure this was true, but he wanted to see the man's reaction.

Hosk abruptly stood up and left the room. When he came back, his hair was wet and he looked pale. "Okay, here's how it was. I thought Crimea was legitimate. When I found out they were on the shady side, I resigned the account and left the firm."

"Shady in what way?"

"I'm not saying anything more without my lawyer," Hosk said.

"If you haven't done anything wrong, you don't have to worry," Service said. "We're interested in you only for what you know about Piscova and Crimea."

"Not without my lawyer."

The man was sweating and trembling. Service took out a business card. "If you think of anything, give me a call on my cell phone." He used a pen to circle the number and placed the card on a coffee table. "I'm sorry to interrupt your cocktail hour. I'm just doing my job. It's not personal."

He drove down the street and parked to take some time to think. Hosk was badly shaken, but admitted to carrying bags. Good chance he knew they contained money, but that probably didn't matter. Roxy would testify to receiving the bags from Hosk and that they contained money. But Hosk's reaction made him wonder if the man was hiding something more serious, or if he was just badly embarrassed by a past that had caught up to him.

He called Denninger. "I'm just pulling out of Hastings; be there in a half-hour. How's the resort?"

She laughed. "Trashed. You eat yet?"

"Not yet."

"I bought some steaks today, and a bottle of wine. See you when you get here, boss."

Boss? The word jarred him; it was a title for others, not him. He didn't like it at all.

THURSDAY, NOVEMBER 4, 2004

Saranac, Ionia County

The temperature outside was in the mid-thirties and there was a light sleet starting as he pulled up to the resort. The room was filled with cardboard boxes and gear. Denninger had a fire going in the woodstove and had set up four huge erasable boards, labeling them: PEOPLE, EVENTS, CONFIRMED FACTS, TASKS TO COMPLETE: PROCESS / CASE-SPECIFIC.

"Impressive," he said. "You get hold of the Canadian?"

"Talked to her twice. She's part of a task force looking at Americans who may be laundering money in Canadian operations."

"Money laundering?"

Denninger nodded. "She said she's been on Fagan's trail for two years and she knows he's doing something, but she can't figure out exactly what. A lot of his money crosses the border into weird schemes and then disappears. Fagan does everything by word of mouth, no paper trail."

"Huh. She interested in what we have?"

"Very. Everything go okay with you?"

"Roxy doesn't look well at all. I stopped and visited Hosk on the way back."

She looked at the board labeled PEOPLE. "The guy in Hastings?"

"He was not at all happy to see me. He was real hinky but admits to delivering bags for Crimea to Piscova. He claims he only handled immigration issues for the company."

Service walked over to the board labeled CONFIRMED FACTS and wrote, "Roxy claims money from Hosk; Hosk confirms delivering, but not knowing contents of packages." On the next line he wrote: "RCMP confirms 2-yr. investigation of Fagan's money-laundering activities."

Denninger said, "Looks like a good start."

"Why do I get the feeling we don't have enough boards to record what's ahead?"

"Let's eat," she said. "We both need a break."

She poured from a bottle of 1999 Amarone and Service looked at the bottle. "You found a bottle of *this* in Saranac?"

"I brought some from my own supplies."

"Good choice," he said.

"Didn't need your approval," she said, taking a sip and saluting him with the glass. "We gonna run in the morning?"

Her mind was erratic. On the phone she'd sounded needy. Now she was copping a weird attitude. He nodded, knowing that crawling out of bed in the dark would be difficult at best.

"I may be headed up to Traverse City tomorrow. You want to go?"

"You need me?"

"I think it's good for us to spend time bouncing stuff off each other."

"You're the boss," she said, obviously pleased to not be left behind again.

She's young, Service told himself. *Very, very young.* Remember that. Damn feelings anyway.

He grilled two steaks and did two baked potatoes in the microwave. They ate in silence.

It was 2 A.M. and Denninger was kneeling beside his bed, shaking his shoulder and whispering in his ear. "Somebody's outside—I saw a light."

He was out of bed, pulling on trousers and boots and following her downstairs, both of them carrying their gear belts.

"Where?"

"East of the house," she said.

They got flashlights and radios, pulled on their gear belts, and slid quietly out the back door, her going east, and him circling to the west. He had managed to get on a shirt, but no coat, and the wind and sleet were cutting.

"Where are you?" he heard her whisper over the 800 MHz.

"Front."

"Keep coming east," she said.

The sky was overcast, the sleet pummeling them, no light, but he could make out her silhouette toward the woods. When he got to her, she whispered. "Voices."

He listened and thought he heard at least one voice, but he couldn't make out the words. The tone sounded irritated. They went through the woods side by side until they reached a clearing and saw a dim light ahead, and two vehicles. One of them was a CO's truck.

"You dumb punks—I let you off with a warning last time."

A teenage voice challenged, "Big whoop. We were headlighting. We ain't got no gun, dude."

Denninger nudged Service with her elbow, whispered, "I'll look around," and was gone.

"Six of us, man, one of you. What're you gonna do, shoot all our asses?"

Service didn't give the CO a chance to respond. He stepped toward the group and when he got close, switched on his light and shone it in the faces of the teens. "DNR, Conservation Officer. He won't shoot your asses, but I will. Get on the ground, *now!*"

The boys hit the ground in unison. The other CO said, "Who is that?"

"Grady Service. Who're you?"

"Cullen."

Service stepped over to the officer, who looked to be about Denninger's age.

"What have you got?"

"They had a light, and it's after eleven. I'm sure there was a weapon."

"You see them toss it?"

"No. I was running black and the ground was rough. *The* Grady Service? What're *you* doing here?"

Service cringed. "Keep your mind in the moment, Officer."

"Yessir."

"Don't call me sir."

"Nossir, I won't, sir."

Denninger suddenly appeared carrying a shotgun. "Hullo, Joe. Somebody musta dropped this."

"Dani?"

Denninger laughed. "Boo."

"Jesus," Cullen said with a huge grin.

Service went over to the boys. "Get on your feet."

When they were up, Service asked, "Who belongs to this?"

"Never saw it before," one of the boys said quickly.

"Good," Service said. "The state gets a new shotgun." He turned to Cullen.

"Stroke the little wiseasses for shining after curfew and trespass, and add on the ticket there was a shotgun found and that they *insist* it doesn't belong to them."

Service and Denninger watched while the officer wrote the tickets and sent them on their way.

"C'mon," Service said to Cullen. "We're in the place just west of here. Drive over and we'll make some fresh coffee."

"I thought we were going to remain incognito," Denninger said as they walked through the woods.

"You know him?"

"He graduated from the academy class ahead of mine."

When Cullen got there, he looked around the room like he had stumbled into the twilight zone, and raised his hands. "I see nothing, right?"

"Dead on," Service said.

"Am I supposed to know you two are here?"

"Know who's where?" Service said in response.

"Ahhh," Joe Cullen said, nodding solemnly. "Ahhh."

Traverse City, Grand Traverse County

Two days earlier Service had hit a wall. He had the name "Aline Bergey" off the Rolodex files and after a few phone calls had discovered she was president of Farmer's Bank of Michigan. She had been the bank's commercial loan officer when the bank made loans to Piscova. Having discovered who she was, he managed to get a call through to her, explaining that he was with the DNR and investigating one of the bank's customers.

"Which customer?" she challenged him.

"Piscova."

"You'd better have a subpoena," she said in a tone that was more businesslike than obstructive.

"I just want to talk."

"Doesn't matter. Get a subpoena," she said.

Service immediately called Anniejo Couch and explained the situation. She said, "We've got a sitting grand jury in GR. You're probably moving a little too fast for the process. We'll need a list of the subpoenas you want and thorough, precise affidavits of how they relate to the case. I need two days to take care of this request, and I'll need a list to get the rest of what you want. Day after tomorrow for this subpoena okay by you?"

"Have to be," he said. He was jacked on the adrenaline that always came with a pursuit, and suddenly it felt wrong. In his world he rarely had to rely on others, and most of the time could move at his own pace. This was bureaucracy at its worst and he hated it.

He looked over at Denninger. "We've got to slow down and think more about this whole process. We need to create a list of people we need subpoenas for, and why."

They spent the remainder of the day getting better organized. Denninger was easy to work with, but he noticed she constantly looked to him for direction and showed little initiative in substance, only in pushing their organization forward.

They had stopped in Grand Rapids to fetch their subpoenas that morning, and then continued on to the bank on East Front Street in Traverse City. It seemed the prototypical modern bank; that is, low on amenities, designed to demonstrate frugality. Aline Bergey was a distinguished, conservatively dressed woman in her late forties. Service and Denninger were shown into her office, where they introduced themselves and handed the bank president the subpoena. Bergey immediately summoned a lawyer to scrutinize the document, and Service took the opportunity to study the office, which was relatively free of any personal mementos other than a single photograph of a distinguished-looking man in a silver frame behind her desk.

"We could have just talked," Service said.

"I have a board and this business is heavily regulated," Bergey said. "We're happy to cooperate with law enforcement, but it has to be done legally and properly."

The lawyer was a young male, with gelled hair in short spikes. He flipped through the subpoena, nodded to Bergey, and departed.

A secretary brought a dozen or so files and handed them to Bergey, who opened the top one. "Ah, yes," she said. "Ten small loans going back as many years. The loans were a little larger over the past three years, but nothing I would characterize as substantial. The company is in good financial standing—a good and loyal customer."

"They do all their banking with you?" Service asked.

"Just loans," Bergey said.

"Did you deal with Quintan Fagan?"

Bergey smiled. "No. I know him, of course, but the loans were all with Mr. Vandeal, for minor construction for a processing operation."

"Do you know anything about Piscova's business?"

"Fish," the banker said. "They've been in business since the late 1970s."

Service heard a commotion. The office door opened and a silver-haired man barged in, his face bright red. "Who the *hell* do you think you are?" the man shouted.

"Beg your pardon, sir. You would be . . . ?" Service said.

"Judge Leo Bergey. If you'da come to my court, there would be no subpoenas. We don't support government fishing expeditions into local business."

"Your Honor," Service said, exchanging glances with Denninger, "these are federal warrants. Nobody's accused anyone of anything. We are simply serving papers, trying to gather information, doing our job, Your Honor. That's all there is to this, nothing personal."

The judge glared at him. "My wife's done nothing wrong."

The man was the one in the picture behind the banker's desk. "Nobody has accused your wife of anything. We're collecting information for a federal investigation."

"Of whom?" the man demanded.

"I'm sure you know we're not at liberty to say, Your Honor."

"I'm not the unwashed public," Leo Bergey said. "I'm a judge."

"Sorry, Your Honor," Denninger said.

Service kept wondering: why such an overreaction? His wife was the bank officer, not him. Had to be more than wanting to protect his wife. And how had he learned about their visit so quickly? Had the bank's lawyer called the judge?

"Your Honor," Service said, "with all due respect, this is none of your affair, and I think it would be best if you left us alone to do our jobs."

The judge blinked at Service. "What agency are you with, son?"

"DNR," Service said.

"What the hell do you people have to do with a federal probe?"

"Your Honor, you really need to leave . . . *now*," Service said forcefully, "or I will be forced to arrest you for interfering with police officers in the performance of their duty."

"Arrest *me*?" The man began to laugh.

"Yessir. We're here to meet with Ms. Bergey, and you're interfering. I suggest you leave now."

"Leo," the banker said, and the judge turned and went through the door.

She made no apology, and Service wondered if this had been a planned show, something meant to intimidate them—and if so, why?

The judge came back through the door. "I am a personal friend of your director, Officer. I want your badge number."

"It's *Detective*, Your Honor, but I don't work for the DNR. I work for the Assistant U.S. Attorney for the Western District of Michigan out of Grand Rapids."

"You work for Riley Endicott?"

"Anniejo Couch."

The judge looked Service over and departed again.

"Your husband?" Service asked Aline Bergey.

"Thirty years."

"He's way off the reservation."

"Leo tends to be a bit overprotective."

"You don't look like a person who needs protection."

"I'm not," she said with quiet self-assurance.

Service picked up the file folders, signed for them, and they left the bank.

"What the hell happened in there?" Denninger asked when they were out on the sidewalk.

"I don't know. It's starting to look like everywhere we go in this thing we're touching raw nerves, but how the hell do we tell if it's related to what we're doing, or to something else?"

Denninger had no answer.

Leaving the city they drove up the Old Mission Peninsula to look at Roxy Lafleur's house. There was a FOR SALE sign by the driveway. It had not been there the last time he'd visited. The realty firm was called Mission Mansions, and the realtor's name was listed as L. Sparks. There was a phone number.

Service picked up his recorder and left himself a voice note. "Lafleur's house." He dialed the realtor on his cell phone. "Is there an L. Sparks there?"

"That would be Lulu," the woman at the realtor's office said.

"Is Ms. Sparks available?"

"No sir, she's out of town until next week."

Service left his cell-phone number, name, affiliation, and asked for a return call when she got back.

"You're wondering who the client is," Denninger said.

"Lafleur says the house is in her name, but Fagan owns it, and I'm wondering if she signed it back to him or somebody else. This guy never seems to do anything in a straight line."

Driving south past Cadillac he got a call from Captain Ware Grant, his boss in Marquette. "The chief told me what you're doing. There's a big Fisheries meeting at the RAM Center tomorrow. The chief wants you to go talk to them, let them know an investigation is under way, and suggest that they should probably seek some separation from Piscova."

Service felt his temper flare. "Dammit, Cap'n, that's like sending a message to the enemy before you mount a surprise attack."

The captain's voice was measured and calm, as it always was. "They are our *colleagues*, Grady—not the enemy."

Service closed his cell phone, looked over at Denninger, and shook his head.

By the time they reached Big Rapids, Anniejo Couch was on the phone. "Did you rattle the cage of Judge Leo Bergey today?"

"No, we served the subpoena to his wife, who is the president of a bank that does business with Piscova. We collected the records we wanted and the judge showed up, making all sorts of threats."

"He called my boss and raised hell with him."

"What did your boss say?"

"He said he'd look into it."

"Ergo, you're calling me."

"Shit flows downhill," Couch said. "Any idea why the judge wants to get into this?"

"Absolutely none. His wife was fine. He just showed up."

"Our ears only," Couch said. "Bergey is a lush and he's had IRS problems in the past that almost cost him his job. He's a little thin-skinned when it comes to his reputation."

"That's got nothing to do with us," Service said.

"You've not been the tip of the spear for a federal investigation before. People get pissed and make threats. Did you threaten to arrest the judge?"

"Yes, ma'am—for interfering with police officers trying to do their duty."

"My advice, and this isn't a criticism, but let them beat on you, make their threats, whatever. Be polite and keep focused on what you have to do. Every case is tough, and you don't need any sideshows to pull you away from the main event."

"I'll take your advice under advisement," he said, earning a laugh.

"I like you, Service. You would have made a good fed."

"I'd rather have a sister in a whorehouse than be a fed."

"Yikes," Anniejo Couch said with a chuckle. "That one cut deep. Keep digging, and if you need anything more, call. The grand jury is processing your other subpoena requests now. Keep reviewing what you want and forwarding your list to me, and stay ahead of the curve. Are we cool?"

"Most Kelvin," he said, wondering why she was so specific about keeping on top of things.

29

TUESDAY, NOVEMBER 9, 2004

RAM Center, North Higgins Lake, Roscommon County

Grady Service wasn't sure he should bring Denninger with him to the Fisheries meeting and expose her to whatever might result from it, but he eventually decided she needed to see what they might be up against.

They met Clay Flinders, head of the Fisheries division, outside the meeting room. The recently elevated Fisheries chief had sandy hair, ruddy skin, and a walrus mustache.

"I had a call from Ware Grant who said you wanted to talk to my people about something important," said Flinders. "You're on first. Please make it brief. Our agenda's full, and with budgets the way they are these days, I rarely get to gather my people in the same place at one time."

The Law Enforcement Division had the same problem. Flinders had come up through the ranks and Service had met him many times, though he'd never worked directly with him. So far he had the rep of a good leader, but having been in the job only a year, the jury was still out, which made the stuff going on under him seem odd. Flinders was not the one many guessed would get the top fish job. He had always been quiet and seemed more comfortable in the field, not an office.

There were perhaps three dozen people in the room, many of whom Service recognized and had worked with during his career. In back he also saw Captain Grant's counterpart, Captain Edwin "Fast Track Eddie" Black, a former Troop who had transferred to the DNR at the same time as Service and Luticious Treebone. From the beginning Black had made no secret of his ambition to one day be chief of DNR law enforcement. Inexplicably, he had risen quickly, spending two years as a CO in Detroit, jumping to sergeant within five, making lieutenant in less than ten years, and captain at sixteen, his career advancement the inspiration for his nickname. Grady Service thought Black was a complete and utter asshole. He had been known in the Troops as a worthless road patrol officer and a blowhard.

Flinders waved his arms to quiet the room. "This is Detective Service from Wildlife Resource Protection. He needs a few minutes of our time."

Service stepped to the lectern that sat on a table in front of the room. "If you haven't already heard, we are looking at Piscova and we are finding some . . . irregularities," he said. "I can't go into the details other than to say it looks like an iceberg, and we've just started on the visible part. I know Piscova's been a longtime contractor for the state, but I would strongly recommend that you do nothing with them other than what is required by contract."

His words were met with dead silence. Jeff Choate, who had called during the first visit to Piscova and handled salmon contracts for the state, jumped to his feet. He was a small man with thick glasses and a loud voice. "If you're accusing Piscova, you're accusing me—hell, you're accusing *all of us*."

"I haven't accused anyone of anything," Service offered.

"It's bogus," Choate sputtered. "The state's in shit shape fiscally and you're wasting taxpayer money with your witch hunt. You'll *never* get Piscova. Quint Fagan's too well connected and he's got too much dough and too many lawyers. He'll bury you."

Service tried to maintain a neutral face and nodded like a bobblehead. Choate was a jerk. "The frustrating thing about looking for witches is you mostly find assholes," he relied.

Choate started to stand up, but he began laughing. "You're not worth it," he said with a dismissive wave of a hand. "Piscova and Fagan will bury you, and that will be that."

We'll see, Service thought, and turned to Flinders. "Thanks for the time. That's all I have."

Fast Track was waiting outside the meeting room, grinning. "Past as prologue," the southern zone captain said. "You've been unprofessional and overrated throughout your career. That performance in there was a disgrace to LED. This one will put you away for good."

Service had never feared Black. "Thank you, Captain. Your support is greatly appreciated."

Black leaned in close. "Lorne put you over the fence with the U.S. Attorney. You may find it hard to get back."

"Thank you for your advice."

"I piss you off, don't I?"

"Not at all, Captain. When I see you, I feel only shame for all the competent people who have to depend on you to get their jobs done."

"This is the end for you," Black hissed as Service headed out of the building with Denninger beside him.

"I thought we were one team, all dedicated to protecting the state's resources," she said as they walked toward his Tahoe.

"We are, but even on a good team, people end up in the wrong positions, burn out, fall over the edge, and can't or won't do their jobs. The thing is that good teams eventually analyze their problems and fix them."

"You mean that, or are you whistling in the graveyard?"

He only smiled and she whined, "My career is going to be short."

Service grabbed her arm and spun her around. "Stop worrying about your career and keep your damn mind on the job you're doing. The career will take care of itself if you do the job right."

She was sullen on the three-hour drive back to Saranac. It snowed the whole way and neither of them said anything as he fought the wind and icy highways.

30

TUESDAY, NOVEMBER 9, 2004

Saranac, Ionia County

Grady Service got the woodstove going and pan-fried chicken breasts with Thai hot chili and lime sauce, assembled a huge salad, and uncapped two bottles of beer. Denninger had changed into sweatpants and a gray DNR sweatshirt before sitting down with him.

He held up the beer and looked at her. She nodded, accepted the bottle, and touched a finger to her head. "I feel like I just went through a tank fight with a slingshot," she said.

"Either of us dead or wounded?"

She shook her head.

"We kill anybody?"

"Nope."

"Then it wasn't a gunfight," he said. "The chief wanted me to put them on warning to see what kind of reactions we got."

"You did that," she said, sipping the beer. "I'm not sure I'm up to this," she confessed.

"You want out?"

"I just don't want to let you down."

"Forget me. Keep your mind on the case; that's all that matters right now."

"How long do you think we're gonna be at this?"

"Until it's done," he said.

"Not everyone can bull their way ahead like you. Most of us have fears and insecurities."

"You don't think I'm afraid? My legs were like Jell-O in that room today."

"It didn't look or sound that way."

"It was," he said.

"I know you're trying to reassure me, but if you're afraid, I'm not so sure that makes me feel better."

He held out a pack of cigarettes but she shook her head. He lit one and sat back. "Everybody has to face fear, and it's never the same fear. We're all different, but the only way to handle fear is the same for all of us. You put your face into it and keep pushing."

"Sounds like a platitude."

"Simple truth, but damn hard to put into practice."

They ate their meal without talking, and he wondered what Denninger was thinking. She had withdrawn again, and after waiting for her to talk, he let his mind drift back to the day's events.

One thing was certain: His old nemesis, "Fast Track" Black, was after his scalp. He also knew this was personal, not part of the case, except that Black was seeing this case as an opportunity. He had not butted heads with Black in years, but he knew the man had had it in for him for a long time. He could ignore Black. Fisheries chief Flinders seemed unaffected by all the emotion in the room. The salmon guy, Jeff Choate, had lost it, and seemed convinced that Fagan and Piscova were untouchable. Choate had more or less declared his loyalty to the contractor, but Flinders had said nothing, and Service wondered where he stood on the potential scandal.

So far Service had done nothing but piss people off—most of the Fisheries group, a county prosecuting attorney, and a judge. He guessed there would be a lot more angry people and wondered if there was a way to avoid hard feelings and negative reactions. After a moment he decided there wasn't. If he couldn't avoid it, was there a way to increase fear and disunity among the opposition, whoever they might be?

"I'm going to see this through," Denninger declared forcefully, breaking into his thoughts.

"Dinner?"

She laughed. "This case, you, the job—everything I signed on for."

"That's good," he said, and tried to return to his thoughts, but she wasn't going to allow it.

"The thing is," she said, "I want to actually play a meaningful role, not just be your personal gofer."

"I took you with me to Traverse City and the RAM Center."

"Exactly. You took me with you—your exact words. To do what? Bottom line: I was just there."

"Are you proposing something?"

"We've got our list for the subpoenas. Let's talk our way through it and divide them up. You do some and I'll do some. We can cover more ground if we're both moving."

"Serving subpoenas isn't exactly brain work."

"It's movement. If I have to sit here endlessly at our resort, I'm liable to lose it. Don't get me wrong. I don't mind being alone, but there's alone and there's hermit. Understand?"

"There's a difference between *alone* and *hermit*?" he said with wide eyes.

"Only you wouldn't notice," she said.

"Okay," he said.

"Okay what?"

"Okay, I cooked. You get the dishes."

"What're you going to do?"

"Visit the edge." He had decided to find a reporter he could use to plant stories. The idea had popped into his mind as he was talking to Denninger.

"Define *edge*," she said.

31

WEDNESDAY, NOVEMBER 10, 2004

East Lansing, Ingham County

After doing their run in the morning dark and wet snow, Service showered and called veterinarian, Summer Rose "SuRo" Genova, founder and operator of the Vegan Animal Rescue and Reclamation Sanctuary near Brevort. Now sixty, Genova was well respected among COs and animal rehab personnel, despite her alleged affinity for radical environmental causes and organizations. Service had met her years before, and though their relationship had started off rocky, it was fairly solid now, based on mutual respect and even a degree of amusement with each other.

"Grady Service," he said when she answered.

"How *are* you?" she asked quietly.

"Not Rockhead?" She almost always called him Rockhead.

"People should cut you some slack when you lose people dear to you."

"Sympathy . . . from you?"

"That's over, Rockhead. You're exempt. What the hell do you want?"

"I'm looking for the name of a reporter, someone who covers environmental issues who might be interested in a potential story, and capable of doing something with it."

Silence on the other end. "Beaker Salant," she said after a thoughtful pause. "Knight Center for Environmental Journalism at Michigan State."

"I'm not looking for a student. I'm looking for a real pencil, somebody who actually *works* in the business."

She laughed. "Always the rockhead. Beaker is the director for special investigations. He's only twenty-five and already has the sort of reputation in his field that you do in yours. You try to push bullshit at him and he'll shove it back up your ass."

"I was actually thinking more along the lines of somebody who can actually publish things."

Genova laughed. "This kid started getting published nationally when he was fifteen. Two years ago he was named a MacArthur Fellow."

"A genius award?" He'd heard of the MacArthurs, but didn't know details.

"One of the youngest ever named. Got him half a million over the next five years, no strings. If Beaker decides to pursue something, anybody and everybody will want to publish it. The trick is convincing him to do anything."

"Sounds like a prima donna."

"Be like looking in a mirror for you," she shot back.

Service wrote down the man's name and his office and cell-phone numbers, and thanked Genova for her help.

"You're probably gonna really piss each other off to start with," she said. "Wish I could be there."

He called Salant's office and got an answering machine that instructed callers to use his cell number.

"Asshole," Service thought, dialing the cell-phone number. Over the years he had not had a lot of contact with environmentalists, but what he'd seen mostly were arrogant, often naive zealots who growled and gloated when they thought they had the upper hand and whined when the tide turned against them.

"I haven't got all day, dude," a voice said on the other end of the cell phone.

"Beaker Salant?"

"That's the number you dialed, dude, unless you're one of those who can't figure out how to correctly key in a simple seven-number sequence."

"My name's Service."

"Like the poet," the voice said. "That's cool."

"I'm a detective with the Wildlife Resource Protection Unit in the Michigan DNR."

"I don't hunt, fish, trap, gather, or do anything else in your purview, dude."

"Maybe I have something that would interest you."

"Dubious."

Service didn't care for the man's attitude. "Maybe you're right. I was told I'd be talking to somebody who knows how to jump on a good story."

"Told by whom?"

"Summer Rose Genova."

"SuRo sent you to me?"

"She recommended you."

"Okay, that helps my interest. What do you have?"

"Not over the phone. Can we meet?"

"I'm busy, dude."

"Fine," Service said. "I can find someone else."

"Wait, wait, okay. I'm tied up with a hearing at the Capitol until three. How about we meet at Paul Revere's at four?"

"The bar on East Grand River toward Okemos?"

"Only Paul Revere's I know of."

Service was surprised to hear it was still around. It had been a landmark at one time, but landmarks had a way of disappearing. "Four—I'll be there."

Service arrived fifteen minutes early and ordered a draft beer. The bar was dark and relatively empty. The bartender brought the draft. "Menu?"

"Libations only," Service said.

The bartender rolled his eyes.

A gaunt young man came into the bar one minute before four and looked around, trying to accustom his eyes to the low light. He wore hiking boots, blue jeans, a black toque, and a ratty, old-fashioned red-and-black-plaid hunting coat. Service waved at him.

The boy sat down without taking off his coat or wool hat. "How'd you recognize me?"

"Your uniform," Service said.

"Witticism from a game warden?"

"I never met anyone in your line of work who doesn't dress similarly. Simple deduction."

"So, whatchu got?"

"You want a beer?"

"I don't consume much alcohol."

Apparently he didn't eat much either. "SuRo highly recommended you."

"You don't have to butter me up. I called her after I talked to you. She said you're Attila the Hun for the Good Guys. She doesn't say that about many cops. You are a *real* cop, right?"

"As much as you're a real journalist."

The young man laughed. "I also used my BlackBerry to do some quick research. You've been credited with solving some very high-profile cases, but I get the feeling you like stepping on toes."

"Got the same feeling about you—without the BlackBerry."

Salant actually smiled and signaled the bartender. "Virgin Mary."

He looked at Service. "I was raised Catholic and I love the name of the drink."

"It's not a real drink without booze," Service said. "Congratulations on the Genius Award."

"Fellowship, not award."

"Whatever. The money change you?"

"Never had money, never really wanted it. Mostly it just sits there in a green mutual fund, accumulating interest. The only thing I bought was the BlackBerry—and some CDs. Man's gotta have his tunes." Service's son had felt the same way about music.

The bartender delivered the drink and left them alone.

"Why did you want to talk to me?" Salant asked.

"What would you say if I told you that there's an investigation of a Michigan company who is allegedly importing contaminated salmon eggs from Lake Ontario, mixing them with Lake Michigan eggs, and selling them as red caviar to an outfit on the East Coast, which provides them to cruise lines?"

"Interesting, but hardly compelling. Contamination in the Lake Ontario eggs is a generalization. Want to be more specific and precise?"

"Mirex."

Salant nodded. "Mirex is some totally bad shit. My interest level riseth."

"There are unsubstantiated allegations of favoritism and maybe some graft among state employees."

The young man grinned. "Getting warmer. What allegations?"

"Not until we get the ground rules straight."

"I don't bargain."

"Sure you do," Service said. "You accepted my invitation, checked my bona fides with SuRo, and researched me. That shows interest and a willingness to hear what I have to say. Willingness to hear requires a degree of cooperation, and cooperation is just another word for trading."

"Where did you go to school?"

"Northern."

"Majoring in?"

"It was a long time ago. Nothing significant."

"What ground rules?"

"See how easy it is to bargain?"

"I'm just asking."

"That's the first step."

"You're not what I expected," the young man said.

"I'll give you some information with some detail. If you're interested, we'll see what else I can do for you. But if we go the next step, my name and all details have to stay out of it," said Service.

"That's called 'on background.' If I publish, that means I can say 'a source close to the investigation.' "

"Too close. I *am* the investigation. It's possible there's an organized crime connection in this, too. Did I mention that?"

"Okay, 'on background' won't work. The other choice is 'off the record.' "

"Which means?"

"It means you tell me, and I can't write about it unless I can get it from another source."

"How do you do that?"

Salant sucked in a breath. "I call someone up and I say, 'I've heard yada yada.' "

"And they respond, 'So what?' "

"Most people will say, 'Where did you hear that?'—which usually means they know something about what you want to talk about. So then you say, 'It's going around Lansing.' "

"You lie to them?"

"Not exactly."

"Sounds like a car rental ad."

"Trust me—if you go off the record, I won't do anything to jeopardize your investigation," said Salant. "Most journalists and writers are interested almost exclusively in the story as it benefits them personally and professionally, not the final outcome. I'm different. If someone is fucking with the environment, I'd rather subjugate the story in the interests of the justice process."

"Okay," Service said. "What if I'm just fucking with you and there's no substance to any of this, and I'm just looking for personal aggrandizement."

Salant said with absolute conviction, "First, SuRo would never send such a person to me. Second, if you're bullshitting me, it won't take long for me to find out."

"Piscova," Service said.

"Quintan Fagan," Salant said.

"You know who he is?"

"Plays marbles with a bowling ball."

"That's him."

"This is about Fagan and Piscova?"

Service nodded. The young man pulled out a small recorder and set it on the bar. He took off his hat and coat, stacked them on top of the barstool beside him, and said, "Feed me, big dude."

32

WEDNESDAY, NOVEMBER 10, 2004

Saranac, Ionia County

Service found a note from Denninger when he got back to the cabin: "Couch called. Subpoenas ready in GR. Back later. Don't wait dinner. D2."

He checked the woodpile stack on the deck, brought more wood up from below the deck to fill the pile, and got the stove going. He sat down at the table and started going through copies of Piscova files, trying to cross-reference documents with people, and where needed, adding more names to the subpoena list. He had no experience with grand juries and wondered how far he—or they—could push. Doing this sort of work was necessary. And it was also annoying. *Deer season in five days and I'm making fucking lists.* It was embarrassing.

Roy Rogers called just before 7 p.m. "How goes it out there?" the New York ECO asked.

"Still trying to sort out what we have to do. There's a sitting grand jury and the Assistant U.S. Attorney is helping push through subpoenas."

"Grand juries are finicky, and we're bumping against Thanksgiving. Not a hell of a lot gets done in New York State from Thanksgiving into the New Year. I called Fish and Wildlife and they were glad to hear from us, but they are bulldogging about helping us with subpoenas and warrants for our investigation."

"Just to get in our way?"

"They don't really open up, but I got some signals that they may have somebody on the inside at Crimea, or at least a source cognizant of the company's activities. I think they don't want to blow their setup until they're ready."

Service wasn't surprised. His experience with federal agencies had never been particularly satisfying. "What's that mean for us?"

"Military doctrine number one: Hurry up and wait."

Service said, "There's a hearing here late next week on the Piscova samples."

"The U.S. Attorney in Syracuse thinks you'll lose."

Service cringed. Was it his fault?

"Doesn't really matter," Rogers said. "The FDA will complete the DNA tests, and like you said the last time we talked, then we'll know. Even if we can't use the test results now, we'll still have them, and that will help us focus."

The next call came from Buster Beal. Service could hear cheering and other loud noise in the background. "You sitting down?" the biologist asked.

"Only way to make my ass get as wide as yours."

"Teeny quit!" Beal shouted, and this raised more noise in the background.

"Where *are* you?"

"Party."

"What party?"

" *'Cause Teeny's gone.* You deaf?"

"Getting that way."

"That's great, right?"

"Stalin replaced Lenin," Service said.

"Geez, you're a bloody downer, Grady. Wait. Candi's here."

"So," McCants said, "the animals have circulated a petition asking for custody to be shifted to me."

"They can't read or write."

"Shows how little attention you pay," she said. "This Teeny thing is good for us, right?"

"Could be. Whoever the new director is, they're gonna have a fiscal mess to deal with."

"Boy, you're a tough audience. Word is that the governor is going to ask Cecil Hopkins to step in as interim director."

"He's got to be eighty."

"Eighty is just a number," she said.

Hopkins had been director more than a decade ago and had a good reputation with all parts of the department. "He's coming back to a far different situation than he left."

"You know," she said, "I was out of line the other night. How's Karylanne?"

"Tired, working hard, big as the front of a barrel trap."

"That's an *awful* image. I was pissed at you but I thought about it, and I really do understand that you can't talk about what you're doing with Piscova."

"Where'd you hear that?"

"See," she said brightly, "that confirms it. Somebody got a call from one of the biologists at the RAM Center who said you were there, rattling their cages."

Jesus, he thought. *She played me exactly the way Beaker Salant said he'd play potential sources.* "You ought to become an investigative journalist," he said.

"Huh?"

"Never mind," he said.

"The thing is, I wasn't as interested in knowing what you were doing as in seeing you. There," she added. "I've said it, and I'm not sorry."

Service stared at the phone.

"Are you drunk?"

"It wouldn't take much," she said, "but no, I'm on Diet Coke and still in uniform. Got anything to say about what I just said?"

"I think Hopkins will be good," he said.

"You are such an asshole," she grumbled, and he heard her say, "Chewy, talk to shit-for-a-heart."

"What did you say to her?" Chewy asked. "She looks totally pissed."

"Nothing."

"Yeah, that would do it," the biologist said. "I guess you haven't noticed that she's got a thing for you."

"Have another drink," Service said.

"Don't mind if I do, shit-for-a-heart."

Service stared at the phone. *Candace McCants . . . a thing for me?* It made no sense, and worse, it made him feel like a louse.

Denninger came in a little while later. "There's a blurb on the radio saying Teeny's leaving the department *and* the state. Someone named Hopkins will replace him."

"I just heard."

"You know this Hopkins?"

"Way back. Good man."

"That will be a change."

"Doesn't affect us," he said.

"Sure it does," she said. "If Teeny's out of the department, it will be easier to subpoena him."

He looked at her. Young or not, she was right. He had thought from the start that he wanted to subpoena Teeny just so they could yank his crank and find out how much he knew about the Piscova situation. Now that he had resigned, it would be a lot easier to get to the man, and if they got to him, others would know and some would start squirming.

Service called Chief Lorne O'Driscoll. "Am I interrupting anything?"

"No. Did you hear about Teeny?"

"That's what I'm calling about. He's on our subpoena list."

"He's leaving for Key West tomorrow," said the chief. "A month in the sun. No point chasing him down there. How're things going?"

"You heard about the Fisheries meeting?"

"Ad nauseum. What about the Piscova samples?"

"Too late. They went to FDA for testing," said Service.

"Darn. We won't be able to use the results unless the judge rules the seizure legit."

"I know. But if the eggs test positive for mirex, that will tell us we've got a real case."

"Have you talked to Miars recently?" O'Driscoll asked.

"No."

"He's up in Gaylord getting ready to work an elk undercover investigation. Did you and he have a confrontation with Teeny the other day?"

"Not what I'd call a confrontation," said Service.

"Captain Black and Teeny came to see me; they want Miars reprimanded."

"For what? He didn't do anything wrong."

"I think he hurt the director's feelings, and at the time Black had no idea Teeny was leaving, so he tried to pile on."

"Black wants me."

"I know that," the chief said. "How is it working out with Anniejo?"

"Good so far."

"Make darn sure you're thorough in putting together the case. Her boss is a you-know-what, and if he finds an undotted 'i,' he'll back away."

"Why are we going through this?"

"Is Piscova dirty?"

"Absolutely."

"There's your reason, Detective."

33

THURSDAY, NOVEMBER 11, 2004

Saranac, Ionia County

The phone rang just after 5 A.M. Service fumbled for it and heard Denninger grumble, roll noisily out of bed, and shuffle downstairs. "Service."

"Andriaitis. Roxy's in the hospital and it doesn't look good. I'm in Minneapolis waiting for a connecting flight."

"What happened?"

"I don't know the details. After her last checkup all her blood counts went screwy, and they can't seem to get it under control."

Service heard a catch in the man's voice. "I'll drive up there."

"No, no, just thought you should know. You sure as hell aren't going to do a deathbed interview."

"I wouldn't do that."

"She's going to die," Andriaitis said, breaking into sobs.

"You sure you don't want me there?"

"What the fuck for? I don't even know you."

"Call me and let me know how she is," Service said, ignoring the man's outburst.

"You kick Quint Fagan's ass yet?"

"We're working on it."

"Spoken like a true bureaucrap," Andriaitis griped. "You fuckers are all the same—all talk and no action," he added, hanging up abruptly.

Service was too awake now to go back to sleep and started downstairs. He met Denninger coming back upstairs, naked, and obviously unconcerned about it. "That how you sleep?"

"Yeah," she said, pushing past him.

"I think we ought to talk about our sleeping arrangements," he said.

"Not until I have coffee," she mumbled over her shoulder.

As he put on the coffee he couldn't get the sight of her out of his mind. He thought about how she'd signed her note "D2" and laughed out loud, wondering if it was alliteration or something else? Both interpretations seemed to fit.

She came down in a sweatshirt with her hair mashed to the side of her head.

"Nudity offends you?" she asked.

"Not in the slightest. I'm thinking more about what's professionally appropriate."

She rolled her eyes and poured a cup of coffee.

"I told you I'm not built for this hermit gig," she said.

"We're colleagues. And you don't have to stay around seven days a week."

"You are," she said. "If you stay, I stay. We're a team. You ever get it on with a colleague?"

"None of your business. I just got a call. Lafleur is in the hospital and she may not make it."

"If you keep me here I may not make it either," she said.

"Okay, that's enough," he snapped at her.

She sat down across from him and smiled seductively. "Admit it—you like what you saw."

He did, but he wasn't about to admit it. His mind suddenly shifted to Candi, who was not half as attractive and had a chunkier build.

"You going to Marquette?" she asked.

"No, I think I'm going to go up to Traverse City to see Alma DeKoening. Who's on your list?"

"I'm still too sleepy to read, much less mine files."

"I might swing over to see Miars after that. He's working an operation near Gaylord."

"Okay," she said. "I'll be fine when I'm awake. Sorry about earlier. I may have been out of line, but Nantz used to talk about you guys. You want to know what she said?"

"Absolutely not."

"Too bad. It was real impressive."

He went upstairs, came back down, showered and shaved, dressed, and got into his truck to head for Traverse City, his head muddled by Denninger, but even more so by McCants.

"Celibacy is a good thing," he told himself as he started the engine. "Fewer complications."

34

FRIDAY, NOVEMBER 12, 2004

Traverse City, Grand Traverse County

He called DeKoening at Piscova. "This is Detective Service," he began. "I thought we might sit down and talk."

"You are going to get me fired."

"That's not my intention. The fact is, I might just save your life."

"What's this all about?" she asked.

"Meet me and we'll talk."

"I guess. You know Fowler's in Buckley?"

"No."

"It's a bar. Buckley is south of TC. Say six P.M.?"

The bar was a typical small-town operation, filled with gaudy neon beer advertising, shelves loaded with thirty different flavors of brandy, and an overweight clientele sporting Kentucky waterfall haircuts and wearing jackets advertising their favorite snowmobile manufacturers—the NASCAR-on-snow look. There were no stools open at the bar, but several tables in the shadows in back. Service grabbed the table closest to the door, ordered coffee, and sat back to wait for DeKoening.

She came in a few minutes late. He tried to flag her down as she walked by but she headed deeper into the darkened area and sat down. He picked up his coffee and followed.

She wore a quilted winter coat and a fur hat. "You wanted to talk, so talk," she said.

"You want a cup of coffee? Kind of cold out there today."

She shook her head and crossed her arms in defiance.

"No need to cop an attitude," Service said. "This is a friendly talk."

"He blames me," she blurted out.

"Vandeal?"

"Quint."

"Blames you for what?"

"For you and major hooter girl coming to the plant that night."

Major hooter girl? He almost laughed out loud. "We saw you hand off the eggs."

"What eggs?" she asked.

Was she stupid, or just scared? He couldn't tell yet. "Look, we saw you pay for and collect the eggs at Devils River, and we saw you deliver the eggs and spend a half-hour in Veatch's trailer in South Boardman."

"Shit," she muttered. "I guess maybe I'll take a drink, but not coffee—something real. I'm screwed, aren't I?"

"Not necessarily. Cooperation counts for a lot." Service waved over a waitress who took DeKoening's order for a Captain Morgan and Coke.

"My luck, like, totally sucks," she announced.

"How's that?"

"This job. It was too good to be true."

"You may be right about that," he said.

"Am I, like, busted?"

"For what?"

She threw her head back and sighed. "*Dude*, I don't know. Like, all I want to do is my job."

"You mixed New York eggs with Michigan eggs."

"Just for taste."

"Fagan told you that?"

"Mr. Vandeal."

"You've only been employed for a few months, so you're probably okay."

The waitress brought the drink. "Run a tab, hon?" she asked Service.

"Please."

DeKoening tasted her drink and closed her eyes for a second. "Like, what do you mean, I'm probably okay?"

"You know what's in the New York eggs?"

"Sludge? You know, like mud or something."

"It's not sludge or mud," Service said. "It's mirex."

She took another drink. "We made casseroles in Pyrex dishes when I was a kid."

"Mirex is a chemical."

"What kind of chemical—a bad one?"

"It was used as a fire retardant in plastics, paint, and other things and as a pesticide to kill fire ants."

"That's good, right?"

"It works for what it's designed for, but not so good in the human body."

She gave him the hard eye. "Maybe you're just tryin' to creep me out."

"You can get mirex in your system just by touching contaminated dirt."

"I don't touch dirt," she said. "My last boyfriend always wanted to get it on out on a blanket, but I said, *ewww,* no dirt, no bugs, you know . . . *down there.*"

Could she be this dim? "You've only done the eggs this fall. You should be okay."

"You keep saying that."

He was pretty sure he was getting her attention. "You still running the caviar line at the plant?"

"I don't think I should say," she said. "Do you think I need to call my lawyer?"

"It's your choice and your right to have an attorney."

"What's the chemical do to people?"

"Cancer, maybe. It's been shown to cause cancer in mice and rats, in their livers and kidneys. It also alters reproduction."

She made a sour face and pointed to her lap. "Like, can it do something to how you feel . . . ya know, down there?"

"It affects having babies."

She took another drink. "That's okay," she said. "I don't want kids, but I like the other part a lot." She squinted at him. "How come you know so much? You're not a doctor; you're just the game warden."

"I'd suggest you give your predecessor a call, but she's in the hospital."

"Shuuut up," DeKoening said. Then, "For real?"

"Very real."

"Cancer?"

He nodded.

"My mother had cancer, but she's okay. You think Ms. Lafleur will be okay?"

"That's not in my hands," he said. "Like you said, I'm not a doctor."

"I don't want to talk about this anymore."

"I wouldn't either."

She stared at her drink and stirred it with her finger. "You really think I could get cancer?"

"You're right. I'm not a doctor, but I'm pretty confident if you stop tasting and handling contaminated eggs, you won't get cancer from that source."

"I get paid *real* good," she said. "And I work hard."

"It's your choice," he said. "I just thought you ought to know."

"Maybe I'm not buyin' what you're sellin', dude," she said defiantly.

"Be a good idea if you did. There are a lot of other jobs."

"Not in this state."

"There are forty-nine other states."

"I was supposed to go to New York, but Quint says I'm not fully trained yet. I'll go next fall."

"So you didn't go there to select eggs? You'd think he'd have given you at least one trip this year."

"I didn't say anything about eggs," she said. "And I told him that, too."

"Did you tell him when you had your clothes on, or off?"

"That's, like, *so* rude," she said.

"Lafleur took her clothes off."

"No way," DeKoening said. "Quint said—"

"You were the first?"

"Stop it!" she said. She got up and headed for the door.

Service intercepted her before she could get her car started and knelt beside the driver's seat. She was crying and looked over at him. "For real, what you said about Ms. Lafleur?"

"Afraid so."

She bumped her head softly on the steering wheel. "Dude, this is, like, a *total* mindfuck."

He understood, even felt for her.

"What we're doing is wrong," she said to herself.

Service knew she was trying to make a decision and that she was almost there.

"The last line will run night after tomorrow," she said, looking him in the eye. "I have to go now."

Service had to jump back to keep from being knocked over by the open door.

Strange meeting, but she had given him something solid. He went back inside and paid the tab and started driving toward Gaylord. As he drove he called Rogers in New York. "Piscova's going to run the caviar line two nights from now."

"You're sure?"

"Impeccable source."

"Can you get warrants?"

"Pretty sure."

"What's the probable cause?"

"The new Caviar Queen admits they mix eggs for taste."

"We need to get the samples legally," Rogers said.

"I'll take care of it."

"I'll call Fish and Wildlife. If the shipment gets past you, maybe they can intercept for us."

Was Rogers questioning his competency? He couldn't blame the man, but it hurt.

Alerting Fish and Game made sense, but something about the girl's whole performance and sudden dramatic departure left him feeling uneasy. "You going to call them tonight?'

"Not that urgent," Rogers said.

"I'd do it tonight," Service said. "Err on the side of caution."

"I hear you. Call me when it goes down, okay?"

Service called Assistant U.S. Attorney Couch. "Piscova's going to run another caviar line, night after tomorrow. I just got this from the woman who supervises the line."

"She fishing for a deal?"

"Not sure yet."

"Promise considerations only, nothing concrete."

"Roxanne Lafleur is in the hospital in Marquette. She may not make it. If she doesn't, that changes everything, right?"

"Not necessarily. We could try for negligent homicide, but proving this kind of thing usually regresses into a scientific turd fight. We probably can use it to leverage cooperation if she dies."

"Even if the mirex kills her?"

"Like I said, it's nearly impossible to prove that. We'd have a better chance if she were a mouse or a rat."

Service felt a cold stone in his belly. At least Couch was reading stuff that related to the case. He had just read the scientific papers himself.

He was in no mood to see Miars. Too nervous, too many things to think about. He was heading through Kalkaska toward Grayling and the interstate to the south when his cell phone rang.

"Dude, I'm sorry," Alma DeKoening said. "The line I told you about? It ran last night. I told Quint we were going to meet and he told me what to say, but he never mentioned cancer. I am so fucking out of there."

"Don't run," he said, but she hung up before he could say anything more.

Goddammit! He called Denninger. "Have you got Alma DeKoening's address?"

"Didn't she show up?"

"I met her, but I need her address."

Denninger found it and read it to him and he wrote it in his notebook. He called Station 20 in Lansing on Channel 25 and asked the dispatcher to call the Traverse City State Police Post and ask them to send a unit to DeKoening's address. If she was home, they should hold her until he could get there.

Halfway back to Traverse City he got a radio call from the Troop who handled the call. "Subject's not there, DNR Twenty Five Fourteen."

"Copy," Service said. *Fuck!*

The Troop asked, "You want me to ask the county to sit on this place?"

"That would be good," Service said. "If she shows, ask the county to apprehend and hold her in their lockup."

"What charges?"

"We have twenty-four hours to sort it out," Service said. *Goddammit to hell.* So close, now *this.* Their slam-dunk case was looking more like a desperation shot-at-the-buzzer. Life had been so much easier in his old job.

He called Rogers and told him the bad news. Rogers had not yet called Fish and Wildlife.

He also called Couch and informed her.

"You still want warrants?" she asked.

"No point. The stuff will be gone."

"You sound pissed," she said.

"I am."

"Pissed is good," she said. "I like my investigators to be pissed. It sharpens their wits."

35

SATURDAY, NOVEMBER 13, 2004

Saranac, Ionia County

During the long drive back to the resort Grady Service tried to sort out what he had. They had seen an illegal transaction and the line operating; maybe the court would not allow the sample seizure, but Alma DeKoening had just confirmed once again that Piscova was still operating. The season would be over anytime now. Maybe Fish and Wildlife would get lucky and intercept product on the other end. But it also sounded like DeKoening had split, which meant she could not serve as a witness unless they found a way to track her down.

This case had started with such promise, but every day it seemed to turn more to shit. The whole thing was like flipping on a flashlight in a room full of rats and watching them scatter.

He got back around 1 A.M. and went to bed. Denninger was stretched out naked on top of her comforter. "Get under the damn covers!" he barked at her.

"What's your problem?" she mumbled.

They spent the next morning going through paperwork and records and adding to their list of people to see. Chief O'Driscoll called after lunch. "Have you seen the papers yet today?"

"We don't get a paper here," Service said, making a mental note to add that to their list.

"Headline reads, 'DNR Too Cozy with Contractors? Director Resigns for College Job.'"

"What's that from?"

"*Lansing State Journal*, early edition. Front page."

"Reporter?"

"The byline says Gabriel Salant."

"Anything of substance?"

"Nope—rehash of rumors. Several department people denied it, and two or three hung up on him. You know anything about this?"

"Like I said, we don't get a paper here." He wasn't lying, just answering selectively.

"I'm getting a lot of calls accusing you of putting the reporter up to this."

"People can believe what they want. But it will be interesting to see if anybody takes any unusual actions."

"I had a similar thought. Cecil Hopkins called me from his place in Muskegon. He saw the article, wants to know what the brouhaha's all about. I sketched it in for him, but he wants to meet you face-to-face. Said he can be there in the morning early, on his way to Lansing. Cecil will hit the ground running."

Could eighty-year-olds actually run? he wondered . . . and then, *Great—another thing to juggle.*

"We'll be waiting for him."

"Give it all to him, Grady. He's a very big boy and he can handle it."

"Yessir, Chief."

Roy Rogers called an instant after he'd hung up. "Fish and Wildlife said yes. Apparently they're ready to knock down the door on their own case, and they'll look for our stuff, too."

Finally, a break, though he knew there could be complications. Still, it was promising, and would cancel out any negative decision by the judge on the original seizure.

36

SATURDAY, NOVEMBER 13, 2004

Saranac, Ionia County

The alarm was set for 6 A.M. but there was pounding on the door an hour before that. Service scrambled out of bed and Denninger sat up.

"Get dressed—it's Hopkins," he hissed.

She laughed. "You ever have this happen to you when you were a high school kid?"

"Shut up and *get dressed.*"

He had not seen Cecil Hopkins in more than ten years, and remarkably, the man looked like he had not aged a day since then. "Sorry," Service apologized at the door, "but we aren't quite ready."

"I always did my best work in the morning, and when I retired, I didn't see a reason to change my ways."

"Coffee?"

"Hot and black would be good."

Denninger came downstairs in jeans and a sweatshirt and Service introduced them. If the interim director questioned their cohabitation setup, he didn't say anything.

"Teeny hated your guts," Hopkins said.

"That was a bad thing?" Service said.

Hopkins chuckled. "Hated me too. Enough foreplay, Detective. Tell me, what the heck is going on with Piscova."

Service took him through the case step by step.

Hopkins said, "Back in my day I questioned Piscova's contracts, but they had already been in place a long time by then, and it would have taken a major, very messy—and very public—fight to get them out. When you sit in the director's chair you have to pick your battles."

"What about principles?"

"The first principle for a director is to keep the department alive and functioning, even if some of the parts could work better than they do. That reality bother you, Detective?"

"It does."

"Good. A detective needs passion, but let the director sort out the politics, internal and external."

"This isn't about politics," Service said a bit more forcefully than he meant to.

Hopkins tilted his head and grinned. "We shall let the evidence fall where it falls, my boy. But trust me—state government is *always* about politics."

At the door the octogenarian clutched Service's arm and whispered, "I see folding cots. Might be a good idea to put one of them to use. I heard you come down the stairs. Let me just say that I'm from a different generation and I don't know beans about baby boomers, generations X, Y, or Me, or any of the sociology and psychobabble that goes with them. What I *do* know is that it's not a good idea to get your meat the same place you get your bread. It may be perfectly innocent, but sleeping in the same room isn't the image we want for our department. Am I making myself clear?"

"Yes, Director," Service said, feeling like a fool.

"What did he say at the door?" Denninger asked.

Service began unfolding a cot.

"Shit, I knew it! My career's burned!"

"Can the drama queen act," Service said with a growl.

"Is he going to back us?"

"He'll back the evidence," Service said. "We're not the point."

"Meaning?"

"We're expendable."

She sighed. "Does this mean I have to wear jammies?"

"Wear as much or as little as you want. I'll be down here tending the stove."

"The upstairs stove could use some attention," she said, then, holding up her hands in supplication, said, "I'm sorry. I'm trying to be cute and it's just not appropriate. It won't happen again."

"Good," he said.

"Even though it's true," she muttered.

As he nursed his coffee and the shower ran in the background, it dawned on him that brash D2 was in fact very insecure, both personally and professionally, feeling vulnerable, and trying to toy with the edge by testing herself. Sexual innuendo was meant to bolster *her* confidence. *Jesus,* he told himself, *you think like a father.*

What to think of Hopkins? No way to tell. He'd once been a good director, but the department these days had some rats on the loose. It had become politicized and had split from the Department of Environmental Quality, which under Bozian had become a rubber stamp for businesses looking for easy approvals and minimal red tape.

Andriaitis called. "Hey, asshole, good news: Roxy's okay. They got her white count under control for now, but her doctor told me the long-term outlook is iffy at best. I'm going to drive down to Grand Rapids to fly out of there. You want to palaver?"

"When?"

"My flight's tomorrow at noon. How about breakfast at seven? I've got a room at the Pantland Hotel."

"I think it's called the Amway Grand Plaza now."

"Don't remind me," Andriaitis said. "See you at seven."

"I'll be there. You hear Teeny resigned?"

"I heard."

"Hopkins has the interim job."

"I heard that, too."

"You know Hopkins?"

"Never met the man. Lobby at seven."

37

SUNDAY, NOVEMBER 14, 2004

Grand Rapids, Kent County

Service was ten minutes from the hotel when Roy Rogers called. "The thing is, Fish and Wildlife says the Piscova shipment is now at Crimea's Shipping and Receiving, but they want to let it sit."

"How long?"

"They're vague, but promise if Crimea moves to distribute, they'll make the seizure. They say they want to hold off—reasons unspecified—until sometime in the New Year, maybe, probably, approximately, more or less, like that."

"Verbal promises," Service said, "are almost impossible to enforce."

"Without ink on paper, bubkes," Rogers said.

"If they can predict distribution schedules, they must have somebody deep inside."

"That's the read from this government-leased chair, too. I'll call when the FDA has results. Maybe the hearing out there will go our way. Did I tell you Leukonovich has a list of subpoenas to serve? She's coming out to meet with you."

"She doesn't know where we are."

"In the IRS, people call her Special Z, like she has superpowers or something." Rogers sounded odd. "Have you been drinking?"

"I'm only punch-drunk and I don't mean on punch. I haven't slept in forty-eight hours."

"Go sleep."

Service found Andriaitis standing with a look of unvarnished disgust in the Amway Grand Plaza Hotel lobby. There was a huge sort of bronze sunburst on the wall behind the reception desk, and a giant chandelier twinkling above a round leather couch. The lobby walls were done in dark wood, a fanciful architect's notion of an English gentleman's club.

Andriaitis wore a faded, stained Carhartt coat, ragged corduroys, and knee-high leather boots, with his trousers tucked into them. "You're on time. You believe this fucking place? Amway makes a fucking megafortune selling pyramid schemes and now the founders are enshrined in this town like a couple of homegrown Dutch saints. Questionable money cleans itself over time. Quint Fagan knows that. You get enough, you can fend off legal challenges and the stink eventually starts to go away. If you don't take down his ass, one day he'll be building a Royal Fagan Arms."

Hotel guests were staring. "Breakfast," Service said, trying to break the rant.

"Not here. Let's take a walk."

It was spitting snow outside, under a light, steady northwest wind. They walked east and north and west again until they reached Fish Ladder Park off Monroe—a half-mile from the hotel. Below them several fishermen in parkas and foul-weather gear were working the frothy yellow-white foam below a low dam that stretched a couple hundred yards across the river.

"Early steelhead," Andriaitis said. "Half the people throwing spawn get their eggs from Piscova. If there are fish eggs anywhere, Piscova won't be far away: Salmon, paddlefish, you name it, Fagan's in the middle of it. The big money's always in the eggs."

"Paddlefish?"

"Not much of a population left in the Great Lakes, but plenty out in the Dakotas and eastern Montana."

"Paddlefish caviar?"

"A blue-collar offering."

"A Piscova product?"

"Not sure he sells the eggs, but I know he has contracts to collect them for a couple of states out that way."

"Funny business?"

Andriaitis shrugged. "Other than a known cheat sucking on the public teat? Who knows?"

The comment gave Service an idea, which he tucked away for later.

They ended up in a café in a touristy section of Monroe Street. The place was called Twenty Four Seven. They ordered a jug of coffee and the same breakfast, fried eggs and hash.

"Roxy's over the crisis?"

"This one. There'll be more. The cancer's like an unstoppable slow leak."

Service turned on his recorder. "Did you work for Piscova when they were making caviar?"

"Last couple of years, but my little outfit was centered on egg collection at state weirs. I didn't hear about what Fagan was doing with caviar until later."

"From Roxy?"

"I told her to quit that piece of shit, but once she gets something set in her mind, there's no dislodging it. She always dreamed of building a shack on a mountaintop, but what the hell good is *stuff* if you ain't alive to enjoy it?"

Service had no answer. "Did Teeny get anything from Fagan?"

"Don't know the answer to that. Your job to figure it out."

"Fisheries people?"

"Fella named Bob Carruth and a biologist named Hoyt Grip. They both liked to party and they both drove brand-new, top-of-the-line trucks every year—on state salaries. You do the math."

"What about Clay Flinders?"

"He's of the if-it-ain't-broke-don't-fix-it school of management. As long as his department's meeting its goals and staying within budget, he won't interfere. He thinks its enlightened management, but all he cares about is the bottom line, which means next year's budget getting approved."

"Jeff Choate?"

"Captain Sleaze. Should have been a recycled condom salesman. Word is he lives way above his income and he travels a lot, mostly to Florida. I guess he likes the sun, and broads and dogs—especially broads."

"They run the caviar line at night," Service said.

"That should be about done for this year," Andriaitis said.

It occurred to Service that the man still had sources inside the company. "Alma DeKoening?"

"Young, dumb like a fox. I heard she quit," Andriaitis said with a grin.

Definitely a source inside. "Vandeal?"

"Loyal to Fagan and he's made a bundle. Bent like a coat hanger on the job, but he's Mr. Straight Arrow outside work."

"Fagan?"

"Wants to be like the jamokes who built Amway. He's as twisted as a grapevine but damn smart, and he hires gunfighter lawyers to cover his six. Somewhere along the way he learned that lawyers are like the H-bomb between us and the Russkies— mutually assured destruction, deterrence and all that. He keeps a bunch on retainer and he'll sue over anything and everything."

"Local lawyers?"

"Some, but the heavy guns are out of Chicago, Detroit, and New York."

"Shamrock Productions?"

"His latest venture, a video production company. Heard they made a trip to the Ukraine to film a show."

"When?"

"Last August."

"DeKoening go with them?"

"Not sure. There's a bimbo named Genie Starr who runs it for him. He hired her away from a Fox affiliate somewhere."

"They have offices?"

"Ann Arbor or Plymouth, somewhere over that way."

Same place as Fagan's convenience store chain. "What about Piscova's Canadian operations?"

Andriaitis grinned. "Not the company's. Quint's personal investments. You've been doing some homework. All I heard is that a lot more money crosses that way than comes back this way, and where it goes in Canada, or why, nobody knows."

A waitress brought their breakfasts. "You headed back to Anchorage?"

"For a couple of weeks, and then it's off to Florida to see the wifey and sit on my ass with all the other snowbirds"

"Have you been to Fagan's place in Florida?"

"Which one?"

"There's more than one?"

"Got the one near Pensacola Beach for the rank and file, and a swanky place smack in the middle of Key West strictly for the big hitters."

Eino Teeny was in Key West for a month, according to the chief.

"I doubt you'll ever make a case with your inside probe," Andriaitis said. "Was me, I'd stick with the egg case. That one you can win. You attack inside, they'll circle the wagons, even your friends."

"You'll testify if we need you?"

Andriaitis chuckled. "Not a chance. Do your job right and you won't need me. Can you drop me at the airport?"

Service took the man to Gerald R. Ford Airport and felt like they departed on good terms. The man had even apologized for his outburst during the phone call about Roxy.

Overall assessment of the morning: some names, some allegations, some smoke. But would there be fire? His mind turned from the case to Karylanne and the baby. *You need to call her every day,* he told himself.

38

SUNDAY, NOVEMBER 14, 2004

Saranac, Ionia County

There was a gray sedan parked at the resort, black letters on the door, UNITED STATES INTRA AGENCY.

He found Zhenya Leukonovich inside, tapping furiously on a laptop. "I sent your girl away," she announced. "I told her we have important business, you and I."

"That's not your call. And she's my partner, not my girl."

"Nonsense; she is a mere child. Zhenya will, of course, domicile here. She has subpoenas to deliver, interviews to be made. This will be a most convenient arrangement."

"How did you find us?"

Leukonovich flashed a sly smile. "I am employed to find the unfindable."

Service made a pot of coffee and brooded. The woman was a pain in the ass. "Fagan has two places in Florida," he said, sitting down with her, "one in Panama City, one in Key West."

"Also a house in Grand Forks, North Dakota," she said, "which is in the name of his spouse. There is another in northern Michigan."

"You ran a background check on me," he said, still yanked about that.

"Routine," she said.

"You can do this on others?"

"Only if there is probable cause for their involvement in the case."

"But you ran one on *me.*"

"Zhenya must know those she is to work with. This is a matter of prudence."

"What about other DNR employees?"

"Investigators?"

"Fishery personnel."

"This I believe would be most difficult. We have no interest in the state contract aspects of this case, only federal tax implications."

"The RCMP is investigating Fagan," Service announced, to see how she would react.

She showed no emotion. "I have heard this."

"Are you working with the Canadians?"

"I am unable to confirm or deny."

"Unable or unwilling?"

She smiled. "Language and semantics are interesting. Zhenya would tell you she admires how you learned from her about her agency's interest in Andriaitis. You are clever and she underestimated you. Zhenya reserves admiration for few. I will not underestimate you again, Detective Service."

"Specifically, I would like to know if certain individuals are living within their means."

"Zhenya is regrettably unable to provide you with such an audit," she said. "Do you wish me to find other accommodations, or will my presence be satisfactory?"

"Here will be fine."

She nodded.

"Are you aware of Piscova's contracts with other states?"

"I am in the process of constructing a picture."

"The IRS charged Fagan in Florida."

"Illegal cash transactions of a personal nature. There were five counts and he pleaded guilty to two, which made for me a disappointment."

"Did you notify the other states where he has contracts about the Florida convictions?"

"Florida was a personal fiscal transgression. Where will Zhenya sleep?"

"You can join Dani in the loft; there are two double beds up there."

"You do not sleep there?"

"I'm down here."

"Interesting," she said.

"I can't quite make out your accent," Service said.

"I was born in Gdansk. My parents brought me to America when I was fifteen. I have worked to eliminate all traces of a foreign accent, but vestiges remain. Most people do not notice."

"I think they notice, but they're afraid to say anything."

She smiled. "You are not intimidated by Zhenya?"

"No."

"You are a unique man, Detective. Zhenya prefers blunt and direct people. This is why she chose forensic accounting. There are no secrets, no ambiguities. Columns must tally, reasons must be clear and legal. It is neat and tidy."

"Unlike people."

"As Zhenya is so painfully aware," she said. "Now, may she return to her work?"

"Don't let me get in your way."

"It is impossible for you to get in Zhenya's way," she said, returning to her laptop.

"How long will you be with us?"

She looked up. "A few days, perhaps. Is this question of a personal or professional nature?"

"When you can, we'd appreciate a list of Piscova's contracts and Fagan's properties."

"As you wish."

"Are you looking at Shamrock Productions?"

"What has this to do with Piscova?"

"It's a Fagan company."

"There is no mention of this in the files."

"Alma DeKoening mentioned it the day we were at the plant, and Andriaitis confirms it."

"You have spoken to Andriaitis?"

"I have."

"He avoids me."

"He alerted you to the Piscova Michigan–New York connection."

"He pointed and went away."

"I'm sure he has his reasons."

"Which, of course, makes Zhenya wonder what he has to hide."

"Are you suspicious of everyone?"

"All people harbor secrets," she said.

"Privacy and secrecy aren't synonymous," he countered.

Zhenya Leukonovich pursed her lips thoughfully, and went back to work.

Later, when Dani returned from delivering subpoenas, they had a moment to talk about the deer opener, which was the following day. He promised Dani they would get out on patrol and see what they could find. She nodded. He was excited beyond words.

39

Ionia State Recreation Area

CO Joe Cullen showed up unexpectedly a few minutes after midnight. The temperature was in the mid-thirties and it was sleeting again. Zhenya Leukonovich was gone—whereabouts, destination, and ETA unshared. Denninger was already asleep in the loft. Service was sitting at the table poring over Piscova files and checking lists of people and case events.

Cullen knocked and Service walked to the door and let him in. The young CO's Gore-Tex coat and overpants were shedding ice pellets, his face the texture and color of a Spanish onion. "Sorry to barge in," Cullen began.

Denninger came down the steps looking half-asleep and yawning.

Cullen glanced at her and looked back to Service. "Er, ah . . . I wondered what you guys were doing for the deer opener?"

Service said, "We thought we'd go out in our trucks and see what we could get into."

"Wha—got?" Denninger mumbled.

"I guess what I'm saying is that I could sort of use some help," the young officer said tentatively. "If that doesn't screw up what you had planned."

Denninger looked to Service for a reaction. "Coffee?" Service asked Cullen.

"Yessir."

"It's fresh, over there," Service said, trying to sort out his thoughts. The firearm deer opener was the most significant period of the year for most conservation officers, many of whom even marked their careers by how many deer seasons remained until they retired. It had always been a highlight for Service, and he had been jacked up to get into another deer season. Now that Cullen was here, he would feel even better about stepping away from Piscova for a little while.

"We going to rescue the officer?" Denninger asked.

"Tell us what you need," Service told Cullen.

"You rolling now?" Denninger said, interrupting.

"No, I just wanted to talk to you guys and catch some sleep before an early start."

Service asked, "You got blinds to check in the morning?" Most officers monitored deer blinds in their areas, marked the illegal ones on their AVL computers and handheld GPS units, and visited them opening morning.

"Not so many."

"So what's your plan?"

"I've got this guy, Rhycough Kirbyson, lives up in Palo."

"Pay-low?"

"Spelled P-A-L-O," Cullen said. "Got a beard like Noah, wears Amish clothes and a wide-brim straw hat. Kirbyson has his own little church in a tarpaper-and-haybale shack, with a few hardscrabble parishioners. Claims to be an Olap minister. He hunts and fishes for everything. I've heard from several sources he whacks eight or ten deer a year. The retail sales system shows he's got the right to two. I've sat on this guy several times, but I just can't seem to catch him. Now I'm hearing he's gonna be hunting the Ionia State Rec this morning."

"Olap?" Service asked.

"The way I heard it, early in the 1800s there was a community of religious people up north of Ionia. There's not much information about them, but they kept separate from other locals and pretty much looked out for themselves," Cullen said. "Eventually the community disappeared—even the old post office is gone, though the area still has its own zip code. It's just a convenience store, a few families, and Kirbyson with eighty acres along Prairie Creek. He travels in a buggy with a horse— like the Amish. Two days ago somebody saw him on Eddy Road on the west side of the rec area. That's twenty miles from his place, which is a *long* haul in a buggy. I talked to some landowners around the area and they tell me they've seen him several times since September."

"Many deer there?" Denninger asked.

"Deer are in the park woods in summer and move out to farm fields to eat. Once the shooting starts today, the big bucks will book it for the Grand River to hide in the thicker cover on the floodplain."

"What do you have in mind?" Service said.

"I think we need to look for the buggy. A couple of local deps are willing to drive around out here, but with us, we'd have three more vehicles and our AVLs. Once we find the buggy, we can assess the situation."

Cullen finished his coffee and got up to leave.

"Where do you live?" Denninger asked.

"South of here . . . Lake Odessa."

"Why don't you crash here?"

"It's not that far," he said.

"Save yourself the drive time."

Service pointed Cullen to the folded cots and went back to his paperwork.

The three were patrolling separately around the perimeter of the 4,500-acre state area by 5 A.M., each of them armed with a thermos of coffee and trapper sandwiches Service had put together for them. The temperature was hovering between 36 and 37 degrees, and it was raining.

Denninger went east on Riverview Drive toward South Ionia. Service worked the southern perimeter along David Highway. Cullen worked through the roads inside the area.

At 5:45 A.M. Service's cell phone buzzed. It was Cullen. "There's a fallow-field farm on Tuttle Road, which cuts the bottom of the rec area. It belongs to a guy named Bruno DeVoll. He used to be a guard at Deerfield Correctional Facility, which is a few miles east of his place. He got canned a couple of years back for beating up an off-duty dep in town. Nasty temper, bully, crooked as they come."

"Kirbyson?" Service said, checking his notepad and trying to get the young officer focused.

"Oh yeah. I got a call a few minutes ago from one of DeVoll's neighbors. He says there were a couple of shots on No Name Creek around zero four forty-five."

"Any lights?"

"No, but he saw an Amish buggy turning into DeVoll's entry road around midnight last night. DeVoll's place is close to where the shots came from, and there's an old quarry just to the west."

Service said, "There's more than one buggy around here, I assume."

"Yes, but my gut . . ."

"Always go with your gut," Service said. It had taken him a long time to learn to trust his own instincts.

"We can stash trucks west of DeVoll's, off Highland Drive. That will put us about a half-mile east of DeVoll's place."

"Tell me how to get there," Service said. "You call Denninger."

Seven minutes later the trucks were hidden and they were outside, saddling up in the cold rain and mud. Service saw the bursts from Cullen's exhalations and knew the young officer was nervous and excited. Denninger seemed fairly calm as they put on their orange hats and vests. Service was experiencing his own adrenaline rush and trying to hide it. No more lists and shit today. This was *real* game warden work!

They made their way a quarter-mile through young oak and maple to the base of some small hills sloping south, and stopped. The land was rolling and slippery. "DeVoll's land starts here," Cullen said, and led them for another fifteen minutes and stopped them again. "The creek is down that way eighty yards or so. DeVoll's place is north of the creek about three hundred yards. I'm going to cross here and move south to creep the buildings."

"We'll sweep the creek," Denninger said.

It was the right approach, but he reminded himself he was working with kids, relatively new to their jobs, and talking and moving like they had been doing the job forever, even though they were both relatively green. Still, it was a little depressing to think the old guard was being replaced by young people as competent as their predecessors; in the bigger view, he decided this was a damn good thing.

When the modern DNR academy had been established a few years back, a lot of longtimers and retirees had bad-mouthed it, but from what he was seeing the graduates were damn good, and he felt an odd sense of pride in them. Nantz had wanted desperately to be a CO, but that would never happen now. The realization made his heart feel empty. In his day it had taken two full years to learn your territory and become fully effective. This was no longer true of new officers, who stepped out of training ready to charge full speed ahead.

"What do you think?" Cullen whispered to him.

"I'm just along for the walk."

Cullen slid away silently.

Denninger moved close to Service, nudged him, and started down toward the creek. Service checked his watch. Last night they had checked the sunrise chart. It would come up this morning around 7:40 A.M.; shooting hours would be about thirty minutes before that, which meant there was a period of three-quarters of an hour before hunters could pull triggers legally.

They moved along a ragged line of sumac above tag alders. He stayed high and the limber, younger Denninger steadily wriggled through the heavier cover. Rain helped mask their sound.

"Twenty Five Fourteen," Denninger whispered over the 800 MHz. "I'm within five feet of the creek. I'm going to wade across. You want to move down here and parallel my line on this side?"

"Affirmative. Twenty Five Fourteen clear."

He started into the tags but his boot got caught, and as he extracted his leg it twisted and he felt the muscle in his calf pop again. *Goddammit.* The pain wasn't as sharp this time as it had been at Cedarville, but it had gone for sure, and he knew it would tighten up if he stopped moving for long. He stopped and dry-swallowed 800 milligrams of ibuprofen and moved on.

"Twenty Five Fourteen, I've got two blood trails. Can you cross over? The water's about three feet deep, semi-firm bottom."

"Twenty Five Fourteen clear."

There was a slight current, and the spot he chose to enter had a soft bottom. He felt the pain shoot up his leg from the suction holding his boot when he tried to move. He leaned back to the bank, took out his knife, cut a length of tag alder to use as a walking stick, and started across, grimacing with the pain of each step. "Give me one green," he said on the 800 as he stood next to tag alders on the far bank. He saw a small green light blink to his left, crawled onto the bank on his knees, and used the stick to get back up to his feet.

Looking over his shoulder he could see gray blades of morning twilight beginning and ahead of him, Denninger's silhouette.

She waited for him and whispered, "Two gut piles and two bait piles, about a hundred gallons each—a little over the limit," she said sarcastically, and pointed. "Two blood trails lead to a fresh off-road vehicle trail."

"Cullen?"

"Nothing so far," she said. "You love this as much as we do."

"Keep your mind on the job," he said softly.

"*Me*? What about Piscova. Should we even be here, helping Joe?"

"It will help remind us what real COs do."

"Detectives aren't real COs?" she asked.

"Sometimes I wonder."

"You took the job."

"I wasn't exactly given a choice," he admitted. "Let's stop yakking and do our jobs."

The ORV trail led west-south. As the light improved, Service could see the outlines of a shack and a barn higher up. No lights. Once the ground firmed up, he dropped his stick. They were climbing uphill.

The first voice they heard was Cullen's.

"DNR, Conservation Officer!"

A second voice boomed, "*Cocksucker!*"

Denninger flew toward the sound. Service tried to speed up, but could only shamble and hop. As he moved along he caught a glimpse of movement to his right and immediately dropped to one knee. Someone was moving downhill toward the stream. He waited until the figure was closer and studied it through some saplings. No weapon in sight. The figure paused before pussyfooting forward.

Service angled toward the figure as he heard Cullen, Denninger, and another voice all shouting angrily. He couldn't make out words, but raw emotions were plain.

His mark suddenly angled downhill toward him and Service unholstered his flashlight. When the man was three feet way, he shone the beam up into the man's face and stood up. "DNR, Conservation Officer!"

The man took a roundhouse swing at him, but missed and fell as his momentum carried him downhill. Service crouched, stepped toward the man, swept at his legs, dropping him to the ground, and immediately fell on him, mashing his face into the mud, jerking his arms behind him, and cuffing him. The man resisted, but every time he fought, Service pressed his face into the mud and hissed, "*Stop resisting!*"

When the cuffs were on, he got the man to his feet, but he kicked Service in his bad leg. Service flinched and reacted by punching the man in the head, not once, but twice, catching himself only as he drew back to strike again. "*Asshole*," Service growled.

The man started struggling, trying to escape like a disabled worm, but Service grabbed the man's arms by the cuffs and began trying to drag him uphill toward the dark buildings. His bad leg was on fire and his temper was melding with frustration, bringing him to a place where it felt like he was going to explode.

The farm sat on a plateau with its grass cut; there was a small barn, a tiny shotgun shack, an open toolshed, and a corral on the west perimeter. The door to the barn was open. "Get some lights on!" Service yelled. His prisoner continued to squirm. A horse nickered inside the barn and there was a crash. Lights came on, revealing an immense man on the ground, his nose and eye bloody.

Cullen and Denninger came out from the shadows, dragging another man with them—clearly, DeVoll. Cullen was bleeding from the forehead, and Denninger had a bloody lip that was swelling fast.

Cullen looked at Service's prisoner. "Reverend Rhycough Kirbyson."

"I was leaving the scene of sin," Kirbyson said, spitting out mud. "I am a man of God."

"Aren't we all," Joe Cullen quipped.

DeVoll suddenly tried to sweep Denninger's legs, but she easily stepped out of the way. "You just do not learn, sir," she said. "Assaulting peace officers, overbaiting, shooting before legal hours, untagged deer, resisting, attempted flight . . . You need to suck in a deep breath and *cool* it!"

"You ain't no fucking cops," DeVoll shouted as two sets of headlights came racing up the grass drive. Two state troopers dismounted.

"*They* are," Denninger said.

One of the Troops said, "Bruno, you ignorant fuckstick, don't you never learn nothing? First you pound knobs on a drunk dep, and now you take on COs?"

"Kick *your* ass next time," DeVoll grumbled.

"Hey," the Troop said, "these people are disciplined. You fuck with us, we'll just kneecap your sad ass."

Cullen and Denninger helped the Troops load the prisoners. "See you at the jail," Cullen told one of the troopers.

Service lit a cigarette and leaned against the barn door. The horse continued to nicker and bump around inside.

"You a horseman?" Denninger asked.

"Not in this lifetime," he said. Horses spooked him even more than dogs. She shook her head, turned on all the barn lights, went to the horse, unharnessed it, led it outside, and released it into the corral. The freshly gutted deer were stacked inside the buggy, both small bucks.

"Gotta get back to our trucks," Denninger said.

"I'll wait here. Pick me up and take me back to mine," said Service. He stared at the two deer. Had Kirbyson really believed he could haul them twenty miles back to his place without being noticed?

Denninger said, "You made a collar; you'll have to go to the jail, too."

"Shit," he said. He was trying to hide his injury, didn't want to admit he could hardly move.

"This is fun," Dani said as she and Cullen jogged off briskly down the grass lane, side by side and chattering. Service ate a trapper sandwich and lit another cigarette, found a log butt by a firepit in the grass yard, and sat down. He was drenched and cold and tired and hurting; and more than that, he was sick with the realization that this truly was a young person's job and he was no longer young and there was no sense trying to fool himself. *You're gonna be a grandfather,* he lectured himself, took out his cell phone, and hit the speed dial for Karylanne in Houghton.

"What time is it?" she answered sleepily.

"Don't know," he said. "You okay?"

"I was until somebody woke me out of the first deep sleep I've had in three nights."

"Sorry," he said, feeling like a selfish ass. *Grow up,* he told himself.

Damn leg, he thought. But then he found himself grinning with nobody to see him. Dani was right. This was the ultimate fun for a game warden. Piscova was there and waiting, but at least for one day, in the rain and cold and mud, he had gotten to do the job the way he had done it for more than two decades. All in all, it was worth a little pain to feel so useful, so *alive.*

Saranac, Ionia County

They got the prisoners processed and lodged at the Ionia County Jail and were back to the resort by 11 A.M. Before Denninger dumped her truck and went with Cullen to finish the patrol, Service talked to them.

"Kirbyson had the deer in his buggy. Did he really think he could get all the way back to Palo without being seen? I'd go back out to DeVoll's property and give it a slow, hard look. Is Kirbyson known for whacking *any* deer, or just big ones? The two in the buggy were pretty small."

Cullen looked at him and nodded. "We'll take a look."

Leukonovich's vehicle was back. He limped inside. She was sitting at the table with her laptop. He walked past her, went into the bathroom, stripped, got into the shower, and stayed there for a long time.

He limped over to his bag with a towel wrapped around him, grabbed some clothes, and went back into the bathroom to get dressed.

When he came out, Leukonovich looked up at him. "It was a difficult morning?"

He ignored her, poured coffee, and sat down at the table.

The IRS agent said, "A woman was here earlier and left her card, but she went on to Grand Rapids. I am to inform you she will return tomorrow morning."

Service read the card: EMMA T. JORNSTADT, SPECIAL INVESTIGATOR, MICHIGAN DEPARTMENT OF TREASURY. He dropped the card on the table. "You know, there are big companies, drug dealers, all sorts of assholes the IRS could be going after, so I'm wondering why you—and now the state tax people—are so damned interested in Piscova."

Leukonovich propped her glasses up on the top of her head. "You are, of course, familiar with The Tax Shelter and Tax Haven Reform Act of 2004?"

"No. I don't track legislation."

"Perhaps you should learn to do so. Your Senator Levin introduced it. We in Washington and your people in Lansing are cooperating to prosecute Piscova and others. This is long overdue."

"All you're interested in is the money," he said.

"Yes, of course; it is the most important thing."

"Wrong," he said, not bothering to enlighten her, and wondering if the actual charges with the eggs would somehow get overshadowed by tax issues in the course of the investigation.

"Where is your girl?" Leukonovich asked.

"Officer Denninger is on patrol," he said. "She is not my *girl*."

Leukonovich rolled her eyes. "It is clear to Zhenya that the girl worships you."

He rolled his eyes and was contemplating a nap when his cell phone buzzed.

"You see what I wrote?" Beaker Salant asked.

"Heard about it."

"I'm working on another piece, along the lines of undercover investigation revealing disturbing activities at Piscova, including the selling of contaminated eggs for human consumption."

"The contamination is not confirmed yet," Service said. "The hearing is Thursday in Bellaire."

"What time?"

Service looked through his notes but couldn't find anything. "Ten, I think, but I don't know for sure. It's the Eighty-Sixth District Court in Bellaire. Call the court administrator and he can give you the time."

"You going to be there?"

"Hadn't planned on it." Initially he'd intended to go, but more thought led him to question the value of being there.

"The hearing is aimed at determining if the egg seizure at the plant was legal—is that accurate?"

"Yep."

"Cool. Maybe I'll see you."

"You're going to be there?"

"This is a cool story, dude. An important one. I'm gonna ride it all the way to the barn."

Roy Rogers called five minutes later. "The FDA says the tests show it's definitely mirex in all the samples."

"That's good—if we can use it. You talk to Fish and Wildlife again?"

"Every day. They're still saying it won't be until the new year."

Service weighed calling the journalist back, but decided not to. If the court found in the state's favor, the test results would be relevant; if not, the results were moot. He started to curl up on a cot when another idea struck him. He called Salant. "Here's an update. An unnamed source, close to the Piscova investigation in New York, reports that FDA testing has confirmed mirex contamination in the egg samples taken from the Piscova plant in Elk Rapids."

"What's the source's name?"

"Irrelevant."

"Not to me."

"I'm the source and I just talked to New York, but I prefer that you keep it generic. Can you get this published before Thursday?"

"I can get it out by Wednesday."

"Good—and thanks."

It occurred to Service that the court might interpret this as tampering with the case, but he didn't care. He wanted as much incriminating information made public as possible to put pressure on Quint Fagan, Piscova, and their confederates. He called Chief O'Driscoll and told him what the FDA results had shown. "Our legal colleagues are not going to be happy," the chief said.

Denninger and Cullen came back around 9 P.M., both of them sky-high. "We went back out to DeVoll's property," Denninger said. "Joe found an old wagon track and we followed it to a field and some ruins of an old homestead. The tracks led close to a Michigan basement with a locked door. Joe called a local judge and got a warrant. A dep brought it to us and we broke the lock. There were ten deer hanging, some of them real trophies." She was so pumped that her words were running together.

Cullen said, "I never thought about the buggy and the deer in it. You experienced guys know so much good shit!"

Service pointed at the coffee. "Not fresh, but it's hot."

Cullen and Denninger sat together at the table, laughing, sharing moments from their day. Service said, "Any time you get a suspicious deer, think about what the perp is going to do next."

Cullen nodded gravely. "I never made an illegal deer case before today, and now I have a dozen. Holy shit!"

"Chili in the fridge," Service said. "You can use the microwave."

Denninger said, "I feel so hot I think I can use my hands to warm the bowls."

Service sat back and let the young officers celebrate. He had experienced many such moments over the course of his career and understood their jubilation. There was nothing so personally and professionally satisfying as taking down scumbags. To his great surprise he was as pleased for them as he once had been for himself. He wasn't sure what these feelings meant. He had given them advice, they had listened and done what he suggested, and it had paid off big. There was something unexpectedly pleasing in this, and a feeling he thought he might even get used to, and suddenly the word *leadership* popped into his mind and he shut off the whole flow of thought. *Fuck that leader shit. You're the Lone Ranger. That's how it works.*

"What's our agenda for tomorrow?" Denninger asked.

"You want to work with Joe again?"

"Ya think?"

"It's the first week of deer season," he said. "We'll have a helluva hard time serving subpoenas to anyone. A lot of them will be out hunting."

"Cool," she said. Service knew from experience that deer season was split into two parts for law enforcement: November 15 to 17 was when the most hunters were out and the most activity was taking place, and the second part was from November 18 until season's end. The first three days were the busiest and tended to yield the most cases.

"She's yours through Wednesday," Service told Cullen, who nodded agreeably and loaded a bowl of chili into the microwave.

Service went out on the porch facing the river to have a cigarette. It was cold, but the rain had stopped. Leukonivich stepped out beside him and wiggled her fingers. "Zhenya would beg a smoke," she said. He gave her the pack and watched her light up and exhale gaudily. "I observe you are very good with these young officers," she said. "It is clear they respect you and hang on your sage advice. Zhenya is a loner," she said, "whereas you are a natural leader."

A natural leader with a bum leg who couldn't keep up, which was the only reason he had nabbed Kirbyson. It had been pure luck. "The temperature keeps dropping, we might have some snow in the morning," he said.

Leukonovich looked at him and took another hit on her cigarette. "We are alike, you and I—both uncomfortable with compliments, unable to see ourselves as others see us."

Saranac, Ionia County

Denninger left with Cullen at around 6 A.M., and Leukonovich departed a half-hour later. Service limped through half of his normal run, showered, and started to make his usual spartan breakfast. A woman walked in without knocking and a man came in behind her. She wore slacks, knee-high boots, and a knee-length down coat. He wore a black trench coat over a sport jacket with a loose tie, and old-fashioned black rubber galoshes. The woman came directly over to him and held out her hand.

"Detective Service, Agent Emma Jornstadt. Behind me is Detective Sergeant Aldo Zarobsky of the Michigan State Police. We often work together." Zarobsky went to a mirror, looked at himself, and smoothed his hair with his hand.

"It's Al," the man said, turning to Service.

"Troop?" Service said. "Out of where?"

"Lansing, Michigan RICO task force, Treasury liaison."

RICO was the acronym for the Racketeer Influenced and Corrupt Organizations Act, and Service knew it had been passed by Congress to provide law enforcement with a tool to prosecute the mafia. By adding mail and wire fraud statutes, it became pretty easy for attorneys to file civil claims in federal courts, and over the years the mafia had begun to disintegrate under sustained Justice Department pressure. U.S. Fish and Wildlife employed RICO statutes to combat international wildlife violations.

"You know, of course, that RICO is rarely ever applied to the old mafia anymore," Jornstadt announced. "Today we focus on individuals and businesses."

"There's coffee," Service said, pointing.

"I think we've had enough, right, Al?"

"Our back teeth are singing 'Su-wan-eee River,'" the Troop detective said.

Service's initial impression was that Zarobsky was vain and shallow, the tall, good-looking type who was better at schmoozing and sticking his face in a cocktail than into the dirt of an investigation. Jornstadt was something else, though he wasn't sure what. She looked good, talked smoothly, and radiated huge self-confidence.

"Anniejo tell you we were coming?"

"Leukonovich said *you* had stopped in."

Jornstadt smiled and rolled her eyes. "Al and I are always together. Think of me, think of him; we're one, a team, Frick and Frack. Right, Al?"

"Three years now," Zarobsky said. "Frick and Frack—you bet."

Jornstadt sat down. "So, Detective, where are we with the investigation?"

Service talked them through it while Zarobsky stood and looked inside the refrigerator and made faces. It seemed to Service that he was becoming a tour guide for the investigation rather than the lead investigator for the case, and this realization bothered him.

"You screwed up the seizure," Jornstadt said. "Right, Al?"

"Fucked," the Troop said. "Jumped too soon. Should have waited a bit. Timing is everything."

Service felt hair pop up on his arms but fought to maintain a calm demeanor.

"The RCMP investigator," Jornstadt said. "We've talked to her. Tell us more about the confrontation with Judge Bergey."

"Boozehound," the Troop investigator said. "Worthless on the bench. Once good, now . . . not so much."

Service went through the meeting with Aline Bergey and her husband at the bank in Traverse City.

"Seem like a bit of an overreaction to you?" Jornstadt asked him.

"Pretty much."

"Keeps a bottle in his private chambers," Jornstadt said. "Right, Al?"

"Absolut. Belts it straight, at room temp—sure sign of a lush. Went to a couple of AA meetings, but dropped out. He's got a lot of questionable investments and so forth."

Service was amazed. They knew what brand of vodka the judge drank? "Other questions?" Service said.

"You haven't made that much progress," Jornstadt said. "Am I right, Al?"

"Just digging in, making himself a beachhead, getting set up, et cetera."

"Are you two staying here?" Service asked.

Jornstadt looked around the room. "Not our kind of place. We prefer a more commercial setting."

"Good hotel with room service," Al said without prompting. "Good walls. Privacy to think."

"We'll let you know where we are," Jornstadt said.

"When we get settled," Zarobsky added. "Right, Em?"

"When we get settled," Jornstadt said, standing up and offering her hand to Service. "We'll be in touch."

Service watched through a window as they got into a state van and started up the resort driveway. When they stopped at the road, he saw them lean toward each other and embrace.

"Good walls, privacy," he said out loud, mimicking Zarobsky. "*Right, Al?*"

Saranac, Ionia County

Chief O'Driscoll called a few minutes after 11 A.M.

"No go," he reported. "The judge went ballistic over the article yesterday, said he would not let cases be tried in the media when they belonged in *his* court! You know anything about the article?"

"Haven't seen it."

"The reporter claims FDA tests in New York were positive for mirex—positive on the very samples, the judge pointed out with great enthusiasm, that are supposed to be impounded. How do you suppose the reporter learned *that*?"

"Reporters are sneaky. I guess New York and the FDA moved pretty fast," Service said, trying to deflect the inquiry.

"The acting director received two letters this morning: one from Piscova, claiming they're being targeted and harassed by an undercover DNR investigation; and the second from the BAO, announcing that they are commencing an audit of all DNR-LED undercover investigations—that given the state's budget crisis, all such activities except those with the highest priorities should be eliminated or reduced in scope."

"You agree with such crap?" asked Service.

"These actions have no teeth."

"If Fish and Wildlife gets new samples for us, we can press forward, right?"

"Just make sure the seizure is legal this time."

"It wasn't *illegal* last time," Service shot back. "We were there. They were mixing the damn eggs."

"I'm not a lawyer, but they're saying that absent yesterday's news article, the judge might very well have ruled in our favor."

Fuck, Service thought, cringing. Was the chief just yanking his chain?

"Who signed the BAO memo?" Service asked.

"Julia Gates."

"Not Langford Horn?"

"Gates works for Horn. He was copied."

"Don't you find the timing just a little suspicious? Fagan and Piscova complain about an undercover investigation, and one of Horn's people decides an audit is in order?"

"Coincidences happen," O'Driscoll said.

"Horn is up to his ass in this Piscova business and is part of this investigation."

"BAO operates independently. They decide who to audit, when, and why."

"Even if it's politically motivated?"

"That's the system."

"It sucks," he said.

"I won't dispute that view," the chief said.

"It's not an undercover DNR investigation," Service said. "It's through the U.S. Attorney."

"Rest assured I will make those very points to the BAO. When will Fish and Wildlife effect the next seizure?"

"After New Year's."

"Let's hope that whoever is stimulating news coverage will cease and desist. These articles are *not* helping us."

Calling off Salant, Service guessed, would be like trying to call back a rock after you'd launched it at a plate-glass window. The question was, should he even try?

43

FRIDAY, NOVEMBER 19, 2004

Lansing, Ingham County

The conversation with Chief O'Driscoll had left Service in a funk, and he'd spent all day Thursday going through files and transcripts and making phone calls.

He called Roxy Lafleur, hoping she was home from her stay in the hospital. She was.

"Heard you had a rough ride," he said.

"Calm water for now," she said. "It wasn't that bad, and it was great that Tas came all the way from Alaska. What can I do for you?"

"Patricia Allard. You mentioned her at our second meeting. How can I get in touch with her?"

"Like I said, when we needed girls, she gave a track phone to Quint who gave it to me, and when the arrangements were done, I threw the phone away."

"You never met her?"

"Not that I know of."

Not that she *knew* of? "Where'd Fagan meet her?"

"Could've been anywhere, but it was just about three years ago. I really don't know exactly when, where, or how."

"Does Fagan have favorite hangouts in Lansing?"

"Several. Galollypops in Okemos, that's out on Grand River past the mall. The Seiche is on Grand River about a block from the Lansing Center. And there's a place he calls the North Lansing Country Club. It's actually called Almancio's, out on Comfort Street. It's run by a man they call El Fontanero, the Plumber. It's a total dump."

"You've been to all these places?"

"Sure."

"But you never met Allard?"

"Not that I know of. But Quint's secretive, and I might've had a drink with her for all I know. Why?"

"Just wondering," he said.

His next call went to Tree. "You know any good vice cops in Lansing?"

"Best one I know retired last June. Name's Gunnar Robuck."

"He still in town there?"

"Lives on an old farm out in DeWitt, just north of Lansing."

"You got a number for him?"

"Somewhere; let me look. You get your tree made yet?"

"It's growing."

"When you call Gunnar, make sure you use the name 'Backtrack.' "

"Inside joke?"

"Like you, that sonuvabitch can find anyone. Here's his number."

Service wrote it down and dialed the man, who answered after several rings.

"Backtrack Robuck?"

The man chuckled. "You must be a friend of Treebone's."

"Long time. Name's Grady Service. I'm a detective with the DNR."

"Service? I heard him talk about you. Together in 'Nam, right?"

"Right. I'm looking for a woman who runs escorts. Her name's Patricia Allard."

"She *get some* out of season?"

Pathetic joke. "Something like that."

"Heard of her," Robuck said. "They call her Mama Cold. She works out of Almancio's."

"The North Lansing Country Club," Service said.

"That's the place."

"She been busted?"

"We hauled her in a couple of times, but nothing stuck. She's smart, real cautious, and coated with Teflon, meaning she has friends in high places."

"You know where she lives?"

"Nope, but I could find her if I had to."

"How?"

"Trade secret," Robuck said. "You want help?"

"I'll see if I can make contact at the bar."

"El Fontanero is her gatekeeper."

"Paid?"

"I think he trades service for service, if you get me. His real name's Sentio Agular. Made a fortune off his dive and he don't take chances, but if he can make a buck or thinks he can get an advantage, he'll cooperate," Robuck said. "Don't sit at the bar. Sit at the far tables and order a beer, and when the waitress asks you if you want a menu, tell her you're looking for special ice cream. That will bring Agular over to check you out. The flavor you want is tutti-frutti, which means you like all colors and types. Don't squeeze and don't be in a hurry. Be polite and smile a lot, *comprende?*"

"Affirmative."

"You can't find Allard, call me. I like finding people."

"Thanks."

"Tell Treebone now that he's retired, he's worthless like the rest of us."

"I'll tell him."

He sent Denninger to Traverse City to find realtor Lulu Sparks and get a showing of Fagan's house on the Old Mission Peninsula.

"Stop in TC and buy some knockout threads," he said, digging in his wallet and passing her six one-hundred-dollar bills. "You're a trophy wife. Act the part," he explained. "Your old man's a film writer, looking to move to the area from LA. You got a gifted kid you want to put in the private school at Interlochen. Your kid's a genius, your old man's a stud, and you are so hot, people can get burned just standing next to you."

"For real?" she asked with wide eyes. "This sounds really off the wall."

"You haven't done it yet. I want to know what Fagan's asking for the house and how willing he is to make a deal. Find out if Lulu knows him, and how well."

"They didn't prep us for this at the academy," she said.

"Women don't need to be prepped to look good," he said.

"Sexist comment?"

"Am I wrong?"

"Not as far as I'm concerned."

Late that afternoon Service drove to Lansing and did a drive-by. The neighborhood had probably never seen good days. Most of the shops around the bar had signs in Spanish. There weren't many people on the street. A Budweiser truck was backed into the alley beside the bar.

He drove out near the airport, bought a salami sub sandwich for dinner, and sat in his truck and ate it. He disconnected the radio and computer units and stashed them in back under a blanket and assorted debris.

The inside of Almancio's was dark and cavelike and he stood inside the entry and let his eyes get accustomed to the light conditions. It was 8 P.M. and there were a few people at the bar, frantic Spanish music squawking on the juke. He made his way to a table in back and sat down. A waitress sidled over. She wore satin pants and a vest over a white shirt. Her blouse was unbuttoned far enough south to advertise. "You new?" she asked.

"Do I look new?" he said.

"I don't mean age," she countered.

"I'm looking for some special ice cream," he said.

"This is a bar, not a dairy," she said.

He gave her a smile. "I guess I'm out of luck. I really wanted ice cream."

"Let me talk to the boss," she said. "It's not on the menu."

The man who approached the table was thin and wolfish, clean shaven, with long black hair streaked silver on one side, and tied back in a ponytail. "What can we do for you?" he asked.

"Special ice cream."

"Try Baskin Robbins or Ben and Jerry's."

"Neither has the flavor I want."

"What flavor's that?"

"Tutti-frutti."

"Easier to find that particular flavor in summer."

"You ever get a craving?" Service asked.

"Only when I'm pregnant," the man said with a grin. "But it truly is most difficult to find tutti-frutti, and this time of year it can be quite expensive."

"Price isn't a barrier," Service said.

The man looked at him and grinned. "Perhaps that will make it easier to locate. You want this tonight?"

"If possible, but if not . . ." Service held up the palms of his hands.

"Like I said, costs a lot this time of year, even more to find on short notice."

"Not a problem," Service said.

"You had dinner?"

"What would you recommend?"

"*Biftek*. Very nice. Grilled with special spices and sautéed in a nice Rioja. You don't like it, it's on the house."

"Can't beat an offer like that."

"We cook it medium rare."

"Works for me."

"What're you drinking?"

"Rioja sounds good."

"A glass?"

"Bring a bottle. I'm filled with hope and good cheer tonight."

The man brought the wine and poured it for Service. "Your first time here?"

"Not my last, I hope."

"You work?"

"Pilot," Service said.

"For an airline?"

"Company pilot, not commercial airlines. Ford Motor Company."

"You fly for Ford?"

"Yep."

"Enjoy your wine. The food will take a while, but it's worth the wait. You got a name?"

"Ford Travers."

"Your name is Ford and you fly for Ford?"

"Ironic, huh."

It took an hour to get the food. The place filled up. He nursed his wine and wondered how Denninger had done with the realtor. At midnight he was full and ready to go to sleep. To think Miars wanted him as an undercover barfly up north turned his stomach. No chance. He'd had less than a third of a bottle and could still feel it in his blood. Why the hell was this dragging out so long? His gut said something was wrong.

Agular came back to the table a few minutes later, looking agitated, but trying to hide it. "*Hombre*, Senor Travers, I am most sorry, but there's no tutti-frutti tonight."

"Price isn't important," Service said.

"I am sorry."

"Tomorrow night?"

"There is no tutti-frutti. No offense."

"None taken."

Service limped to his truck, four blocks away, got in, swallowed some ibuprofen, and reconnected his radio and computer. Something had soured the deal. He'd played it the way he'd been told. Had Agular looked him over and gotten hinky? Or had Allard been there and nixed the deal? Frustrating.

He drove west and called Robuck. "I wake you up?"

"Thirty years in vice. I sleep more in the day than at night. How did it go?"

Service related what had gone down and his opinion of why no connection had been made.

"Somebody recognized you," Robuck said. "Busted. You want me to find her?"

"I could use the help."

"Take some time."

Service gave him his cell-phone number and headed for Saranac.

Denninger's truck was parked in front, but not Leukonovich's vehicle. Shit; he'd sent Denninger to Traverse to the city to play big shot, forgetting that all she had was her truck with the big gold shield on the doors. *Idiot!*

She was sitting at the table when he walked in, dressed in a dark green dress and four-inch heels, with her legs crossed and a long leg sticking out.

"How'd it go?" he asked.

"I was nervous as a virgin guest of honor at an orgy," she said. "But it was a total *hoot!*"

"Lulu bought it?"

"No question. Fagan wants three-five, but for the right buyer and fast turnover, he'll let it go for three-one. I think we could get it for two-nine if we press them, honey." She put her head back and laughed.

"I forgot you didn't have a civilian vehicle," he apologized.

"Not a problem. I called Helen Gallow—we went through the academy together, and she's got west Grand Traverse County. She loaned me her husband's Jaguar XK; he's an emergency room doc."

He was impressed by her initiative. "What did you learn about Fagan?'

"Officially, nothing, but Lulu and I stopped for a drink out on the peninsula and she doesn't hold her liquor very well. She's doing Fagan, or vice versa, or whatever. If she can sell this place, she stands to make a ten percent commission. The usual is seven."

"How often does she see Fagan?"

"Not much, but when he's in town he gets a room at the Sands Hotel on One Thirty-One, and I get the feeling she spends a lot of time there—in 'conference' with her client."

"She seen him recently?"

"No, and she's not happy about it. Says he's been in a bad mood, but she's sure it will pass."

"Bad mood, huh?"

"Yeah." Denninger got up and yawned. When she got to the stairs she put one foot up and struck a pose. "Between us, hot clothes make my juices flow, and there's just us here tonight," she added.

"I have a headache."

She laughed. "Don't steal my lines." She went very slowly up the stairs, vamping it to the hilt, and making him smile.

He was badly tempted to follow her up to the loft, but resisted. He started to call Karylanne, but held up. She needed rest. He called McCants instead.

"I just now walked in," she said breathlessly. "Sixteen hours. We've got a ton of overtime for deer season."

"You'll earn every penny," he said. "Anything interesting?"

"The usual fools. Three wolves are down so far, no leads or arrests."

"How's the Mosquito?"

"Quiet. I sometimes think you terrorized everyone you ever came across in there."

He hadn't, but he also didn't deny it. "You on again tomorrow?"

"Just a short eight."

"How're the beasts?"

"Moody, practicing peaceful coexistence."

"Did Karylanne call you about the animals?" he asked.

"Was that *your* bright idea?"

"Hers," he said.

"I talked her out of it, reminded her she needs to focus on school and getting her rest. She doesn't need two animals to complicate her life right now."

"I agree."

"Then why didn't you tell her that?"

"Didn't think fast enough."

"Bullshit. All this makes me wonder sometimes if you think *at all*. How's your assignment?"

"Plodding along."

"The animals will be glad when you get home."

"All this *what* makes you wonder?"

"You are thick," McCants said, adding, "hopeless and thick." And slammed the phone down.

Service remembered what Chewy had told him and moaned out loud. All these women! *God!*

44

TUESDAY, NOVEMBER 23, 2004

Lansing, Ingham County

Retired Lansing detective Backtrack Robuck called Monday night. It had taken him four days to find Patricia Allard.

"Guess I'm out of practice," Robuck confessed. "I always thought it would be like riding a bike, but it's not, and Allard is one slippery tootsie—more wary and careful than she needs to be, which suggests a heavy dose of professional paranoia."

"You found her?"

"I'm tryin' to tell you. She doesn't turn tricks and she doesn't suck profits up her nose through straws. She drinks and eats in moderation, and very few people ever meet her face-to-face. She keeps three very modest places around the city and never spends more than two consecutive nights in any one of them—like those assholes Castro and Saddam Hussein."

"How do I find her?"

"She shows up at the North Lansing Country Club every night at eleven, goes upstairs, and stays exactly one hour. Sentio Agular, *El Fontanero*, screens all potential clients and handles all negotiations after she looks them over and gives the green light."

"Meaning she must've seen me that night."

"For sure. Customers never see her, only her girls. I'm thinking she saw you and recognized you because she's altered her whole routine, and is taking a vacation from doing business on Comfort Street."

"A vacation from all business?"

"She's still working, my sources say, just out of a different place."

"Where?"

"Doesn't matter. I know where she's sleeping tonight."

"Spit it out, Robuck."

"White Thunder Estates on the Grand River, just west of Grand Ledge. She's working now out of a bar called Walpole's in Mason. She'll leave there at midnight and be at the house by twelve-thirty. It's a gated community with live security; you could badge your way in, but then every asshole would know you're there. You can get past security by boat. The house sits right on the river."

Service wrote down the address and passed it to Denninger. "Goaler Lane," she whispered, thumbing through her notes. "Sweet! It's *Fagan's* place," she said, beaming a smile.

"No shit?" Service said.

"I worked hard to get that information," Robuck said on the phone.

"Sorry about that. I was talking to another officer," Service said. "Thanks for the help," he added, and hung up. Service looked at Denninger's note, and at her.

"A little luck finds its way home now and then," she said.

"We'll need a boat. Who's the CO there?" he asked.

She opened her laptop and pulled up a state roster. "G. Laramie."

"Grundoon Laramie."

"That's his nickname?"

"His given name. He comes from a big family. His folks named all their kids after Pogo characters."

"Pogo?" she said. "Oh, that geeky lizard cartoony thing?"

"Alligator," he said, feeling old.

"You know Laramie?"

"We were LED teammates at the Michigan All-Cop Shootout one year."

"You were on our pistol team?'

"Just that one year. I don't like guns."

"I *like* guns," she said.

"Good for you. It's your constitutional right. Give it a few years, and a few hundred assholes packing illegally, and let's see how you feel then."

She ignored him. "Who won?"

"Not the paper targets," he said.

CO Grundoon Laramie met them at Island Park, a block off the main drag in the center of Grand Ledge.

"How far?" Service asked.

"A couple of miles, give or take."

Service and Denninger helped Laramie carry the canoe down to a shoreside eddy on the top of the island. The air was at 27 degrees. There was ice along the shoreline and some rafts of skiff ice floating in the water. "I hate canoes," Service announced.

"Thought you Yoopers were born to them."

"You don't have to like them to use them. This ice gonna be a problem for us?"

"Nah," Laramie said. "Might hear it scrape the sides, but it isn't cold enough yet."

"What's the place like?" Service asked.

"No one in the DNR gets called here very often unless the rezzies got deer eating their precious gardens. I'll take stern; Denninger, bow. Service, park your big ass in the middle like a living god and don't be wiggling around."

Service said, climbing in, "Don't tip us over."

The house looked dark. It was set on a limestone bluff one hundred feet above the river. Wooden steps switchbacked their way up the bluff. Laramie remained with the canoe while Service and Denninger made their way to the top. The steps made Service's leg ache to the point where he began limping, cold air burning his lungs. The house was immense, two stories, turrets, showy; it looked old, a modern-day knockoff of something historical. A circular drive swung up to the house, which included a built-in garage underneath the main structure. The lawn was huge and extensively landscaped with shaped hedges and trees.

"Midnight in ten," Denninger said.

"Get out to the street, and bump me on the 800 when the car comes in. Stay there and bump me again if a second vehicle arrives."

"Are we expecting more than one?"

"I worship at the altar of what-if," he said.

"Laramie told me you shot a perfect score," she said.

"So did he; paper doesn't shoot back."

Denninger headed along the shadows of hedges. Light snow was beginning to fall but there was virtually no wind. Service positioned himself beside a tree to the side of the garage and stomped his feet to keep circulation going. It didn't matter what time of year it was, or what conditions he faced; it seemed to him that he was

always wearing the wrong boots. His calf muscle was sore from the canoe and the stair climb. When he retired, he told himself he would not miss night work—cold feet, achy muscles, chest congestion, snot-cicles hanging from his nostrils, windburn, frostbite, hypothermia—all the things civilians rarely faced and COs accepted as normal. He wished he had coffee and settled for a cigarette, which he cupped in his hand to hide the ember.

Damn you, Denninger, he told himself. You're too young, too tempting, too damn willing. She and Nantz had been competitors before Nantz had been forced to drop out of the academy. He shuddered to think how Nantz would react to his even working with her.

"Vehicle turning into the driveway," Denninger's voice said softly over the radio. "Honda, I think."

"Souls?"

"Just one."

It was a small import, moving right along, the only sound its tires on the slushy driveway. The garage door began to rise, triggered electronically. He hadn't counted on this. The vehicle drove inside and the door began to come down. He made a quick decision, rolled through the opening, and smacked his elbow on concrete, sending a sharp pain up his arm.

The lights came on in the garage, also remote-controlled. Interesting. He got to his knees and moved over to the rear of the Honda. The door opened, the driver got out, and it struck him that he had no legal reason to be inside. If she told him to leave, he would have no choice but to comply. There were no wants or warrants on her, and no probable cause for entering the premises.

When she shut the car door he stood up and walked around the rear of the vehicle toward her. "DNR, Conservation Officer."

The woman turned and stared at him.

The face left him speechless. *Honeypat Allerdyce was Patricia Allard!*

Honeypat was the daughter-in-law of the U.P.'s most notorious poacher, and after her husband's death, his sometime squeeze. A tangle with clan leader Limpy Allerdyce years ago had resulted in a gunshot wound for Service's leg and a seven-year stint in Jackson Prison for the old poacher.

Honeypat had run things in his absence, and when Limpy got out, she resented his taking control again. There had been an alleged family war. Honeypat had tried to starve her father-in-law to death, and an Allerdyce enforcer named Jukka "Skunk" Kelo had sided with her and later disappeared without a trace. Kelo had once been described as a lamprey on ice. There was circumstantial evidence that Honeypat might have killed Kelo, but nothing solid.

Honeypat was a fine-looking woman, and a chameleon: She could look like trailer trash one minute and high-class the next. She was smart, cold-blooded, and a sexual predator, trying more than once to seduce Service. She had once told him they were a lot alike.

Honeypat had disappeared in the fall of 2002 at about the time Lorelei Timms was elected to replace Sam Bozian as governor. Honeypat had been seen in the U.P. only once in the two years since then—last summer at the Ojibwa casino in Baraga.

"Been a while," Service said, turning on his tape recorder.

"Shoulda known youse'd keep on plowin' ahead," Honeypat said.

"I just wanted to talk to Patricia Allard. I had no idea it was you."

She looked him up and down. "Youse're here, might as well come in and I'll make us some coffee. Stupid ta stand out here in grudge and yak."

She led him through the house into a kitchen half the size of the entire ground floor of his cabin, made coffee with her winter coat and boots still on, and left him alone. She came back minutes later with fresh makeup, in a black dress and high heels. She looked like she fit the house.

"There're warrants out on you," he said as she poured coffee.

She sat down across the table from him. "Don't bullshit me," she countered with a grin. "Technically I'm a person of interest, but dere's no warrants. I know how ta keep track of such tings."

"Jukka Kelo disappeared," he said.

"Youse tryin' ta say somepin'?"

There was no evidence Kelo was dead, and little doubt she had tried to kill Limpy, but the old poacher would never admit to it or press charges. "Let's talk about Fagan," he said.

"Youse gonna read me my rights?"

"I'm talking to Patricia Allard, not Honeypat Allerdyce."

"Your mind always drove Limpy batshit," she said with a grin. "What *aboot* Fagan?"

"You provide services for him."

"I don't know what youse're talkin' about."

"Mama Cold," he said.

"Who's dat? I read in da papers Quint might have his ass in some hot water. Dat true?"

"This is Fagan's house," Service said.

"Really? A friend arranged for me ta stay here. I didn't know Quint had a place near Lansing."

"The shit Fagan is up to is hurting people," Service said. "We're investigating, and when the charges come out, it will be messy as hell and your name will get dragged in, and from what I hear, your business operates best under the radar."

She paused and studied him. "I'm not sayin' I know anyting, but I mighta heard some stuff."

"Fagan uses escorts for business contacts."

She smiled. "I tink I heard dat."

"You hear names?"

"Try me."

"Langford Horn?"

"Could be."

"Eino Teeny?"

"Not him."

"Clay Flinders."

"Never heard of 'im."

"Jeff Choates."

"Yeah."

"Horn and Choates. Fagan got women for them?"

"I tink I *heard* dat," she said, feigning like it was news.

"You want to confirm those names under oath?"

"What would I get out of it?"

"Peace of mind."

"I got plenty of dat already."

"I could talk to cops in the Yoop, tell them you say you know nothing about Kelo."

"Dat ain't no guarantee."

"Best I can do."

"Guess we got nuttin' more ta talk about, you and me."

"I can get a subpoena."

"How'd youse find me?" she asked.

"It's what I do."

She nodded. "Yeah. How 'bout we go jump in bed and talk aboot dis, eh?"

"Word is you don't turn tricks, or snort coke, and you drink and eat in moderation."

"Not talking business here," she said. "You and me in bed is personal ting, been long time waitin' ta happen."

"I don't think so," he said, getting to his feet.

"Someday youse'll find out what youse're missin'," she said.

"I'll have to live with the loss," he said, and toggled his radio.

"All quiet out there?" he radioed Denninger.

"Very," Denninger said.

"Join me at the house."

"Shoulda known youse'd have reinforcements."

"Nature of the work," he said.

"Your recorder ting on?" she asked.

"Yep."

"Okay. I procured escorts for Quintan Fagan. The two you mentioned were among 'em, Horn and Choates. Dere wass a coupla udders in the DNR, but you'll have ta find dem names on your own."

"Why'd you decide to cooperate?"

"Guess I got a ting for Boy Scouts. I done you a favor. Now you owe me one."

"I don't think so."

She smiled and lowered her eyes. "It's gonna happen, hey."

He let Denninger in a few minutes later, and Honeypat looked her up and down. "You poundin' dat?" she asked.

Denninger snarled silently.

"Got fire, big tits under dat ugly cop coat; I bet she's a good one. Honey, you ever get tired a playin' out in da snow wid woods cops, youse let me know. I'll get youse nice warm work and good money."

"Who *are* you?" Denninger snapped.

"Da big Boy Scout over dere's an old fuck buddy," Honeypat said.

"Let's go," Service said, grabbing Denninger's arm and pushing her through the door, which closed quietly behind them.

"That was Allard?"

"Yep."

"You *know* her?"

"Knew her way back."

"Knew her, *biblically* speaking?"

"None of your business."

"Working with you is a trip," she said.

They met Laramie at the river's edge and got within five feet of the landing at Island Park when the canoe rolled over, dumping them all in three feet of icy water. They got the canoe out and helped Laramie put it in the back of his truck, thanked him for the help, got into their truck, got out the thermos of coffee, and started drinking it. Service turned the heater and blower to high, but even with the coffee in him, felt cold all the way back to Saranac.

No sign of Leukonovich. He let Denninger use the shower first. After ten minutes he poked his head in the door. "You're using all the hot water."

"Plenty of room in here for two," she said.

"No."

"Too bad," she said, and moments later came out wrapped in a towel, her hair still wet. He stripped and got into the shower. The hot water did its work, and he felt all his aches start to fade. Honeypat was Patricia Allard, and he had her on tape confirming Horn and Choate as clients, paid for by Fagan. The question was, how could he best use this information to push the case forward? First he needed to talk to Miars and tell him what he had learned.

When he came out of the bathroom Denninger was at the table in sweats, drinking coffee.

"That was Allard, for real?"

"Yes, but that's not her real name."

"You used to scromp with her?"

"I told you, that's none of your business."

"She's older, but definitely hot," Denninger said.

"She's a black widow," Service said. "She'll have her way with you and cut your throat in the afterglow."

"Every woman feels like that after bad sex," Denninger said. Service looked at her and knew she wasn't kidding.

"Not just bad sex, *any* sex," he said.

"You get her to talk?"

"She confirms Fagan used her to get escorts for Horn and Choate." He handed her the recorder and she took out the tape.

"Leave out the irrelevant stuff," he told her.

She raised an eyebrow.

Denninger's teasing was driving him crazy. So was Leukonovich. And suddenly he remembered a couple of comments McCants had made. Years back, after he'd gotten together with Nantz, his relationship with Candi had changed subtly. She had been good friends with Nantz, but there had been an edge after Nantz came into his life. Had Candi been jealous? *Holy shit.* He dialed McCants's cell and got her voice mail. He then dialed her home phone. A male voice said, "Candi's Sweet Shop." He hung up.

What the hell is wrong with you?

45

WEDNESDAY, NOVEMBER 24, 2004

Saranac, Ionia County

What the hell was going on with the women around him? Honeypat was the only one he thought he understood; she had always been unstable and off the wall. But McCants? She had definitely made vague overtures, and as he thought back, it had been going on for a long time. But last night a man had answered her phone. Geez.

Leukonovich was a complete puzzle, and his instincts told him to avoid her at all costs. Denninger, on the other hand, had him in a frazzle, and as long as they were working and living so closely, he decided they needed to set clear rules—ironclad ones.

He had only once ever had an affair with a colleague and that had been with Lisette McKower; he was determined not to repeat *that* screwup. She had not only been a colleague, but also married. The memory of his own stupidity still made him cringe. It might make sense to send Denninger home, but she was now at risk because she had been with him the night of the seizure, and they were both now linked to the U.S. Attorney's office. He didn't have the authority to send her home, and he didn't want to risk getting her into a mess that could potentially hurt her career. He liked the fact that she showed good instincts as an officer, and he trusted her. He just had to have a talk with her and hope for the best.

His worries about women aside, he spent most of the night thinking about Eino Teeny. If Fagan had not gotten women for him, what connection had led Fagan to underwrite an academic chair for Teeny? There had to be something. And now Teeny was vacationing in Key West after resigning as director. What were the chances he was at Fagan's place down there? Fagan had loosed his lawyers on the department, all because he, Service, was investigating Piscova.

The DNR's lawyers believed they had lost the egg seizure hearing because of the story Service had planted with Salant. Chief O'Driscoll seemed equally unhappy about the articles, but so far seemed supportive—at least in a don't-ask, don't-tell frame of mind. Should he plant more—put things out in the public light and see how people reacted? This was risky business, and the thought of playing it this way made him nervous in ways he had never quite felt before. In the past he had preferred to keep everything close and inside the department where it belonged. But now . . .

He also needed to sit down with Julia Gates, the BAO woman who wrote the letter to the director announcing an audit of undercover operations. Also risky to talk to her, but he felt he had to in order to gauge what prompted the move.

Most of all, he needed to talk to Miars and see what was happening with him. Miars had pretty much disappeared from the Piscova investigation ostensibly because of more pressing work, but had he done anything more about the internal stuff?

The faster this case seemed to move, the more it seemed to bog down and become more complex. Most of all, he needed focus and there wasn't anyone to provide it.

He also needed to talk to Karylanne more, and he decided to set a schedule so that they had regular contact.

A secretary answered for Julia Gates, and after some contentious-but-polite door-guard questioning, put his call through to her boss.

"Grady Service," he said when Gates answered. "We haven't met."

"I know your name," she countered, not offering any further information.

"I've been told that you're about to commence an audit of all DNR undercover operations and investigations."

"If we were, what business would that be of yours?" she asked sharply.

"It's my unit."

"As far as I know, you're not in a supervisory position."

"That's true. Do you work for Langford Horn?"

"Yes."

"Then neither of us is supervisory."

"You have no idea what my position is," she said. "I suggest you get what you need to know through your supervision."

The woman had a voice as sharp as cracked ice and was clearly nervous. He sensed her wanting to duck any direct questions. Why?

"Look," he said, "I'm not trying to interfere, and I don't know what motivated the audit, but I need to tell you that it would behoove you to bear in mind that your boss figures prominently in this investigation. I'm not saying he's done anything wrong, but I *am* telling you as clearly as I can that there's a lot of smoke that needs to dissipate before we can know what we have. All I'm requesting is that you ask yourself when you got the order to initiate your audit, and what else was happening at that time."

"This conversation is inappropriate and therefore concluded," she said.

"Your call, but do yourself a favor and think about what I just said."

She hung up without further comment and Service exhaled loudly. Either she'd think about it or she would come after him, full claw.

Denninger came down to the kitchen looking half asleep. "You run yet?"

"Have some coffee, then we'll run."

"I'm all about that," she said.

He poured coffee for her and sat down across the table. "You and I need to get something straight between us."

"That's what I've been saying," she said.

She was a lot like Nantz, but much younger. "That's exactly what I'm talking about. All this innuendo has got to stop. It's fun and it's flattering, but nothing's going to happen."

She winked. "I can think of a great way to end it."

He glared at her. "It's not going to happen, Dani. I'm not saying I'm not attracted to you, but given my personal situation, I'm just not ready to tackle a personal relationship right now. I had Nantz and she died. I still think about her all the time. My job has always come first in my life. You have the makings of a great officer, and you need to get your job in perspective right now. Relationships between officers can work, but they're risky for all parties. Comments?"

"You're *serious*."

"Absolutely. Living like this puts a helluva strain on both of us, and I think we need to resolve it to avoid any entanglements."

"Forever?"

"Honestly? I don't know," he said. "But definitely for now. You're worried about your career. You should be. My dragging you into this has put you in a difficult spot. If we don't bring this case home we're probably going to be under a microscope, and if the relationship is more than professional, that will come out."

She had a serious face. "I hear you," she said. "I won't lie: I'm attracted, but to be completely honest, I don't know if it's proximity, or what Nantz used to say about you, or if it's your status in the department. I mean, you *are* a star."

"I'm old enough to be your father—or grandfather."

"Don't sell yourself short," she said.

"Are we going to fix this, or are we going to wait until it all explodes in our faces?"

"What do you suggest?"

"Keeping it totally professional, nothing more, nothing less."

"I can do that," she said.

"Good. Ready to run?"

After a forty-minute run around the area, they returned to the resort, showered, and dressed. His leg was aching again, so he took another 800 milligrams of ibuprofen with a piece of bread. Denninger made breakfast and they talked while they ate.

"I want you to go to Lansing and see Jeff Choate from Fisheries. Inform him that he's a person of interest in an ongoing investigation and that he should consider sitting down with us and talking informally," said Service.

"Can we do that?"

"Legally? I don't know. But if we can get him talking about Piscova, he may shed more light on what we're dealing with."

"He's supposed to be a real asshole."

"Just deliver the message forcefully. Be polite, but don't take any shit from him."

"What're you going to be doing?" Dani asked.

He was still in a quandary about how much to reveal about his own activities. She didn't formally report to him, but he felt responsible for her, and if she knew about some of the things he was doing, like planting stories in the media, she could also be held liable.

"I'm going to go see Miars and bring him up to speed."

"Meet back here tonight?"

"That's the plan. If Leukonovich is here when you get back, see if she's got a list of Piscova contracts for us yet. If Jornstadt and Zarobsky show up, ignore them."

"Can we do that?"

"I don't think they're digging all that hard in this case. I think it's just an excuse for them to get a room."

She lowered her eyes. "Backpackers?"

He had no idea what she was talking about and his face must've shown it. "You know, scromping, getting it on . . . ?"

He nodded dumbly. She spoke a different language.

He called Salant on his way north to find Miars.

"Yo," Salant said, "Po-po, how it be?"

Po-po? What the fuck was he talking about? *Stay calm.* "Might have an interesting little angle for you. Word is out that Fagan underwrote an academic chair for Teeny at a college near Seattle."

"Why would he do that?"

"I don't know, but it does make one wonder. Teeny's on vacation in Key West, and Fagan owns a place down there."

"You sayin' he's at Fagan's place? This info cold, or what?"

Service closed his eyes, tried to assume he was getting through. "I'm stating two facts. How they connect, I don't know; I just thought you might be interested."

"I am, man. This story is crunk. Same ground rules?"

"Has to be."

"That's cool, but at some point you gotta crawl up into the light."

"At some point," Service said, with no intention of ever going on the record in the media.

It had been a long day, and it was 5 P.M. by the time he found Milo Miars at the Gaylord district office. "Have you eaten yet?"

"Can't remember my last regular meal. My wife thinks I've moved out."

"How's the elk case?"

"We've finally got a lead that looks promising. Let's take a ride."

Service got into his sergeant's unmarked truck and they drove east through town, eventually pulling up to a purple house with a green roof and white trim. "Big Bear Deli," Miars said. "Prices aren't bad and the food's pretty good."

There were only two people in line ahead of them, and Service wondered why there were so few customers if the food was so good. The two officers remained silent as Service studied the menu, and discovered the place was smoke-free. "Let's get it to go," Service said. "First Traverse City, now Gaylord; this smoke-free bullshit is spreading faster than bacterial kidney disease in salmon."

Miars grinned.

Both men ordered albacore tuna on rye bread, no mayo, and large Diet Pepsis. They took their food outside, drove down a side street, and parked.

"Happy Thanksgiving," Miars said.

"*Thanksgiving?*"

"Actually, it's tomorrow, but we'll probably both be working."

Good God, I'm missing everything, Service thought. It had never even occurred to him that he should be in the U.P. with Karylanne for Thanksgiving.

After a pause, Miars asked, "Are you behind the articles?"

"Do you really want to know?"

Miars shook his head. "Not really. I've got enough on my plate."

"The chief call you?"

"The BAO investigation? We talked."

"What's your take?"

"You're stirring the pot pretty hard," said Miars.

"You think it will happen?"

"The interim director is a straight arrow. I think it will happen."

"Anything I need to know about?"

"Things were pretty quiet before you popped up."

"Sorry about that. Have you done any more work on the case?"

"Too busy with elk, and it looks to me like you've got a head of steam."

"Not as much as people might think," Service said, and talked his sergeant through what he had found so far.

"This escort service madam will testify?"

"I think she'll give us a statement, but actually getting her to a trial might be tough. My guess is that she'd disappear."

"It's going to get rough," Miars said. "Zins and I met internal resistance like you wouldn't believe when this thing got going eighteen months ago."

"Enough resistance to make you back off?"

"Zins, not me; but alone, I had to scale back and take it easy. I hounded that bastard. Fagan paid for the operation of three weirs on the Platte and Manistee rivers and Van Etten Creek. He built them, paid the power bills, repairs, everything. He was supposed to reimburse the state for eggs. At one point we had a count of two million fish coming through those weirs. We had probable cause for a misdemeanor search warrant—not accurately reporting fish numbers, and so forth. We got the warrant and served it at the Elk Rapids plant. We even got BAO to do a three-year contract audit, and they found Piscova owed seventy to eighty thousand to the state for year one, and one-twenty to one-thirty for year two, and in year three, which was two years ago, even more—all this based on Piscova take records.

"We went to the Fisheries division. Choate was the contract coordinator. In his office we found records of Florida trips and so forth. We took all this to Teeny, who told us to relax, but I wouldn't. I went back to Elk Rapids, and all the records were gone and Piscova had suddenly been granted a ten-year contract. There was a big party at the plant and Teeny was there, and Choate and the assistant governor and all sorts of state legislators. After that Zins threw up his hands, decided it was as futile as pushing a rope, and that was that. He didn't terminate the investigation; he just let it go dormant."

"And you?" Service asked.

"Not much I could to, but I kept snooping. I found that Fagan had two partners: a fish guy named Amonte out of Milwaukee and another one named Jingles Steinmetz."

Miars said Steinmetz's name like Service should be familiar with it, but Service only shrugged.

"Steinmetz is out of Detroit, king of the fish business, mobbed up, brains, and muscle. As I looked at the transactions I found evidence that Piscova was underreporting and underpaying. Fagan would make five sales in a day, but report only two. He was shorting the state and his partners, but I couldn't prove it without more resources."

"Did you talk to his partners?"

"Couldn't. Steinmetz would have him whacked and the state would have gotten nothing."

"So you backed off."

"Then you came along with your egg thing and I could see the case was getting legs again"

"But you didn't jump back in with your angles."

"Been there, done that. No point to hopeless causes. Thought it better to see what you turned up and then jump in if there was room."

"Is this what we signed on for?" Service asked, taking a bite of sandwich, holding his napkin at his chin to keep from dribbling. "Only going after sure things?"

"The job and environment are so different now, it's sometimes hard to remember *what* we signed on for."

Miars was clearly having second thoughts and Service couldn't blame him. "Eventually Fish and Wildlife will raid Crimea. You want in?"

"No."

"You want me to keep you tuned in to what we're doing?"

"From time to time. How's Denninger doing?"

"Good officer." Service related her visit to the realtor in Traverse City.

"Where did the money for the clothes come from?" Miars asked, snapping to attention in his seat.

"My wallet."

"Jesus, I couldn't afford anything like that. You'll never get it back from the state, or the feds."

"I know," Service said.

Service was headed south to Saranac by 8:30 P.M. Beaker Salant called him when he was passing St. Louis. "Too cool, dude. I talked to Teeny, and he is indeed staying at Fagan's place in Key West, and he went, like, total crunk. I asked him if he'd stayed there before and he actually said, 'No comment.' Can you believe *that?* I also asked him about the chair endowment and he said he had no knowledge of Fagan paying the way, but if it was true, he was grateful."

"You buy it?"

"Not a chance. I talked to the vice president of development at the college and he confirms that Fagan's the primary contributor, though there are others as well. That's all he had to say, and when I gave him chapter and verse on Teeny's nonperformance here, all he would say is that Teeny had a wide range of experience that will be invaluable to their students. I think he wanted me to split. I asked him to confirm the contributors to the Teeny chair by snail mail, and he said he would, but I'm not going to hold my breath."

"Thanks, Beaker."

"You have any more brainstorms, call."

"That door swings both ways," Service said, not at all sure that it did. There was no guidebook for leaking information to the media.

It was just past midnight and Leukonovich's staff car was parked out front. No sign of Denninger's truck, but it was probably in the barn. Service found the IRS agent reading newspaper clippings. Denninger was sitting at the table, looking morose.

"Your handiwork?" Leukonovich asked, holding up the clippings.

"What are they?"

"The sort of interference in an investigation that can manifest severe repercussions," she said.

Service caught Denninger's eye. "Happy Thanksgiving."

"That's tomorrow," Denninger said. "Your day go okay?"

"I had dinner with Miars. He's busy with another investigation."

"Is he looking for cover?"

"Not sure yet. Could be, I guess."

Leukonovich put the clippings in a briefcase, got up, and went upstairs.

Denninger came over to Service. "That woman totally creeps me out."

"She's a little different, but she's supposed to be good at what she does. How did the meeting go with Choate?"

"He got in my face initially, but after a minute or so he sat back in his chair and stared."

"You think he got the message?"

"His hands were shaking like he had Parkinson's."

"You okay?"

"Not a problem. It wasn't fun, but I guess it needed to be done. That which doesn't kill us, makes us stronger, right?"

"Absolutely. We'll give Choate a couple of days to stew and then we'll go see Clay Flinders."

"You get the sense this will end in a mess?"

"It's already a mess," Service said. "What we need to do is bathe it in light and let processes work."

"You say that like you're confident it will all work out."

He was anything but confident, but kept quiet.

Leukonovich came down in a ratty gray terrycloth robe. "You put together that list of Piscova contracts yet?" he asked.

She went back upstairs and brought back the list. "I gave them to your girl earlier."

The women were in bed. Service looked at the list. Piscova had contracts in North Dakota, South Dakota, Missouri, and Oklahoma. He went to the truck, got his laptop, brought it inside, plugged it in, and began surfing the Net for information. *This is not what a game warden does*, he told himself.

46

THANKSGIVING DAY, NOVEMBER 25, 2004

Saranac, Ionia County

Service fell asleep with his head on the table next to his laptop. He was awakened by the scent of fresh coffee and Denninger trying to creep quietly around the kitchen area. "I'm awake," he said.

"I'm convinced," she said.

They sat quietly. Snow was falling outside and beginning to accumulate. "We're not going to get anything done this weekend," he said. "You want to head home, go."

"Alone there, company here, even if it's you. I'll stay. What about Flinders?"

"See if you can locate him and request a meeting for Monday."

Leukonovich came downstairs in tights and a loose blouse, her feet in baggy wool socks.

"Coffee's ready," Denninger said.

"Can you administer caffeine to Zhenya through IV?" the IRS agent asked.

Service thought she looked exhausted. "Sleep bad?"

"Zhenya always sleeps poorly," she said. "Her mind has no off-switch—I think a design flaw on the part of God."

There was a light knocking on the door and Denninger yelled that it was open.

CO Joe Cullen came in, looking sheepish. He was out of uniform, decked out in a down coat, snowpants, and Sorel boots. "Coffee on?"

"Grab a cup," Service said.

The four sat in silence, nursing coffees, navel gazing, engulfed in a morning fugue. "You work out yet?" Cullen asked Denninger.

"Caffeine titers aren't high enough. You?"

"Thought I'd do a snowshoe run in the rec area. There are some good hills on one of the bike trails."

Denninger smiled and perked up. "I'm up for that."

She went upstairs and got dressed. Service looked at Cullen. "Have her home before midnight, Joe—or I'll have to kill you."

Cullen looked like he couldn't decide if it was a joke. Service didn't know either. It had just popped out.

After the young officers were gone, Leukonovich said, "All of this sort of raw physical exertion is for the young. You do not accompany them?"

"I'll run later."

"You seem old to be doing this work with such young people."

"I am," he said.

"Zhenya has decided to grant herself a day of rest."

"Good for you."

"But you, of course, will work. I see that you are highly motivated to fulfill the obligations of your work."

"It's what I do."

"The list was what you wished?"

"Yes, thanks." Why was she being so solicitous?

He picked up his cell phone and saw her frown. He punched in Lisette McKower's home number and one of her daughters answered the phone.

"Is your mom there?"

"Mommy, it's *Godzilla!*"

"Grady?"

"What's up with that Godzilla crap?"

"They are convinced Godzilla is the coolest. Anybody they think is cool they call Godzilla. It's a compliment."

"Godzilla's a big, ugly lizard."

"But cool," she said. "It's Thanksgiving. Why aren't you at home—or more to the point, in Houghton?"

Jesus, everyone had advice for him. "What's Harvey Ghent's phone number?"

"Leave Harv alone," she said sternly. "He's probably at his hunting camp, and there's no phone out there."

"I need information."

"What you need to do is take a deep breath and listen to me. Your name came up at the LED management meeting on Tuesday."

"You were there?" The law division's management group was comprised of the chief, his captains, the assistant chief, and senior district lieutenants from the north and south regions. McKower was relatively new and low in seniority.

"Captain Grant sent me to represent him. Black is gunning for you."

"Fast Track can't hit shit."

"You are singlehandedly turning the department upside down. The word is out that since Nantz died you've become more of a loose cannon, and you're off the reservation pursuing your own agenda. They're calling your case a witch hunt. The paranoia was palpable."

"Only the dirtbags should be paranoid," he countered.

"Grady Service, listen to me! When you allege corruption in state government, all employees suffer."

"Are you telling me to back off?"

"I'm saying you need to be surgical in your approach."

"What's Harvey's number?"

"You are so goddamned stubborn. Black wants all your records audited—gas card expenditures, expenses, equipment, time cards, everything. They're coming after you," she said.

"I work for Captain Grant," he said.

"Not anymore you don't. You're now an actual part of Wildlife Resource Protection and your report is in Gaylord."

This fact stopped him. "Tree and I got sent into Laos one time. Our scout showed us a valley and said the enemy was down there, and if we went into the valley we would die. We told him if we didn't go into the valley, people who needed to die would live. We went."

"You're talking crazy," she said.

"I'm talking *reality*. The mission is the mission is the mission. When you start factoring in personal and professional risk, the mission is fucked."

"They'll try to destroy you."

"Does that mean you'll have to choose sides?"

"I hope not," she said, "but I've got a family, a career, responsibilities. Most of us are in the same boat."

"Lis, every bent motherfucker in the DNR diminishes all of us. They're a fucking cancer. You don't cut it out, it takes over and kills the whole shebang. Now, can I *please* have that number?"

She gave it to him and he hung up without further comment. He sat for a few minutes trying to reduce his heart rate, and when he had calmed down, started to punch in Harvey Ghent's number. He stopped after two digits and closed the phone. Why drag Ghent into this? He looked for Tassos Andriaitis's number and hit the speed dial.

He got the man's service and a message: "Can't make money gabbing on the phone. Leave your name and number."

Service did as he was instructed and hung up. Andriaitis had said he would be in Alaska for two weeks before heading back to Florida. Was he in between now? *Shit.*

Zhenya Leukonovich went upstairs and came back down with a rubber mat, which she spread out on the floor. She peeled off her clothes and sat naked on the mat, her back straight, head up, legs crossed, her limp hands over her knees, palms up, eyes closed.

She was not exactly thin, but . . . He looked away. "Can you take that upstairs?"

"Silence please. Zhenya must meditate."

"At least put on some clothes."

"Zhenya must align her chakras. Please, there must be silence."

He stepped outside on the balcony and had a cigarette. The wind was whipping from the southwest, the snowflakes wet and heavy.

When he finally went back inside Leukonovich had shifted her position. The bottoms of her feet were pressed against each other, her hands holding them in position. She was bent slightly forward, her breasts dangling heavily over her feet.

He sat down at his laptop and began trying to find information on paddlefish hatcheries in Montana, North Dakota, South Dakota, Missouri, and Oklahoma. The most information concerned a national fish hatchery in North Dakota and it appeared that the state depended on paddlefish eggs being reared there. How did the state work that with the feds?

"You are uncomfortable with the human body?" Leukonovich asked from her mat.

"You're done?"

"Yes," she said. "Zhenya believes that all of nature is unclothed. Only man covers his body."

"Some people need to," he said.

"You are sexually repressed," she said.

"I don't think so," he said.

"I was in such a condition for many years, but now I have freed my sexuality."

"Is that part of CPA training?"

"You amuse me," she said. "A born leader, you hide all but your most aggressive feelings from others."

His cell phone buzzed.

"Andriaitis."

"How do states work with federal hatcheries?" Service asked.

"Lots of ways. Are you talking about Piscova?"

"They've got several contracts."

"The most lucrative is North Dakota. The state pays Piscova to collect eggs, which they deliver to the Garrison Dam Federal Hatchery. The feds raise the eggs to planting size and then state Fish personnel handle the planting."

"Do the feds collect eggs?"

"They take what they need from collectors paid for by the state. It's part of their payment," said Andriaitis.

"Are you back in Florida?"

"Seattle. The weather is lousy. I'll probably be here for six hours or so until airports east of here clear up."

"Do you know who handles the Piscova contract in North Dakota?"

"You should talk to the director, Gar Kochak. He's been there a long time, and all contracts, fish or game, eventually cross his desk."

"How do you know so much?" asked Service.

"It's a small universe and those of us on the commercial side talk a lot and pay attention to what's going on. You snooze, you lose. Roxy said you two talked again."

"We did. She seems all right, sort of resigned to whatever comes along."

Andriaitis grunted. "Fucking Calvinist upbringing, predestination and such shit. Nothing's written. You write your own fucking life."

Service agreed. "Not everyone buys into that."

"Sad but true. You got what you want? I need a goddamn five-dollar beer."

"Jingles Steinmetz," Service said.

There was another audible grunt on the other end. "By God, you're starting to get somewhere, but be careful. Fagan's slippery, but Steinmetz is one vicious motherfucker."

"Steinmetz and Fagan are partners."

"Steinmetz staked him in the biz when he got started. I don't know what their deal is now."

"Thanks."

Cullen and Denninger came in as he closed his phone, walked over to the kitchen area, saw Leukonovich, and immediately turned away. "Geez," Cullen mumbled.

"She's meditating," Service said.

"Isn't she cold on the floor?"

"Apparently not."

"We're gonna make hot chocolate," Denninger said. "You want some?"

"Sure."

Denninger went about making the drink and Cullen sat down next to Service, glanced at Leukonovich, turned back to Service, and rolled his eyes. "The detective business always like this?" the young officer asked.

"No," Service said. "Sometimes it gets weird."

Lansing, Ingham County

Beaker Salant called as Service and Denninger were getting ready for their morning run. Service sent her ahead and told her he would catch up.

"Dude, this story is like *so sick!* I filed a Freedom of Information Act request for Teeny's travel vouchers while he was in office, and it was like running into a wall, *full stop!* I've got legal contacts who'll put the squeeze on the department, pro bono. With the department's budgets in such shitty shape, they'll fold pretty quick rather than invest a lot of manpower in withholding an FOIA request. Thanksgiving night I got a call from a man named Boyd Scow, general counsel for Pacific Green College. Boydie-boy wanted to let me know that because the college is private, it's not required to make the names of donors public. I think he labors under the assumption I'm some lowly, lame undergrad. I pointed out to him that PGC has about four million in federal grants, which automatically and legally obligates the institution to place donor lists and amounts in the public domain. The dude was, like, totally freaked. We'll get the list, just like we'll get Teeny's travel vouchers."

"Sick?"

"Big, cool, sick—it's growing thick, hairy legs, dude."

"Can you report the conversations you had?"

"Absolutely. The story will run statewide tomorrow. The storyline is, former director vacations at contractor's place in Florida and DNR stonewalls FOIA for the director's travel vouchers. Part two, attorney for Pacific Green College tries to dodge making donor lists available. The owner of Piscova, Quintan Fagan, recently alleged to have funded the academic position soon to be occupied by former DNR director Eino Teeny. It's further alleged by credible sources that Piscova, a company with a long-term contract with the DNR to collect salmon eggs for state hatcheries, is under investigation for violating IRS and FDA laws. A Michigan DNR seizure of contaminated Piscova eggs was recently overturned by a judge, despite DNA tests of those samples by FDA showing the presence of the pesticide mirex in the eggs.

The banned mirex has contaminated Lake Ontario fish eggs for years, and because of this, they're banned for human consumption; Michigan eggs are not banned. You catching any heat?"

"Some," Service said.

"Put on your fire-retardant drawers, dude; this deal's going to get a whole lot *hotter.*"

It bothered Service that he was opening the door to a reporter to trash the DNR he loved, but he couldn't see a better way of bringing everything into the public eye. Behind closed doors, the power brokers could control everything and would ultimately prevail.

Earlier this morning Denninger had called the office of Clay Flinders and was told that the Fisheries director was out for the day. She immediately called a woman she knew in the Parks Divison, who talked to an acquaintance in Fisheries and learned that Flinders was speaking to an organization called the Resource Rescue Group, a collection of staffers from various committees in the Michigan House of Representatives. The RRG met quarterly to review various natural resource issues. The meetings, open to all House staff personnel, were described as "background," with open give-and-take between invited guests and staff.

Service cut through the woods and caught up to Denninger, who was plowing through fresh snow under a stand of oaks, her face bright red. "If the RRG meeting is open only to House staff personnel, how do we get in?"

They kept running while trying to talk.

"Badges," she said.

He hoped she was right.

He parked his vehicle on a ramp off North Grand Avenue and they walked down Ottawa Street toward the Capitol Building. The Anderson House Office Building was just west of the Capitol. They checked in with the security detail in the lobby and took an elevator to the fifth floor, to the Mackinac Room, which was laid out in an ellipse, a half-moon with a stage in front.

There was no security in the meeting room. They found seats in the back row right before Flinders was introduced. He did a thirty-minute PowerPoint presentation on the condition and operations of state fish hatcheries. Questions followed. For a known introvert, Flinders looked comfortable in front of the audience, sallying around the stage with a lavalier microphone. The questions were all softballs, and Service wondered if they had been planted. After answering several questions, Flinders and his host, a middle-aged woman with straight blond hair, invited the audience for refreshments in an adjoining room.

Service waited until the room was crowded before easing in. The group loitered in clusters, attracted by forces Service couldn't decipher. There were cookies, coffee, tea, and soft drinks on a series of tables along a wall. Service wandered over and got a Diet Pepsi and noticed a small sign on one of the tables: REFRESHMENTS COURTESY OF PISCOVA, INC. Service nudged Denninger and went looking for Flinders.

"Mr. Flinders, Grady Service," he said, announcing himself and pointing to his partner. "Conservation Officer Dani Denninger." Flinders blinked and tugged at his beard. "Chief, Piscova is being investigated for illegal activities with eggs owned by the people of Michigan. Don't you find it ironic, if not offensive, that this is the company sponsoring the refreshments here—or is your organization changing its name to the Resource *Rape* Group?"

Flinders sucked in a deep breath and hissed, "You sonuvabitch!"

"No argument with that characterization, Chief—but you're not answering the question."

"You are not authorized to be here," Flinders stammered.

"Conservation officers are all about rescuing and saving resources. That authorizes us."

The blond woman who had introduced Flinders tried to intervene as people began to gather. "Would you gentlemen like a private room to continue your discussion?" she asked.

"The gentlemen would *not*," Service said. "This thing has been kept in private rooms for too long. It needs to be out where people can hear about it."

"Call Security," Flinders said to the woman, his eyes on fire.

Service said, "We're officers conducting a legally authorized investigation, Chief."

"Are you happy? Are you *happy?*" Flinders said, his voice rising. "Jeff Choate turned in his paperwork to retire this morning. Is that what you want? They'll get me next!"

"Who will?"

"You *know* who!" the Fisheries chief said, wheeling around and departing the room at a brisk clip.

"What's going on?" a man in a white shirt and tie asked.

"Just business."

Service and Denninger returned to his vehicle on the parking ramp. Service called the North Dakota Game and Fish Department and asked to speak to director Gar Kochak. The department receptionist didn't ask any questions and put the call through. The director answered his own phone. "Gar."

Service couldn't imagine Eino Teeny answering his own phone, much less with his first name. "Director Kochak, I'm Michigan DNR detective Grady Service. I understand North Dakota has contracted with Piscova, Inc. for paddlefish egg collections."

"That's correct," Kochak said.

"Are you aware that Quintan Fagan has been convicted of IRS crimes in the state of Florida?"

There was a long pause. "What kind of crimes?"

"Illegal cash transactions and tax evasion. There were five counts, and he pleaded to two."

"Is that right?" the North Dakota director said slowly. "What's your name again, and your phone number?"

Kochak hung up, and called back ten minutes later. "Detective, thank you for the information. I can't say that Piscova's ever done anything but honor the contract here, but I'll be damned if this state is going to award contracts to felons."

Service hung up and looked at Denninger.

"Why didn't you tell him about the eggs?" she asked.

"We haven't proven anything in court, but the convictions in Florida are a matter of public record."

"Are we going to have everybody in the state of Michigan pissed at us?" she asked.

"Maybe," he said. "You still in?"

Denninger nodded.

Next, Service called Law Enforcement Divison chief Lorne O'Driscoll. "I just heard Jeff Choate is retiring."

"Turned in his letter this morning and cleaned out his desk. He's going to take unused vacation."

"Sort of sudden," Service said. "What happens to the salmon contract liaison?"

"Like you said, it's sudden. Too soon to tell how Fisheries will play this."

"What kind of reaction are you hearing about his retirement?"

"Some astonishment, I'd say. People are surprised."

"Chief, Officer Denninger met with Choate last week."

Silence on the other end. "Do you think that precipitated his decision?"

"I'm going to try to find him and talk to him."

"I'm not sure I agree with that," O'Driscoll said. "Let me talk to the interim director before you do that."

Service was not pleased by the response and wished he had not told his chief what he was planning to do. "All right."

They were on their way out of Lansing when the cell phone rang. "Detective, this is Cecil. Lorne told me about Officer Denninger's meeting with Choate. What exactly did she say to him?"

Service handed Denninger the phone. "Acting Director Hopkins wants to talk to you."

"Director Hopkins, this is Officer Denninger. Yes, sir . . . Cecil, I understand. I told him he was being investigated, and that we have evidence he was provided female company by Piscova."

Service saw that Denninger was sweating. He reached over and patted her shoulder supportively. "Yes, sir, there's a woman who runs a call-girl service in Lansing, and she confirms that Choate and Horn were clients, paid for by Piscova. The person who provided the arrangements confirms it. We have her statement. She left us with the impression there might be more personnel involved, but this is as much as we have so far."

Denninger looked over at him and tried to smile as she listened to the voice on the phone. "No, sir, I didn't threaten him. I only stated the facts of the investigation. He was huffy at first, then he sat back in his chair and didn't say anything. All right, sir."

She handed the phone back to Service.

"Why did you send her to Choate?" Hopkins asked.

"I wanted to get a reaction."

"Well, I guess you got one. I don't think you should talk to him again. I'm sure he will lawyer up and that will just make it a mess. If you think your evidence is solid, let it speak when you lay out your case. You with me on this?"

"I was hoping to convince him to share details," Service said.

The interim director took several seconds to respond. "I'm going to have to overrule you on this one. Leave the man be and develop the case. How many others are involved beyond Horn?"

"I don't know."

"All these articles keep coming out. You think Teeny is staying at Fagan's place in Florida?"

"I only know what I read in the funny papers," Service said.

Cecil Hopkins laughed. "Ware Grant told me you're a piece of work."

"You know the captain?"

"Long time. Tell me you're going to leave Choate alone."

"If that's your order."

"It is. Have you heard that your activities are dividing the department?"

"I heard something along those lines."

"It's hard to remove bad apples without bruising a few good ones along the way," Hopkins said. "Keep at it and let me worry about morale and attitudes."

"You're telling me to take it all the way?"

"I don't know what *all the way* is, Detective. I'm telling you to take the case to its natural conclusion, no less, no more. Keep it professional at every step."

"And keep pissing people off?"

"That's the risk you run."

In one way he was getting a vote of confidence, but if so, why did he feel so out on a limb, all alone? "Thanks," Service said, closing the phone. Hopkins hadn't said *we*.

"We're really swimming in shit, aren't we?" Denninger said.

"We always swim in shit," he said. "We just need to pay attention to the direction and strength of the current."

Saranac, Ionia County

Service and Denninger had finished their run, showered, and were drinking coffee. Leukonovich sat at the table, working on her laptop.

"Fish and Wildlife are unlikely to prosecute Crimea over the adulterated caviar," the IRS agent announced. Her pronouncement came out of the blue.

"You have contact with Fish and Wildlife?" Service asked.

"Zhenya will graciously ignore your crude attempt to pry. The point is that Fish and Wildlife will use Crimea for leverage against bigger fish."

"If that's true, what does it mean for our investigation?"

Leukonovich looked up at the ceiling and sighed. "Impossible for Zhenya to say, but if Fish and Wildlife does not pursue Crimea, Zhenya will not allow their decision to affect the outcome of her case against Piscova. I believe there will be a satisfactory outcome for you and for me." She took two sheets of paper out of a folder and slid them over to him.

Service scanned the pages, which contained two names. "Askin and Hough?"

"They are fish technicians in your department. It has been alleged that they live somewhat beyond their means. An audit shows no trust funds or exogenous income adequate to explain their lifestyles."

"They're on the take?"

"I deal in numbers," Leukonovich said.

Service and Denninger spent the rest of the day trying to gather information on the two names, Dewayne Askin and Darwin Hough.

WEDNESDAY, DECEMBER 1, 2004

Platte River State Fish Hatchery, Benzie County

Service and Denninger left Saranac at 6 A.M. and drove north in a dusting of snow toward Honor, 130 miles away. The hatchery that employed Askin and Hough was four miles east of the resort town. Not wanting to risk spooking the biologist manager of the facility, Service last night had placed a call to Sergeant Jed Ernat, whose area included Benzie County, and who had been a CO almost as long as Service.

"Jed, Grady Service."

"The witch hunter," Ernat said. "Or is it shit disturber—I always get those two confused."

Service cringed. Word was spreading fast, as it always did. "I need help."

"We all knew that years ago," Ernat joked. "What's up?"

Service asked if he knew the two fish technicians at the Platte River Hatchery.

"I've met them, but can't say I know them."

"Are you in a position to find out if they're working tomorrow?"

"Shouldn't be a problem. I'll call you back."

Askin was scheduled to work. Hough wasn't.

Denninger used a laptop to find Hough's home address. He lived south of the hatchery near a village called Wallin on Aylsworth Road.

They found the address just before 9 A.M. There was a new Ford pickup truck under a carport next to a double-wide trailer. There was also a small pole barn on the property, a trailer with a snowmobile, a trailer with a Honda ATV, another trailer with a personal watercraft and a dirt bike, and another trailer with a bass boat under a cover.

"Up-north yard decor," Denninger said, deadpan.

"Give him a call, see if he's home," Service said.

She dialed the number and a man answered.

"Who am I talking to?" Denninger said.

Denninger hung up. "Male voice. Someone's there. You want me to creep the property?"

"Not without a warrant. Let's just go knock on the door and see what happens. I'll talk, and you look around."

They hammered on the door for a long time. A man finally cracked the door. "Wha—?"

"Darwin Hough, we're conservation officers; can we come in?"

"Is there a problem?"

"We just need to talk, and it's kind of cold out here."

"I'm trying to sleep, sirs."

"It won't take long," Service said. He smelled marijuana smoke wafting out of the trailer.

The man reluctantly opened the door. The interior was unremarkable except for being relatively clean and well kept. The man didn't offer coffee or even for them to sit. "What?" was all he said, looking nervous.

"Where's the doobie?" Service asked.

The man looked like he was in pain. "Doobie?"

"We can smell the damn thing, Darwin. Go put it out."

The man shuffled toward the back and shuffled back, sputtering. "I don't smoke regular. Just when I need to sleep."

"You work at the hatchery?"

"Yeah, when I'm not out at the Platte weir."

"You have contact with Piscova people?"

"Sometimes, but not all that much, ya know?"

Denninger picked up a photo. "Sweet Vette. Oh-three?"

"Oh-four. It's my brother's."

Denninger set the photo down. Service said, "Some contact with Piscova people; like, how much is some?"

"You know, we just see each other around."

"At the weirs."

"Like that."

"You got some nice toys in the yard," Service said.

The man shrugged.

"Tech ten, eleven?" Denninger asked.

"I'm an eight, but I should be a nine," Hough said, clearly unhappy with his civil service rating.

Service said, "You make what, fourteen, fifteen an hour?"

"What's this about?"

"Seems like a lot of hardware in the yard on thirty grand a year," Service said.

"My truck's paid for; I live in a trailer. What are you sayin', sir?"

"What I'm saying is that I figure your Polaris goes for around ten grand, your bass boat around twenty, the Honda ATV, six, the dirt bike another six, the WaveRunner close to seven. Four trailers at four each, probably on the low side. If my math's correct, that's close to sixty-five grand, and the Vette's another fifty. So how does a guy making thirty grand afford all the brand-new toys?"

"I live on a budget, sir. What business is it of yours?"

"You sell weed, maybe, generate a little side cash?"

The man looked horrified. "No, man, I swear, I just use. I don't deal and I'm not answering no more questions."

"Where's your dope?"

"Man, what the *fuck* is your problem!"

"I don't have a problem, Darwin. You do. State employees can't smoke dope."

"You busting me?"

"Not if I don't have to."

"This isn't right," he said.

"I know, life's a bitch. Word's out that you know the Piscova folks more than just a little."

The man reached into his pocket for a cigarette. His hand shook as he lit it. "Can I sit down?"

"Go ahead."

"Man."

"You got something to tell me?"

"Am I gonna lose my job, sir?"

"I'm thinking you ought to be more concerned about losing your freedom."

"Fuck, man," he said. "Okay, Piscova slipped us a little cash if we looked the other way when they were over their collection limit. I mean, what's the big deal— they had more than we needed. We're just gonna dump the surplus in the river, and if we made a little off it . . . not a big deal, right?" He looked at Service, dropped his eyes, and said, "I need a lawyer, right?"

"That's your right," Service said. "Who's *us*?"

"Look, sir, I'm not naming no names unless my lawyer tells me to."

"Have it your way, Darwin."

"Man, we're just talking about a bunch of nasty old eggs."

Service motioned Denninger to the door and turned back. "You want to show us the Vette?"

"It's my brother's, sir."

"No problem; let's just look at the registration and proof of insurance."

"It's not there. He's supposed to bring the paperwork. The Vette's new."

Service looked at Denninger. "Go run it through the computer, check Sec State, and let's see what pops up."

"Wait," Hough said, holding up his hands. "Okay, it's mine, but it's registered and there's insurance."

"Why'd you lie?"

"You make me nervous, sir."

"Okay, Darwin. Here's the deal: We're going to get some paper for you and you'll write the details of your interactions with Piscova—how much they paid, when, how often, everything. When you finish writing, read it into the tape recorder."

"I'm gonna get fired, sir."

"That could happen," Service said, "but if you've been scamming the state and doing dope, you could get worse than fired. What say we forget the dope?"

It took an hour to get Hough's statement on paper and tape.

Denninger said, "He rolled easy."

"Let's hope Askin does the same."

When they got to the plant they talked to Askin's supervisor and discovered Dewayne wasn't there; he had called in last night and asked for a week's vacation.

"You always give vacation on such short notice?" Service asked the supervisor.

"Slow time of the year," the man said with a shrug.

"Askin say where he's going?"

"Probably fishing. He's always headed south to fish for bass. He's in tournaments all the time, thinks he's gonna make it to the big time and become the next KVD."

KVD was Kevin VanDam, a Kalamazoo boy who had broken into what was then pretty much a Southern bass tour and risen to become the all-time biggest money winner on the pro bass tour. "We all gotta have dreams," Service said.

"Dewayne couldn't catch a goldfish if he emptied the bowl into a net."

"Good worker?"

"Gets the job done, more or less," the man said.

"Thanks," Service said.

"Dewayne in trouble?"

"Thanks," Service repeated as he walked away.

They had the man's home address from the computer and drove to a house on Thompsonville Highway, two miles south of the hatchery. There was a rusted, ancient black Ford Escort in the driveway.

A woman answered the door, with a child on her hip. "Yes?"

"Is Dewayne home?"

"He took off to some bass tournament in Florida."

Service said, "One I've heard of?"

"Florida Panhandle somewhere. He's gotta be there Thursday for a Friday start."

"He fish a lot of tournaments?"

"What he does is not win any, but he always seems to have enough money for his stupid toys, and I gotta work to put clothes on my kids. What did you say your name was?"

"Service."

"You want me to tell him you stopped by?"

"Not necessary," Service said. "Does he have a cell phone?"

"When he decides to answer it."

"Think I could have his number? I'll just call him and we'll do our business over the phone." She gave him the number, and Service and Denninger started south toward Saranac. Denninger called the number, which went over to a message service. She didn't leave a message.

"What's it cost to enter big bass tournaments?" he asked.

"No clue, but we can find out."

"Let's do that."

"We're getting there, aren't we?"

"Looks okay for the moment." Deep in his mind he was worried. How come Leukonovich knew about these guys, and why had she passed along their names?

Service called Roy Rogers in New York. "Leukonovich told us that Fish and Wildlife are going to play Crimea to get a bigger fish; you heard anything about that?"

"Not officially, but I've been picking up hints."

"We need those samples, Trip."

"I know; I'm working on it."

Service looked over at Denninger and shook his head.

50

THURSDAY, DECEMBER 2, 2004

Mount Pleasant, Isabella County

First thing in the morning, Service and Denninger logged onto the Internet with their laptops and did some quick research. They called Florida and made contact with the Florida Fish and Wildlife Conservation Commission law enforcement division and got the name and cell-phone number for the conservation officer who handled Pensacola Beach in Escambia County.

Service made contact with officer Joanelle Lox, told her briefly about the investigation, and asked if she had time to check out Fagan's place. She said she would, took down the address from him, and called back thirty minutes later.

"I'm out front now."

"What's it look like?"

"Beachfront, moderate size, maybe a million-eight. Y'all got you a camera phone?"

Service looked over at Denninger. "Do you have a cell phone that will handle photos?"

"My personal phone." She gave him the number, he relayed it to the Florida officer, and hung up. Lox called the line a minute later and talked to Denninger, who put it on speaker. "Can y'all see?"

"Comes through good," Denninger said, showing the photo to Service, who was leaning over her shoulder.

"Y'all don't mind, I'll just leave it on and go on up and make contact, and y'all can listen in."

"We're here," Denninger said.

They saw the front door on the phone and heard a bell ringing.

"Moanin'," the officer greeted a clean-shaven man with wet hair. "Ah'm Officer Lox of the FWC. We're conductin' a survey of the horned northern viper—tha's a kinda snike. Y'all the owners?"

The phone camera shifted to show a young woman, disheveled, with mussed hair.

"We're on vacation," the man said.

"My plat book shows this here's the property of Mr. Quintan Fagan," Officer Lox said, "that right?"

"Yes, ma'am. We're his guests."

"Who're you?" the officer asked.

"Dewayne Askin."

The camera went back to the woman.

"Ya'll married?" the officer asked.

"No, ma'am, just good friends," Askin said.

"My name's Edie," the woman said. "These snakes you're lookin' for, they dangerous or anything?"

"No, ma'am. They just sort of migrate down this way ever' winter to breed, and we like to keep track."

"You want to come in?" the woman named Edie asked.

"No, ma'am, jes didn't want you folks ta panic when I commenced ta walkin' ya'll's grounds."

"No problem," Askin said. "Thanks for stopping by."

"Like ta keep folks happy," the officer said.

"What's so special about these snakes?" the woman called Edie asked.

"They aren't endangered or anything, but they're kinda interestin'. They make the most god-awful sounds when they're matin'."

The woman giggled.

"I best get on," the officer said.

"Me, too," Edie said, giggling.

Out in the yard, the officer said to Denninger. "You get all that?"

"We did. What the heck is a horned northern viper?"

The officer laughed. "Could ya'll hear what was goin' on inside when I got up at the door?"

"No."

"Let's just say it give me the idea for namin' the snake. You see their hair?"

"We get it," Denninger said. "Thanks for your help."

"Glad to. Just keep on sendin' them tourists south with beaucoup cash."

Denninger hung up. "Press this anymore?"

"No, you can talk to Askin when he gets back to work. We know he and Hough are dirty, but in the greater scheme, I think they're small fish. Let's keep working our lists and see what develops."

Beaker Salant called between Service's calls. "I've got a source telling me that Michigan DNR seals were found at a New York state hatchery. That true?"

Service did not remember mentioning the seals and was pretty sure he hadn't, which meant the journalist had another source. Or he was fishing. "I haven't seen any seals," Service answered, trying to hedge. Working with a reporter was a real strain.

"But you knew there were seals."

"I just heard it from you."

"You're being evasive," Salant said.

"It seems to me that the seals aren't the story," Service countered.

"They're part of it. A story is like a jigsaw, and reporters like to get all the pieces in the right places."

Service wanted to redirect him. "Jeff Choate is retiring."

"Because of my articles?"

"I don't know."

"If he retires does that mean you can still go after him?"

"I assume so," Service said, feeling a sudden surge of panic. *Why had Cecil Hopkins ordered him off Choate?* "Any more stories in the works?"

"Maybe. I got an e-mail from a former Piscova employee, who claims she took cash from Fagan, went to Chicago, and bought Krugerrands for him."

"Have you confirmed she was an employee?"

"Not yet."

"What's her name?"

"Whoa, dude. We're partners, you and me, which means we share. Michigan seals were or were not found in New York?"

"They were, but like I said, they're secondary to the main story."

"How did they get to New York? It's my understanding that only a state biologist can use them."

"We're pursuing that, but it's not a priority. Who's the former employee?"

"Lauren Gladieux. You'll keep me tuned in to the seal thing?"

"You bet," Service said, wondering who was using whom.

Denninger asked, "Who was that?"

"We need to get back to the Rolodex names and look for a woman named Lauren Gladieux."

Denninger went through the file. "She's here. Beulah address and phone number."

Service called the number and got a message that it had been disconnected. He terminated the call and said, "Keep at it. What did each employee do for Piscova, for how long, and when? Any connection to caviar production? Did they work with Lafleur, Fagan, or Vandeal?"

They spent the rest of the day on the phones, talking, scratching notes, finding a few people they might interview later, but none with the potential interest of Lauren Gladieux. Mid-afternoon Denninger began waving frantically at Service and he hung up from his call and listened to her.

"You're still in touch with her? Where was that? Why'd she change her name? She get married? No, okay. Thanks much. We appreciate it."

She looked at Service. "Lauren Gladieux is now known as Lauren Glad. She lives near Oil City in Midland County and works at Soaring Eagle."

The Soaring Eagle casino was the largest Native American gambling operation in the state. It was operated by the Saginaw Chippewas and located in Mt. Pleasant.

"She tribal?" Service asked.

"Don't know. Her friend said she changed her name because the old one was too long. What's *that* all about? You want to get phone ear, or go up there?"

"Let's roll," he said.

"I'm all over that," she said. "Want me to get us rooms at the casino?"

"We'll come back here, or sleep in the truck. We're spending money like crazy."

"Don't think I've ever slept double in a patrol truck."

Service wondered if this was a double entendre, but it seemed straightforward and he put it out of his mind.

They got to the casino around 6 P.M. It was a Thursday night and the lot was close to full, most of the space taken up by what had to be one hundred buses from all over the Midwest. They parked and made their way under a wooden beam entrance into the main lobby. In front and below them were rows of one-arm bandits, most of them occupied. Service saw at least three wheelchairs with oxygen bottles, elderly women with slot cards on lanyards around their necks. There was a sandstone wall with flying eagles in relief. "Uplifting," he grumped. He had always found casinos depressing. What did people expect—that hope and eagles would carry them up to the good luck god?

"Hey," Denninger said, looking at a wall turned bulletin board, "The second annual indigenous Upper Peninsula farming conference will be here in January, and the Michigan Mosquito Control Association conference in February."

"Weather sucks for farming in the U.P.," Service said, "and judging by our mosquito populations, the control association must be hauling them up there and unloading them. Let's find the manager's office."

The casino manager was too busy to see them, but an assistant manager came out. She was young and bouncy and did not appear to be tribal. Service badged her. "We're looking for one of your employees, Lauren Glad."

"Is she with the casino or the resort?"

"Soaring Eagle is all we know."

"This could take some time. Why don't you go into the Water Lily and have a drink."

"We're on duty."

"We have coffee and soft drinks," the woman said, showing them into the dark restaurant and seating them before talking to a waitress who brought a carafe of coffee.

"They must think we're gonna be here a while," Denninger quipped.

The manager came back after they had each had a cup. "Sorry to take so long. We're short-handed. Lauren Glad works rolling stones."

Service glanced at Denninger. "Rolling stones?"

"Crap tables."

"Is she working tonight?"

"Tomorrow; she has the morning shift. Is there a problem?"

"No, we just need to talk to her."

"Try tomorrow morning. She comes on at eight."

"Thanks," Service said.

On their way out to the truck they found that light snow had turned heavier. "Let's find her residence," Service said as they got in.

Oil City was ten miles east on M-20. Though named, there was no actual town and never had been. Back in the sixties it had housed a slew of bars populated by oil and natural gas roughnecks exploiting the fields in the area, and Central Michigan University students looking for a little excitement and action. Oil City had been a tough place back then. Today, there wasn't much to see. They found a trailer set back from Greendale Road, a green VW bug parked in front. The parking area had not seen a shovel recently, but lights were on inside.

They went up into the mudroom that led to the front door and knocked. There were two pairs of heavy boots, probably women's, Service thought.

The woman who opened the door had wide eyes and long black hair. "Yes?" she asked.

"Lauren Gladieux?"

"Cops?"

"DNR."

"Game wardens?"

"Yes, ma'am."

"What do you want?"

"You used to work for Piscova."

"I don't know nothing," she said.

"We haven't asked a question yet," Denninger said.

"It don't matter. I got nothing to say."

"It's about Krugerrands and Quintan Fagan."

"That sonuvabitch. He claim I stole from him?"

A sore point, Service thought. "Stole what?"

"Krugerrands. It's not true. I never took none of them dumb coins."

"Why don't you tell us about it?"

"I'm still trying to forget that bastard."

No sign she was going to invite them in. "Maybe we can help."

"I don't want no help. I just want to be left alone."

"Fagan accused you of stealing Krugerrands?"

"I never stole nothing. He accused me so he could fire me."

"Why?"

"I wouldn't go to bed with him."

"So he accused you of stealing?"

"After he chewed my ass he told me I was either gonna go along or that would be the end of me."

"What did he mean by that?"

"He always says things so they can be interpreted differently."

"And you said no."

"No; I said yes, and I went with him one time and that was enough for me. No job's worth that."

"You bought Krugerrands for him?"

"He gave me Northwest Airline bags with cash and I went to Chicago and bought them at a bank down there. I made maybe four trips and he hit me with the fuck-or-be-canned speech." She looked up at Service. "Is he trying to claim I stole them?"

"Not that we know of," Service said.

"He scared me, so I moved and changed my name. How'd you find me?"

"We can't say."

"If you found me, he can, too. You don't know what he's like."

"He's not looking for you," Denninger said. "It would be good if you talked to us. When did you buy the Krugerrands, where, from whom, all of that. We don't want to cause you a problem."

"What's this about?"

"Fagan, not you. Did you keep records?"

"On my calendar."

"Do you have it?"

"Somewhere."

"Think we could take a look?"

"I suppose," she said.

The woman let them inside. The furniture was in bad shape. There was a Native American spirit wheel on one wall, made of wooden strips—probably white ash, Service thought—and decorated with feathers. "You make that?"

"A guy I dated give it to me, said it would heal my spirit. It worked for a while, but then he started showing up drunk and that ended that. I got no time for drunks."

She showed them the calendar.

"You're sure these dates are right?" Service asked. The calendar was from 2003.

"I quit last April and moved. I was in Chicago in the fall."

"So you did this four times?" Service asked. She nodded. "He send anybody else?"

"He keeps everything secret. I don't know."

"You could file charges," Denninger said.

"Wasn't no rape. I give it up."

"He coerced you."

"I guess, but I don't want to talk about that no more. I'm making a new life and I don't want nothing to do with all that old junk."

They thanked her for the information, and left. It was 10 P.M. by the time they got into Service's truck, and snowing hard. "We'll take it slow heading back," he said.

"Safer to get a room."

Service raised an eyebrow and Denninger did likewise. "You think those spirit wheel things work?"

"They work for those who believe they work," he said. "Otherwise it's a good place to hang feathers."

She laughed, said, "You're cold, dude."

"Is that cold as in hot, or cold as in cold?"

"Depends on what you believe," she said.

He was no longer sure what he believed in when it came to the department and its mission. The mission, yes. The department? Not sure, up in the air, a sea change coming—great waves like Superior's fabled Three Sisters. He believed in Nantz, and his dead son. Brook trout remained beautiful and predictably unpredictable. He would always believe in brook trout and tannin-stained water. What else? Even the list of possibilities was short. Only one thing declared itself, to take the case all the way, no matter what. He was not sure it was a standard that would be achievable, and that alone made it worth pursuing. He kept all these thoughts to himself.

Denninger was young and he had already seen a slight negative streak in her. She didn't need his baggage.

Saranac, Ionia County

It is a Rowlandsonian scene of domestic bliss: morning run complete, showers and breakfast done, Zhenya in a sheer leotard on her meditation mat. Service and Denninger were at a table, pecking at their laptops.

Emma Jornstadt came through the door without knocking, letting in a wave of cold air. Her partner, Aldo Zarobsky, nosed in behind Jornstadt, looked down at Leukonovich, her breasts suspended over her feet like blood oranges defying gravity, begging helping hands. Jornstadt glared at her shadow, who continued to lag and stare.

"Time for an update," Jornstadt announced, plopping an obese briefcase on the table. No thin reed of a portfolio announcing its owner as too important to carry more than only the most significant and important papers; this was a real bruiser of a briefcase announcing its sherpa as a woman who faced quantity and quality and relished bearing the whole load. The briefcase's spine swayed like an overworked nag. "Right, Al?"

Al, transfixed by Zhenya's various angles, did not take the prompt as adroitly as usual.

"*Aldo*," Jornstadt said again, no question this, no prompt, an order in one word.

"Right," he chirped, momentarily fighting off the considerable distraction.

"We have met with Anniejo, who has in turn met with U.S.Attorney Endicott, who has minimal knowledge of the case, and even less enthusiasm for seeing it go forward. Fagan's wallet opens to Republicans, a not-insignificant fact for U.S. Attorneys appointed by Bushies and expected to stay in step with the tribal drums. Am I telling this accurately, Al?"

"Same page of the songbook, same steps on the dance floor," Zarobsky said.

"Bottom line?" Service asked.

"As always, money is politics. The golden rule—him who controls the gold, rules—and Light Brigade charges, militarily or politically, although noble and undeniably romantic in retrospect, are no longer in vogue. A good Bushie fights only the fights Big Bushie directs."

"You agree with this?"

"Not my call. Facts are subject to interpretation. I find facts, others interpret and reassemble. Accurate job description, Al?"

"Spot on," Al said. "Never been a fight when everybody didn't get bloodied somewhat. The US of A isn't interested, why waste the state's treasure? Time to cut and run: It's unassailable practical logic."

Leukonovich laughed out loud, something between a pack animal's bray and the feral snarl of a hyena. "Zhenya does *not* run. The *IRS* relishes fights, blood, tissue rotting in the sun."

Service noticed Denninger's mouth hanging open.

Aldo chipped in on his own, pointed a finger at Service. "Word's out your neck's on the line—maybe more to the point, your anatomy further south."

"That has nothing to do with the case," Service said.

Special Agent Jornstadt declared, "Damaged goods cannot deliver an airtight, hermetically sealed case. Endicott finds fault with toilet tissue not properly installed in the federal building."

"Gotta roll off the front, not the back," Zarobsky chimed in. "Like Brobdingnagian arguments over bread and which side to butter. Endicott won't shit if the paper's not unrolling properly."

Service refused to wilt. "This case isn't finished. We haven't pulled it all together yet."

"Input streams through endless apertures like light rays into an abandoned homestead," Jornstadt pontificated. "Damaged goods, damaged case against staunch supporter of the Grand Old Party, and that means this party is over. I'd offer condolences, but we are professionals and team players. We do not take such things personally."

Service was steaming, fighting to hold back his temper, without success. "She need a new view, Al, a change of scenery? She starting to notice the ceiling needs repainting or cobwebs in a corner while you're giving her your probe? She need to recharge the old you-know-what?"

Zarobsky turned burnt umber, swelled his chest, and took one step forward, but Jornstadt was on her feet, readjusting her eyeglasses. "Boys, boys," she said. To

Leukonovich, "Put on some clothes, seek professional help." She started toward the door, not looking back and barking, "Al!" He seemed transfixed, torn between his exiting sure-thing partner and the near-naked possibilities of Zhenya Leukonovich. He eventually broke off his stare and shifted his eyes to Service. "Yours is coming, smart guy."

"Yours is leaving," Service countered.

Denninger was stunned, speechless, Leukonovich almost giddy—for her.

As if orchestrated by a demented creator, Service's cell phone rang.

It was Anniejo Couch. "Before you hear about it via the drumline, I want you to know that there is resistance to this case above my pay grade. It will not be going to the grand jury. I don't support this, but team is team."

"Can't be a team unless they get on the field and play."

"I can imagine your disappointment."

She was wrong. There was no disappointment, only rage—an old friend, and one that had always served him well, stepping up in the darkest moments of life to bring hope. He hung up without further comment, knowing instinctively that the calls were not finished, that the legendary and perhaps mythical Three Sisters of Lake Superior had come to him, each wave successively larger and potentially more demoralizing than the last.

But what he expected as the next and final call was not that at all. It was Roy Rogers.

"Sunday afternoon, noon. Crimea. Fly into JFK. Get a cab to the Hotel Garibaldi. Crimea's in Brooklyn. We'll meet beforehand, get our act together."

"It'll just be me."

"Bring a vest," Rogers says. "We are going into Indian country, where they talk with Slavic accents."

Leukonovich remained on her mat, raising her thin arms high above her head, a pose far to the east. Denninger had not moved, was barely breathing.

Proactive, preemptive, forward-looking, whatever, Grady Service speed-dialed his chief's cell phone. "We go to Crimea Sunday," he said, and hung up, leaving loose ends hanging limp like battle pennants in the Sargasso Sea. The chief was a team player, wed to the chain of command. Service thought of casinos, rolling stones, the click of dice muffled by thick felt, war declared as silently as a nun's prayers. He thought: *Me or them, to the finish, all the way, no quarter.*

He told Denninger, "I'm going to bite a chunk out of the Big Apple's ass."

"I don't understand," she said.

"Head for home, water your cat, shovel your snow—do whatever you do on your own time. It's time to count your blessings."

"Am I out?"

"Not until the chief brings us both back to the DNR."

Zhenya looked up at him, nodded ever so slightly, a smile that was not quite a smile; it was something else, a look of recognition, one warrior to another. Her looked seemed to say she had been blooded in this kind of thing, and not only understood it, but was cheering him forward without words.

Service thought: *New York on Sunday. Motion, not progress. Sometimes it was all you had.*

As if the phone had taken on a life of its own, acting director Cecil Hopkins called. "Detective Service, I have an assignment for you. You and Denninger will be in my office tonight at twenty-one hundred hours, fifth floor, Mason Building; understood?"

"Understood, Director."

He turned to Denninger. "Hopkins wants us at his office at nine P.M. tonight."

"Is that, like, a bad thing?"

"We'll find out," he said. His gut gave him no reading on it, but after hours on a Friday night? It was at the least very unusual.

PART III

ANIMATO

Chance has put in our way a most singular and whimsical problem,
and its solution is its own reward.

—Sherlock Holmes, "The Adventure of the Blue Carbuncle"

Lansing, Ingham County

The parking lots surrounding the Mason Building were mostly empty. Service and Denninger went to Security on the ground floor and were greeted by three people—a uniformed woman handling night security, and two straight-backed men dressed in tactical black. The taller of the men stuck out his hand and said gruffly, "Detective Service? Sergeant Votruba, CPD." CPD was the Capitol Police Division of the Michigan State Police. The sergeant didn't bother to introduce his partner. Service introduced Denninger.

"We're to accompany you to Director Hopkins's office," Votruba said. Denninger raised an eyebrow but said nothing. They rode the elevator in silence.

When the door opened, Hopkins was standing there, waiting for them. He nodded for them to follow and led them into a conference room. There were two black tactical canvas bags on the floor, shotguns on top. "Seats," the director ordered.

There was a pot of coffee on the table, five cups.

"You look puzzled," Hopkins began. "Any idea what's about to happen?"

"Either you're about to give us bad news and you're expecting an extreme reaction, or we're going to invade a small country."

Hopkins laughed. The CPD men showed no emotion.

"The sergeants, you, and your partner are going to BAO director Horn's office on the seventh floor. There you will examine Horn's files for evidence relating to your case."

"We don't have a warrant," Service said.

Hopkins said, "We are *public* servants. These buildings and all within them *belong* to the public. As representatives of the public, we can enter and investigate where we wish."

"Somebody has to approve it," Service insisted.

"Governor Timms has approved it," Hopkins said. "Anything that relates in any way to your case or our division may be removed and copied. We have legal personnel standing by on the fifth floor. Documents you want are to be brought to them to be copied and logged. They will see that the documents are returned when copies are in our files. Questions?"

Service glanced at the tactical bags and shotguns. "With all due respect, is all that necessary?"

"Our colleagues are responsible for the entire Capitol complex. Like us, they have procedures to follow. They are along to assist, not hinder. Once you are into the office, you are in charge."

"Why are you doing this?" Service asked.

"I have closely followed everything you've done, Detective. I've read the media coverage and noted reactions within the division and the legislature. I see no actual flames, but there seems to be considerable smoke everywhere I look. I'm old-fashioned, started my career as a fire officer. When I smell this much smoke and can't find the source, it makes me professionally and personally uneasy. I don't like those feelings. If we can't see the flames, it's time to get out the shovels and Pulaskis and dig down to see if it's in the roots. Take your team to Horn's office and do what has to be done."

At 10 P.M. they were in the hallway outside Horn's office. The two sergeants were in tac vests and headsets, and carried shotguns and sidearms. "You gonna blow the door?" Service asked Sergeant Votruba.

"No need." The sergeant held up a key. "Stand aside, please, and wait for us to clear the room."

Clear the room? Of what—dust motes? Sergeant Votruba was all business and Service hooked Denninger's arm and pulled her to the side. The sergeant's partner stepped to the right side of the door and quietly racked a round into the chamber of his shotgun. Votruba turned the key, the lock made a click, and he shouldered open the door. Both men charged inside, hunched over, ready to rock and roll.

Denninger whispered, "I don't know whether to wet my pants or laugh out loud."

"Shut up, Dani."

Votruba came out of the office and said, "The space is clear, sir," and waved them in.

They were in a suite that contained the desk of a receptionist, a large office, a small office lined with file cabinets, a conference room, and a safe. "Geez," Denninger said. "Where do we start, and what do we look for?"

"DNR files, Piscova, Fagan, contracts. You take the office with the file cabinets. I'll start in Horn's office."

Service looked at Votruba. "How much time do we have?"

"We'll hold it as long as you need it."

"At least unchamber the rounds."

"Procedure, Detective. You do your job, we'll do ours."

Denninger went into the smaller office, Service into Horn's. Votruba stepped in with a key and flipped it to him. "This opens desks, files, everything."

Service hit the jackpot in the third drawer. The file was marked DNR: SALMON CONTRACTS. It was six inches thick. Service spread the documents on Horn's desk and began to read. Halfway into the pile he found correspondence from Fagan talking about the ten-year contract and clauses that should be included. Further down there was boilerplate for the contract itself, amended in handwriting, the exact changes Fagan wanted. Near the bottom were three letters from Fagan suggesting certain investment opportunities, with a prospectus attached to each letter.

Denninger came in. "There's a file on the Wildlife Resource Protection Unit, a document from Horn directing a unit-wide audit. What do we do with the stuff we want to copy?"

"Make a note of where you found it and start a pile."

Denninger stuck her head through the door before she left. "Boxes are coming up from the fifth floor."

Service finished going through Horn's files. There was also a folder in the man's in-basket marked PERSONAL, but he couldn't bring himself to open it; people had to have some privacy. There was a photograph of Horn holding a salmon in front of a boat. Service added it to the pile.

Denninger came back at midnight. "Been through everything, and there's nothing in the conference room. You need help here?"

"I'm about done."

At 1 A.M. they were back in the office of Cecil Hopkins. "Two copies of everything will be made," the acting DNR director said. "One for here, one for your investigation. Your set will be delivered tomorrow. The originals will be returned to Hopkins tonight, left in boxes with a memo instructing Horn to call me when he comes in on Monday. Did you get what you needed?"

"We won't know until we have time to read and digest everything, but it looks promising," Service said.

The two sergeants and Hopkins accompanied them back to the lobby of the Mason Building. Service looked at Cecil Hopkins, but didn't know what to say. After years of Teeny's political toadying, the eighty-year-old acting director had stepped up. The DNR in the old days had been one of the best fish and game operations in the United States, and the department had always had strong leaders. A final look at Hopkins gave Service a surge of hope he had not felt in a long time.

Votruba said, "Great mission—our pleasure. You two want to grab a brew?"

"Thanks, but we've got a ways to drive."

"Understood."

In the truck Denninger said, "Did that really happen?"

"Apparently," Service said.

"I'll start on the documents as soon as they arrive tomorrow."

"*We'll* start."

"You're leaving town," she reminded him.

He had forgotten.

53

SATURDAY, DECEMBER 4, 2004

New York, New York

There was no sun, and the temperature was hovering just above freezing at Detroit Metro Airport. It had rained and sleeted all night, and airline maintenance crews were working feverishly at de-icing aircraft, one at a time, causing flight delays. Service's flight was affected, and he and his fellow passengers milled aimlessly around the velvet rope gate like cattle piled up in front of a wooden chute.

Service's cell phone rang. He expected it to be Dani, but it was Tassos Andriaitis, who said in a voice barely qualifying as a whisper, "Roxy's dead."

Service tried to process the information, and felt immediately conflicted, part of him wanting to scream at Fagan, the other part almost smiling because Roxy's demise changed everything and might actually make the case easier. The unexpected mix of anger and shame left him speechless. "How?" he managed, an insipid question at best.

"Last night—her heart," Andriaitis said. "The cocksuckers killed her." Andriaitis hung up.

It was 3 P.M. before the Northwest flight touched down at LaGuardia. The airport terminal and baggage-claim areas were a madhouse, an international smorgasbord of mankind in motion: bearded Sikhs in bright turbans, Muslim women in black chadors, purple and latte-skinned blacks in dashikis and kaftans, Manhattanites in Armani, soldiers and sailors in uniform, duffels on their shoulders, a fat man with a cat in a red plastic crate, both of them crying. The smells of sweat, body odor, curry, garlic, and perfume blended in nauseating ratios. Wet shoe leather and stinking feet grabbed at his nostrils. The only thing that really registered for Grady Service was the military personnel in uniforms—a far cry from Vietnam, when returning warriors were cursed and spit on and men took off their uniforms and medals and threw everything away so they wouldn't be harassed.

He collected his bag, stepped outside to the taxi stand, and found himself first in line. The cabbie who pulled up had teeth filed to points, and the pinkie fingernail on his left hand was four inches long and painted bright red. His BO was a mix of unwashed goat and sun-rotted roadkill. He wore a multicolored striped toque tilted on the left side of his head, the right side filled with petrified pigtails, sticking up stiffly like stalacmites or exposed punji stakes.

Service tossed his bag in the backseat and got in. The cabbie looked back. "I dry, you rye, o-gay? Bo-tel?"

"OK," Service says. Bo-tel? "Hotel?"

"Jess, Bo-tel, pless sid beck, suh?"

"Garibaldi in Brooklyn Heights, o-gay?"

"O-gay, suh; sid ewe back," the driver said with a menacing grin before mashing down the accelerator. The taxi barreled into the traffic with NASCAR commitment, surging and surfing past slower vehicles, leaving behind a startled and cranky wake of honking horns and single fingers being waved angrily.

At the hotel the cabbie tapped the meter with his magic pinkie. "I dry, you rye, boss say him you pay thet mush." The amount was $24.76. Service gave him a buck tip, not sure if it was too little or too much, and dismounted on rubber legs, thinking the man could be anything from a paroled mob wheelman to a closet vampire. As a cabbie, he doubted the man's professional career would be either long or venerable.

There was a note at Reception from Roy Rogers: "Meet in the lobby, seven P.M."

Two hours hence. A bellman wanted to carry his bags, but Service told him thanks-but-no-thanks and got a dirty look. His ninth-floor room looked out on the Brooklyn Bridge if you ignored most of the vista being blocked by two high-rises in the foreground.

His mind was on Dani. She was unhappy with her exclusion from this trip, seemed to take it as involuntary exile, but also seemed committed to mining Horn's files and documents in his absence. He had no time—and worse, no facts—to reason with. What he felt was in his gut, a sense that taking this trip together would have been a mistake, and though Anniejo Couch had not made a peep about expenses, why spend what you didn't need to spend?

Rogers arrived with a six-footer in tow. The other man wore a brown leather coat that draped his thighs, six tiny gold stud earrings lined up on the rim of his right ear, stacked like monkeys on a totem, a grimy Mets hat, knee-high brown leather boots, tattoos extending above his shirt collar, the rest hidden like an iceberg.

"This is Eco 'Down-Deep' Depp," Rogers announced. "We call him Three-D."

"Caw me Three-D or caw me Deep, not Depp; I share no blood wid faggot actors."

"Deep," Service said, shaking his hand. "Grady."

"Yo, I think I caw you whatever you say, man," Deep said, craning his neck to look up at the taller, more hulking Service.

"I'll pick up warrants in the morning," Rogers said. "Your flight okay?"

Service shrugged.

Rogers said, "Crimea will know we're coming; they'll have their lawyers there to greet us."

"I thought it was a raid," Service said.

"Yo," Three-D said. "We raid the Ukes, guns come out, and shit happens. We don't want no rounds exchanged. Someone at the court will tip them, or it will come from the precinct house, it doesn't matter who. This is a simple professional business transaction, paper for product samples, in and out, no hard feelings."

"You're saying we're compromised?" Service asks.

"Yo," Depp said. "Not compromised. This be fac-il-ih–TAY-shun, yo. Crimea a victim, see, like they customers victims, of Piscova caviar. Ain't no reason we dis our Uke brothers."

Service understood. Someone had told Crimea they were victims in order to get the samples. "What time?" Service asked.

"High noon," Rogers said.

"Like the movie."

"Without hardware," Depp added.

The two men disappeared into the night, leaving Service alone. He grabbed a beer and some popcorn in the lobby bar, checked the menu, decided he wasn't hungry and needed sleep, and called it a night after a quick call to Karylanne.

He fell asleep with the regular sound of jets departing the city and arriving from all around the world.

The Crimea warehouse was between Brooklyn Heights and Williamsburg, a sooty low building in a block of warehouses with one major difference: It was the only one without graffiti on the walls. A tall man in a suit met them at the loading-dock entrance. Depp carried two large and garish red, white, and blue backpacks for the samples.

Rogers presented the warrants to their greeter, who read them slowly, word by word, page by page. He wore a suit, not new. His hair was neat, his face clean-shaven, his black leather shoes a little pointy, but freshly polished.

Warrants verified, the man led them inside and down a long green corridor to a room with metal shelves and a hundred forty-five-pound red, white, and blue buckets marked PISCOVA: CAVIAR ROUGE. Depp selected six buckets from various parts of the stash, pried off the lids, took six packages from each, placed the samples in the backpacks, and put the lids back on the buckets.

Their black-suited watcher was joined by four others, dressed identically, all of them looking like they were trapped between faintly devout and severely bored. They looked like clones or identical quintuplets.

"Crimea bosses?" Service asks.

"Their lawyers," Rogers said.

The visit lasted twenty minutes; ingress to egress seemed to be over before it could even get started. "You outta here today?" Rogers asked when they got outside.

"Tomorrow, noon."

"Grab a bite and a beer tonight?"

"Thanks, but no."

"Where's your partner?"

"Couldn't make it."

"You don' like New York?" Depp asked.

"No feelings one way or the other," Service said.

"I hate the fucking place," Rogers volunteered.

"His office in Syracuse," Depp said, grimacing. "Wouldn't recommend no tourist walking 'round here after dark, yo."

"I thought Giuliani cleaned up the city."

"Maybe tourist Manhattan; rest of the boroughs, not so much. He gone, got his eyes on the White House. We run that greasy fuck out and he moves up. Go figure. Nine-eleven bin bera-bera-good to Rudy-baby," Depp said.

"Samples to the FDA," Rogers said interrupting the rant. "Ten days to two weeks for results. We don't have priority on caviar. Not enough consumers."

"Even if they squirtin' mercury columns out their butts," Depp adds. "Fucking FDA."

Service made his way from the hotel to Sid's Fish House on Fulton Street. What attracted him was a sign that read OUR CUSTOMERS CAN *STILL* SMOKE IN OUR BAR! He ordered blackened sea bass and steamed veggies and ate alone. He smoked and tried to think about the case, but couldn't generate the necessary concentration. Things seemed to be closing in on him, an unspecified sea change under way, magnitude undetermined. He hoped Denninger was finding good stuff in Horn's files, still felt disconcerted by the silly firepower show of the Capitol cops. He had envisioned a bit more drama at Crimea, but it had been more like going to the Secretary of State's office to pick up extra blank forms. Shit was happening. No grand jury to look at his stuff, Black after his ass, Roxy dead, not a fucking inkling of anything positive in any of it. How the hell had Fagan built his empire?

A block from his hotel he encountered three men in black leather jackets. They spread out across the sidewalk, a human fence blocking his way. "Can you spare a dime?" one of the men asked.

"I doubt a dime would buy a single square of asswipe in this city, which means the real question's not *if* I can spare a dime, but if I *will*, and given the virtual worthlessness of a dime, I gotta ask, what the fuck for?"

"You got 'tude, man?"

"Depends on you Three Musketeers," Service said. "What you really want to know is how good I am, and more to the point, if I'm willing. You look like smart guys. Go ahead and figure it out."

"You Clint-Fucking-Eastwood," one of the men said.

"Clint reads lines somebody else writes," Service said. "I don't."

Seconds passed and the men gave way. "Where you from, man?"

"A place where we'd carve 'pussy' on your forehead and make you walk around with it the rest of your life as evidence of what you are."

Service walked on, waiting for a rear attack that never came, got to his room, and opened the door to find a man sitting at the table next to the window. The man was in a black suit and wore the whitest shirt he had ever seen, and a black yarmulke. He was smoking a small green-black cigarette. A razor-thin cell phone sat on the table.

"You've got fifteen seconds to tell me who you are and what you want," Service said. "I'm not even going to ask how you got in."

"I am Krapahkin," the man said. "I wanted to see face-to-face this man from the *taiga* who alone makes so many things happen."

Krapahkin, the big boss of Crimea. "Now that you've seen what you came to see, it's time for you to walk out."

The man raised an eyebrow. "Or?"

"There's no *or*. Just go."

"You are not intimidated."

"It's a genetic flaw."

Krapahkin smiled. "I share this flaw. Did you get your samples?"

"You know we did."

"Did you ever imagine one man's efforts could reach so far?"

"I never think in such terms," Service said.

"I think this way all the time—how I began with nothing, built it into something."

He wants something, Service thought.

Krapahkin held out his pack of cigarettes. Service took one, sat down across from him, and lit up.

"We have been told Piscova is your target," Krapahkin said. "But we are not so stupid, and in the end, the feds will come after my company. But my lawyers will drag it out and we will pay a token fine and continue to do business."

"That's between the feds, the state of New York, and you."

"To be sure," the man said. "I had no idea Quintan Fagan was mixing good eggs with bad."

"You didn't know and didn't care to know."

"Had I known, we would not be here now."

"You see yourself as a victim?"

"I came alone to this country at twelve, from the Ukraine through Israel. I stopped being a victim when I stepped off El Al."

"What is it you want from me?"

"A sentimental lapse," Krapahkin said. "There was a woman who worked for Piscova."

"Roxanne Lafleur?"

"*Da.*"

"She's dead."

Krapahkin's eyes flashed.

"Just yesterday," Service added. "Cancer."

"God kills all of us," Krapahkin said.

"God didn't kill Lafleur. Quintan Fagan did—with the same eggs you've been selling to cruise lines."

"It is said you are not a man who allows his focus to be diluted. Lafleur was *special* to you?"

"I barely knew her."

"Then this is not a simple matter of revenge."

"No."

The Ukrainian nodded. "A zealot's life is not a happy one. I will pay a fine. What price will you pay to get what it is that *you* want?"

"Whatever it takes," Service said.

Krapahkin mashed his cigarette, picked up his cell phone, and flipped it open. He dialed a number and said, "Five minutes," then closed it. "All these badges running around, swelling with testosterone," the head of Crimea said, "and it falls to one policeman from the *taiga* to undo so much. You and I, Detective, we are not so different."

Krapahkin left his cigarette pack on the table. Service put it with his own and called Karylanne to check on her. She was still tired, but still upbeat and she wanted to know when he could get over to Houghton again. "I'll be there when you need me," he told her. He was tired, and sick of everything to do with work.

Rogers was waiting for him in the lobby the next morning. "Got a ride for you," the New York ECO said. There was a cab outside, driven by the same psycho who had brought him from the airport the day before. Service found himself balking.

"It's cool," Rogers said. "Get in."

The driver looked back and grinned, "I dry, you rye, o-gay?"

Rogers looked amused. "Grady Service, meet Fish and Wildlife Special Agent John N'Dinga, son of a diplomat, MS in wildlife biology from Cornell, law degree from Colombia, the finest, sneakiest sonuvabitch undercover Fish and Wildlife ever had the good luck to hire."

Service nodded.

N'Dinga said, "Didn't mean to frighten you, mate, but gots to play the part, sayin'? I heard Krapahkin wanted to meet with you."

"He came to my room last night."

"Have anything interesting to say?" Rogers asked.

"Not really. He's convinced you guys and the feds will come after him, but his lawyers will make sure he'll skate with a fine."

"On this point, he may be right," N'Dinga said, "but he's got a dirty operation with beluga out of the Caspian area, and it won't be long before we bring him down. He'll do real time on that one. The thing you should know is that he looks and talks like a businessman, but he's *Organizatsiya*, hard-core Russian mob, very connected to the Lev Lazarus group out of Tel Aviv. L-Two plays dirty and rough. If they decide you're hurting business, you disappear."

"Is that a message for me?"

"Dose guy dey mi' lye meg you die mon," N'Dinga said.

"Theoretically?"

"Consider it real," Rogers said, "and let that thought have a prominent and permanent seat at your table of shit to be on the lookout for."

N'Dinga drove with the same recklessness back to the airport and even Rogers looked pale when they got out. "You're not going back with him?" Service asked.

"That motherfucker's certifiably insane," Rogers said with obvious admiration, tapping the roof of the taxi, which raced away.

The two men stepped over to a floor-to-ceiling window next to the entrance. Service groped for his smokes, but found the Ukrininan's pack and held it out to Rogers. They each took one and the pack was empty. Service started to crumple it, but saw some writing on the paper and stuffed the pack in his pocket. Rogers said, "When you get inside, go to the Lufthansa lounge."

"What for?

"Just go. You're expected."

It took some time to find the lounge. He went inside and announced his name to one of the blond, blue-uniformed women at the desk.

She said, "This way, please," and led him to a private room. There was a man sitting at a table pounding on a laptop. He had gelled hair, looked fortyish, was short with manicured nails, an expensive suit, and a thin gold wedding band. "Manny Florida," the man said, not bothering to get up. "You the woods cop?"

"Grady Service."

"Whatever. Piscova's *my* case. That pussy Endicott wouldn't know how to prosecute fucking Hitler. I heard he was making noises about my case, called him up, and injected him with a dose of reality. New York is a green state. The contaminated eggs are ours because the mirex comes from our waters, and the eggs came back here to Crimea. *Ours.* End of discussion. *Comprende?*"

"Without us, there would be no case."

"Big fucking deal. We'll make sure a bone gets thrown your way."

"A woman is dead," Service said.

"You have an MD? How about a PhD in toxicology? I didn't think so. The woman died. Maybe from the mirex, maybe not. Or maybe she had shitty genes, or her lifestyle sucked the big one. I don't know, and I don't care. This is my case and it's solid, and I'm not gonna complicate it with morality of dubious veracity."

"What about the IRS?"

"What *about* them? It's my case. They'll stick to my sheet music."

Manny Florida looked at the door. "Get the fuck out. I'm working."

Service felt like he'd gotten a chicken bone stuck in his throat as he went through Security and out to the gate. He pulled out Krapahkin's cigarette pack, smoothed it out, and saw what was written: "Costa Rica." What the fuck did that mean?

He had time before his flight and needed something to eat, so he went into a nook café and sat at a tiny counter. A waitress asked, "What is you wand?"

"Truth and justice," he said, "but I'll settle for a beignet."

The woman made a huffing sound. "*Beg*-ney—what that?"

"You have or no have?"

He felt like he was back in Vietnam, drowning in pidgin. "No got no *beg*-ney."

"Okay, how about a breakfast pasty."

"We got cheese Danish pastry," she said. "You want?"

"Just coffee. Who knew LaGuardia was an epicurean wasteland?"

"We *got* peppercorn," the server said, smiling.

Her rage and confusion had fled, replaced by resignation to deal with reality, weird as it was. "You pick for me," he said.

"You see, I pick good," the woman said.

His flight was called before the coffee came. He left a five-dollar bill and headed for the gate.

54

MONDAY, DECEMBER 6, 2004

Dayton International Airport, Dayton, Ohio

Service's flight stopped over in Dayton en route to Grand Rapids and his cell phone buzzed. "Where are you?" Gus Turnage asked.

"What's wrong?"

"I just put Karylanne in the hospital. Bad cramps and some bleeding. The doctor thinks the baby may be coming early."

"But she's okay, right?"

"They're pretty closemouthed. You need to get here as quick as you can."

"I'm in Dayton, headed for GR. I'll get there as fast as I can, Gus."

"Shark, Limey, and I are right here with her."

Service wanted to grab the pilot and tell him to leave late-boarding passengers, but forced himself to calm down. He called Anniejo Couch in Lansing. "I'm on a commercial flight in Dayton. I need to charter a plane from Grand Rapids to Houghton as fast as I can. Got any suggestions?"

"No-Hassle Charters," she said immediately. "This on the federal dime?"

"No."

She gave him an office number and he punched it in.

"NHC," a man answered.

"I need to charter a flight from Grand Rapids to Houghton."

"How many passengers?"

"Just me."

"One-way or round trip?"

He had no idea how long he would be there. "If I need to catch a plane back, can I get another one?"

"The price will be round-trip for that."

"Just book me one way," Service said.

"Purpose of flight?"

"To get there fast."

The man said, "Please hold for a minute." When he came back on the line, he said, "We've got a Cessna four-twenty-one available now. Flight time will be one forty-five at two hundred and thirty knots, wind permitting."

"I'll take it."

"When do you want it?"

"I'm in Dayton now, will be in GR in three hours or less. Will the bird hold for me?"

"You'll be the only passenger. Call from the terminal and we'll send a vehicle to bring you over to General Aviation. How will you pay for this?"

"Credit card work?"

"Which one?"

"American Express."

"That will work."

"How's the weather look?" Service asked.

"Manageable."

What the hell did that mean? Now he could stew over it until he got to Grand Rapids and could talk to the pilot. He had gotten so used to flying with Nantz, he wasn't sure he could adjust to a stranger, but there wasn't any other choice. It also occurred to him that had Nantz not left him her money, he couldn't afford to do this, and maybe this was all meant to happen—a thought he quickly banished from his mind. He did not believe in fate.

55

TUESDAY, DECEMBER 7, 2004

Houghton, Houghton County

There was a storm along the entire north-south coast of Lake Michigan, and another near Houghton coming in off Lake Superior; the chartered flight could not land until after midnight. Gus Turnage was waiting for Service at the Houghton County Memorial Airport, which was actually in Hancock. They ran out to Gus's truck and headed for the hospital, on the same street as the ice rink at Michigan Tech. Gus drove with a set jaw and said nothing during the drive.

They got to the Family Birthing Center and went through the blond double doors to find Limey Pyykkonen and Shark Wetelainen standing outside one of the birthing rooms.

"Dr. Priva will be here in a minute," Limey said.

"Is she okay?" Service demanded.

"Calm down," Pyykkonen said. "You getting all jacked up isn't going to help anyone."

Service felt his heart sink. *What the fuck was wrong?*

The doctor arrived in a smock decorated with clowns, a pale blue mask over his nose. Service thought he looked like a deer that couldn't catch its breath.

"You the father?" the doctor asked, tugging his mask down to his neck.

"Grandfather. The father's deceased."

"I'm sorry," the doctor said. "Karylanne is doing fine in post-op, and your granddaughter is strong. She just decided to come a little early."

"Premature?"

"Early, not premature. Technically she's considered full-term."

"Post-op?" *Granddaughter?* His mind was not connecting things.

"Karylanne had a hemorrhage and we had to do a C-section. They'll both be fine, but there may be a problem with Karylanne having another child. Testing will tell us more over time."

Service looked at his friends, saw them watching for his reaction, willed himself to calm down. "Can I see Karylanne?"

"Give her a half-hour . . . but you can see your granddaughter."

They went into the nursery. The baby was in a glass container that looked like an aquarium. She wore a pink hat. A card said BABY PENGELLY.

"A little small, five pounds eight, but that's not a problem," the doctor said.

She was red and shriveled and had a head full of black hair that looked like Cat's when he had rescued the kitten from Slippery Creek many years before. "She's beautiful," the doctor said.

Was the man blind? The baby looked more like a rat dipped in Mercurochrome than a human.

Service went outside to smoke a cigarette until he could see Karylanne. Gus and Shark went with him. "She is *so* ugly," Service said.

"They all are," Gus said. "Every one of mine looked like a waterlogged possum. You'll get used to it."

"They talk to you about Karylanne?"

"Privacy laws wouldn't allow it. You're the only one on her form. The doctor said it was an emergency is all."

Shark said, "The kid's got great hands. She'll be able to tie great flies."

"She's shorter than a big brown," Service said.

"She'll grow soon enough," Gus said.

Service felt a combination of shock and relief and was trying to sort it all out when he finally got in to see Karylanne, who was in a bed with oxygen tubes clipped to her nose, an IV in her wrist. He put his hand on her arm and her eyes half-opened. "I made a mess of it," she said.

"There's no mess," Service said. "Everything's fine. The baby is beautiful."

"You really think so?"

"Not really," he said, and she managed a half chuckle. "No bullshit; that was our deal. But she'll be beautiful if she grows up to look like her mother or her father."

"Listen to you," Karylanne said. "Such sensitivity. I promise not to tell."

She went to sleep without saying any more. She slept with a smile on her face and Service found himself grinning. He went back to look at the baby.

"She tell you the name?" Limey asked.

"Baby Pengelly."

"Doofus," Pyykkonen said. "It's going to be Maridly, if you agree."

The tears came out before he could stop them, and his friends stood next to him, patting his arms, and the baby started screaming and turned bright red.

"She's hungry," Pyykkonen said.

"Maridly fits," Service said, suddenly sobbing, trying unsuccessfully to emotionally balance the staggering gains and losses of his life.

"The first motherfucker that tries to date her better have *sisu*," Shark said seriously.

"*Yalmer*, your language," Limey said.

"Well, it's true, and it ain't a *dirty* four-letter word."

Sisu was a Finnish term that translated roughly to willpower, a resolute will to see things through to the finish.

"*Sisu*," Service said out loud. He could use a healthy dose of it as well.

56

WEDNESDAY, DECEMBER 8, 2004

Houghton, Houghton County

Denninger called before 6 A.M. Service was stretched out on a couch in Gus Turnage's den and fumbled with his cell phone. "What?"

"Where are you?"

"Houghton. My . . ." He couldn't think of the right term, and said, "My daughter-in-law had some problems having her baby."

Long pause on the phone. "You're a grandfather?"

"Scary, huh?"

Denninger laughed. "I don't know who to be most sorry for—you or the kid."

"I'll be here for a few days," he said, "to make sure everything's all right. You okay?"

"I'm back at the resort. Back home I had a call from Captain Black who wanted to know if you and I have been sleeping together."

Asshole, Service thought. "What did you tell him?"

"I told him first, we report to the U.S. Attorney's office, and second, and more important, it's none of his damn business who I sleep with."

"He probably didn't like that."

"He called me a cunt."

Service sat up. "He *what*?"

"Called me a cheap, spoiled cunt and said my career's going into the crapper with yours."

"You're sure he said that?"

"You want to hear? Since I started with you, I automatically record everything."

She turned on the recorder and Service listened to what Black had said.

"What should I do?" she asked.

"Put that tape in a safe place and don't worry about it."

"I'm afraid," she said.

"Don't be." Black had gone over the line this time. "Have you seen Leukonovich?"

"She had to go to Detroit. Supposed to be back tomorrow. You want her number?"

"You have her itinerary *and* her phone number?"

"She gave it to me. For a long time I was your 'girl'—now she's making nice. I don't get it."

"Don't try," Service said, writing down the number. Leukonovich was inscrutable.

"Girl or boy?" Denninger asked.

"Girl. Her name's Maridly."

"That is *so* cool!" Denninger said, her voice breaking.

Service made coffee and found a note from Gus, who was on patrol in the Lake Linden area east of Hancock. He poured a cup and punched in Leukonovich's number.

She answered on the second ring and sounded half-asleep. "Yes?"

"It's Grady. Someone gave me information that I think is supposed to link to Fagan. Costa Rica. Does that ring any bells?"

"Zhenya call you back when her mind is clearer," she said, hanging up.

An hour later they were on the phone again and he told her about the meeting with Krapahkin and the cigarette pack with "Costa Rica" written on it, and she said nothing until he had finished.

"Krapahkin's morality aside, he is a man to be admired for his organizational skills. His seeking you out is significant, as is the questioning about the dead woman. I believe he is telling you something to make amends for the woman's death," said Leukonovich.

"But what?"

"Zhenya will find out," the woman said. "Perhaps Fagan has hidden accounts there. Whatever it is, I will find it. Where are you?"

He told her about the baby, the crazed race to get back, everything.

She said, "I offer my congratulations and thank fate for making Zhenya incapable of procreating. She thinks there is too much emotion over such a pedestrian thing."

"If it was your granddaughter you'd be feeling differently," he said.

"Zhenya will not argue with you, and she will be in touch."

The next call went to Chief O'Driscoll, and when he finished telling Denninger's story the chief asked, "She has this on tape?"

"Yessir. I heard it."

"Black was pushing the audit of your affairs and I told him to stop. He was not happy. I think this was his attempt to press his career forward in another way."

"It's a shitty thing, Chief."

"It's my responsibility to take care of it."

"Denninger and I have not slept together," Service said.

"I didn't ask if you had. What happened in New York?"

Service told him, and O'Driscoll said, "You should heed the warning."

"Krapahkin doesn't want a piece of me, Captain. He met with me to help me get Fagan."

"The Ukrainians are known as much for their duplicity as for their brutality."

"I can't worry about that now, Captain."

"Langford Horn has announced that he's leaving state government to take a position with Bozian in New York."

"When?"

"Today. It's not public yet, but I expect it might make the late news cycle."

"Any reason given?"

"He finds it—and I quote from his letter—'uncomfortable to work in a disorganized, fiscally incompetent, liberal democratic administration that puts ideology ahead of its citizens.' End quote."

"What about the audit of WRPU undercover programs?"

"Up to his successor, I would think."

"Endicott's not going to take any of this to the grand jury here, but the New York U.S. Attorney in Syracuse is chomping at the bit to push it."

"You have a problem with this?"

"It's *our* case, Chief."

"Try thinking in terms of justice being done, not the hand administering it."

"What about our rats?"

"I think your threats have driven them out."

"Meaning they get to retire with their reputations intact?"

"Few solutions are perfect," O'Driscoll said.

57

SUNDAY, DECEMBER 12, 2004

Saranac, Ionia County

Service had been back at the resort for less than six hours. He had made a stopover to see McCants, who was elated about the baby and not so elated about seeing him. Newf and Cat seemed to side with her.

Leukonovich was with him when Beaker Salant called.

"I talked to Teeny in Key West. He says he's going to sue for defamation of character."

"You can't sue for what you never had."

"What do you think about Langford Horn?"

"Good riddance."

"I mean the reason why."

"No idea."

"How about one of his direct reports refused to do an audit he ordered and announced she was going to the governor to recommend Horn's records be audited? You getting close to filing charges?"

"More or less." Who's the direct report, he wondered. He did not mention the Friday-night incursion into Horn's office and had the feeling that when Horn found out his files had been copied, it would push him out.

"I get the exclusive, on the record."

"That's what I promised," Service said, knowing that the story would be out of his hands and in Syracuse or Albany, not Grand Rapids.

"I hear there's been some resignations from the DNR."

"A certain amount of turnover is fairly normal."

"You make it hard to work with you," Salant said.

Leukonovich sat quietly at the table, and after he'd hung up, said, "I am hearing a state representative sold a house in Costa Rica to Fagan."

"Confirmed?"

"I have an appointment today. Your company would be welcome."

"On a Sunday?"

"It is informal—what I am calling a pre-audit meeting."

"Is there such a thing?"

"For today at least."

Denninger came downstairs. "Keep working the list," Service said.

"A lot of people still left."

"Just stay with it."

"Who are we seeing?" Service asked when they started east on I-96.

"L. Bradley Angledenny."

"You told him what this is about?"

She tilted her head. "More or less."

"Does he have a past with the IRS?"

Leukonovich answered with a smile.

They met Angledenny at Bravura, a steak house on Washington Avenue, not far from the state office complex. He had arrived ahead of them and was perspiring heavily. Leukonovich took her time setting up her laptop, letting the anticipation build.

"I prefer not to waste your time, or mine," she began. "If you will agree to plead guilty, I will see what I can do for you."

Angledenny almost clutched at his heart. "Plead *guilty!* What the hell are you talking about?"

"Is old IRS joke,"she said, "no doubt in questionable taste. The special agent apologizes."

Angledenny tried to smile but failed.

"There is a certain condominium in Costa Rica."

"I sold it this year and took a small profit, maybe twenty-five K."

"Sale price one-million, one twenty-five," she said.

"Yes."

"Purchased by whom, and at what price?" She let the question hang.

"One-point-one. Why are we talking about this? I haven't even filed the return yet. It's not due for five months."

She ignored his question. "Sold it to whom?"

"A broker."

"Brokers acquire real estate?"

"They invest like the rest of us, do a little speculation. Costa Rica's been pretty hot."

"Yet you took a very small profit."

"A cash-flow issue for me. I couldn't wait, and I don't mind paying the taxes."

"This broker's name."

"I'd have to look that up."

"Please," she said, crossing her hands in her lap.

"I'll have to call my accountant," Angledenny said.

"Thank you," she said.

The man stared at her and fled the room.

"What's going on?" Service asked.

"Fagan is the broker-buyer."

"That's legal?"

"Costa Rica says the paperwork for his broker's license is in progress and therefore active. The Costa Ricans don't willingly cooperate with U.S. authorities, except under special circumstances. I would guess that Fagan fronted the money for Angledenny, and now he is buying it back. Angledenny will make twenty-five thousand for doing nothing, and the condo will now belong to the brokerage. It will be very difficult to detect Fagan's name."

"You detected it."

"I have gone as far as I can."

"Fagan greased palms there?"

"It's an old and revered Latin custom."

Angledenny came back fifteen minutes later and handed Leukonovich a slip of paper.

She read it silently, then out loud. "*Refugio Seguro.*"

"That's it," the representative said.

"May I ask how you came to know this broker, *Refugio Seguro?*"

"Through a friend."

"His name?"

"Langford Horn."

"This Mr. Horn has had dealings with this broker?"

"I don't know. Said he'd heard good things about the company."

"Of course you checked into it?"

"Called them; we talked."

"When did you see the property?"

"Digital photos."

"You did not visit?" she asked, raising an eyebrow to make her point.

"No need. it was a spec investment. The photos were good enough for me."

"Your purchase was when?"

"January this year."

"And the sale?

"Late October."

"You held it less than a year?"

"Like I said, I had a cash-flow problem, and this was entirely legal."

"Are there tax advantages in Costa Rica?"

"I don't know the details. My financial advisor told me it was a good deal." Angledenny suddenly stiffened. "A pre-audit?"

"Yes."

"To hell with you. I haven't even filed my return. It's not even due for five months. You want to audit, wait until it's filed."

"You force me to report an uncooperative attitude."

"Call it what you want—we're done here."

The representative left without paying his part of the bill and Leukonovich said, "I am sure the link to Fagan is Horn, but I will investigate further. There is, however, another connection I'm sure you recognize."

He didn't, and shook his head.

"Representative Angledenny's father wrote the bill that outlawed the practice of snagging in the state."

"Which gave the legal egg harvest market to Fagan," Service said.

"Zhenya would call it a monopoly. The records show that even in unusual years when Piscova did not get the contract, Fagan was the majority shareholder in the companies that did."

"Belated payback," Service said.

"Perhaps. I will eventually know."

"But nothing for us to act on now."

"Do you speak Spanish?"

"No."

"*Refugio Seguro* means 'safe haven.' "

"But Fagan already has all sorts of real estate holdings."

"Perhaps he needs a particular domicile in a particular location for a specific reason—perhaps in a location that does not extradite."

Service rolled his eyes. "His own rat line. The sonuvabitch smells what's coming down."

"Media coverage has made that abundantly clear," she said.

Grady Service had no comeback. Had he shot himself in the foot?

Houghton, Houghton County

Charles Marschke was wearing a flame-orange parka that reached below his knees and boots that made him look like he was headed to the Iditarod. Since Nantz's death, her personal financial advisor/manager had assumed the same role for him. Over the past couple of weeks they had spoken several times, culminating in this morning's meeting. It was Marschke who had chosen the bank, one of the smallest in the U.P., to handle matters.

The meeting was at the Iron Range Bank & Trust Company on East Montezuma Avenue. Present were Arlo Maki, Iron Range president, trust officer, and general counsel; Marschke; Karylanne; Service; and an unidentified woman.

Service had told Karylanne nothing in advance other than he wanted her to go to a meeting with him. She was well on the road to recovery, and Little M (as the baby was now being called) was healthy, alert, and happy, as long as she was fed regularly on *her* schedule.

Karylanne had missed finals and arranged to take them late, in January. She would not return to school until the next fall, which would give her nine months with the baby before diving back into the academic grind.

Maki, the bank's virtual one-man band, had a sheaf of papers on the table. Service helped Karylanne sit down and Marschke got the meeting started. "Grady wants to provide for you and your daughter. The papers here this morning create a trust for which you will serve as executor until your daughter's eighteenth birthday. You will receive an annual salary as executor. In the event of Grady's death, you and your daughter will inherit his assets equally. Questions?"

Karylanne looked stunned, unable to speak.

Marschke said, "Good. Let's get started signing the paperwork so we can get everyone home for Christmas Eve. I will serve as your financial advisor and manager. Mr. Maki here is the bank's trust officer, and will actively manage both the trust and your investment portfolio."

Maki began pushing papers at her and Karylanne began signing. Maki took the signed pages, peeled off copies, and put them in a folder. When the stack was signed, the woman stepped to the table.

"What's this?" Karylanne asked.

"Just sign," Service said.

Karylanne looked at the paperwork. "This is a deed."

"Sign," Service said, and she did as she was told.

Meeting concluded, the participants split up. Service drove Karylanne to a neighborhood west of downtown and pulled into a subdivision of new homes. He pulled into a driveway, got out, went to the front door, and opened it. Karylanne stepped inside. "This is your new home," Service said. "Three bedrooms, well built but not fancy." He handed her the keys. "It's paid for. If you decide you and Little M want something different down the road, it's your decision."

She turned and looked at him, tears in her eyes, shaking her head. "I don't . . ."

"You won't have to worry about money for the rest of your life, which means you can go after whatever you want."

"I haven't earned anything," she said.

"It's not about earning. It's about family," he said.

They celebrated Christmas Eve at Gus Turnage's house, along with his three sons, two of them with their wives, Marschke, Shark, and Limey. There were people sleeping all over the house.

On Christmas morning Shark was already sitting by the tree, anxious to start opening presents. Limey said, "The big red one's for you," but Shark shook his head and picked up a package and held it out to the baby. "This is yours, kid."

Karylanne said, "She can't open a present, Yalmer."

He looked puzzled, mouthed, "Oh, yeah," and ripped the wrapping away. He opened a box, took out a double-barreled shotgun, snapped together the pieces, and held it out to the baby, who stared up at him and the weapon.

"*Yalmer*," Limey Pyykkonen said. "You got a shotgun for a newborn?"

"Not *just* a shotgun. It's a Beretta S687, twenty-six-inch barrel, four-ten gauge. We'll get her started on it."

"The barrel's longer than she is," Limey said.

"She'll grow into it. I got it off eBay. It's a work of art!"

Service said, "The baby is two weeks old."

"Hey, youse gotta get 'em started early, eh."

Limey shook her head, tacit admission that she knew she would never be able to change the strange ways of her husband.

Service saw that his friend was as proud as he had ever been and he knew that whatever happened to him, his granddaughter would have a support system second to none, and the knowledge warmed him.

Later in the day he called Roy Rogers in New York.

"I'm on a little Christmas break, but we'll have the reports all done and in your hands two days after the New Year."

"Based on the samples I've already seen, we should have everything ready for indictments by early February."

"Trial?"

"Florida's pushing hard for April, but it could be May, and if Fagan's attorneys get cute, they could push it into summer."

"You want Denninger and me out there?"

"That's the U.S. Attorney's call, but one thing's for sure, and this is my call alone: When the time comes to arrest that sonuvabitch, I'm going to fly out there and watch you do the honors."

"*That* will be a pleasure."

59

MONDAY, DECEMBER 27, 2004

Alba, Antrim County

They had started compiling the criminal case report, double-checking transcripts against tapes, detailing charges against Vandeal and Fagan. The package was nearly two feet tall, and by the end of the week would go by overnight messenger to the the Northern District of New York's Syracuse office. Leukonovich was working alongside them and assembling her own case report and evidence.

Despite the deadline, Service continued to fret. They had a list of two dozen former employees, half of whose phone numbers and whereabouts were no longer known; they could still talk to the other dozen, however, and Service didn't want to close the report until they had done so. The Syracuse U.S. Attorney wanted the criminal report but Service felt like they needed more. Denninger tried to argue with him and Leukonovich just smiled. He left the women in Saranac and headed north.

Max and Travis Seti were on the list, with separate addresses in Antrim County. Service called Max, identified himself only as an investigator for the U.S. Attorney out of Grand Rapids, and said he wanted to talk to the man about Piscova. The man said, "No," and hung up. He called Travis next, and opened the same way, but Travis vacillated and hestitated. "You related to Max?"

"My older brother."

"Max says he's willing to talk."

Travis agreed reluctantly. Service then called Max back and told him he was going to talk to Travis and if necessary would get a subpoena to talk to him as well. Max then agreed.

The meeting was at Galwa's Tavern in Alba. Max and Travis looked to be in their forties, and like they had never seen the break-even side of life. They were short and sturdy, with stringy gray hair and sparse gray whiskers, silver earrings, and noses that suggested they'd been flattened by too many fists. He let them order coffee and got right to the point.

"You both worked at Piscova."

Nods, no words. This was going to be like pulling teeth. "Doing what?"

Shrugs, still no words.

"Okay, boys; it's your turn to talk, and here's how it works: I ask a question, you answer. If not, we'll head for the Troop post in Mancelona and do this formally. I don't know that either of you have done anything wrong. You worked in processing at Piscova. Processing what?"

"Fish eggs," Max said.

Travis nodded.

"What kind of eggs?"

"Salmon," Max said.

"Kings," Travis added.

"For what?" Service asked.

"Piscova," Max said.

"The company," Travis said.

The brothers were uptight. "Eggs for customers?" Service asked.

"Yeah," Max said.

"Customers," Travis echoed.

"What customers?"

"They didn't tell us that stuff," Max said.

"Salmon eggs," Travis said, catching a glare from his brother.

"Describe your jobs—what you did in the process," Service said.

"Just the regular stuff," Max said.

"Salt vats, drying racks?" Service asked, trying to lead them into specifics.

Max gave no indication of hearing the question. Travis nodded almost imperceptibly and Service locked eyes with him. "You were making caviar."

Silence. "Who was the customer, Travis?"

"Criminy," Travis said.

"Criminy?"

"Da Bright Brigade guys."

"It's the *Light* Brigade, you moron," Max said.

"Yeah, Light Brigade; I get them two confused."

Service said, "You mean Crimea?"

Travis nodded. "Right, Criminy."

"You made salmon caviar, which Piscova sold to Crimea."

"Yeah," Max said.

"Criminy," Travis repeated, old habits dying hard.

"All Michigan eggs?"

The brothers looked at each other. "No," Max said.

"Other sources were involved?" Service asked.

"New York," Max said.

"Why were they mixed?" Service asked.

Max said, "Taste."

"Did you taste the mix?"

The brothers made faces, shook their heads. "Looked too gritty," Max said.

"Like the bottom of a fish tank ain't been cleaned," Travis offered.

"You see containers from New York?"

Nods in unison.

"The ones saying 'Bait Only'?"

More nods. "You never asked why Michigan eggs were being mixed with bait eggs?"

"Fuckin' A, we asked," Max said sharply.

Sore point. "What did they tell you?"

"Taste," Max said.

Travis agreed.

"How many years did you make caviar?"

"Three seasons," Max said.

"Why'd you leave the jobs?"

"Heard things," Max said.

"Such as?"

"Like it wasn't too cool to mix the eggs."

"Who said this?"

"Rex Towne, Calvin Lumette."

Both were names on his list. "Processors with you guys?"

"Yeah," Max said, "till they was fired."

"Did you two get fired?"

"We quit. Had enough of Vandeal and his holier-than-thou bullshit," Max said.

"Asshole," Travis chimed in.

"Know anybody still there?"

"No," Max said. "We in trouble?"

"Piscova's got trouble."

"You gonna get Vandeal?" Travis asked.

"Hope to, and Fagan."

"The asshole and the prick," Max said, nodding his approval.

"You have words with Vandeal when you quit?"

"Just left," Max said.

"Got our paychecks and out the door," Travis said.

"We gonna get dragged into their shit?" Max asked.

"I don't think so, but I'd like to get statements from both of you—what you did, with whom, where—all the details."

The men agreed, took nearly an hour to handwrite their statements. Both men knew the egg mixing was illegal, but had done it for three years. When it started to be clear that it might not be safe, they quit. Their statements provided more names for follow-up; Service wondered if there was any way to get to the others.

When he got back to Saranac, Denninger was typing up a report on her phone interview with Mary Quet, a caviar processor who had worked for Piscova for seven years. Denninger said, "She claims the FDA tested the eggs and ruled them safe."

Service stared at his partner. "*Really?*"

"Claims she saw the FDA inspector, a woman."

If there was only more time, he thought. "At least she confirms mixing. That helps."

"Fagan fired her."

"Not Vandeal?"

"Fagan. She's good-looking, built. Met Fagan in a bar, he macked on her, she fell for it, and did the nasty with him. He gave her a job, would drop by from time to time to tell her he needed to talk privately, take her into an office, unzip Big John, tell her Big John was her pipeline to promotion and raises. One day he gives her the same old line and she tells him Big John is more like Little Jack, and she wants a raise or no more pipeline maintenance. He said okay, she took care of him, and the next night she showed for work and Vandeal told her she was being laid off because demand was down, but they would call her back when the business turned around."

"Let me guess," Service said. "It never got better."

"You must be a detective."

Service asked, "When was this FDA meeting?"

"Ninety-six, ninety-seven, she thinks."

"When was she laid off?"

"Oh-one."

"She thought the eggs were safe?"

"She had some doubts because she saw the New York containers, but Vandeal and Fagan both said the mixing was for taste, and the FDA inspector seemed to agree with the company."

"We have to talk to the FDA."

"You want me to bird-dog that?"

"No, I'll go after it. Add Rex Towne and Calvin Lumette to your interview list and get them on paper. I talked to the Seti brothers today, and they say Towne and Lumette got fired because they were questioning safety. I'll type my transcripts tonight and you can have them to help you. Let's try to keep all this shit organized, one folder per individual, each folder containing lead source, tape, transcript, and written statement. We can fold what we need into the main report electronically."

"We're running out of time and using a lot of paper."

"It's too late for the trees," Service said.

He called Roy Rogers in New York. "We have the statement of a former Piscova employee who claims FDA inspected Piscova's plant in ninety-six or -seven and ruled the mixing safe and legal."

"Not possible!" Rogers said.

"Some way to check it out?"

"I know someone in the Syracuse FDA office. Maybe they can point us. We don't have much time."

"Make time," Service said. "This could be important."

"It has no bearing on the case," Rogers said.

"You don't know that yet."

60

TUESDAY, DECEMBER 28, 2004

Lansing, Ingham County

The report package had not yet gone to Syracuse and Service and Denninger had spent the previous night and all morning trying to pull it together when the call came for them to report to Chief O'Driscoll's fifth-floor office in the Mason Building.

"Your part of the case is finished," the chief said. "Effective January fourth, you're both transferred back to the DNR. Officer Denninger, I've already talked to your sergeant and lieutenant. You'll have a couple of pass days and go back to duty next Friday. Call your area supervisor to discuss details." The chief looked at Denninger and said, "Can you give Detective Service and me a moment alone?"

Denninger left.

Service had a bad feeling in his gut. O'Driscoll said, "Clay Flinders is threatening to retire and he's saying it's your fault, that he's being railroaded. He swears he's done nothing wrong."

"What am I supposed to do about it?"

"Go talk to him, hear him out. He's in his office."

Service found the Fisheries chief looking like someone had knee-capped him. Flinders said nothing when Service walked in and sat down. "I heard from Lorne you're thinking about retiring."

Flinders shrugged. "Time for me to go. I never wanted this job."

"You haven't been at it very long."

"Long enough to get my butt caught in a backfire."

"Look, for what it's worth, we don't see you as part of this case, except that some of the people involved report up to you. I'm sorry about showing up at the meeting at the Anderson Building."

"I think we both lost it a little up there," Flinders said. "If I stay with the job, they'll get me anyway."

"Who's *they*?"

"Certain Natural Resource Commission members appointed by Bozian, the new director, whoever. I was chosen for the job by Teeny. That automatically makes me shit, and Piscova just adds to my problem, even if I just caught the tail end of it on my shift."

Flinders had assessed the situation fairly realistically, and Service couldn't find anything to say that might appease the man. Flinders understood the politics a lot better than he did. "I just wanted you to know," Service said, ending the meeting.

"Appreciated," Flinders said with a tone Service couldn't decipher.

61

WEDNESDAY, DECEMBER 29, 2004

Ann Arbor, Washtenaw County

Rogers had called at 5 A.M. "I think this is a blind alley, but an FDA inspector named Arlette Arwaddy inspected Piscova's Elk Rapids facility on May ninth, 1997. She never filed a report and resigned in June from the agency. She's part of Pfizer's FDA Liaison operation in Ann Arbor now, been there since July 1997."

"Why'd she quit?"

"Not known."

"Performance problems?"

"Not clear. My contact in Syracuse says we could subpoena personnel records from the Chicago regional office, but we don't have time, and what's the point?"

"If she ruled the eggs safe and legal, and there's a report to that effect in Piscova's files, it could be a major problem for the case. If she didn't, it helps us. Something stinks on this one."

"You think I should fight for more time to file reports?"

"Probably wouldn't hurt."

"How long?"

"Extra week or two?"

"I'll try, but no promises."

"I'll try to meet her as soon as I can."

Which turned out to be that afternoon. The pharmaceutical giant's global research was based in Ann Arbor on a grassy, landscaped campus at the corner of Plymouth Road and Huron Parkway, the company's property abutting University of Michigan land. The building where Service was to meet Arlette Arwaddy was a stone facade and glass monstrosity that looked like a parking ramp

Arwaddy met him in the lobby, a tropical atrium minus birds and animal life. She was tall, well groomed, and carried herself with a straight back, chin tilted upward.

He introduced himself as working for the U.S. Attorney out of Grand Rapids, made a production of setting his recorder on the table in front of them and clicking it on. "I don't want to waste your time. Thanks for seeing me on such short notice, Ms. Arwaddy."

"It's *Dr.* Arwaddy," she countered, correcting him and declaring formality for the conversation.

"You did a plant inspection at Piscova's Elk Rapids plant on May ninth, in ninety-seven," he opened.

"I was with the agency for ten years. I did innumerable inspections."

"You never filed a report, Doctor."

"I'm certain I did," she said after a pause. "I scrupulously filed reports in a timely manner."

"It's not in the FDA's files. How do you explain that?"

"The agency's incompetence in such administrative matters is not without substance or precedent."

"Odd that the report's not in their files. Do you remember the inspection?"

"As I said, there were so many."

He let a little silence set in and said, "The company insists you ruled that mixing mirex-contaminated salmon eggs with Michigan eggs was safe and legal." This was like fishing. Throw out the fly, let it sit, twitch it slightly. "Is that right?"

The woman seemed to swell. "I made *no* such finding," she said through clenched teeth.

Hook-set time. "I thought you didn't remember the inspection."

"I remember it," she admitted. "I found the eggs being mixed and knew the New York eggs were contaminated. I recommended that the agency charge the company with adulterating a product intended for human consumption."

Hook set, it was time to smack it hard and set it deep. "They're still mixing eggs," Service said, "which makes it hard to believe you recommended they stop."

"I resigned to express my displeasure," she said.

"Because the agency didn't take action?"

"There was no DNA footprint for mirex then. I made my recommendation because I found New York containers and was told by employees they were mixing eggs. My supervision reprimanded me for inadequate and improper analysis lacking the requisite supporting scientific data. This was not my first clash with supervision, and I had had enough."

"Do you have a copy of your report?"

"I think I should consult my attorney."

Service clicked off his recorder. "Send it to me overnight; otherwise, there will be a subpoena from the grand jury. I'm after Piscova, not you."

The woman's face was suddenly splotched. "If this becomes public, my position here will be compromised."

"Why? According to you, you did the right thing."

"I *did* do the right thing," she insisted.

"Shouldn't be a problem then."

"You don't understand the complexity and nuances of liaising with a federal bureaucracy."

"I know this: go along to get along. Did your report go to the DNR?"

"Not from me. Procedure required that it come from another department at FDA. I don't know if it was sent or not."

"What happens if a report isn't accepted? They just throw it away?"

"No; it goes into a permanent historical file on the company."

"Meaning it should be there, even if they took no action."

"Correct," she said.

Service wondered if Fagan's tentacles were embedded in the FDA as well as the DNR, and the thought made him cringe at how far Fagan's activities might reach. If only he would be allowed sufficient time to flesh it all out and expose everything, piece by piece.

He handed her his card. "Overnight mail."

He sat in his truck for a long time, thinking. He'd been focused on the DNR, but this new evidence seemed to point to the Food and Drug Administration. Maybe Arwaddy's report did not go to DNR, but to the state agency responsible for food, the Michigan Department of Agriculture. Unable to think of anyone else to talk to, Service called acting director Cecil Hopkins in Lansing.

"Sorry to bother you," Service said when he finally got through.

"Lorne says you're wrapping up the case," Hopkins said.

"Yessir, we're just trying to nail down some details. I've learned that an FDA inspector recommended closing down Piscova's caviar line in 1997 because she learned of the egg mixing. She filed a report, but no action was taken by the FDA. Would we have gotten the report?"

Hopkins paused. "She's required to file her reports jointly with her own agency and the Michigan Department of Agriculture. Our getting a copy would depend on who in the MDA got the report, and what they decided to do with it."

"How do I find that individual?"

"Why do you need to do that?"

"For the case."

"Do you have the FDA report in question?"

"A copy's being sent to me."

"Reference it in your narrative and append it to the report. Use it as a footnote to make your point. If you're thinking there's hanky-panky at the FDA and the MDA, let that be investigated downstream as a separate investigation—otherwise, you'll never finish what you've started."

"This is like drinking from a spittoon," Service said, and Cecil Hopkins laughed.

"I imagine it is," he said, still chuckling. "Just make sure you get a copy and put it in the report. Anything else?"

"Nossir."

"I wouldn't like to see this leaked to the media," Hopkins said.

"Me either," Service said.

"There's been enough turmoil, Detective. Let's get this case into the courts and let the process work."

"Yessir," Service said. He was tempted to call Beaker Salant, but restrained himself. The DNR was already roiling at a slow boil. The governor didn't need a riled-up Ag Department as well. Hopkins was right. It was time to put this thing to bed and be done with it.

62

THURSDAY, DECEMBER 30, 2004

Saranac, Ionia County

They had spent all day yesterday putting together the report, and Denninger was now hard at work on an inventory of supplies and equipment to be submitted to Anniejo Couch once the investigation was formally concluded. Leukonovich was still with them, working on her part of the case.

Karylanne called around lunchtime. She was back to her bubbly self, filling his ear with baby trivia, including the nitty-gritty of breast pumps and nursing, details he had no desire to hear. Nevertheless, he tried to listen with one ear while his mind kept sweeping the case, looking for holes and weaknesses. The FDA report from Arwaddy had arrived by messenger that morning, and was just as she had claimed. She had recommended shutting down Piscova, and her report referenced similar problems for the company's operations in Wisconsin, New York, and California. He had nearly fallen off his chair as he read Arwaddy's words. Having this document at the start of the investigation would have let them cast their net a hell of a lot more widely. It felt like the case as it was would hit only the tip of the iceberg, and the realization made him angry.

"Say hi to your Bampy," Karylanne said, jarring him back to the phone call.

"Bampy?"

"It's an old East Coast Canadian term of endearment for grandpas," she said.

"Leave that shit on their side of the border," he growled.

"What *do* you want your granddaughter to call you?"

"Grady," he said.

Silence. "That's not very grandfatherly."

"Exactly."

"We'll let her decide," Karylanne said, trying to get in the last word.

"Just as long as it's not Bampy."

He was smoking on the balcony, getting more and more worked up over additional crap that apparently had gone on for a long time under Bozian, when he heard a crash inside. He turned to see Denninger falling backwards and someone on top of her, flailing away. He fumbled to open the sliding-glass door just as Denninger brought a knee sharply upward between the attacker's legs, the blow resounding like a bocci ball dropped on a tile floor. Denninger rolled out from under the man, popped to her feet, blood pouring from her nose, legs apart, knees bent, hands up, ready to fight, but Zhenya Leukonovich walked calmly over to the man, leaned down, and took hold of his neck with some sort of pinch-hold. The man let loose a short, intense shriek and blacked out, his head thumping the bare floor.

Service saw that it was Captain "Fast Track" Black, went over to him, pulled his hands behind him, and cuffed him. Leukonovich looked down at Black, shrugged, and sat down to continue her work. Denninger was panting with adrenaline, blood all over her chin and shirt.

"What the hell happened?" Service asked.

"He came through the door, called me 'cunt,' and knocked me off my chair."

Leukonovich looked up, said, "He will begin to recover in less than one minute," and went back to typing on her computer.

Black's first mumbled words: "I'm so sorry."

"I would be too," Service said, "if a couple of girls kicked my ass." He looked at Denninger. "Dani, you want me to call the county deps?"

She was sitting with her head down, trying to stanch the nosebleed. "Just get him out of here."

"Charges should be pursued," Leukonovich said. "Such behavior is no doubt part of a long-term behavioral pattern. Without punishment this creature will continue to mistreat women."

"Just get him out of here," Denninger repeated.

Service helped Black out to his car, put him inside, buckled his seat belt, and leaned down close. "You're retiring. Be satisfied with that. For my part, I wouldn't have called the county. I would have taken you out back, kicked your fucking head in, and left you there . . . but I guess that's a guy thing. Leave it to women to have level heads."

He stood in the doorway until Black had recovered sufficiently to drive away. He turned back to Leukonovich. Denninger was in the bathroom. "What the hell was that hold you used?"

"I haven't always worked for the IRS," she said, leaving her statement hanging in the air.

Denninger came out of the bathroom, opened a can of Diet Pepsi, uprighted her chair, and sat back down to work.

He looked at her. "You need anything?"

"A better early-warning system?" she said, laughing and gingerly touching her nose. "It's not bleeding anymore."

Service watched the women nod to each other in recognition of what had happened. They were grinning. "Thelma and Louise," he said.

"We required no firearm," Leukonovich said, which made Grady Service laugh out loud.

Denninger looked up at him. "Did you call us a couple of *girls?*"

Service held up his hands in submission. "Slip of the tongue, I swear."

Denninger looked at Leukonovich. "Sexist pig."

"Possibly salvageable," the IRS agent said.

63

NEW YEAR'S DAY, 2005

Saranac, Ionia County

The report and supporting documents had been sent both to Syracuse and Grand Rapids, but Anniejo Couch continued to insist in no uncertain terms that the indictments would be refused, that U.S. Attorney Riley Endicott in Grand Rapids wanted no part of a case that could loose defense lawyers into the bowels of the FDA, DNR, MDA, and Michigan legislature. Service was certain he had barely scratched the surface of all the wrongdoing, and this gut feeling put him in a deep, dark place.

Zhenya Leukonovich was scheduled to leave Monday morning. Denninger had already departed. Equipment and supplies would be picked up Tuesday, which gave him a weekend with nothing to do but second-guess himself. It had been snowing for two days, and the night before, they had been sitting at the table when Leukonovich had announced, "I find meditation helps."

"You ever worry that looking inside your mind will show you things you'd rather not see?"

Her answer was calm and assured. "Meditation clears the mind, centers it, allows us to become one with the universe, to find peace, albeit momentary and temporary."

"There's nothing peaceful about this universe," he'd countered. He did not understand the IRS agent, but she had stepped up when it counted. There was a tenacity in her that he admired.

"Zhenya has observed your work and reviewed your case. You could do no more with such limited resources."

"You work alone," he said, "yet you get things done."

"I am merely the point of a gigantic government spear. Here, there was just you and Denninger. She's young, but there is substance there, unlimited potential under the right guidance and leadership."

"Who leads you?" he asked.

"You and I lead ourselves, and are guided by the mission and our sense of duty."

"I keep asking myself how much we didn't even get to, and then I wonder if our limited results are by design."

Leukonovich shrugged, and for once, broke out of her third-person voice. "I feel similarly after each investigation."

"That's when you meditate?"

A bottle and two glasses appeared on the table. "Zhenya finds that alcohol helps dull the mind. Luksusowa is inexpensive Polish potato vodka, triple distilled, very smooth. I carry my own into the heartland and keep it available for special moments."

The bottle had a silver, almost metallic label with the name printed vertically. Service opened it and tipped some liquid into each glass. He pushed one glass to her, using the bottle, and picked up the other. "To the dulling of minds."

"And elevated senses," Leukonovich added. "A delicious paradox."

He'd awoken upstairs, semi-dressed, in one of the double beds, with one of Leukonovich's long legs draped over him, his head pounding. "Are you awake?" he asked.

"Not again," she mumbled. "It is too early to declare wakefulness with any certainty. More data are required."

Again? He felt his heart jump. "Did we . . . ?"

Zhenya ran her hand over the contour of his hip and put her head lightly against his shoulder. "Zhenya makes a joke and requires sleep now. No more talking."

He had snippets of memory from the previous night, but nothing close to a full picture, and lingering inside him, guilt and a sense of betrayal lay like tumors. He gently shook her. "Seriously, did we . . . ?"

She exhaled deeply. "We did nothing to shame the souls in our pasts. Zhenya distinctly remembers every moment except the one where scrofulous nomadic camels found a way to deposit excrement in her mouth."

"Neither scrofulous, nor sleeping," he said. "Dead camels."

"Zhenya finds no consolation in further specificity," she said.

"Where do you go next?" he asked.

"Where duty requires."

"Did I tell you about my granddaughter?"

"Sleep," she said. "Zhenya has no patience for pillow talk, especially when no pillowing has occurred."

His head hurt, but he couldn't sleep. Not like this. Her skin was warm and soft and he was tempted, but he said, "I'm going to make coffee," and slid off the bed.

The sound of the coffeemaker made his head ache more, and he did not hear Leukonovich come downstairs. She was standing by the sliding-glass door, staring out at the snow, her body backlit by a dreary sky. "Do you believe each snowflake is structurally unique?" she asked.

"Never thought about it," he said.

"Zhenya loathes snow," she said wistfully.

"This is nothing. Try three hundred inches a year."

She turned, grinning slyly. "Zhenya would require a minimum of twelve hundred. I would have coffee now."

Service stared at her. "*What?*"

She filled a cup for each of them and sat down across the table from him. "The woman you lost—she was remarkable, but she is gone, and you must continue to live."

"I told you about Nantz?"

"And your son, and the girl he made pregnant, and your granddaughter, and your late father, and a superhuman called Tree, and an Asian woman called Candi, with an 'I,' not a 'Y.' Zhenya suffered a night of alcohol-induced domestic abuse by personal information overload."

"I'm sorry," he said.

"You are sad, you are mourning, and you bury yourself in work. All these feelings will fade. You are trying too hard to analyze and fulfill your obligations, but in this, you miss the most important factor: obligation to self."

"It's only been seven months."

"Nonsense," was her only response.

Service saw a bottle on the counter. It was empty. "What's that?"

"Krupnik, a Polish honey liqueur; it's a scientifically and time-proven aphrodisiac."

"But you said that nothing—"

"I believe that science has not taken into account a constitution such as yours. In Gdansk we had a long history of alcoholic beverages. A Dutchman called Vermoellen made a liqueur called *Der Lachs*, which means 'salmon.' Zhenya is thinking that a bottle of salmon would have had a stronger effect on such a *leśnik myśliwy.*" She looked him directly in the eyes. "Yes, Zhenya tried to seduce you and failed. Zhenya loathes failure more than snow. Go back to your forests and swamps, Detective. Your soul and memories are there. Someday, perhaps, when your wounds are healed, we will meet again."

She was a very strange woman, but he found himself drawn to her.

"I think I'd like that," he said.

Bellaire, Antrim County

His work was done, the package was in New York, and he was alone for the first time in weeks. Yet somehow, he still couldn't let go. He had called former FDA inspector Arwaddy in Ann Arbor that morning. "Sorry to bother you again," he began, "but who in the Michigan Department of Agriculture would your report have gone to?"

"I sent the copy you asked for. You question its veracity?"

"No, not at all—but I'm curious about what happened to it after it left your hands."

"My reports went to my supervision and from there, back to relevant state agencies."

"But where in MDA?" he pressed.

"Often, but not always, the local contact was the agricultural extension service agent."

"Did you interact with the agent in Elk Rapids?"

"No. If there's nothing more, I have a meeting."

He sat and thought: May 9, 1997, was seven and a half years ago, and a lot could have changed since then. He could go to MDA and play bureaucratic phone tag, or try another route, and hope. He looked up CO Venus Wire's cell number and called her in Antrim County.

"Service here."

"How's it going?" she asked.

"Day by day."

"I hear what you're saying."

"How long have you been in Antrim?"

"Since ninety-five; why?"

"Can you remember who the ag extension agent was in ninety-seven?"

"Same one as now, Abe Hostetter."

"Good guy?"

"Too smarmy for my taste, but the farmers up here seem to like him. I stroked him for a tagging violation a couple of years back. Found him with a nice buck at his truck, still untagged. Said he'd gotten excited and forgotten. He's been pretty cool toward me since then."

"You know where he lives?"

"Right in Bellaire." She checked her computer and read off an address and phone number.

"He married?"

"Divorced. His wife left him for a golf pro who got a job in South Carolina. Definite trade up for her."

He thanked Wire and drove north with only a general plan in mind. At 8 P.M. he was parked across the street from the address; the house was dark. The outside temp was 23 degrees and there was a steady wind out of the west. He turned up his heat, cracked his windows, opened his thermos, and poured a cup of coffee, settling in to do what experienced game wardens did best: wait.

He awoke to lights on in the house. His dash clock said 10:14 P.M. Decision time: call or knock? He was tired of treading lightly and got out of the truck.

"Geez, hold your horses," a voice keened as he pounded on the door.

A man with sparse red hair and a pathetic mustache opened the door and stared out at him.

"Conservation Officer, Department of Natural Resources," Service said, showing his badge.

"I know who you game wardens work for. What do you want?"

"A little chat."

"It's past my bedtime."

"Sleep in tomorrow," Service said, stepping toward the threshold.

"You can't just walk in," the man said.

"Something to hide in there, Mr. Hostetter?" Service said, making a show of leaning over the shorter man to look into the house.

"I resent that. How do you know my name?"

"If there's nothing to hide, you won't mind inviting me in."

The man held the door open, nodded, and Service stepped inside. The man left the door open.

"Burning energy," Service said.

"You won't be here that long. What do you want?"

"May ninth, ninety-seven. FDA Inspector Arwaddy went to Piscova. She filed a report. It's not in the FDA's files."

"I'm Michigan Ag, not FDA. What's your question?"

"FDA calls for you to receive a copy."

"Did you check with MDA? I don't keep copies of reports past current year plus one. That's our agency's policy statewide."

"This report never made it to MDA," Service said. He was guessing, but so far things seemed on track. The man started to shake, and not because the door was open.

"Are you making an accusation?" The man's shaking seemed to be worsening.

"You remember the report," Service said. Statement, not question.

"I want my attorney."

"Fine, call him."

"Her," Hostetter said.

Bingo, Service thought. "Let me guess: Constance Algyre, attorney at law."

"Sweet Jesus," the man said. "You've already checked MDA."

He had no idea what the man was driving at, but decided to let him think whatever it was that he was thinking. "The report?"

Hostetter was shaking all over and trying to keep it in check. "Okay, here's the truth. I'm a people person. My administrative skills aren't so hot. I try, but stuff gets lost, okay? Not intentionally. It just happens; know what I'm saying?"

"The thing is," Service said, "the report said Piscova was engaged in illegal activity, specifically and willingly adulterating food for human consumption. That's a felony. The report should have closed down the company, but it's still operating."

"Honest, I don't remember," Hostetter said.

"You have so many reports like that, you can't remember this particular one?"

"I just can't recall, okay?"

"Not okay," Service said menacingly. "The other thing is, your lawyer is also Piscova's lawyer, and I'm wondering if a little grease helped that report slide into the circular file."

"I'm calling my lawyer," Hostetter said, reaching for the phone.

Service put one of his business cards by the phone. "Tell Algyre I'll talk to her before we take the next step."

"We?"

"Didn't I mention, I work for the U.S. Attorney?"

The man shook his head. "*What* next step?"

"Abe, Abe . . . what step do you think?"

Service left the house and sat in the truck, waiting for a call from Algyre, which never came. He was willing to bet that Hostetter's phone records would show a call to someone at Piscova.

Arwaddy wrote her report. Presumably she had sent it—he'd seen the copy. Presumably the FDA sent it to MDA, which sent it down to Hostetter, which meant there should be a copy in MDA's files—unless the FDA had sent it straight to Hostetter, which he doubted. FDA was an up-down organization from what he knew of it. But what if it had been stifled at FDA? Would that mean Fagan had somebody there? Or had Arwaddy never sent the report? *Stop it*, he told himself. There was enough to stir the pot, and there was one more person he needed to see. The criminal report he'd filed contained numerous charges, including thirty-eight counts of failure to report cash transactions. Roxy Lafleur had lived well off the Piscova caviar skim. How much money was going elsewhere, and for how long had it been going on?

Petoskey, Emmet County

Service called Glen Sheppard, editor of *The North Woods Call*, the state's small, most influential outdoor periodical. A Korean War vet, editor Sheppard was a longtime friend of DNR law enforcement, the kind of fearless and principled editor who took on any and all power brokers if he thought they were in the wrong—including DNR Law Enforcement. The paper's small circulation belied its influence among a broad cross section of people interested in everything from hunting to bird-watching. Sheppard, his wife, and their pets lived and worked out of his house on an isolated drumlin near Ellsworth, in northern Antrim County.

Service worried about waking up the old curmudgeon, who was an early-to-bed type, but he needed help, and Shep was the man to provide it. Service had originally considered giving the Piscova story to Shep, as the most influential outdoor editor in the state, but the man's publication ran on a shoestring, and he was known to be extremely close to certain elements in the DNR. Service felt this might have made it easy for Shep to accidentally reveal that Service was the source, so he'd gone with Beaker Salant instead. His reasoning at the time: Why put Shep in the middle of a shitfight he hadn't asked for?

"Sheppard," a man's voice growled over the phone.

"Grady Service."

"Seems I've been hearing that name a lot recently," the editor said.

"Highly complimentary things, I'm sure."

"Depends on who's doing the talking," Sheppard said. "Why the call?"

"I need information on Angledenny."

"L. Bradley or G. Wilson?"

"L. Bradley's old man."

"That's GW. Term-limited in ninety-eight. His kid took the seat on his old man's coattails and GW's old man had it before him, a great example of political power as a family hand-me-down."

"What's GW doing nowadays?"

"Mostly retired. He owns a construction company that builds high-end summer homes on the lakeshore. Got a grandson running the outfit."

"GW sponsored the snagging ban."

"Rammed it right through the legislature and pissed off a lot of people who couldn't understand all the fuss over a bunch of stinky, dying fish."

"Black hat, white hat?"

Sheppard chuckled. "Gray, like most of them we send to Lansing. All his time as a solon aside, GW's a pretty good man. Not perfect—but who among us is?"

"What was the motivation for the bill?"

"The Michigan Salmon Society thought snagging was a serious problem for long-term salmon reproduction and with all the money salmon fishermen were bringing into the state, the state chamber of commerce and tourism bureau jumped on the issue."

"Is it a coincidence that Piscova ended up with a monopoly on egg harvesting in the state?"

"You looking for a scrap with Quint Fagan?"

"Just asking questions. Where's GW live?"

"Bay View in Petoskey. Got a show house with a paint job that looks like somebody puked up a Christmas cookie."

"He winter in Michigan?"

"Far as I know. He's a tough, outspoken old bastard. Don't think he ever got into that Arizona-Florida snowbird baloney; plus, the grandson who runs the construction company's young, and the old guy likes to keep an eye on him."

"How old is GW?"

"Gotta think . . . mid-eighties, give or take, still sharp as a brand-new Swedish hand ax."

"Thanks, Shep."

"Want some advice from an old fart?"

"You bet."

"You're a Vietnam guy. You can take the best damn GIs in the world and send them into battle, but if the civilians who give the orders don't have their act together, you can't win."

"Copy that." Service took this as a warning that it would be hard to find consensus in state government to pursue Fagan. He'd already seen the evidence.

It was late, and there was no point trying to find the retired lawmaker tonight. Service drove to the Petoskey state police post, checked in, and let the dispatcher know he'd be sleeping in his truck in the parking lot.

After a shower, shave, and coffee at the post in the morning, he drove to Bay View, a collection of expensively renovated Queen Anne homes in the northeast part of town. There had been two inches of fluffy snow during the night, and the neighborhood looked like something out of a kid's storybook. He found the house, which was red, green, and white, and noticed someone in a parka and pac boots stooped over a snow scoop, clearing the driveway. The scoop was like those used by Yoopers, but plastic rather than metal.

Service parked on the street and walked up the driveway. "Nice scoop," he said in greeting.

"Neighbors think I'm nuts, but what the hell do I need a snowblower for? Work's good for the old ticker."

"Is Representative Angledenny here?"

"That depends. Brad's in Lansing. I'm GW."

"Grady Service, DNR."

The old man laughed and wiped a pearl of mucous from his nose. The son looked nothing like him. Angledenny propped the snow scoop against a snowbank by the garage and took off his choppers.

"Service," he said with a smirk. "I heard you rattled hell out of my son's cage, you and some female IRS freak. Game wardens still drink coffee, or have they sissified to latte?"

Service grinned, said, "We're still on coffee." He followed the man through the garage and into a large kitchen with a breakfast nook. A small white dog began barking and the old man said, "Ignore her. She was my wife's idea. Lost Sally in July, inherited the dog. Lousy trade."

"Sorry about your wife."

"Alzheimer's; no idea what planet she was on at the end."

No emotion, just straight facts. The old man poured coffee in mugs that said HERS and HER DOG'S.

"I know about you. A marine in Vietnam, state police, DNR; you've maxed out your pension nut and got more than enough time to retire, so what keeps you going? You one of them crusader types?"

Angledenny was nothing like his son. The man put an ashtray on the table, took a half-cigar out of his pocket, and said, "Watch this." He flicked a Zippo lighter open and the dog came charging into the room, barking, yipping, snarling, hopping around like it had been injected with speed. Angledenny lit the cigar and blew a puff at the dog, which retreated, whimpering. "Beat it, ya four-legged cotton ball. The queen's gone. Long live the king."

Angledenny took another puff. "It's a good thing to rattle my kid's cage. Do it myself as often as I can. I held that seat a long time, and he got it because of me, but he'll be out on his keister come next election. He doesn't believe that, but I know the voters here and he's done. Runs with a crowd of assholes and everybody knows it. You asked him about that stupid Costa Rica investment . . . I told him to stay the hell away from Horn and Fagan, but kids don't listen." The old man tilted his chin and blew a perfect smoke ring.

Fagan's name had never come up with Angledenny. He and Leukonovich had talked about him, but not to L. Bradley. "You don't like Fagan?"

"Can't say I care about the sonuvabitch one way or the other, but a sleazeball is a sleazeball, and we've got some sad history. Term limits came in and I was six months out from my last election; my PAC got a check for twenty-five grand from an outfit called the Michigan Salmon Society. I'd held this seat so long I could tell you within ten the final vote count every time, and name the people who voted against me. I never spent more than ten grand for a campaign, and only spent that on radio spots just before Election Day, to make sure voters knew I was still interested. Twenty-five grand was way over the top and made me wonder what the hell was going on. I took the check, put it in my desk, never cashed it."

Angledenny took another sip of coffee and kept talking. "Soon after I got that check, the MSS began a statewide PR campaign against snagging salmon. Good stuff, got your attention—so I told my people to call the MSS in to give me their spiel."

A puff of smoke. "They come in, looking like good old boys in plaid shirts, but they put on the damnedest dog-and-pony show I ever saw, stuff to make Detroit's car ad boys drool. I was impressed, and the message made sense. They showed me graphs that talked about the estimated egg loss yearly from snagging, and what the long-term effect would be on natural reproduction by the fish. Even though I liked their cause, there was a disconnect: Here were these plaid-shirt guys, average Joes, giving me this high-powered, knock-your-socks-off presentation. It was too slick by half. Still, I supported them, so I called Legislative Affairs and they sent over a young sharpie who drafted the legislation for me. I introduced it and ramrodded that sonuvabitch all the way to Clearcut's desk. When he signed it without protest, I thought maybe he was beginning to have an outdoor conscience."

More coffee; the man was in the groove now, talking, not bothering to see if Service was listening or getting any of it. "Bill got signed, MSS went out of business. I called one of the plaid-shirt boys and asked him what the hell was going on. He told me they'd run out of money, that their sugar daddy had pulled out. The guy says their main funding came from Shamrock Productions, the same outfit that did the dog-and-pony show and media campaign. I asked my people to find out who and what Shamrock Productions was."

"A Fagan company," Service said.

Angledenny looked at him and arched a brow. "Took a little pressure, but the plaid-shirt boys eventually told me that Fagan funded them, and gave them the twenty-five K for my PAC. So I called Fagan."

"You'd met him before?"

"Never really met. Seen him here and there. The capital's a small place. Turns out that the analysis we did on the bill showed only the upside. We didn't know there was a connection between Shamrock, Piscova, and Fagan, or what a monopoly on egg harvesting meant. Our focus was on Michigan sportfishermen and the economy, and based on that, the ban was the right thing to do. I saw it as my legacy to the people of the state—until the Shamrock-Fagan connection popped up.

"So I set up a meeting. The greasy little bastard came to my office and I passed his check across the desk and told him to stick it up his ass. He just laughed at me, took the check, and left. A few weeks later Sam Bozian pulled me aside at a reception and told me he was disappointed. Said he'd signed the bill as a favor to me, and since then, he'd heard I wasn't a team player. Nothing more, no names—just that. I lost it. I told Sam he'd been a politician his whole damn life and had never had an actual job, but when his term was up he'd find life a little different than the damn cocoon he'd been living in. I learned later that Shamrock Productions created all of Bozian's political ads. Sam didn't give a shit about sportfishermen. He just wanted to support his pal Fagan."

The man's bitter soliloquy was not at all what Service had expected, and he was trying to sort it out. His gut said the old man was telling him the truth, and either this was the way it was, or the man was the most accomplished liar he'd ever met.

"So," Angledenny said, "what is it you want? You met my son, figured the apple wouldn't fall far from the tree?"

"Something like that."

Angledenny laughed sarcastically. "I think my Sally-girl let the mailman get in her pants to make that kid. Always been different. You looking for dirt on Fagan?"

"Information."

"You think he bribed me to push through that bill?"

"I didn't come here with a preset notion."

"He didn't have to bribe me," Angledenny said. "I bit on the line, pushed it through, and made it easy for him. I got snookered, and if you think that makes me feel like a dope, you'd be right." Angledenny studied him for a moment. "You want dirt? I've heard that Fagan got his start with dirty money. He went to school at Florida International University and didn't have a pot to piss in. He took out student loans, did all sorts of odd jobs, did all that crap a starving student has to do to keep himself in school and afloat. Then he graduated, and within six months all his loans were paid off and his business was up and running. I called Fagan one time and asked him if the rumor was true. Know what the bastard said? 'Your wife's got a cute little black dog.' A week later somebody threw mothballs on the lawn, the stupid dog ate them, and that's all she wrote. I said to hell with it; I'm not screwing with this guy anymore."

"You never went to the cops?"

"With *what*, 'Your wife's got a cute little black dog'?"

"According to the rumor, what was the source of his start-up cash?"

"What I heard is a guy named Amos Grenchev was his banker. Grenchev's an Israeli from the Ukraine, the moneyman for a crook named Lev Lazarus."

"L-Two out of Tel Aviv."

Angledenny stared at him. "Son, the word on you is that you're one tough, honest hombre, but the world's never been a place for an army of one. Ask Jesus himself."

He left the retired legislator deep in thought. Krapahkin was connected to L2 and to Fagan. Was it a triangle, and did Zhenya or Rogers or anybody else know anything about this? Or was it just rumor? Not rumor, he decided, too many specifics—some of which might be off to some degree, but the level of specificity was suggestive of a rumor with real roots.

He tried to call Leukonovich, but got a recording and decided the time had come to go home. As he crossed the Mackinac Bridge, he felt like he had failed and was running away with his tail between his legs. It was a feeling that left him angry.

66

MONDAY, FEBRUARY 14, 2005

Slippery Creek Camp

He had been home just over a month. He'd fetched Newf and Cat from Candi, and had had a less than satisfying talk with her.

"Called you. Some guy answered, 'Candi's Sweet Shop.' "

"Your point?"

"No point; just telling you I called."

"How lucky for me," she said icily.

They had not talked since then. Captain Grant had not asked about the Piscova case and he'd not volunteered anything. Service called Karylanne every night, but had not yet been to Houghton to see her and the baby.

Denninger called a couple of times, said Cullen had asked her out and what did he think about it? Her decision. He liked Denninger, felt momentarily jealous of Cullen. They were both good kids.

Leukonovich never called back.

He'd gone to see Lafleur's doctor to ask questions about her cancer and a possible link to mirex. He'd been rebuffed, told in no uncertain terms that he needed a subpoena to overturn the privacy law. Without Anniejo Couch's backing, he couldn't get the records. It was another dead end and more disappointment.

Beaker Salant called twice, looking for more stories, but he had nothing more to give the reporter.

That morning's run had been nearly an hour in the snow, with Newf plowing a path ahead of him. He lifted weights, shoveled snow away from his truck, split some kindling, showered, and had his regular breakfast

When the phone rang, he wasn't in the mood to pick it up, but relented. "Trip Rogers here. You want the bad news or the bad news?"

"Nice to have a choice."

"Wrong answer. The decision was made here—not by me—to *not* pound doors to arrest Vandeal and Fagan. The U.S. Attorney's office called the men's attorneys and told them there were warrants and they needed to turn themselves in. Vandeal came in Friday, was charged and bonded out. Fagan's coming in today. Sorry, buddy. I really wanted you to be the one to arrest that prick."

"Projected date for trials?"

"One trial, two accused, each with his own legal team. Syracuse is pushing for May, could be later, but Manny Florida seems motivated. Someone in Florida's office said he thinks the defendants' lawyers will drag things out."

"You want me there for the trial?"

"Nope. Your report was thorough. Manny Florida said it's the best he's ever seen. He kicked sand in my face over mine."

"What charges did they go with?"

"Dozens of counts of de facto Lacey Act violations and conspiracy to violate the Lacey Act, conspiracy to defraud the United States government with cash transactions exceeding one hundred K, causing financial institutions to fail to file currency transaction reports, structuring illegal transactions at financial institutions. They're also charged for substantive financial crimes in violation of federal codes and with forfeiture. If Manny Florida can bring this home, they're gonna do serious time and pay the piper big time."

"Sounds like Leukonovich's work is a big part of the case."

"That woman is *unbelievable*," Rogers said. "Cold-blooded, efficient, unbending, no wasted energy. The IRS calls her Super Z. The name ought to be Walking Dead. Gotta be nothing but coolant in her veins."

"She been around there?"

"I'd think so, but I don't really know. I turned in my report and I'm done there except to answer questions. I'm back on other stuff. You?"

"Back to the grind, too, more or less."

"Listen," Rogers said, "I'm sorry about this arrest thing, but that's how she goes sometimes, yes?"

"Yep, way she goes."

"Great working with you. Maybe we'll get to do it again."

"Maybe."

"You know, we learned from the Piscova files that they have a big business for their caviar with the Japs out of Seattle. Fagan has an office and warehouse there."

Service suspected Rogers had known this for a while and had kept the information back. He was sick of the case, sick of pushing against the wall.

He put the dog in his truck, loaded his ice-fishing sledge, and drove to Black Cedar Pond. He augered a couple of holes in the ice, baited two rods, set up his tip-ups, turned his gear bucket upside down, and sat down to wait for the eyes to cooperate while Newf raced around the lake and through the cedars along the bank. He had been there about an hour, and had caught a pair of fat, twenty-inch fish, which were plenty for him, but he liked fishing through the ice and still hoped to catch another keeper.

"This is a pathetic sight," a voice said.

Service looked over his shoulder to see Candace McCants standing behind him.

"You on patrol?"

"Just checked out of service."

"Have any fun?"

"Absolutely none."

"You always have fun."

"Not recently."

He thought he detected a catch in her voice. "There a problem I need to know about?"

"Well, I've considered hiring a skywriter to put it up for you to see, but the weather sucks for that, and I hate billboards on ethical grounds, so I'm sort of limited in how I get this across to you."

He turned around on his bucket and faced her. "You want some coffee?"

"Not really."

"Want to fish? I got a couple of nice ones."

"Me too," she said.

"We're not talking about fish?" he said, sensing her tone and seeing a sparkle in her dark eyes. Less sparkle than predator's glare.

"You're right, it's not about fish," she said. "You know what today is?"

"Monday, right?"

She pulled out her telescoping baton and he flinched, but she extended it and used the tip to make an outline in the snow. The sky was yellow and purple, clouds coming in, light snow beginning to fall. At that moment Newf barked and Service turned to see the tip-up flag bouncing. He grabbed for the rod, but something knocked him off his bucket to his knees.

"You are so pathetically lame. Read the damn snow," McCants said with a growl, pointing.

He saw a crude heart. "Valentine's Day?"

"Well, *duh*."

He looked back at the tip-up. The fish was still on.

"You reach for *that* rod and I will kick your ass right here, right now. You and me have business, Grady Service."

It hit him like a hammer—the hints, her changing moods. He felt stupid. "You mean?"

"Yeah," she said, nodding, a smile forming on her face. "Hallelujah. My place or yours? Get naked, get drunk, and so forth and so on."

"And walleye on the grill?"

"All the sensitivity of a cinder block," she said, taking a step toward him.

"You know . . ." he said, but didn't finish. They were in the middle of a kiss rolling around in the snow on top of two feet of ice and the dog was circling and raising hell at something in the air, and they stopped long enough to look up and see a pair of bald eagles soaring over them.

Grady Service said, "But—"

McCants said, "Finish that statement and I will personally stuff that big fish down your throat. You want to keep rolling around on the ice or shall we go act like normal people on Valentine's Day?"

"This *is* normal," he said.

"You scare the hell out of me," Candace McCants said, reaching for the tip-up and pulling another walleye through the ice. Service patted her on the rump and they started collecting his gear.

"I'm not sure this is the right thing for us," Service said.

She glared at him. "Who makes you the arbiter of right and wrong?"

Newf stood at McCants's side, her massive tail swinging, Candi's hand on the top of her head. "Your dog and cat love me."

"They love me, too."

"There you go: A plus B equals C," she said.

"I flunked algebra."

"Okay, what's one plus one?"

"Two," he said.

"Wrong," she said. "It's one, stupid."

"I guess I need a refresher."

"Lucky for you," she said with a huge grin that warmed him in a way he had not felt in a long, long time.

"The guy on your phone?"

"My big brother. I have four, you big dope—remember?"

67

SUNDAY, FEBRUARY 20, 2005

Gwinn, Marquette County

Simon del Olmo called about a gray wolf shot in Iron County during deer season. An anonymous informant had called the state's report-all-poaching line, said a man named Presley Corvo had been drunk and bragging it up in a local gin mill. Del Olmo had found the skinned carcass. Could Grady check out the guy?

The area had gotten almost eighteen inches of snow in the last thirty-six hours, and county trucks were working overtime to keep the main roads clear. The temperature was eight below zero Fahrenheit, the warmest it had been in four days. Snowbanks in Gwinn were seven feet high and pure white from the new snow. Most of the winter they were the color of sharkskin. Service found the house, pulled into the unplowed driveway, and hit an ice bump, which jolted the Tahoe as he bounced over it. *Shit!*

He got out, looked back at the bump, and saw a hand sticking out of the snow. His heart began to race as he dropped to his knees and frantically began to brush snow away. His last thought: *It's frozen?*

Marquette, Marquette County

The voice to his left was faint and growing louder. Service felt like his whole head was trying to explode and he was blind.

Candi McCants said, "I know you've got a quadrillion questions, but you're not supposed to talk. Just lay there and listen. The body you ran over was Presley Corvo's mother. He was tweaking on meth, beat her to death two nights before you arrived, and dumped her in the driveway, thinking it was the backyard. When you pulled in he thought you were after his lab, so he charged you with a softball bat and started pounding away."

"What brand?"

He could hear her gasp. "Easton, you jerk. Linsenman was cruising by, saw your Tahoe, saw Corvo pounding somebody in the snow, jumped out, and took the asshole down. Corvo swore you'd just run over his mother and totally wigged out. Linsenman saw that the body was frozen solid and Corvo's eyes sunk in his head like red coals. He cuffed him, went into the house, and found the meth lab. Apparently Corvo was one of his own best customers. There was also a wolf pelt. Linsenman got it over to Simon who sent it to Michigan State's lab for DNA to compare with the carcass tissue he found in November."

Linsenman was a longtime Marquette County deputy, an outdoorsman who loved dogs, and he'd been in several misadventures with Service over the years. His first name was Weasel, but everyone called him Linsenman.

"My head," Service said. "I can't see."

"Major concussion, no fracture to your head, but Corvo got some licks in on your face. Your nose has been reconstructed and he shattered the orbit of your left eye. They've wired that back together. Probably be a couple more surgeries to finish the job and make you pretty again. What I want to know is how the hell do you make a wolf case, a murder, and bust a meth lab all when you're flat on your ass and out cold? Every CO in the state is talking about you!"

He wanted to laugh, but even the thought of trying made him ache. "My eyes."

"Temporary thing. They've got a bandage over them and everything will be fine over time. Linsenman told me he thought you were dead and he just about lost it. Corvo's lucky he got pinched by a pro. What else? Oh yeah, Linsenman's getting promoted to sergeant, but not because of this, so don't congratulate yourself."

"Little M?"

"The baby and mom are fine. Karylanne was scared to death, but Simon and I talked to her and calmed her down. She and the baby are at your cabin."

He cringed. His camp was no place for a baby. There were no real beds and it was not very well insulated. Shit. "Take them to *your* place," he mumbled.

"I tried; no go. Karylanne insists on Slippery Creek. The doctors are saying you'll be here another week, then it's home and four months off."

"Overload," he whispered. "Shut up, Candi."

Who is this woman? he asked himself, reaching out with his hand, which McCants pressed to her face. It was wet.

69

THURSDAY, APRIL 7, 2005

Slippery Creek Camp

Roy Rogers called around noon. Grady Service's head still ached for extended periods each day. "Heard you ran into some trouble," the New York ECO said.

"Some."

"The trial here is looking good, but I have to tell you that Manny Florida's using your indictments to bargain with Fagan's and Vandeal's lawyers."

"Bargain how?"

"He'll drop a bunch of your charges in order to press ours."

Service stared at the phone. Throw them away? Weren't they *all* valid? What had been the point of the whole fucking exercise? New York didn't have shit until he'd caught Baranov selling salmon eggs and Baranov had told him about the Piscova egg business. He'd let Baranov's ticket drop in exchange for information. But this shit in New York wasn't the same degree of bargaining. Baranov was small. Fagan was big.

"You don't have much to say," Rogers said.

"More like too much to say, and this isn't the right time," Service said.

"I hear you, man. I thought you'd want to know."

"You go along with Florida?"

"Since when do federal prosecutors look for input from state employees?"

"Ever wonder why we do this?" Service asked.

"A lot more nowadays than in years past. The trial's scheduled to start May first, and Florida's office is saying two to four months to put it in the jury's hands."

What happened to the concept of swift justice? Service wondered.

70

Slippery Creek Camp

Leukonovich called. "I am in Syracuse. The trial is progressing satisfactorily. Zhenya has informed U.S. Attorney Florida about Costa Rica, but Mr. Florida is personal friend of Mr. Fagan's attorney, who has assured him that Fagan will not flee if the verdict comes in for the government. Florida believes fervently that Fagan is only an overreaching businessman, not a thug."

Words popped into Grady Service's mind: *Your wife's got a cute little black dog.*

"You waited a long time to call back," he said, leaving it at that. Z was Z; she offered no excuses, no defense. He immediately called Manny Florida, left a message, and did not get a callback until almost midnight.

"What's the matter, hotshot, you feeling left out—want in on the glory?" Manny Florida had obviously been into the sauce.

"Write this down," Service said. "Fagan's going to run and leave shit on your face."

Manny Florida exploded with derisive laughter. "Yo, Ranger Rick, hunker down and leave the heavy lifting to the pros."

"Up your ass," Service said.

"Whatever," Florida said, and hung up.

Why was nobody listening to him? Krapahkin had tipped him about Costa Rica and Leukonovich had confirmed Fagan's recent and somewhat murky purchase of property there. He was going to run. Why couldn't the others see what was so plain to him?

The surgeon made him wear a clear plastic mask to protect his handiwork. Service felt like a goalie for the short-bus team. His head still ached. Without whatever painkiller they'd given him, he felt like his head was freezing or boiling, with no in-between. There was medicine to "manage the discomfort," but there was no drug that could stop the pain in that part of the soul dedicated to being right.

"Five months off duty," the doctor was saying now over the phone.

"Three," Service countered.

"This is *not* a negotiation," the doctor said.

"Bullshit. Everything's a negotiation."

"This one's nonnegotiable. Maybe we should have you talk to a psychiatrist."

"Fine; tomorrow will work for me."

"I don't think it can be arranged that quickly."

"See, we're negotiating," Service said with a snarl. "We all do it, every day."

"Do you or do you not wish to consult with a psychiatrist?"

"No. Tell him to use the time he might have had with me to heal himself."

Service made another call, this one to Rogers. "Fagan's going to run."

"We've already talked about this. Manny Florida doesn't buy it."

"Do you?"

"By fiat, not so much. Team, team, team."

Intimating that he *wasn't* a team player? This hurt so sharply he couldn't give voice to his feelings.

McCants came over after getting off patrol, peeled off her outer shirt and body armor, and looked him over. "You're all worked up again."

"We're in a plague of assholes."

"You're supposed to rest, recuperate, grow new brain cells."

"I hate this case."

"There is no case," she reminded him. "You're on the bench."

"Says you."

She held out his pills. "Be a good boy."

The next day Sergeant Milo Miars dropped by in uniform, shiny new lieutenant's bars gleaming on his collar. Miars held out two sets of green chevrons. "For when you come back."

He was still undecided about Miars, harbored a vague suspicion the sergeant had sidestepped to let Service and Denninger carry the puck and absorb all the abuse from the Piscova case. He ignored the chevrons, left them sitting on the table.

It was good with Candi, even though she wasn't Nantz. Not great, but nice . . . okay. He was distracted, she was working: stasis of sorts. He couldn't be around his granddaughter—too much risk to his face. The surgeon had been clear in his instructions: No sex, no running, and no weight lifting. His jaw was wired shut, and he was on a liquid diet of pureed crap, like baby food virtual calories and nothing more. He had dropped twelve pounds and was continuing to lose weight. But there was good news too: No need for his dentures right now.

Only Fagan and Vandeal charged out of how many? A helluva lot of people were going to skate free, with their reputations intact, and this rankled. He'd barely scratched the wrongdoing, felt this in his gut.

"Whatever you're hatching," McCants said out of the blue, "don't."

He shrugged and glowered.

She said softly, "Have you checked your dog lately?" Her voice had a strange tone and he looked at her. "I think she is with puppies," she said.

"Bullshit; she was spayed when I got her."

"Wrong. I talked to Kira."

Kira Lehto, his former girlfriend, DVM, full-time vet, BN . . . Before Nantz. Before Candi.

"She never spayed her. She thought you were going to take care of it."

Service looked at his humongous dog. "With our luck the father will be a Chihuahua."

"You said 'our,'" McCants said. "That's sweet. Actually, I've seen a wolf hanging around here."

"God, no," he said.

"Just reporting what I've seen," she said.

"What's the gestation time?" A wolf? Jesus.

"Nine weeks," she said. "You're getting to be a regular midwife." After taking a breath, she added, "Whatever it is that's eating at you, you need to let it go."

"I've pissed off a lot of people in the department."

"Only those who deserve it. The rest of us are cheering."

"This is tectonic," he said. "A major fault line."

"Plates shift open, close. The big gaps are rarely permanent. There's a lot of angst in the department. Always will be. Stress; making tough, fast judgments; lousy working conditions; it all piles up and sometimes the angst gets loose." She laughed. "I don't even know what it is we're talking about."

"But you've heard rumors."

"The holier-than-thou crusader."

"The alleged witch hunt."

She shrugged. "You find any?"

He nodded. "Not enough."

"One's enough, Grady. It warns the wannabes."

Maybe, he thought. But miss a few cancer cells and the disease comes back. He couldn't get Roxy Lafleur out of his mind. Her death had to count for something. Didn't it?

"Candi?"

"Yeah?"

"If there's really a wolf in this thing, I'll have to get rid of the pups."

"I know."

"Do me a favor. Call SuRo Genova, see if she knows a good refuge for wolf-dog pups."

"Not a problem. 'Course, we don't know for sure there is a wolf involved." She looked over at him. "How the heck do you know if a pup's a wolf-dog or not?"

"Animal control people look at the animals and decide if they look wolfish or not."

"Are you kidding?"

"Nope. All there is to go on. The DNA of a Chihuahua and a wolf are identical."

McCants shook her head.

Grady Service glared at his dog and said, "Tramp."

Slippery Creek Camp

Captain Grant dropped by unexpectedly. Service invited him in and made fresh coffee while Newf sniffed around, trying to decide if the captain's formal air was a wall or something else.

"Recovering?"

Service's jaw was swollen from his latest and to-be-last surgery, but his jaw was unwired and his eye nearly open again. "Getting there."

"That Corvo thing came out of nowhere," the captain said, and Service heard in his former supervisor's voice that there was more to come. "You had occasion to interact with a Troop detective named Zarobsky during the Piscova case."

"Unfortunately."

"Want to tell me about it?"

"What's to tell? He works with a state treasury agent named Jornstadt. He's banging her. We saw them only a couple of times: to announce their arrival on the case, and then, to announce their departure when U.S. Attorney Endicott got cold feet."

"Words were exchanged between you and Zarobsky?"

"Not really. He was being an asshole and I reminded him that banging his girlfriend was not synonymous with work."

Service felt the captain studying him. "Zarobsky filed a complaint, alleging unprofessional conduct on your part and recommending you undergo anger management training."

He felt no anger over hearing this. He felt like he was getting beyond anger over anything in his life. "And?"

"Acting Director Hopkins had a call from U.S. Attorney Florida, who alleges you were also disrespectful to him. Given these allegations, Cecil has decided you will attend the class."

"Shouldn't this be the chief's decision, or yours?"

"The chief was in opposition, as was I, but Cecil is the boss."

"Great. Do you think I have a problem with my temper?"

"In my opinion you have almost perfect emotional control. Maybe too much. You are one of those rare individuals who seems to be able to control his emotions and focus on central issues and the mission."

A thought came to him. "Is Hopkins trying to force me to retire?"

"No. I'm certain that there are some residual hard feelings in the Fisheries division, but it seems to me this is meant more as a sop to the New York attorney general, the Troops, and the DNR internal audience than to the Michigan State Police."

"Sacrificial lamb."

"Purely symbolic," the captain said.

"When does the inquisition begin?"

The captain opened his briefcase, took out a folder, and placed it on the table. "Don't go into this with a negative attitude. Trust in the chief. There are several dates. Pick one and call Dr. Purloy. He's in East Lansing, provides this service to a number of state agencies."

What was this talk about trust? "I should've gone when my jaw was wired shut," Service said, which earned a smile from his captain.

Miami International Airport, Florida

Grady Service had driven to Detroit, spent the night with Treebone and Kalina, and caught an American Airlines flight early that morning to Miami, where he would catch a connecting flight to San José, the capital of Costa Rica.

He hadn't been able to get the Costa Rica link out of his head. Two weeks ago he'd called a former FBI agent turned lawyer who had helped him on several occasions, and asked if she knew anyone in law enforcement in Costa Rica. Shamekia had referred him to a retired FBI agent named Fernando Fischer, who had enjoyed a long career in the New York field office. Fischer's father was Puerto Rican, his mother from Costa Rica. He had been born in Queens and retired in 1995 to San José, where he did some part-time PI work and ran an outfit called Azul-Verde Aventura, some sort of ecotourism outfit in Puerto Limon on the Caribbean coast.

A call from their mutual friend led Fischer to contact Service.

"Shamekia don't hand out a lot of compliments," Fischer said. "But you're top of her list of good guys. You looking for a tour?"

"Tour?"

"Blue-Green Adventures. We can take you into the rainforest or onto the big water, or drop your ass in a mudbath and make your skin all pretty."

"More in the line of fact-finding. There's an American named Quintan Fagan, who holds property under a brokerage called *Refugio Seguro*."

"Never heard of him. He dirty?"

"Trying to find that out," Service said, holding back, not wanting to surrender too much information too quickly. "You know the environmental folks down there?"

"NGO or government?"

"Government, I guess."

"Dolores del Rio."

"Sounds like a movie star."

"She's the senior investigator for the Ministry of Environment and Energy, and she's got the reputation of Eliot Ness among the Ticos. Down here, Dolores is the man."

"Ticos?"

"What the Costa Ricans call themselves. What is it you're looking for?"

"I'll start with knowing something about Fagan's property, where and what it is, and so forth."

"He lives here, of course."

"Of course?"

"One cannot purchase real estate in Costa Rica unless one is a resident."

Unless one is a resident, Service thought. *Interesting.*

"I will call you when I have something to share," Fischer said, and hung up.

That call had taken place three weeks ago. Ten days ago, Fischer had called back and suggested Service come down for a visit to observe some interesting things. Fischer did not elaborate. Service had immediately called Yooper Travel in Escanaba and made arrangements. Candi was keeping the dog and cat, and though she had a lot of questions about where he was going, all he told her was that he had to get away—not exactly a lie, if not the whole truth.

Rogers had been calling in every few days with updates on the Fagan-Vandeal trial. The new guess for completion was sometime in late August. He suspected his own management, New York, and the feds would not be happy with his continued interest in the Piscova case, but he was beyond caring what others thought.

He ordered half an avocado on a piece of full-grain dark Swedish rye toast, salted and peppered, and added a glass of orange juice to wash down his medications as he waited for his Miami flight to be called.

THURSDAY, JUNE 16, 2005

Puerto Limon, Costa Rica

Service flew into Juan Santamaria Airport, only a few miles north of the capital's downtown, slogged through customs and immigration, and caught an orange cab to Pavas Domestic Airport, also called Tobias Bolanos, a one-hour ride, to cover what he estimated to be no more than four or five miles as the crow flew. At Pavas he caught a flight on a twin-engine aircraft operated by Nature Air, the name in English on the pointed nose. One pilot, no other crew. The skies were lumpy, gray, threatening, the ride fairly wild with a lot of up and down and skidding through the air. His fellow passengers carried on as if this were normal.

Fischer was close to six foot, with silver tips to his thick black hair, and a pencil mustache; all in all, a distinguished-looking man with an almost regal bearing and intense, gray eyes. "Your trip was without incident?"

"Flying," Service said with a shrug, feeling Fischer examining the fresh scars around his eye and jaw.

"Come," the man said. "We are at the beginning of the rainy season, and when the rain comes, it is often like a lover's temper: quiet, then there, right in your face, without warning."

The man drove a beat-up Ford Explorer with AZUL-VERDE AVENTURA painted in bright red script along the side. "I have arranged for a place for you to stay, but this will not be until later. If you wish, I can arrange for a room here until you're rested."

"I slept all the way down."

"A good habit," Fischer said.

Service patted his pocket to rattle his pain pills. "Drugs."

"You are not well?"

"I'm fine. Where are we going?"

Fischer smiled, did not answer, and concentrated on driving. The traffic seemed totally disorganized, with potholed streets and suicidal drivers following no observable traffic laws.

They drove up the coast to a small restaurant and went inside. The waiter was haughty and attentive to Fischer, who ordered in rapid-fire Spanish. The waiter brought a glass of rum.

"From sugarcane," Fischer said, "a local specialty." Too syrupy for Service's taste, but he drank it out of politeness. The waiter brought them four eggs about the size of Ping-Pong balls.

Service could smell the pickling and waited for Fischer to eat. The man salted and peppered an egg, raised his eyes to the ceiling, said, "God forgive me," and popped the whole egg into his mouth.

Service did as his host had done. The flavor was impossible to describe—sweet, tart, smooth. "*Huevos tortuga*," Fischer said. "Turtle eggs; specifically, green sea turtle eggs, of the endangered species, *Chelonia mydas*. Our government allows for a modest harvest of the creatures by licensed fishermen, but there is poaching at unknown and presumed high levels. These eggs could be legal or illegal. If illegal, the fines are extremely high, but the government lacks the resources to track poachers with either enthusiasm or effectiveness."

Eggs, Service thought. What had Tas Andriaitis said? Fagan was never far from eggs. "Is there a point to this, or are we just breaking the law for sport?"

"The point at this moment is that neither you nor I *know* if we are breaking the law. So we may eat in good conscience—and good health, God willing."

Meal complete, they got back into the vehicle and drove into a village, the buildings all one story and painted bright colors. Fischer stopped the Explorer and got out. Service joined him.

"You see," the retired FBI agent said, pointing. "The yellow wooden steps leading up the side of the cliff? The blue house on top belongs to your Mr. Fagan, and the two blue buildings directly below the stairs are part of it—one is a grocery, one is a fish house."

"All Fagan's?"

"The house on top is his; the places below are under the brokerage of *Refugio Seguro*. The one place buys fish from local fishermen and ships them around the country, as well as to destinations outside the country."

"How far outside?"

"I've been told as far as Japan."

"Tuna?"

"Some, to be sure."

"You're trying to make a point here, and I may be a bit too thick to get it."

"The man who manages the fish house is called Yaya da Costa. Senor da Costa is an extremely interesting man who was called Marvy Block when he lived in New York. He was part of a mob operation that used to beat the shit out of the airport in Newark, trafficking animal parts, but neither U.S. Fish and Wildlife or the Bureau could get anything on him. Curious that he ends up here, working for *Refugio Seguro*."

Fischer took out a cigarette case, opened it, and offered it to Service, who shook his head while the retired agent lit up. "It is said there are turtle eggs in the fish store," Fischer said, exhaling. "I called an associate, Juan Carlos Nevar—the chief enforcement ranger at Tortuguero National Park—and talked to him about Senor da Costa. I've put one of my employees on this, and he has observed a boat going north every two days. It leaves late in the afternoon, too late for sightseeing, and there is no commercial activity of note to the north of Limon. This is not a licensed fishing boat. It could be that local poachers are selling turtle eggs to Senor da Costa, or that he is harvesting them himself. He travels with a crew of three, the ideal turtle unit," Fischer said. "Juan Carlos has an informant who claims a group is taking nesting turtles and eggs on a beach called Green Moon, which is in an exceptionally isolated part of the national park—one never visited by tourists, and only rarely by scientists."

"You have university scientists studying green sea turtles?"

"Our academics study all fauna and flora, and especially green sea turtles, because they are endangered and therefore sexy, which means *mucho* grant money for their work and institutes."

"Does *Refugio Seguro* have a license to catch fish?"

"Not that I have been able to ascertain."

"What about a license to collect eggs for the academics who study the turtles?"

Fischer gave him a funny look. "Such a possibility never occurred to me, but I shall make inquiries. My colleague Juan Carlos Nevar is preparing to interdict the activities on Green Moon Beach."

"Possible for me to go along?"

"This is a most strenuous undertaking, and you have no law enforcement authority here."

"I can be an interested observer."

"This is possible, I think."

"When?"

"Tomorrow night."

"How do I get there?"

"You fly to Tortuguero. It is a beach village of perhaps three hundred people. It lives off tourism and the nearby national park. Juan Carlos will fetch you."

"When do I leave?"

"Let us return to the airport," Fischer said. "I will arrange a flight, and talk to my colleague. While you are gone I will check on Senor Fagan and licenses."

74

FRIDAY, JUNE 17, 2005

Green Moon Bay, Tortuguero National Park, Limon Province, Costa Rica

Juan Carlos Nevar was barely five feet tall, with missing teeth and enormous hands. He met Service at the small airport next to the village of Tortuguero and drove him to his quarters on the edge of the massive park. The small frame house sat on a channel looking across at a towering dark green rainforest, which looked more forbidding than any cedar swamp Service had ever faced in the Upper Peninsula.

Nevar spoke halting English, but talked slowly and listened to make sure Service understood his plan. "We go by boat in the morning. Then we climb a mountain and go down other side. One of my men placed ropes, which we been using. When rains, she come, the mud turns to *helado*, ice—yes?"

"Ice, slippery."

"*Si, mucho-mucho.* We lower ourselves to beach and stay edge of forest. I have a man above, up high, like God? We have marked where this boat is coming. This time we will be close, and if they come ashore for turtles, we will be waiting." Nevar picked up a piece of carved wood with a long handle and a knot on the end. "No guns; only this. *Comprende?*" Nevar popped his hand with the club for emphasis.

"No guns."

"You watch only," Nevar said. "Observer."

"Understood."

The man made them a dish of beans and rice with tomatoes, gave him a hammock, and showed him how to hang it. Grady Service went to sleep staring at geckos moving around the ceiling, defying gravity, thinking that whatever kept them up there might be a good thing to have on his own feet in a muddy jungle. Nevar hadn't needed to warn him about the mud in the rainforest. He and Treebone had been in jungle mud beyond description for an endless, bloody year. It was something sane men weren't eager to go back to.

The boat they took was a twenty-foot-long dugout with a fifteen-horse Yamaha engine that ran almost without sound. Nevar steered and two other men sat forward with Service in the middle as they slid quietly through an unending series of canals filled with black water. On occasion Service could hear surf crashing to their east, but he never saw the big water. Mid-afternoon they beached and hid the boat and made their way into the rainforest. Nevar moved with ease and kept a hard pace. Service found himself puffing, but keeping up. Two hours later they started up a ridge, got to a knotted rope, took hold, and began to climb. There was no talking. Sweat poured off him and he congratulated himself on being smart enough to bring waterproof boots and nylon clothes that were light and would dry out quickly.

From the apex of the ridge they took a new set of ropes downward. The ground was slippery, but manageable. Nevar and his men did not use flashlights, which suited Service. He rarely used lights at night either.

By 2 A.M. they were in a small clearing, and Nevar left them for a few minutes, came back, sent his men one way and took Service in another. They moved out into high grass, overlooking a dark beach against a black sky and dark water.

"Sleep," Nevar said. "They come in two hours, no sooner."

Service was too geeked to sleep. Behind him he heard a strange grunting, barking sound like nothing he'd ever heard before. "*Mono Congo*," Nevar said quietly. "Howling . . . monkey. No danger. Only noise, much noise."

Despite himself, Service fell asleep, and was awakened later by Nevar. "Come, come."

They moved through the grass, and Nevar slid off his pack and took out infrared night-vision binoculars. He set them on a small tripod, looked through the viewfinder, and said, "You look, *quick*."

Service slid over. The scene was green. He could see a lot of boulders on the sand, and less than fifty feet away one of the boulders moved. There was a quiet thump and he saw a flurry of blurred movement and something dashing back into the grass to their right. "*Jaguar*," Nevar said. "She eats the head of the turtle." The cat was red and yellow in the thermal imager.

"Doesn't she smell us?"

"Like big bears in Alaska, yes? When salmon come, they eat salmon, not people. Turtles taste better, I think."

The scene finally clarified. "Those boulders are turtles?" They looked to be three to four feet around.

"*Ochenta* kilos," Nevar said. "Not so big."

"What are we waiting for?"

"Small girl turtles lay eggs. They come from sea toward forest, dig hole, lay *ciento huevos*. Poachers come by boat, catch turtle early, turn on back, drag to boat, lift in. When enough, they leave. Get close to water, tracks gone, yes. *Ondular*; you say wave, yes? Wave?"

Ondular. Wave. Service nodded. No wonder the poachers were difficult to catch. It was an in-and-out deal, like walleye poachers in the U.P., who would descend on a stream, hurriedly spear some fish, throw them in a bag, and be gone—in ten minutes, max.

A jaguar had eaten a turtle's head so close to him it was hard to believe.

At 4 A.M. Nevar nudged Service. "We go."

Nevar took off at a full run, brandishing his club.

Service struggled to keep up, despite his much longer legs. He saw two silhouettes and heard the sounds of men struggling and the flat *whomp* of the club striking flesh, or sand, or both; and then Nevar was up and running toward another man and it happened again. Near the water's edge Service heard a motor fire up, but he couldn't see a boat.

Nevar had handcuffs on the second man and when he struggled, struck him once on the head and added a kick. The second man stopped resisting.

At creeping dawn there was fair light, and Service went to the dead turtle and saw where the head had been severed. Blood was faint in the black sand, hard to distinguish. Had the cat been out there watching them as well?

"We climb out?" he asked Nevar.

"No, a boat will come. We eat now."

The man dug up some green sea turtle eggs, broke them into a small pan, and fried them over the fire with some sort of thin red meat. The man who defended the turtles also poached them. It was a disconcerting moment, but Service ate and relished the taste.

The boat came at 7 A.M. and took them south toward the village, two hours away. Nevar kept the men belowdecks. Service could hear the club working, an occasional scream, a lot of whimpers, Nevar talking emphatically but never shouting.

At the village, they loaded the two prisoners in a plane and took off for Limon. Halfway there, Nevar opened a hatch and began pushing one of the men toward it. The man screamed and clawed with his feet to resist, but Nevar stopped only at the last second and let the man collapse to the flight deck. "Yaya da Costa," the man said. "Yaya, Yaya, Yaya!" the man whimpered.

Policemen met the plane in Limon and Nevar walked with Service to meet Fischer, who looked him over. "Are you all right?"

"I'm fine." He turned to Nevar. "You were going to push that man out of the plane?" He made shoving motions with his hands.

Fischer translated into Spanish, but there was no need. "Law says *tortugas* matter. Man is not so important. Others make law; I keep it. You understand?"

"*Si*," Service said. It had been that way once in Michigan, but now people got lawyers and fought everything, like it was their right to do whatever they wanted in the woods. He understood Nevar, but didn't like him threatening to turn the prisoner into a flyer.

"Your Mr. Fagan, I am still unable to determine his precise involvement in *Refugio Seguro*," said Fischer. "The fish house, I am told, has no license to collect eggs from universities and professors, but it is said perhaps such a request is in the works."

"Fagan?"

Fischer shook his head. "Who knows?"

"Would it be possible for me to talk to Ms. del Rio?"

"She is very busy, but I will tell her of what you have done with Nevar and we shall see."

Two days later they flew to San José and went to a sky-blue stucco building that looked more like a church than a government building. After going through security, they were taken to a small office filled with paperwork and showing no apparent signs of organization. A woman stepped out from behind a pile of papers and exchanged kisses with Fischer. She turned to Service, pushed a chair toward him with her foot, and said, "Please be seated. I am not much for formality. Coffee?"

Service said yes. The woman didn't call a secretary; instead, she stepped into an anteroom and came back with two cups, one for each of the men. She lit a cigarette and said, "I'm listening."

Grady Service took her through the Quint Fagan–Piscova case, from finding Blinky Baranov selling eggs, to the visit to Brooklyn and his encounter with

Krapahkin. When he had finished, the woman asked, "Fagan was convicted of tax violations in Florida?"

"Illegal cash transactions. I don't know all the details."

"But this other thing in New York—the trial goes on as we speak?"

"Yes."

"According to your constitution, I believe Senor Fagan is an innocent man at this time."

"Innocent until proven guilty," Service said. "But he's also purchased property here, and it's my understanding that in order to do that legally, your law requires the purchaser to be a resident of Costa Rica."

"What you say is true," she said.

Service looked at Fischer. "Has he filed for residency?"

"Perhaps, perhaps not. In time we will know."

"Why do you tell us this story?" del Rio asked.

"Because I'm guessing that if he gets off the charges in New York, he's going to come here and do the same thing with green sea turtle eggs. I don't know that he will mix them with contaminated eggs, but he will find a way to harvest illegally and add to his profit. If he's found guilty, I believe he will flee to your country."

"Perhaps you harbor a personal grudge against this man?"

"No, ma'am, I just want to uphold the laws."

"I see. You are very kind to come so far to share this with us," del Rio said, turning back to some papers on her desk as she bid them farewell.

On the way to a hotel Fischer said, "You will seek extradition for Fagan?"

"Not me, but the feds probably will."

"Very difficult," Fischer said, "very difficult, but perhaps there will be a miracle."

The flight home the next day was not a pleasant one. He had taken it as far as he could. What happened now was in the hands of whoever took responsibility for miracles. In his own life, especially recently, there had not been many incidents that qualified. It occurred to him as he waited for his connecting flight to Detroit that his first task when he got back was to send the entire case report to del Rio. Then he would have done all he could do, and he could forget about this. It was time to get his boots back into the dirt and get on with his life.

WEDNESDAY, JULY 20, 2005

East Lansing, Ingham County

The anger management session was scheduled with Dr. Lance Purloy at his office in the Three Winds strip mall on Lake Lansing Road, at 8 A.M. The strip mall was one minute off US 27, the psychologist's office sandwiched between the Polaris Transgender Internet Café and Lunella's Parisian Bistro. The door in front of him said: L. PURLOY, CONSULTING SERVICES, BY APPOINTMENT ONLY.

There was a receptionist behind a desk in the entry area. Beige carpet, clean, beige walls, no color, no distractions. The woman had short brown hair and so many strands of colored plastic beads that she looked like a Mardi Gras refugee.

"Detective Service?" she greeted him, checking her wristwatch.

He nodded.

"Scooter will be with you in a minute."

What kind of doctor was addressed as Scooter?

The doctor came out wearing a gray shirt that had the word MARMOSETS emblazoned across the chest in blue and white. "You stay in town last night?" he asked.

"Just drove down from the U.P. Today's my first day back on duty."

"Lorne said you'd had some trouble." He could sense the man looking directly at his new scars. "C'mon in," the doctor added, waving him into a room furnished only with a green-and-white wrestling mat and a couple of speed bags used by boxers. "I have a real office, too," the man assured him.

The doctor was six-foot-two with the heft of a serious weight lifter.

"Scooter?" Service said.

"Played ball for the Spartans until my knee blew out. Understand you played some college hockey."

"You play Four-Square or volleyball?" Service asked, digging deep.

The psychologist grinned. "The way I heard it, you pounded some poor fuck half to death in a game. Was there any acting out before that?"

"It didn't feel like acting," Service said.

The doctor sat cross-legged on the mat and patted it as a signal for Service to sit down. Service remained standing.

"Anger doesn't just show up one day like a migrating bird," Purloy said.

"You want to hear how my old man beat me?"

"Sure."

"He didn't."

"Got a bit of a chip on that shoulder," Purloy said. "Being here a problem for you?"

"Is it for you?"

"I'm getting paid."

"So am I."

"Do you know why you're here?"

"Orders."

"You always follow orders?"

"The ones that make sense."

"Meaning the ones that don't piss you off?"

"I don't get pissed off."

Purloy stared. "You're pissed off right now."

"I'm irritated right now, not pissed off."

"They look the same to me."

"You're you, *not* me."

"Point taken. You've had a couple of incidents."

"I'm a cop. We have incidents almost every day."

"I can imagine."

"I doubt that."

"I *was* a cop," Purloy said. "ATF, seven years."

"Short career."

"By choice. I'd had enough of gun nuts. I went back to school."

He didn't want to hear the man's life story, and he never liked hearing why an individual quit being a cop.

"Can we just get on with this?"

"More irritation?"

"Perturbation."

"You've got the rep of a cowboy."

"Our reps aren't us."

"True enough, but our reputations often affect how others deal with us."

"Our reputations affect how people *think* they'll deal with us; then they meet us and have to reevaluate."

"Your captain says you're a bit introverted, both analytical and instinctive, extremely intelligent, and that you rarely act on impulse."

"Am I supposed to say, 'Aw, shucks'?"

"That's generally how a conversations works. Cooperate to graduate."

"Keep your sheepskin."

"No cooperation, no graduation, no job."

"Like *that* would be the end of the world," Service said.

"You don't like your job?"

"I *love* my job."

"And you'd risk losing it by not cooperating?"

"There it is," Service said. "It's a job, not a life."

The man grinned. "Do you even *have* a fuse?"

"Fuses don't do anyone any good."

"How do you cook off pressure?"

"I bear down harder."

The man got up, left the room, and came back with a piece of paper. He held it against a wall and made a flourish of signing it. "Well done."

Service ignored the paper.

"You're graduated, top of your class."

"What the fuck is this?"

"Both your captain and your chief said your being sent here was bogus, that you have no anger problems. I told them everybody has a flashpoint and I bet them each fifty bucks I could find yours. You cost me a hundred smackers."

"Jack up your rates."

The man laughed out loud. "Get out of here."

Dr. Purloy followed him out to the parking lot. "Emotional control is admirable, but too much leads to other problems. We all need outlets, safety valves, someone we can confide in."

"I have a dog."

"What's your dog's outlet?"

"Sex with wolves."

Atlanta, Montmorency County

Service called Milo Miars on his way north. Miars was working in Atlanta with some biologists, planning for next year's elk hunt. They agreed to meet for lunch at Bucky's in Atlanta.

"You get the dirty elk guide this year?"

Miars shook his head. "Next year, I hope."

They were halfway into their salads when Service's cell phone rang. It was Roy Rogers. "Guilty on all counts. The judge passed sentence on the spot. Fagan got eighty-seven months in the federal lockup, Vandeal seventy. Vandeal skated without a fine, but Fagan got bit for a quarter million cash. The judge fined Piscova one million, and Shamrock Productions one point two. Piscova also has to forfeit just under a half-million more. Both plants are closed. How about *them* apples?"

"Good," Service said, mouthing "pen" to Miars. "Give me those numbers again, Trip." Service wrote them on a napkin as Rogers read them off and passed the napkin to his lieutenant, who raised his eyebrows and pumped a fist in the air.

"How long until they report?" Service asked.

"The judge gave them sixty days to get their acts together, and I know what you're going to say, but Fagan gave a speech at sentencing and apologized, and well, it was pretty damn convincing."

"He's an asshole, Trip."

"I understand your frustration," the New York ECO said. "You did a great job. Without you, none of this would have happened."

"Fagan and Vandeal going to appeal?"

"Probably. Manny Florida says Fagan's lawyer is a genius with appeals. He'll find a lot to argue, even if the courts will never buy it. That will cost Fagan even more."

"They *killed* a woman, Trip."

"You don't know that. Nobody knows that. It's not provable."

"Neither is God, but a helluva lot of people believe anyway."

"This is a good thing," Trip Rogers said. "Look at the glass as half full."

"Fuck that. I've never been much on the things-happen-for-a-reason school of thought. Fagan's going to run to Costa Rica."

"Did it ever occur to you that you could be wrong?" the New Yorker asked.

"You bet. But not this time."

He closed the phone and told Miars what Rogers had said.

Miars studied him for a long time. "You're sure Fagan's going to run."

"The issue's not *if* he'll run, but what the feds will do if he does. And by the way, I dropped by to tell you thanks, but no thanks on the sergeant's stripes."

"We need people like you to teach and lead our younger officers."

"You can do that a whole lot better than me."

Miars was visibly upset. "The U.P. is still yours. You'll report directly to me."

"Nothing personal, Milo, but not too often, I hope."

Miars grinned, said, "Cowboy," and went back to eating his meal.

Grady Service thought: *I'm the last of the old-time cowboy game wardens, whose decisions turn solely on what's best for the resource.* It was something to be proud of, and fuck anybody who didn't understand.

As for Fagan, what had Fischer, the retired FBI agent said—that maybe there would be a miracle? Maybe there would be, but he wasn't going to count on it. Time to turn his mind to more important things. In the time he'd been on medical leave, a builder from Rock had brought in a crew and finished Slippery Creek Camp. Now there were real bedrooms, with beds instead of footlockers, real bathrooms, one with a tub, new living room furniture, and a brand-new kitchen with top-line appliances. If Karylanne and the baby were going to be around, they deserved a real home—not the empty shell he had lived in for so many years.

"You got anything in your hopper up there?" Miars asked as they ate.

"No, but you know how it is. There's always something."

Upper Fishdam River, Delta County

McCants had stopped by the night before. She'd found a trot line in a feeder creek off the Fishdam River, about two miles south of County Road 442. It had been freshly set and baited, but there were no fish on the hooks she'd checked so far, and she told Service she was pretty sure the line belonged to Craine Koski, who had a dozen DNR priors and had done four years for meth manufacture and distribution. An officer had once called Koski, "double-digit stupid and triple-digit mean."

They parked a half-mile away and made their way west to the Fishdam, then south until they found the feeder creek. There was an old two-track running south from the junction. "I think he parks west near Frying Pan Lake and hikes in," she said. "The trot line's about a quarter-mile north, and the water temp's fifty-four degrees."

Which meant brook trout would migrate out of the warmer Fishdam during this part of the summer. Service followed her west through tag alders and popple stands until the creek was just below them. They found blueberry bushes loaded with fruit, mixed in with waist-high ferns, and sat down to wait. It felt great to be back in the woods, but he kept this to himself. Working with Candi was a diversion. It wouldn't be long until a case came in that would absorb all of his time, and he would find himself in an office doing stuff he didn't like.

"You've seemed a little better in the last month or so," she said.

He nodded.

"Better," she added, "but the two of us—we're not working out, are we?"

"This isn't the time," he said. "We're in the middle of something here."

"When *is* a good time?"

"Shhh," he said.

"The thing is, you're not over Nantz. *Duh!* Stupid me: I knew this, but didn't really grasp it. Didn't want to, I guess. You don't think you'll ever get over her, but you will."

"Shush, Candi."

"Life goes on, Grady. It really does. You have to deal with it."

Why couldn't she just be quiet? This guy Koski was bad news, and she needed to have her mind on the job.

An hour after dark they heard splashing in the small creek. Movement in the water, but not quite right, Service thought.

McCants started to move and he grabbed at her arm, but she was too quick and was on her feet, her SureFire light on, and yelling, "DNR, Conservation Officer," followed by, "*Holy Mother of Jesus!*"

Something dark came up the embankment, banged into McCants, brushed Service's leg, and disappeared into the ferns going north. McCants picked herself up, said, "You *knew* it was a goddamn bear, didn't you?"

"Something didn't sound quite right." He wanted to laugh, had to hold it in.

"Jesus, he could've attacked me."

"No bear's *that* stupid," he said.

She giggled, then guffawed. "I'll take that as a compliment. Man, that's one fur coat in *bad* need of dry cleaning."

A voice from below said, "What the the bloody devil's goin' on up dere?"

It was a challenge tinged with fear. "DNR, Conservation Officers," the two of them said in unison, switching on their lights and charging down to the creek to face Craine Koski, who stood there dumbfounded and blinking in the glare of their lights. They immediately cuffed him.

"This is too fuckin' weird," Koski mumbled. "I ain't done nuttin'. Why's youse cuffin' me?"

"For everyone's protection," McCants said. "You're not under arrest . . . yet."

Service said, "The trot line's empty."

"Where are the fish, Koski?" McCants asked.

"In da creek, where dey live."

McCants illuminated the monofilament in her hand.

Koski said, "Holy wah, is dat trot line?"

"Braided line, treble hooks; your style, Craine."

"Not bloody mine. I don't need no more bullshit tickets from da likes a youse."

"Where's your vehicle?" McCants asked.

Koski nodded west, providing no clear verbal direction.

"You mind if we take a look?" Service asked.

"Ain't no reason for you ta look in my truck," Koski shot back.

"There's this trot line," McCants said.

"Ain't mine. I brung a rod."

"Really? Where is it?"

"In da grass; youse scared da shit outten me."

McCants shone her beam along the grassy bank. "Show me."

Koski bent over and groped in the grass with two hands and pivoted suddenly with something a lot fatter and more substantial than a fishing rod, but McCants anticipated something. She chopped the man's legs with her baton and sent him facedown into the dark mud along the creek's side, where he began shrieking. Service jumped on the man and rolled him onto his back. There were two treble hooks hanging out of his cheek, the monofilament reflecting the flashlight.

"Hurts!" Koski yelled. "Fuckin' hurts!"

"Hold still," Service said. "You're not gonna die. We'll take you into Manistique and get the hooks removed."

"Looks to me like he's in possession of illegal gear," McCants said.

"Chickenshit!" Koski yelled. "Dis won't stick."

"Assaulting a police officer will," Service growled.

Koski reluctantly led them to his truck, a rusted and ancient Willys. In the cluttered back Service found monofilament and a mason jar filled with treble hooks. There were twelve brook trout in a cooler, most of them under legal size. "You got more than one line out, Craine?" Service asked.

"I ain't sayin' shit," he man said.

"Even when you're talking you're not saying shit," McCants said. And to Service, "You want to go grab my truck? I'll keep Craine company."

It took a half-hour to walk to Candi's truck and drive back to where she was holding her prisoner, but when he got there, the Willys was gone and there was no sign of McCants or Koski. His heart sank. *What the hell?* This area was a crosshatch of two-tracks. He got out of her truck and shone his light on the grass and saw tracks. The truck had gone west, spinning its tires. *What the hell had happened?*

He jogged along, looking around; several hundred feet west, he saw a silhouette staggering along the road. He ran to catch up, lit the figure with his light. It was McCants. Her face was covered with blood.

"Where are you going?" he asked her, wanting to judge her condition.

"To kick Koski's ass," she said, slogging along.

"How about we drive?" he said, grabbing her arm and steering her east toward her truck, holding her firmly until he had her in her seat. He gave her a towel. "Pressure."

"Fucker had a pipe sitting on one of the fenders. I looked away and next thing I knew I was seeing stars. I came to hearing him grinding the gears, trying to get out of there. I got hold of a window, but I couldn't hold on. He was trying to shift and steer with both hands cuffed."

Blood continued to course from her head wound. Service reached over and pushed hard on the towel. "*Pressure!*" he said. "Stop talking."

"He'll run home," she said. "Like most men, he *always* runs home."

Service cringed. Had that comment been aimed at him?

Koski lived in a small house on Cemetery Road, east of the village of Cooks. No lights, no Willys. Service drove in dark, got out, and found the Willys back in the trees behind the house, which was dark.

"Vehicle's back in the trees," he told McCants. "Let's call the Troops, get backup. He's not the most stable individual in the world."

"Fuck the Troops," she said, getting out. "This is personal. Let's do a front-back," she said. "I'll yell at the house, see what he does."

Service knew better than to argue with her and got into position behind the house.

He heard McCants shouting out front. "Koski, we know you're in there!" Service heard the crack of a bullet followed by its sonic boom, and his first thought: *Candi.* Then, *Fuck, that was at* me!

He dropped to the ground and fumbled for his SIG-Sauer. Seconds later he heard a crash, another shot, and a lot of cursing. He got up and charged the house with his light in hand.

McCants had Koski on the floor and was pummeling him, the man holding his cuffed hands above him to protect himself. Service grabbed her by the collar and pulled her away.

"Fucking psycho bitch!" Koski screamed.

They called the county to tell them they were transporting a prisoner to Escanaba. Service helped McCants blot the blood off her face. The cut was beginning to coagulate.

They put Koski in the front seat and strapped him in. Service rearranged her gear and squeezed into the backseat of her truck.

"We should have driven the Willys, cuffed him with the loose hooks," Service said.

"Well, we *didn't*," McCants said.

"I'm just saying."

"Don't fucking second-guess me."

"We should let the deps haul him in."

"Bullshit! It's my job, he's my prisoner. *Fucking psycho bitch*?" she said to Koski, letting out a grunt. She reached over and thumped him with her finger on the side of his head, making him wince.

"*Candi*."

"I didn't hurt the asshole. Maybe if you paid more attention to things, this sort of shit wouldn't happen."

What the hell was she talking about? "You're not making any sense."

"Right; you're the only one who knows all the answers."

The truck swerved. "Keep your eyes on the road," he said.

"I mean, what's so damn difficult about taking care of the people you care about?" she said. "My goddamn heart is coming apart and you don't want to talk about it."

"Youse guys need privacy, youse can just drop me off anywhere along here," Koski said.

"Shut the *fuck* up!" McCants shrieked, and Koski flinched.

Passing through Rapid River, Koski got up the nerve to talk again. "Youse two like an item, or what?"

Grady Service jabbed the man in the back of his head with the heel of his hand.

After getting the man fingerprinted and processed, McCants cleaned her head. The cut wasn't bad. They got two butterflies from the jail's first-aid room, closed the wound, and stopped at an all-night coffee joint on Ludington Street, Escanaba's main drag.

"You *knew* it was a bear," she said, after sipping her decaf.

"The sound wasn't right. I didn't know it was a bear, but I thought maybe it wasn't a man."

"You should have told me."

"You moved too fast."

"How fucking long are you supposed to wait?"

"I'd wait to see a silhouette or something."

"I'm not talking about Koski," she said.

"You handled him good."

"Not that asshole. *Us.* I can't keep my mind on the damn job because of you, and I tell you we're not working out, and you don't have a damn thing to say, one way or the other."

"You're still pumped on adrenaline."

"Goddamn right I am."

"I think we're doing okay," he said reluctantly.

"There's a huge difference between thinking and knowing, Grady, and if you don't know that, you're clueless. I'll drop you at your truck, and then maybe we need to take a time-out."

He was smart enough to know that there was no acceptable response to this, and he kept his mouth shut and drank his coffee.

They were in the truck leaving Escanaba when his cell phone rang.

"You're going to like this call," Roy Rogers said. "Vandeal reported in with his lawyer today. Fagan didn't. The judge will give his lawyer until Monday to get him in."

"That just just gives him three more days to run," Service said, clicking the phone shut.

"Bad news?" McCants asked.

"The last year or so, it's been nothing but," he said.

78

MONDAY, SEPTEMBER 12, 2005

Marquette, Marquette County

Zhenya Leukonovich called. "After Fagan went AWOL, Mr. U.S. Attorney Manny Florida went ballistic. He accused New York of malfeasance and they accused him of professional incompetence. It took ten days for the accusations and counter-allegations to stop and to get the FBI on the case. As expected, they traced Fagan to Costa Rica. Mr. Florida and the Bureau were in the process of seeking extradition when Costa Rican officials called and announced Mr. Fagan was in their custody and the U.S. could come claim him at its earliest convenience."

"Did they say why they grabbed him?"

"He was implicated in a conspiracy involving unspecified environmental felonies. Apparently you can murder anyone except a politician in Costa Rica and they will make extradition difficult, but their environment and ecotourism are sacrosanct. Mr. Fagan is not the class of immigrant they seek. Technically the charge against him is purchasing property without being a resident, or even having filed paperwork toward that end. Astonishing, yes?"

"I guess it sucks to be Fagan," Service said, grinning. Apparently del Rio had been listening during their meeting; he was pretty sure the case reports he sent had sealed the deal. "Are they fetching him now?"

"The U.S. Marshals Service has been given the task. Mr. Fagan will arrive in Miami September fifteenth, where New York personnel will take possession. Zhenya finds it most sad to reach the conclusion of this case. She grew attached to the resort and company. Perhaps we will have another opportunity for collaboration."

"Never say never."

"Of course. Never is a theoretical and rhetorical construct with no statistical basis, the equivalent of proving a negative or a totally motionless object."

"Took the words right out of my mouth." He had no idea what she was talking about, but Z was Z and he truly liked her. Didn't understand her, but liked her and had learned to trust her.

As soon as he hung up he called a travel agent and got all the times for Costa Rica arrivals in Miami. There were four flights, spread out over the course of the fifteenth. He booked a flight for the fourteenth, despite the travel agent's vehement warnings about hurricanes. He understood her concern: Katrina had struck Louisiana and Mississippi less than two weeks earlier, and the media were still gagging out post-storm horror stories.

79

THURSDAY, SEPTEMBER 15, 2005

Miami International Airport, Dade County, Florida

The travel agent booked a room for him at the Miami International Airport Hotel. A room with a king-size bed was a hundred and fifty bucks, but he didn't care. The hotel was inside Terminal E, right at the airport, which made it convenient. He flew in on the fourteenth, checked into his room, and went down to the lobby bar to sit among the travelers and the potted palms. He sat at the bar and was joined by a woman who introduced herself as Gal Sal, a forty-something realtor, and borderline anorexic. She matched him Jack for Jack, and smoke for smoke

"How do you make your living?" Gal Sal asked.

"Professional observer."

She eyed him suspiciously. "Don't think I've ever heard that one."

"I get paid to watch things, report whether they go right or wrong. You know, the way the Indians always had a few guys sit out the battle to watch what happened and carry the news back to the tribe?"

"Indians down this way," the woman said, "Semen-Holes? I heard they fought us white people to a standstill. Me, I'm from Long Island. What do I know from Indians? What's the most interesting thing you've seen?"

"I once watched a wolf mother teach her pups to dance."

She grinned. "Yeah, what dance?"

He shrugged. "I'm from Michigan. What do I know from dances?"

"You make cars in Michigan."

"Fewer and fewer."

"*Japs*," she said touching her glass to his.

"Real estate, eh?"

"The most precious money can buy: Me."

"You sell it?"

"Technically, I suppose it's more of a short-term lease."

"Tough job," he said.

"Better than my last one. I flew Blackhawks in Desert Storm. The government paid me so it could fuck me over. I decided to become an independent contractor. Pays a whole lot more and the working conditions are better. You want to observe what I get paid for?"

Service liked Gal Sal. "I'll have to pass."

He woke up the next morning with a slight headache, showered, shaved, and went to find the Transportation Security Administration office. He talked his way in to see a shift supervisor named Wagner, showed his badge and credentials, explained what he wanted.

"Extraditees are taken to a holding cell in the security holding area we call Gitmo North. They stay there until their forwarding flight, but you can't get in without specific authorization, which we can't grant. But you can wait outside." Supervisor Wagner had the air of a package expediter.

Fagan came in on the third Costa Rica flight of the day. The marshals escorted him down the hall to Gitmo North. Thirty minutes later Roy Rogers and another man came out with Fagan cuffed and in tow. Rogers's jaw dropped when he saw Service, who walked up to Fagan and blocked his way.

Fagan had a full head of hair, a short, compact man with a perpetual sneer and dark eyes that served more as a mask than lenses. "*Refugio Seguro*," Service said. "Guess it wasn't either."

"Who the fuck are you?" Fagan asked.

"A friend of Roxanne Lafleur. When you get inside I'm going to make sure the fudge-packers give you a proper welcome and a lot of attention."

Fagan looked at ECO Roy Rogers. "Who is *this* asshole?"

Grady Service smiled and walked away. This wasn't the outcome he wanted, but it would have to do. Closure was closure.

Rogers caught up to him. "Didn't expect to see you here."

"I bet."

"We got a call from a woman named del Rio. She knew everything about Fagan. How do you suppose that happened?"

Service shrugged. The two men touched fists and Service watched them lead Quintan Fagan down the hall. The judge had given him eighty-seven months. His failure to report would add a couple of years, which potentially could keep him out of circulation for almost a decade. It was a lousy trade for a life, but it was something.

His flight back to Detroit wasn't until the next morning. Gal Sal was in the lobby bar on the same stool where he'd left her last night. "Observe anything today?" she asked.

"A miracle," he said.

"That's cool," Gal Sal said. "Way cool."

"You?"

"No miracles in my business," she said.

Slippery Creek Camp

Karylanne was back in school, but had skipped classes from Friday through Tuesday and brought the baby over for the weekend, escorted by Shark and Limey and Gus. McCants was also there, as was Newf and her twelve very active pups, which looked wolflike enough to be purebreds. He hadn't seen Cat in days.

Grady Service loved having all the animals around, despite the bedlam. One night he sat down and figured the animals would probably grow to an average weight of a hundred pounds each, which meant he'd have to feed more than a half-ton of eager, active canines daily. The cost wasn't a concern. SuRo Genova had identified a wolf-dog sanctuary in Wisconsin to take all of the animals, and he had arranged through Marschke to provide a substantial grant to the sanctuary, not just for his animals, but for the entire operation, enough to secure the place's future for at least five years.

The Fagan-Piscova case was done, but some loose ends remained.

Early that morning he'd driven to Limpy Allerdyce's isolated compound in southwest Marquette County.

"Youse ain't been around much," the old poacher said.

"Been busy. I ran into Honeypat."

"Youse fuck 'er?" Allerdyce asked without a pause.

The old man was disgusting.

"Nah," Limpy said quickly. "Youse're da Boy Scout. Told youse I din't do nuttin' to her. I changed my ways."

There was a time when he'd suspected that Limpy had murdered Honeypat. He did not apologize for having entertained that thought, but owed it to the old man to let him know he now knew he'd told the truth.

Visit to Limpy complete, he returned to Slippery Creek and placed a call to Benny Baranov, who answered the phone on the second ring.

"Baranov."

"Grady Service, Benny. You're not out fishing?"

"I have been for early steelhead once or twice. I have had interview for job as caretaker for rich man's property close to Onaway. I am finalist. I gave your name as personal reference."

Service started to complain, but stopped himself. His gut told him that Benny was a good guy pushed to desperation, doing the best he could, given his circumstances. "That's good. I hope you get it. Did the ticket disappear?"

"Yes, no problem."

"I thought you'd want to know that Vandeal and his boss are both in prison. Our report-all-poaching operation sometimes pays rewards for information leading to arrests and convictions. I put you in for a reward. I can't guarantee you'll get anything, and if you do, it won't be large, but it's our way of saying thank you."

He heard Benny's voice catch. "*Spasibo.*"

"Let me know if you get that new job, and take care of those girls."

"Yes, of course. I have your card."

Service hung up and felt pleasure. Dropping Benny's ticket and not confiscating his equipment had turned out to be one of the smartest moves he'd ever made.

He sat with Little Mar in his lap. She frowned as she looked up at him with her huge blue eyes.

The puppies were all trying to gang up on Cat, who had reappeared and was on her hind legs and angrily smacking at them. "Dammit, Newf, get your kids under control."

One of the puppies, the largest male in the litter, wriggled up to Service's leg and put his head next to the baby. "I guess you've got a fan," he told his granddaughter.

Newf looked at the cat and her pups and showed no interest in intervening in the fracas.

The baby reached up to touch her grandfather's chin.

"Geez-o-Peto," Shark said. "Youse're cryin' like a little girl, Grady!"

"*Yalmer,*" Limey Pyykkonen said in a shrill whisper, "will you *ever* learn to keep your mouth shut?"

It was warm, in the high seventies, the tail end of Indian summer. Winter would soon arrive and the long, brutally cold months would begin. The love of his life was dead, as was his son. Roxanne Lafleur was dead. Fagan and Vandeal were in prison, and he would retain the U.P. as his responsibility. He still had all his friends. He and

Candi were no longer an item, but their friendship would survive—he hoped. Most important, he had Karylanne, whom he considered his daughter, and he had Little Mar. Grady Service looked down at his granddaughter, and for the first time in a year and a half, felt nearly at peace. *Everything is perfect,* he told himself.

"Bampy?" his almost ten-month-old granddaughter said loudly, enthusiastically, and clearly, with perfect enunciation.

Well, almost everything.